Anchors Aweight

by

A. Ross Morris & J. Holden Jenswold

Bloomington, IN authorHOUSE™ Milton Keynes, UK

AuthorHouse™
1663 Liberty Drive, Suite 200
Bloomington, IN 47403
www.authorhouse.com
Phone: 1-800-839-8640

AuthorHouse™ UK Ltd.
500 Avebury Boulevard
Central Milton Keynes, MK9 2BE
www.authorhouse.co.uk
Phone: 08001974150

First published by AuthorHouse 3/27/2006

ISBN: 1-4259-1967-7 (e)
ISBN: 1-4259-1966-9 (sc)

Library of Congress Control Number: 2006902023

Printed in the United States of America
Bloomington, Indiana

This book is printed on acid-free paper.

Foreword (Caveat)

The incidents and characters in this book are fictional because, although, we were both in the Navy at the same time, neither one of us can remember a damn thing about it. This book is the result of two over-active imaginations and any similarity between any of the characters to any person or animal, living or dead, is simply coincidental.

If you are paging through this book and haven't made the conscious decision to buy it, then stop it!! Go buy it. It's worth it, and we need the money. If you've bought it, we congratulate you on your impeccable literary taste. When you, with the impeccable taste, have finished reading this tome do <u>not</u> pass it along to friends. No, make those cheap son-of-a-bitches buy their own copy. Yes, once you've read it, place it on the mantel, next to a trophy, or heirloom, or something and just admire it. When those cheap bastards (friends) show their face at your house, just gloat. Yes, my friend, just drink your toddy, beer, cheap whiskey, or whatever, and gloat.

If you've bought it and don't like it, give it to that perpetual thorn in your ass: your mother-in-law, because you sure as hell aren't getting our money back.

A & J

Table of Contents

Introduction: Anchors Aweight

1969 was a strange year. There have been plenty of other strange years to be sure, but 1969 had to be the strangest. Like Jim Morrison had sang about a year earlier, "strange days have found us; strange days have tracked us down."

It was a time of conflicts and contrast. A time of peace and war. Love and hate. Sexual freedom and VD. Drugs and natural highs. Woodstock, Frank Sinatra, Frank Zappa, and frankness. The Doors and the Cowsills. Jimi Hendrix and Scott MacKenzie. Hurry up and wait. Calmness and chaos. Ferraris and foodstamps. Astronauts and Appalachia. Them and us. It was a time of wondering why a government would send teenagers into battle but not allow them to legally drink beer or vote. Of wondering if the government was telling us the truth or telling us lies. Of wondering who was going to end up in Vietnam and wondering who would be coming back alive, or in a box. 1969 was the end of the infamous sixties. It was the sixty's final hurrah. For many young adults it was the end of innocence, the passing of the carefree days of youth, and the acquisition of the freedom to make our own choices. Time to grow up, we were told.

Sexual innuendoes dominated the year. Sticky fingers, sticky floors, sticky everything was hard to avoid wherever young people gathered. 'STICKYYY, GOTCHA'!!! Edible underwear made some innovative person a lot of money. Jim Morrison entertained the good people of Miami with an exercise in very public flagellation. Sex, drugs, and rock and roll RULED.

Graduating and non-graduating seniors bragged of being the "Class of 69". Creative graffitists passed on the "69" message to the public via walls, water towers and overpasses, reveling in the delusion that they were shocking all who passed by and read their work.

1969 was a long time ago. It's now old news, immortalized in book, film and song. The endless inspections, dissections and vivisections done on the year have both criticized and romanticized the time. Most of the stories have been told and most of the skeletons freed from the closets.

Many coming of age stories have been heard and the past is slowly but surely being buried. But one more story has yet to be told: the story of two young men who were, looking for the meaning of life, freedom of choice, and a good time.

All this happened in that strange year of 1969 when these two thought they took a detour off the road of young adult life, and joined the Navy.

Chapter 1: <u>And so it Begins</u>

It was New Years morning, 9:00 am. It was a cold, dreary Mendota, Wisconsin morning; the first day of 1969. It could just as well as been Siberia as far as Jay West was concerned. The world outside the window looked bleak. Jay looked around the familiar room. It looked bleak. Jay felt bleak. This could be a long bleak year, he thought to himself.

Mostly he felt bleak because he could no longer drive, legally. He had a car but no license. The State thought he drove too fast. He'd pointed out to them that he had only broken the speed limit three times-honest, the same three times he had gotten the tickets. He thought they'd be impressed with his honesty and would forget the whole thing. The state was quick to point out that, although Jay had paid them enough money in speeding fines to pave at least three hundred miles of interstate, they thought that it was still in both his and society's best interest to suspend his license for three months. Having no driver's license could plunge any 18 year old into the deepest of despairs, even those upwardly mobile types who were no longer mobile.

Having been 18 for a whole 6 months and finally able to drink legally, Jay had already hit most of the bars in town. That scene had gotten old. He was about to start a second semester of college, but that too was getting old. The shining idea of being a college graduate had initially been appealing but lately had dimmed to a dull glow. To further complicate things, Jay had stupidly forgotten to get the all-important student deferment and was currently 1A.

1

He was sitting at the top of the draft list. The post New Year's Eve hangover didn't help matters. This could be a long year, he thought again. He felt the weight of the world on his shoulders. Jay pulled the covers over his head and hid from the world.

Two weeks later, Jay was back in school. He started a second semester, but his heart wasn't in it. He joined ROTC because they promised big money, more girls, and an easy life, or something like that. Jay lasted one day. After having to get up early to "assemble" at 6 am and marching in circles for two hours, he decided that was enough of that. Besides, until they could come up with a uniform that included flannel shirts and blue jeans, Jay wasn't interested in the military or their monkey suits. As a matter of fact, the last thing he wanted to do was get involved in any military business. He was more anti-war than pro-war; more liberal than conservative. If anything, he was a dove with an aggressive streak. He was more interested in surviving young adulthood and having a good time as much as anything else. Jay didn't think much of what the government was up to in Vietnam and agreed with the protests against the war. He had been involved in several demonstrations (enough to get gassed) but, in 1969, Jay was too busy with nothing in particular to get adamantly involved in anything of real social importance.

Jay loafed through college until just before Spring break. One day, while sitting around waiting for the snow to melt, Howard Valentine, Jay's best friend, came up with an outstandingly good plan. Like Jay, Howard was also without much of a life plan for his future.

"We need a vacation," he announced. "Let's go to New Orleans for a while."

So they went on vacation. They liked it so much they stayed. And stayed. And stayed. They stayed until they ran out of money so they worked at Manpower. The hell with college. After a couple of months, the jobs ran out, so they headed back to Wisconsin. On their second night back, they were sitting in a bar on Madison Street.

"Things don't seem any different than before we left," Jay observed.

"They aren't," Howard agreed. "Nothing ever changes around here."

"What's changed is that I don't have any job and I'm out of money. Besides that, I've been kicked out of school and now I'm 4F or whatever it is that gets you drafted and sent to Nam." Jay was remembering how bleak things looked back on that New Year's morning 5 months ago. Damn, he thought, things still look bleak.

Howard thought a minute. "Let's do something different."

"Like what?"

"Let's join the Navy."

"Sure thing," Jay chuckled at the joke. "Which Navy?"

"The U.S. Navy, dipshit."

"How about the Canadian navy? I know, the Polish navy. No, wait, the Ubangi navy. They could all get pissed if we don't consider them too. Or how about the Hungarian or the Chinese navy. They all must have wonderful opportunities for two downwardly mobile guys like us."

Howard wasn't laughing as hard as Jay. He actually looked somewhat serious. Jay choked on his beer as reality hit. "No fucking way!"

"Listen, this would be ideal." Howard had convinced himself that he had a good plan. "Really! Its ideal. It fits right in the picture. You're afraid of heights, so the Air Force is out. You don't like getting up early and marching so the Army is out. Even though you're an asshole, you aren't real fond of killing people so that eliminates the Marines. And nobody seems to know who, what or where the Coast Guard is so that leaves the Navy. It'll be a piece of cake."

"Howard, your logic sucks. Listen to me, 'cuz I'm only saying this once: NO FUCKING WAY." Jay was getting a little nervous.

Three weeks later, they did it! They enlisted in a *special* program. By then, Jay had convinced himself that the draft board was stalking him, waiting to snatch him up without warning. To further his paranoia, he had received a form letter from someone named Dean Robert Dean at his former college. Instead of congratulating him on his 0.69 grade point average and thanking him for all the money he had paid the university, Dean Dean also informed him that he was not welcome back at the school and suggested that Jay grow up and do something else before he tried college again. Something mature, like working for a living or joining the military. Jay was furious!

"Those assholes! They were more than happy to take my money. Tuition money, dorm money, food money, locker money, special event money, student ID money, towel money, postage, shipping and handling fee money and who knows what else over the past year! They have some serious bull fucking balls to tell me that I'm not mature enough for college life! How fucking mature do you have to be for panty raids, beer parties, lighting ass farts, and all that other shit? And just how does joining the service and going to Nam and killing people make you ready for college? What's wrong with this picture? What's wrong with these assholes?" Jay was pissed and on a roll. "They want me to grow up, so maybe if I'm mature, they'll let me come back, pay them all the money they want again and start all over again. "Fuck them! I'm as mature as the next guy! " He threw an ashtray at the wall, breaking a bar mirror. "Fuck this, fuck that and fuck you!"

"Seven years bad luck," Howard observed. "You really are the picture of maturity," he added.

Jay clamed down, switching into a more depressed mood. He was in a bad spot. A sitting duck and good old Uncle Sam had a loaded shotgun, just waiting for him to raise his head. Just like shooting fish or ducks or whatever in a barrel. Jay promised the bartender he'd pay for the mirror. The bartender, thinking Jay to be a responsible enlistee, naturally, believed him.

A week later they signed up on the Navy's "Buddy Plan." Jay figured that the recruiter wanted them to so he could get the double bounty that the recruiters obviously received for each victim they captured. They also signed up for what Larry, their friendly recruiter (they were all on a first name basis by then), called the 120-Day-Delayed-Entry-Program. As Larry explained it, 120 days was actually 2,880 hours, plenty of time to party and relax before taking the plunge. "Hell, boys, that's longer than some wars that have been fought."

It seemed that everyone was Dee Jay's friend, but he made Andy nervous. Here was this short, long haired, long bearded, weirdly dressed man selling dope right on campus. In broad daylight. In front of God and everybody. What about the student police? Or narcs? Or Captain Kirk, head of the university police? Andy wondered a lot about that.

DJ just didn't care. He was a character out of the <u>Hobbit</u>; he was Bilbo Baggins reincarnate. Andy asked him about the boldness of it once.

DJ just said, "me and Captain Kirk got an understanding'. He don't fuck with me and I don't fuck with him."

Andy asked, "How'd you get that?"

"Hey! I went to his home one night, with a quart of tequila, and told him what I was gonna do. I said I'm gonna sell a little pot on the campus here from time to time. I'm not gonna cause any trouble, just sell a little pot. I'm in; I'm out, that's it. Now, Captain Kirk, you can come ahead and bust me if you want, but if you bust me, I'm gonna' come lookin for you and it won't be pretty. I ain't gonna' cause no trouble. Just sell a little pot. When the quart was empty we had a deal. Then I left."

Andy couldn't imagine anyone saying that to Captain Kirk, head of the University police force. That wasn't common, Andy thought, but it was bold. Was it bull shit or what? How do you know when someone is bullshitting you? Andy thought it was bull shit.

Andy began to learn more about DJ as time went by. DJ would share things that others on campus were never privy to. It was at a party at his own house where DJ started opening up to Andy. He was really talkative and Andy didn't know if it was the pot, acid or the wine, but DJ was really getting into it.

His real name really was Dee Jay. It was on his Texas driver's license. He wasn't bull shitting about that. He said he was abandoned as a kid and Indians in northern Mexico took him in. They all raised marijuana and sold it north of the border. When DJ was little, they taught him how to roll joints. He became good at it and it soon became one of the ways he paid his way. When he got older, because he wasn't Mexican or Indian, but Norte Americano, they had him run the stuff over the Rio Grande into the U.S. He said those

Indians could run for 50 miles at a whack. That had to be bullshit, Andy thought, nobody can do that. 26.5 miles maybe, if you were in shape for a marathon, but 50? Get real, Andy thought. Some years later, Andy would learn that there are Indians in Northern Mexico who can run that far and even further, barefoot.

There was just enough of an element of validity to DJ's stories that lent credibility to the ones that stretched to the fantastic. Andy struggled with what was true and what wasn't. Man, what a character, he thought time after time. Is DJ for real? What was bullshit and what was serious truth? Andy didn't know, but DJ sure had good stories; every one of them.

Andy had never taken anything too seriously that concerned school work since the beginning of High School, unless of course, you counted football as school work. He wasn't big and he wasn't a star, but he always wanted to play bad enough to make the starting team. His six foot frame barely held 160 pounds of meanness in place long enough to slam it against the lower legs of an opposing, and almost always bigger lineman. When he could knock the first one down, he'd get up as quick as he could, and go after another pair of knees to slam into. That's how he got along practically everywhere. Hit 'em hard, low, and hit 'em fast. Catch 'em off guard. Many people loved his enthusiasm; off the field, it could escalate into an excitement that to Andy was just plain-old-good-natured-fun, gregariousness. Others though, weren't quite so sure because maybe it was too gregarious. Maybe too mischievous. Some said it was over the line because it had a quality that might just put it on the edge of an eerie insanity. On the football field, however, there was no doubt. It wasn't good natured; it wasn't gregarious; it wasn't bullshit, it was serious madness. Hit someone low! Get up! Find another, do it again! Hurry! Hit again! Sometimes the ref's whistle blew before the next one could be found. Sometimes you get caught; sometimes you don't. But you always try, and try and try.

Andy just couldn't channel his normal enthusiasm toward college academics. Who could, in a world where you were finally, really on your own. Where the pot, LSD, beer and vodka were easy enough to get, even if you were only 19 in a 21 year old's world.

Where there were more pretty girls than you could ever possibly hope to see, let alone meet, in a semester? The pleasures were all out there, beckoning and tempting. There was just too much living to do to find time for the actual school stuff. Make the hit! Get up! Find another! Do it again! Hurry up! There isn't enough time! Yeah, Andy had plenty of enthusiasm for what seemed more real and alive than working on boring math problems or memorizing phylum, genus or some historical dates for a test, only to forget them 30 minutes later.

The only scholarly high point of Andy's academic exposure was Professor Scholp, an older professor of 50 or so, from Germany. He had a thick shock of hair and a huge bushy, broom-like mustache. He was about average in height but stocky, and looked like a middle-weight boxer. Professor Scholp would begin his lectures behind the podium on the stage at the head of the lecture hall. Before he was finished however, he would use the whole stage, pacing back and forth, jabbing the air with his fingers, smashing his fist into his hand and pausing from time to time for effect. His voice, which he had no trouble projecting, would rise and fall. He could fill the whole lecture hall with his booming baritone and thickly accented German voice. He lectured about real things. He related what he wanted to teach about Camus and Sarte to experiences that Andy could relate to. He knew about the rich and the poor; the owners and the workers; the drafters and draftees. He knew about the War. He piqued Andy's attention when he talked about conscription in Germany, when he was younger, during World War II and how it was wrong then. "… taking young men from der families to fight! Not to defend or protect der Fadderland, but to be der aggressor! Fadders were taken! Uncles were taken! Brruders were taken! Whole classes and cultures were taken! And so many died! For what? So Hitler could have a few more gypsies or Jews to build another road or dam; to glorify der facist state? IT WAS WRRRONG!

"AND TODAY!" He was yelling now in that deep, rumbling, booming baritone voice. "YOUR CHILDREN, YOUR BRUDDERS, YOUR BOYFRIENDS ARE BEING TAKEN! Not by conscription but by der DRAFT! Yes, der DRAFT! He spit out the word draft like you would say *shit* as if the word were in your mouth and had to be evacuated-quickly and not-so-quietly before you wretched or before anyone else could smell the obnoxious, vile filth. "Taken! Taken for vhat? To defend der families? NO! To defend der homes? NO! To defend der country? NO!" And now he was slowly walking the stage like a lion on the prowl, looking at the students, from one to another and almost whispering, but loud enough for all 250 to hear. "Dey are *drafted* so a few corrupt Vietnamese families can add to der personal wealth by stealing from poor Vietnamese farmers and der families. Farmers, workers, merchants and students, not unlike yourrrlesves!" Andy was in awe. This old man was always impressive, emotional, animated, peace loving, yet he was also, very strong. Andy had a great deal of respect for the strength of Dr. Scholp.

"Yes," his voice building to a crescendo, "I tell you dis truth! A rrrose is a rrrose, and by any oudder name it smells just as sweet." Pausing for effect, he lowered his voice and, almost spitting out the words, "but conscription, by *any* oudder name is rrroten and IT STINKS TO HIGH HEAVEN!!"

He's right, Andy thought. The old son of a bitch is right. Professor Scholp was still lecturing, but Andy was deep in thought. We can't vote. Shit, we can't even legally buy beer and we have to hide the drinking of it. Might as well smoke some grass and do something really illegal, if you're going to risk getting busted. Even a small decision like choosing what courses to take has restrictions. You can only take these classes, and can't take others. But BY GOD, we're old enough to get sent off to some strange land and get our asses shot off.

Take my buddy Moe. We used to play basketball all summer long, and look what happened to him. He was hanging some wire on a telephone pole in some place called Bin Wau and they shot his ass off. Killed him. No more basketball, for Moe. No more girls, for Moe. No more family, for Moe. No more nothing for Moe. Damn. He could really shoot the old round ball too. Give him half a second in the corner and you always had two points. And we can't even vote. Then there was Gary and his twin brother, Gus. Gary goes. Gus doesn't. How do you figure that? Twins. They take one but not the other. Shit man, they're twins for chrissake. Gary

Chapter 3: Taking the Plunge

Jay had never been noted for his patience. He hated to wait. He also hated not knowing what was happening next. He hated surprises, especially bad ones. It had something to do with a need to feel in control of his life. But the two cornerstones on which the military are built are waiting and keeping people in the dark. Taking away their sense of control of their life. The Navy and Jay were less than a perfect match.

Jay began the fearful apprehension of waiting for the Navy the day he and Howard took the bus to the Induction Center, October 31st. It was a cold, gray Halloween day. They were told to be at the bus station at 7 am. The bus didn't leave for Milwaukee until 8:30. That figures, thought Jay.

The bus trip was uneventful. Jay slept most of the way. It had been a long night. The last hurrah before the serious shit started. It would be their last night of freedom. There had been the tearful farewells and some fatherly advice at the bus station. Christ, Jay thought, I'm not leaving forever. I plan on being back before too long. This is just a temporary deal, he reminded everyone, including himself.

Once in Milwaukee, they were soon at the Induction Center. It was Milwaukee's answer to Alcatraz: a large, cold, impersonal building left over from the depression. The epitomization of depression was never more poignant as now. "So what else would you expect?" Jay asked of no one in particular.

21

They were shepherded into the Center as soon as the bus stopped.

"Move it! Move it! Move it!" A skinny, young asshole in a uniform screamed at them.

They were herded into a large locker room and ordered to remove all their clothes. They then were put in line with a lot of other young naked men, waiting for THE PHYSICAL. The physical, a true psychological masterpiece: take off the clothes to eliminate the individuality and enhance the vulnerability, stand in line forever to strengthen their power to delay, face to the wall to enforce humility, and screamed at by strangers at the tops of their lungs to dehumanize. The lambs heading for the slaughter. The physical was performed by slightly demented, and no doubt discredited doctors or sawbone impersonators. They examined, probed, evaluated and generally belittled whoever was standing before them. After almost 6 hours of nonstop fun, the subjects were sent to a room to get dressed and await the results. Everyone passed (Surprise!! Surprise!!), but not everyone ended up going where they thought they would.

Jay was a little unsettled when, in the midst of the process, a hundred new, naked subjects were ushered into the large room and lined up against the far wall. It didn't look good. Jay fully expected them all to be offered a last cigarette before the execution began. These were draftees: a species somewhere between flies and shit on the food chain. A mean looking Staff Sergeant, in starched uniform and crew cut, strutted into the room and marched down the ranks.

"YOU! YOU! YOU! YOU!" He randomly screamed as he passed down the line. He got to the end of the line. He looked at Jay who happened to be standing there, in the wrong place at the wrong time. "YOU TOO!" he screamed.

"Me too, what?" Jay wanted to know.

"You, too Asshole!" He turned around. "The Marines I pointed out will now fall out. The rest of you scumbags are Army cannon fodder!"

"S'cuse me, but I can't be in the Marines," Jay offered.

"You talking to me, shitbag?" Big Mouth asked incredulously. His eyes were almost bugging out of his face. He wasn't used to people talking to him, only hearing him.

"Well, yeah. See, the Navy already got me. As much as I'd love to be a Marine, I can't cuz the Navy'd be real pissed if I did." Jay was scared shitless, but he couldn't stop talking.

Big Mouth looked at Jay. He was bright red; his veins were almost popping in his neck. He turned around abruptly and stormed into another room. He returned a few minutes later. "You're lucky shithead! Nothing but a fucking Navy pussy.....Semen!" He snorted as if he was proving a point. "Go ahead and hide on a ship. You are nothing but a candy ass seaman! I'd love to see your ass in a rice paddy!"

"Oh well," was all Jay could think to say.

Big Mouth turned to his new victims. The dazed boys were looking at each other. After a moment of quiet confusion, followed by more screaming by Big Mouth, the 50 naked, soon to be Marines were herded together. The remaining cannon fodder was also herded together into another group. Both groups were herded out of the room through separate doors.

Jay wanted to laugh at the absurdity of what he just saw, but figured he had better not.

Once dressed, they waited some more. Finally, Jay and Howard were called and given a pile of papers and told they were "processed." Another little man with a big mouth stepped up to address the remaining troops.

"Awright! Ya'll now go to the hotel and go right to bed then ya'll be up by 0500 when a bus'll take ya'll to the YMCA for chow then ya'll ship out to Great Lakes fer yer new life! DISMISSED!"

Jay looked at Howard. "What the fuck...?"

Howard shrugged.

"Why do all of these little men have such big mouths? And why do they all yell? We aren't deaf."

"Not yet, but we will be. Its the little man complex. Shitbag!" Howard started chuckling. He couldn't stop. He thought he was pretty funny.

"No shit. And fuck you to the extreme."

The Whitetail Hotel was a leftover from the early 1900's. It was a dive. Perfect for the Navy and its soon-to-be sailors. It was big, old, ugly and far from inviting. They got to the Hotel and checked in. Checking in consisted of lining up in front of a small front desk with a half-cage window while the 200 year old alcoholic clerk gave them a key to their individual rooms. They filed up the stairs: some to the second, some to the third and some to the fourth floor. Each room was furnished with a single, stained bed and a beat up dresser. A bare 75 watt bulb hung from the middle of each room's ceiling. The community bathroom was down the hall. As they walked down the hallway, a couple of doors inched open and they could see anonymous eyes follow them to their respective rooms.

"Top shelf," Jay exclaimed. "Not exactly the Hilton, is it?"

That night, they wandered aimlessly around downtown Milwaukee. Looking for something to do, they checked out a couple of theaters; nothing looked appealing.

"What we need is a good war flick to get us in the mood for tomorrow," Jay suggested. They stopped in a couple of 18-year-old beer bars and drank some tasteless beer. Things weren't right. Try as he might, Jay couldn't shake the funk he was in.

They ended the night in a greasy spoon that was disguised as a bar. A cop sat at the counter reading the paper with his coffee. A drunk, middle aged couple was arguing in a booth. And a drunk was passed out over a full, cold coffee cup at the end of the counter.

"This place may not be more expensive than George Webb, but it has a hell of a lot of atmosphere." Howard was trying to be upbeat.

"The atmosphere in here stinks. The room stinks. This building stinks. This whole thing stinks! We're probably being watched by an army of roaches as we speak," Jay said. "This is like a perverted last supper."

"Yeah," Howard agreed, stuffing a greasy hamburger into his mouth. "Like the last dance, shitbag." He really liked Jay's new nickname.

"Last call."

"Last chance."

"Last of the Mohicans."

"Last train to Clarksville, Last stan...." It didn't get out. Jay cut him off.

"Oh, Christ, gimme a break." Jay hated the Monkees.

They finished their hamburgers and headed down the street. Jay was still in a major funk. He couldn't get rid of it.

It was quiet for 10:00 on a Monday night. On a street corner, they passed a couple of interested hookers. At least Jay figured they were hookers. Who else would take an interest in a couple of obviously doomed young men?

"Hey boys, looking for some action?"

Jay's funk switched to a bad mood. "There's an original line," he said. "You got action?

"For 25 bucks you could get all the action you want."

"I don't fucking think so. Never paid for it; never will."

"How about 15?"

"How about free?" Better yet, why don't you pay me?'

"No way! Fuck off."

"No! You haggie-bags can fuck off! Who the fuck needs you?"

"Have fun with Rosie Palm and her twin sister. See ya' little boys later." Then, the hookers huffed, puffed, and strutted away.

"Fuck you!"

"Nice negotiations," Howard observed. "You sure have a way with words and women."

"Aw, shit, come on. I 'm not in a real good mood right now."

"I couldn't tell, shitbag." Howard was the kind who, once started with the needling, he couldn't quit until he got drunk or something happened and he just forgot. Or, you got in his face. And Jay wasn't up for the latter.

They headed on down the street. The thought of being picked up at 5:30, in less than 7 hours, by a bus that would start their trip to finally meeting Uncle Sam was heavy on both their minds. The prospect of having to get up early, plus the dehumanizing things they had gone through that day made it hard for them to get fired up about much of anything. Things looked bleak.

At 11:00 they found themselves back at the hotel. They climbed the stairs, walking past the doors that had inched open earlier. Several inched open again as they approached. Jay glared at the eyeballs in the doorjamb cracks. "What the fuck you looking at?' he demanded. "Get outta' my face!" The doors slammed shut.

"Who do you suppose is in this fire trap with us?" Jay asked in a loud voice. "Besides fucking perverts?"

"Besides perverts? I suppose some winos and some soon-to-be military fighting machines-like us," Howard responded. "You know, the usual riffraff. Plus a few serial killers, child molesters and life insurance salesmen."

"Thanks. That'll make it even easier to sleep tonight."

There wasn't much sleep to be had that night. Jay couldn't get his mind to stop working. He spent most of the night drifting in and out of sleep, dreaming about prisons, circuses and torture chambers. Twice someone tapped on his door. "Get the fuck out of here! I've got a gun!" He yelled, half asleep. The tapping quickly stopped. Throughout the rest of the night, he'd hear the noises of people trying to find their way down to the community bathroom. Finally a loud, authoritative knock on the door jarred him awake. He felt like he'd slept a whole half hour all night.

"Get up!" The desk clerk (or whatever he was) was following Jay's instructions. Earlier the previous evening, Howard had called Hardy Slater, a former regional supervisor from a gas station chain they had worked for in Milwaukee a year ago. Hardy now lived in Milwaukee and managed a tiny gas station in a bad neighborhood. To some it may have seemed to be a demotion, but not to Hardy. He didn't give a shit. According to him, there were lots of horny divorcees in the neighborhood.

Jay and Howard had kept in touch with Hardy over the past year. He thought they were good guys and would buy them beers. They had to listen to his stories about all the women he had laid. Jay figured Hardy was lonely and needed someone to impress. But he was ok, and fun to listen to.

Hardy had informed them that he was busy that night. He had a hot date with at least two women, but promised he'd meet them in the morning at 4:40 sharp in front of the Whitetail Hotel with a going-away present. "I'll be up all night anyway," he bragged. "These women won't let me sleep."

"Do you think he'll actually show up?" Jay asked Howard.

"Sure he will. He has to be up anyway. He's got to open the station at 5 am."

The next morning, at 4:40 sharp, there he was. Hardy pulled up in front of the hotel in his old Cadillac. "Get in." They headed down the street.

Halfway down the block, he pulled out a big jar of booze and tomato juice. (Jay would realize later, after he had become a man of the world, that the jar was one giant Bloody Mary minus the celery and Tabasco).

"Here's a little going away gift. It'll get your day started on the right foot." Hardy then began to talk about the night he had. He was getting into graphic detail when Jay interrupted him.

"Jesus Christ, Hardy! We're going to disappear in a few hours for the next four years-maybe the rest of our lives-and you're talking this bullshit stuff." Jay sounded a little stressed.

Hardy looked -honest to god- hurt. "Aw shit, I know. I respect you guys for what you're doing. It'll be fine. Look, I made it through a tour in the Army. If I can do it, you guys can."

Howard glanced at Jay. This was a new Hardy they were hearing.

"Just go along with the bullshit," Hardy continued. "Swallow your pride once in awhile and keep your head above water. Score as many women as you can. Keep your back to the wall in the gin mills. And hang on to your wallet and your sense of humor. Don't take anything too seriously and always use a rubber."

Jay and Howard were trying to digest this barrage of advice. "I plan on keeping my wallet, but I'm not sure about going along with all of the bullshit," Jay said finally.

"You have to. At least with some of it; they'll fry you otherwise. There's more of them than you. Remember, they hold most of the cards. Its up to you to get as many of those cards as you can."

"Hey man," Howard interrupted, "This is getting pretty heavy."

"Its a heavy time," Jay muttered. They sat silent for minute and chugged down the rest of the Bloody Mary mix. They pulled up to the hotel again and raised a last toast to Hardy. They got out of the car. "Careful, boys," Hardy said. "Keep it cool on the tool and straight-fuckin'-A all the way, man."

"Thanks man, for the advice and all," Jay said. "And thanks for the farewell. It helped. And you take it cool too."

The Cadillac pulled away and headed down the street. They walked over to the bus that was now parked in front of the hotel. It was an old black bus with only its clearance lights lit. It was completely unmarked: no signs, nothing. It sat at the curb in an ominously threatening silence. It was the most menacing bus Jay had ever seen. A line of very somber, depressed looking young men, were filing into it. All this under the watchful eye of a mean looking weasel in a uniform. Jay and Howard joined the line.

They found their seats as the bus pulled away from the Whitetail, heading for the first stop on the recruits' journey: the YMCA, and a quick breakfast.

By the time they got to the Y, they were feeling the effects of Hardy's early morning eye openers. They both had a weird combination of feelings: a little depressed, angry, stunned and mellow. They were herded into a large room and lined up at several long tables for what was loosely called breakfast. Jay looked at the others around them. Gone was the somber mood of the group who had earlier boarded the bus. Gone was the general sense of doom and depression. The others had gotten noisy. Talkative. The mood around the tables of recruits (soon to be swabs, sailors, seamen, or whatever the hell they were going to be) was surprising. Shocking in fact. There was a gaiety and festive mood like they were all headed for a week of summer camp or getting ready to raid a girl's dorm or something. Jay looked at Howard.

"What the hell...?"

"I don't get it either." Howard shrugged.

"These bastards are crazy. They forget where we're going?"

"Fucking crazy," Howard agreed. "Lets eat as far away from them as we can."

They sat down at the very end of one of the long tables. Bowls of some sort of sludge (oatmeal?) were placed in front of them. Plates of yellow mush (scrambled eggs?), bowls of lumpy brown stuff (hash?) and plates loaded with slabs of flat blackened shingles (toast?) appeared in front of them. "Eat hearty, boys!" A matronly middle-aged woman plopped plates down in front of them. She seemed to love her job and was way too cheerful as far as Jay was concerned.

"Since when does the Y have waitresses?" Jay asked Howard. "Who is this woman anyway?"

"I dunno. Your mother?"

"I can't eat this shit! Just looking at it makes me sick!"

A gangly and gawky looking kid sitting across from them reached across the table as Jay pushed his plate away. "Ain't ya gonna eat your breakfast?" Ain't you hungry? Care if I have it?"

"Help yourself." Jay looked at Howard through his red eyes, and then he rolled his eyes.

The kid was in seventh heaven. Not a care in the world. "Ya know, I always eat a big breakfast. Always. Makes me sharp for the rest of the day. Momma taught me that. Momma always says to eat a big breakfast, says it'll make me a winner. Like Wheaties! I love Wheaties. Breakfast of Champions and winners. I'm gonna be a winner. In the Navy. They told me I'd be winner!"

Jay had had enough. "Who put the quarter in you?" he exploded. "You're a wiener all right. A big fucking wiener! Enjoy your fucking breakfast!" He stood up. "I'm out of here," he said to Howard.

"Wait up!" Howard followed him outside. "You're not leaving me alone in here."

They leaned against the bus, dazed by the booze, angry, but strangely calm and feeling a little lighter. They lit cigarettes and waited for the rest of the group to finish eating.

"I think I'm going nuts," Jay announced.

"I always believed you were already nuts Jay."

From the Y, the bus headed for the train station. From there they would ride the rails south to Great Lakes. From the back of the bus, a group was singing "Anchors Away." They sounded like a group of sixth graders on a field trip to the zoo. From the open windows, they yelled and whistled at girls on the street. Normal girls, going to school, going to work, doing normal things. The normal girls stared as the freak-show-on-wheels cruised by.

29

Jay was getting a headache. "For Christ's sake! It's 7 in the morning! WHAT IS WRONG with these guys?"

"I told you. They're fucking crazy."

"They're lambs heading for the slaughter and too stupid to even realize it."

"Listen to Mr. Sunshine," Howard said. "You shouldn't drink in the morning. It makes you cranky. And let me be the first to remind you that you're on the same bus, heading for the same slaughterhouse...shitbag."

"Shut the fuck up."

The train was a little better. It was large enough so they could get away from the maddening crowd. Jay slouched in a corner of one of the last cars and tried to sleep. After a half hour of fitful dozing, he woke up. He was anything but refreshed. The lack of sleep, the booze, no breakfast and the general sense of doom resulted in a real downer and a pretty bad mood in general.

Bored, they wandered into the next car. This one was packed with soon-to-be-sailors. In the center of the car, an attractive young lady was entertaining a group of drooling young recruits. She had long blond hair. Her mini skirt revealed a pair of legs that seemed to climb all the way up to her neck. Her cute pixie face was perched just above a very healthy set of lungs. She was laughing, giggling, and flirting. She told them she lived in Waukegan and was heading home after a wild all-nighter in Milwaukee. Her daddy was an Admiral and she really loved sailors.

Jay was unimpressed. "So what else would you expect a girl to say when she's center stage in a pack of horny, fired up guys who won't be seeing a female for the next 10 to 15 weeks?" He asked, not expecting answer.

He and Howard watched the show from the back of the car. They heard her say her name was Angel. "The only Angel I ever heard of was a stripper." Jay commented.

"This one sure wrote the book on prick tease," Howard said. "Wonder if she's going to sign autographed copies for the boys."

Angel was definitely flirting in high gear, giving her name and address (or some name and address), promising to write back to one and all. She was obviously the Navy's Official Great-Lakes-

Andy stood up and looked out on the sidewalk. "Coast is clear. Nobody out there."

"You sure?" Little Eddie asked. "They're tricky. You have to watch them all the time. Hey! I hear someone coming! COPS!" He ducked to the floor. Andy followed suit. Gus had never gotten up.

"Hey idiot boys! Is that you, Andy? What the hell you doing down there?" Fat Charlie was looking down at them.

They slowly got up and climbed up the three steps. Once on the sidewalk, Little Eddie stopped suddenly. "COPS!" he yelled again, pointing over Fat Charlie's shoulder. Fat Charlie turned to see what he was pointing at.

"Jesus Christ, Eddie! Shut up! Those red lights are just party lights on someone's patio."

Andy looked at a bright red blur across the street. He looked real hard. Sure enough, they were only red patio lights. Man, he thought, this is really some good acid.

"Gus, you drive," Charlie said. "Somebody probably called the cops and I don't want to be the one stopped. I don't have a license. Besides, I've got some beer to drink."

That wasn't a good idea. Gus was wasted. But he headed down the street anyway, determined to give it his best shot. Before long, Andy realized something was wrong. They didn't seem to be moving very fast. As a matter of fact, they weren't moving at all. The VW would move about 30 feet and stop. Move thirty feet and stop. Go and stop. Go and stop. What the hell is this? Andy wondered.

The Benjamin Franklin Insurance Building got ready for Christmas real early each Fall. In order to promote the upcoming festive season, they replaced the white lights in their old streetlamp globes with alternating red and green ones. Gus had seen the red and green street lights and had been responding accordingly. Go and stop. Stop and go. There were about twenty lights along this long block. Gus was about three fourths of the way to the end. Fat Charlie started laughing his ass off. Little Eddie hadn't even noticed. Gus stopped in the middle of a four lane main street to obey some higher, mysterious traffic law. He started up again and finally reached the end of the block. "God this town has a lot of lights," Gus complained. "You'd think they could synchronize the timing better or something." The VW continued down the street.

Fat Charlie was drinking like a fish. It wasn't easy drinking beer and keeping up with tripping acid heads, but he was giving it his best shot. As the night wore on, the acid started to wear off a little, but Fat Charlie was just getting started. He was rapidly heading for a different plane. He got drunker and drunker.

About midnight, they all decided they wanted to shoot some pool. They headed for the Strike & Spare. It had a pool hall attached to the back of a large bowling alley. They found a parking spot close to the door and headed into the building. To get to the pool hall, they had to walk down a wide hall-like-entryway inside the bowling alley and go past a large plate glass window. The window was a good twenty feet long, extending from floor to ceiling and looked into the bowling alley's restaurant area. It reminded Andy of being in a giant fish tank. People on the other side of the glass glanced at them as they paraded by. Andy wasn't sure if he was outside of the tank looking in or inside looking out. The way the people were looking at him caused him to suspect the latter. Fat Charlie was lagging behind.

By the time they got to the entrance of the Pool hall, Fat Charlie yelled from the other end of the hallway. "Hey guys! Waitdafuckup, Igottadosumpin, waitferme!"

Fat Charlie got his nickname because he was over six feet tall and weighed a good 300 pounds in his birthday suit. Apparently, he had now decided to show off all 300 pounds, in his birthday suit, to the diners on the other side of the glass. He had dropped his drawers and was waltzing slowly down the hallway with them down around his ankles. Andy, Gus and Little Eddie all started yelling at him to pull them up, but Fat Charlie was clearly on a mission. A mission he alone understood.

Suddenly he spotted his target. It was an innocent young couple in the restaurant on the other side of the window. Their table was right up to the window; touching the glass. They were obviously engaged in an intimate conversation. It was a special moment. They leaned across the table, holding hands. Their faces drew ever family. The only way this would work would be if someone had to shit real bad. Andy had to shit real bad. So he didn't care at this point.

Fortunately, There was almost no one else in the bathroom anyway. That was fine with Andy. He had plenty of room. This shit is really a healthy one, he thought. He kept on shitting and shitting, working on a real masterpiece. He looked at his creation when he finished. God, it was a trophy. It was just the type that would make anyone proud. I should pick this up, he thought, and put it on display for my..... Andy was abruptly awakened from his reverie.

"Hey! Why's your dick hard? These guys turn you on?" A big, red haired (if Andy could judge by the intruder's shaved skull) guy stood over Andy, staring at him.

Andy came to life. The acid was wearing off; the trip was coming to an end. "No goddamn it! I just finished a healthy shit! That's all. I shit! Ok with you? Andy decided that this guy was just another recruit and he wasn't about to take any jive ass shit from him. "What the fuck you looking at my dick for? You a homo or something? You gotta thing for dicks? Leave me the fuck alone. You ain't shit! You're just another scumbag!"

The intruder hadn't expected that. Andy had looked like just another space cadet to him. He didn't know what to say. "Uh, ok," was all he could come up with.

That was how Andy met Mazon. Mazon was a Jewish kid from New York City. He was the biggest Jewish kid Andy had ever met. Not as big as fat Charlie, but almost and with more muscle. He also had the strongest New York accent Andy had ever heard. Maybe because it was the first New York accent Andy could remember hearing. It was kind of nasal too. For example, Mazon might say: "I'm gwoin' down to the boiber's to get a haycut for a quoiter." But he was more likely to say: "I'm gwoin down to the coirner wid my twenty spot to pick up a whooer." Not being from the big city, and not hearing or seeing the actual word, Andy didn't now that Mazon meant whore when he said whooer. It took Andy a while to figure out what a whooer was. Mazon had a good time laughing at Andy until Andy figured out what a whooer was.

Even though they came from different backgrounds, they had some things in common. Andy liked to laugh; Mazon knew a lot of jokes. They both smoked Lucky's. They both arrived and were admitted to hell at the same time.

Mazon had been raised by his mother. He said she wasn't real Jewish, in the religious sense, but she was in other ways. He didn't remember his dad. His mom had always told him that his dad was a schmuck. Andy wasn't sure what a schmuck was, but he didn't think he should ask right away.

Mazon was either quite worldly or he put on a good show. He could put on that New Yawk, Jewish schtick and be extremely funny. Even though he was raised by his mom, he definitely was not a momma's boy.

They became fast friends and ended up in the same company in Boot Camp. They discovered that because of their age (they were a year or two older than many of the other recruits, not right out of high school), they had a shared goal, to survive rather than to succeed in the Navy. Because of this they weren't that easily influenced by the assholes running the show. Most of the other recruits were right out of high school (or dropouts). You could tell them apart from the older group. Just one or two years of life-after-high-school helped them resist the Navy's "break'em down and rebuild 'em our way" philosophy. This was an important discovery for Andy and Mazon.

It soon became clear that Chief Jones wasn't making them do any of the gung-ho stuff the other companies were being subjected to. He seemed to be going through the motions. As they spent more evenings talking to him, Chief Jones started talking more and more about how phony and messed up the Navy was. He related stories about alcoholism and laziness in the career men and complained that there was a general ambiance of ungodliness throughout the entire system.

Man, Andy thought, this guy's something else. But, he reminded himself, it sure beats the alternative.

The more the Chief talked, the more candid and adamant he became. Finally, one evening, he announced that he couldn't take it anymore. He was getting a discharge.

"An honorable discharge, Chief?" Andy really wanted to know.

"Yeah, I made a deal with them. As soon as I get out, my wife and I are going to be missionaries in Africa. I've had it. I'm getting my tattoos sanded off, too."

Holy shit, thought Andy. That sounds like one painful process, and probably just an exercise in guilt relief. This guy is serious. He's not a bad guy. He's leveling with us about the Navy. He talks to us like equals and answers our questions without any bullshit. He might be ok.

This went on for another week, until one day they came to get the Chief. When the three marines came for him, the entire company was in the barracks, getting ready to go greet the morning on the grinder. Two enlisted Marines and one officer came in, produced some papers, grabbed him by the arms and headed toward the door. Their orders were to escort ex-Chief Jones off of the base.

Chief Jones asked about his papers and was curtly told that they were all taken care of. It was obvious to Andy that the Chief hadn't gotten the deal he thought he'd been promised. He looked from one Marine to another but got no response. Then his gaze shifted to Andy. His eyes weren't focused real well. Looking directly at Andy, he said, "Remember what I've told you, all of you! Get everything in writing before you agree to anything! They'll cheat you! They'll lie to you." The Marines moved him closer to the door. "They'll promise you promotions and then not deliver! They'll promise you bonuses and then lower your pay! They say they'll send you one place but then send you another! They'll look for excuses to write you up! They'll plot and scheme so they can get your wife!" Chief Jones was yelling by now. The Marines had his feet off the ground and carried him out the door. As he disappeared from the sight of his company he yelled," Watch out! I've warned you!"

They never saw him again. Andy felt kind of bad about the whole thing. Chief Jones had honest with them. Apparently he was too honest for his own good. The Chief was the first person Andy knew that the Navy "disappeared." Disappeared: here one minute, gone the next, never to be heard from again.

Company 54 had developed some bad habits with Chief Jones because he knew he was a short timer and didn't watch them real close. So they had begun taking some liberties unheard of in the other Companies. They had more smoking breaks than anyone else. They only participated in about half of the marching drills. No one knew all 21 steps of the "Manual of Arms". Most noticeable of all, their shoes were not as shiny as everyone else's. Most of Company 54 didn't take the whole Navy thing very seriously.

Smoke breaks were few and far between, per Navy directives. Many of the recruits were already slaves to the tobacco habit and the few smoke breaks were just not enough. Since Chief Jones didn't watch them real closely while they were marching, they had taken to lighting up in the middle of the ranks and passing the cigarette around. Also, guys inside the ranks would try to trip those ahead of them or short stepping to screw up the cadence. The Company was usually in chaos when it marched outside. Inside the drill hallway was a different story. Since there were always other companies and Company Commanders watching, they had to try to behave themselves a little more. They had made the mistake of screwing up in the drill hall once and both Chief Jones and Company 54 had gotten a royal chewing out for it. Before too long it seemed that a lot of the other Company Commanders made it their business to watch Andy's company, even though it didn't seem to be their business. In hindsight, Andy realized that the Navy was conspiring it! Come on and meet me, boots! Just what the fuck are your names and what Company are you fuckheads with?"

Man, does he have bad breath, Andy thought, his mind racing. Having Hardeners's screaming face inches from his had gotten his adrenaline flowing. Ok, I'm scared, really scared this time. Shit. Did I fuck up this time or what? What's gonna happen now? Man, this hardass is going to have a heart attack. I hope he does. I'm going to run if he does.

Chief Hardeners turned to the sailor on duty. "Petty Officer Droole, write this shit up in the duty roster! I want names! I want their company number! Shit! Never mind the company number, I bet I know it. They're probably from that rag tag piece of shit company upstairs, 54. The one that pansy ass, crybaby Chief Jones had until last week. Now they've got that candy assed Crane. I've seen them drill and they look like a bunch of fucking retards. They can't march, they can't drill, they can't do shit! He turned back to them. "You scum bags give Petty Officer Droole your names! NOW! Goddamn it!"

They all decided they better cooperate. They began blurting out their names all at the same time. This brought another outburst from Chief Hardass. He ordered everyone to give their names in turn. Kane, Big Lip Wayne, and Hot Dog Terry all gave their names. Then Andy heard Mazon give a fake name to Petty Officer Droole. "Name's Mason, Steven A., Sir!"

That seemed like the smartest idea Andy had heard in a while. "Rogers, Andrew L." he said. It seemed like the right thing to do. LIE!! What else was there?

Chief Hardeners was gaining a little control over himself. He lined them up against the wall. "I'm real interested in seeing how many pushups a pack of candy asses like you can do." He smiled at them, a vicious smile that turned into a sneer. "Hit the fucking deck and give me 50 real quick. Go all the way down, nose to floor, and then all the way back up, or else I see how far I can bury my boot up your ass!"

They finished the pushups, then did situps. They did situps for a long time. Then they did Jumping Jacks. Chief Hardeners' verbal abuse was more controlled, but non-stop. He seemed capable of some pretty serious sadism. By now, he'd forgotten all about Sophia Loren and was really enjoying his job. He had them do more pushups while he read the duty roster that Petty Officer Droole had written up. "Halt! On your feet!" he screamed.

They staggered to their feet. He told them to shout out when he read their names. When he got to Mazon's fake name, Mazon yelled "Yo!" without batting an eye.

Cool, Andy thought. Hardass yelled, "Rogers!"

"Yo!" Andy responded. Good deal, he thought. I got him! He doesn't know our real names and I may just get out of this tight spot after all.

Suddenly Hardass was in Andy's face. "What's your fucking name, sailor?"

"Rogers, Sir!"

"What was that? I don't believe I heard you."

"Rogers, Sir!"

"Scumbag, that makes two times you've lied to me! Do you want to make it three? You know, third time's the charm and all that shit? What is your real name, scumbag?"

Andy was thinking. He was scared. How the hell did this hardass know? "Mathers, Sir!"

"You are not only a scumbag, Mathers, but you are a candy-assed-lying-scumbag. Your ass is grass and I <u>am</u> the lawn mower!"

As scared as he was, Andy couldn't help thinking, What? This guy uses that tired lawnmower phrase. What a puss. An idiot. Yeah, what a fucking idiot.

Chief Hardeners interrupted Andy's thoughts. "Anyone else a fucking liar in here?"

"Yes, Chief, Sir! I am also a fucking liar."

Mazon. He's owning up to it, but Andy could tell through that New York accent that he wasn't as concerned as he was trying to sound.

"What's your name, scumbag?"

"Mazon, Sir!"

"Mazon, your name's not on this list! Are you fucking lying again?"

"No sir! My name was Mason, but my name is really Mazon. Its not on the list sir!"

"I know you're name's not on the list, you fucking idiot! What did I just say? *I* said your name's not on the fucking list!" Hardeners screamed, his face bright red. "You are not only a fucking liar, you are also a goddamned maggot-eating-wise-mouth-jew-prick, aren't you? You can't ever tell the truth, can you?"

"No sir! I mean yes, sir, I am a maggot-eating-wise-mouth-jew-prick! I can tell the truth. I just..."

"Shut the fuck up! Yes, you are a sorry piece of shit, whatever your name is. Do you know what I hate most in this world, Slick? I hate liars! I hate liars more than anything else. Liars lie because they are worthless pieces of douche bag chunks. They lie because they have something to hide! And you and Mathers are two liars who are going to stay a little while after I check out the names of the rest of these assholes. I want to personally show you how much I hate liars!"

"Sir," said Petty Officer Droole. "His name really is Mazon, not Mason. Mason was the lying name he used, sir. It may have seemed kind of confusing, but here his name is, see? Mazon, not Mason like you thought"

Chief Hardeners turned to Petty Officer Droole. He just stared at him for a few seconds. He was still bright red. He started to shake. Andy wondered if he was going to explode. He did.

"Goddamn it, Droole, you're a fucking moron too! I know that. I know his real name and I know his fake name. I know them both and it doesn't mean shit! Whatever name he uses, he's still a lying scumbag maggot. And you, Droole, are a stupid son of a bitch! Now shut the fuck up and stay out of my way while I do my job or I'll nail your ass to the wall!"

Droole looked like he needed a hole to crawl into and hide. He put his tail between his legs and went to stand in the corner.

Hardass turned back to Mazon and Andy. "Aren't you a maggot, Mazon?"

"Yes sir", said Mazon, "I sure enough am that sir, in spades." Andy thought that Mazon sounded a little too cocky.

Chief Hardeners apparently thought so too. Without warning, he kicked Mazon real hard in the stomach. Mazon doubled over and dropped to his knees, in real pain. Andy immediately stopped seeing anything remotely funny about the situation. The situation had just graduated to real serious shit. Hardeners looked at Andy, who braced himself for the assault. But Hardeners looked away and walked to the other four members of the renegade group.

After he decided that he finally had everyone's real names, Hardeners called up to Company 54. He got mad when he found out Chief Crane was gone and a substitute was there in his place. He then had Petty Officer Droole escort the other four back to the company. Hardass left them with some final words, "I'll make a full report to your Company Commander as well as to the Base Commander first thing in the morning. Your life will not be the same because of this severe breech of military law. You are all in a world of shit!"

Mazon and Andy were left alone with Chief Hardeners. No witnesses, Andy thought. He was scared. "All right," Hardeners growled through clenched teeth, "you lying assholes are going to do some more pushups."

They did pushups until they couldn't lift themselves off the floor any longer. He screamed at them. He threatened them. He kicked them. He stood on their backs, but they couldn't do any more. "Try maggots, try! Try! Try to raise your low-life measly little pencil dicks off the deck! You can't do it can you? You're candy-asses, aren't you?" They were too exhausted to reply. Just as well. At this point it was much safer to say nothing.

Next he had them up against the wall, going through his psychological repertoire of verbal abuse and assault. Hardeners was good at this, he'd done it many times before. He had them convinced they were worthless and stupid. They were heading for life in the Brig. The Brig, he said, was not like prison. In the Brig, they don't feed you, much. You don't get shoes, you go barefoot. There's no light or heat in the Brig. There are rats and bugs. Millions of bugs. Some inmates never get out because their cases are "lost" and they are forgotten about. There is no contact with the outside. Andy and Mazon may never see their families again, blah, blah,

blah. Every once in awhile, a well placed smack across the face, just to make sure the lying maggots got the point and were still awake. Although Andy knew better than to believe all of it, he was still scared. And tired and sore. Very sore. His back hurt, his legs hurt, his head hurt and his numb arms had the consistency of cooked linguini.

Hardeners finished up. "Tomorrow you'll be turned over to the Big Dogs" (the authorities). "They'll take care of you two lying maggots. The Big Dogs are rabid. They'll go to work on you until you're chewed-up raw meat. When they're done with you, you'll wish you had never thought about leaving your nice warm rack tonight. You'll wish you'd have never tried to sneak out. You'll wish and wish and wish, but tough shit. You wish in one hand and shit in the other, see which fills up faster. And then I'll make you smell it. You'll learn real quick what's real in this man's Navy and what's shit. You boys are in deep shit! In a world of deep shit!"

Hardeners' speech brought Andy back to life. Not because it inspired him. Not because it scared him. He was already scared. But what the hell, he thought. I've heard that "world of shit "phase one too many times. It's getting old. First it was scary, now it sounds stupid. All this, just because we were trying to sneak out for a hamburger and a beer? Fuck him! Big Dogs? Rabid dogs? Fuck them too. Hell, we weren't hurting anybody. Yeah, it was a dumb thing to try, but come on, the brig? The Navy may be fucked up but it can't be that extreme, can it? Somebody around here must have some common sense. Oh well, he consoled himself, nothing I can do about it now. What's done is done. I'll just have to wait until morning to see how this ends up. Ride it out. This must be what Hank meant by a SNAFU!

Andy felt worse in the morning. A hodgepodge of emotions and thoughts weighed on his mind. He had less than two hours of sleep. His back was worse, his head was worse, his arms were worse. His outlook on life was worse. The morning started out like any other, but worse. Nobody said anything to them. The renegades didn't talk much to each other. They ate breakfast and marched and had a class about tying knots. Andy had almost started thinking that maybe they'd forgotten about the whole thing, when two big Marines entered the classroom. They were there to escort five recruits to the CID (Center for Investigative Detention). The five names were called out and they were lined up into a small formation. The rest of the company sat silent and wide eyed; almost know one knew what was going on.

The CID was in the basement of a building that looked similar to the barracks. As they entered, doors were locked behind them. They were herded into a large room with tables, chairs and a few bunks. They were led past a few other sailors who were sitting at a near table, to a table at the opposite end of the room. They were told to sit down and wait for further orders. The other sailors stared at the newcomers. Andy stared back. There was something strange about them. Beside the fact that they all looked like hardened criminals, some of them had hair. Long hair. Some so long it almost touched their shoulders. Man, thought Andy, maybe Chief Hardeners was right. Some of these guys look like they've been growing their hair for a long time. Here they sit. Nobody remembers them. And this is just the CID. I guess the right to a speedy trial isn't part of the Military Code of Justice.

Nobody talked for awhile. Mazon noticed that the other sailors were smoking. "Hey," he whispered, "the smoking lamp must always be lit in here."

They pulled out their cigarettes and started to smoke. The cigarettes helped relax them a little. Smoking was a familiar activity in a strange and unfamiliar world. They spoke in hushed tones: talking about what they should say. They all agreed that the best course of action was to tell the truth. Maybe it sounded dumb, but the truth is the truth. At least they'd all be saying the same thing: they just wanted to get out for a while, meet some girls, eat real food and have a beer.

They were questioned individually in a tiny, windowless room. Everyone was questioned twice. Then they were questioned in twos. It seemed that the Big Dogs did not like the answers they were hearing. The reasons for the foiled escape were too simple. They wanted something more complicated; they were looking for a conspiracy. The questions were weird: What were the recruits really doing? Where were they really going to go? Who were they really going to meet? Were they antiwar sympathizers? Were they trying to embarrass the Navy? Were they sneaking out to call a press conference? The renegades persevered. The Big Dogs couldn't get them to lie, no matter how hard they tried.

By early evening, the questioning stopped and they were allowed to eat chow. They were escorted to the Mess Hall by Marines (armed Marines, Andy noticed). They ate and were then marched back to the CID in enforced silence. They were each issued a sheet, pillow and blanket and assigned a bunk in a locked room that looked like a jail cell.

Kane, who was weird in a number of ways, was also homophobic, to the max. He had recently adjusted to living and sleeping with a hundred guys in Company 54 and had finally convinced himself that his fellow Company recruits were straight. Now, however, he was in a different situation. Jail. He remembered all of the stories he'd heard about guys in prison and jail and how they went crazy without women. He imagined all kinds of father stabbers and father rapers breaking into his cell and raping him. The others all promised Kane they would keep an eye out for weirdoes. Andy didn't really believe anything like that would happen, but, nervously glancing around, he thought, you never know. Nobody slept very well that night.

In the morning, the Marines appeared to escort them to breakfast. The renegades made up their own little troop. They tried to march the best they could, figuring that they needed to make as good an impression on everyone as they could if they were going to get out of this fix in one piece. However, the other prisoners, the alleged father-rapers didn't care how they marched. They were never in step and talked back and forth to each other, but they stayed in line.

The questioning went on for two days. They experienced a number of emotions: mostly fear and hopelessness, but also some anger and contempt, which was always covered up and never shown. They stuck to their stories. The truth was easy to stick to. The Big Dogs were convinced that a conspiracy existed; that the renegades all knew each other before joining the Navy. Even though Andy and Kane were from the same town, they didn't know each other. Even though Hot Dog Terry and Big Lip Wayne were from Kentucky, they didn't know each other. The Big Dogs couldn't buy it. They believed there was something bigger involved than just sneaking out of the barracks for a burger and beer. Everyone of the renegades was in a recruit leadership position. Possibly their goal was to brainwash the other recruits in the company with communist propaganda. The Big Dogs figured that they conspired to all enlist together, manipulated their way into being in the same company and then disrupt the Base with communist sponsored un-American activities. There was almost a constant anti-war protesting group just outside the gates.

The questioning got more bizarre. Interrogation is a strange experience. Others are in total control of your existence. You can't leave unless they allow. You can't do anything unless they allow. Andy started to feel claustrophobic. He felt choked, cut off from the rest of the world. The activity of answering questions helped take his mind off the strangling feeling of confinement. On the second day, the questioning became real strange. Andy was confronted by three investigators. They started off real nice, then one or two of them started to get a little nasty. The good cop-bad cop routine. They got nastier and more insinuating as the questioning continued. For some reason, they continued to attempt to break the 'code' on the Mathers-Kane connection. Andy had repeatedly told himself, no matter what, tell them the truth. No matter what. And think about the answer before you respond. Don't blurt anything out. Be calculated, deliberate and truthful. He felt he could handle anything they would throw at him.

By the third day, the questioning stopped and the renegades were given the verdict. They were marched into an official looking room. Several officers sat behind a long desk that resembled a judge's bench. The renegades stood at attention in front of them. Armed Marines guarded the doors behind them. The middle officer (a Captain, Andy concluded by his uniform) stood up before them. The room was dead silent as he began to speak.

"It is difficult for us to understand your desire to leave the base before you complete your graduation from Boot Camp. You cannot possibly understand the seriousness of your actions. In your zeal to leave the base, you might well have prolonged your stay. It is especially troublesome that you represent much of the recruit leadership of your Company and you have exhibited a complete disregard for the leadership responsibilities you have to your company. There are those here who still believe that you have connections to those on the outside who are constantly protesting our constitutional military duties. They are at the gates of this base on an almost daily basis and would love to have deserters of your status to parade on television and embarrass the rest of us here on the base. Since you were caught before you deserted, under the Uniform Code of Military Justice, you have broken no laws and cannot be punished in the manner in which you deserve. However, you were not at your assigned duty station when you were assigned to it. We will render some punishment. Consequently, you will return to your company. You will be stripped of your positions of leadership within the company. You will be placed on informal report and your names will be listed for future reference and severe reprimand if you are involved in any further violations of any kind throughout the rest of your enlistment."

The Captain stared at each of them individually for a moment. "If you keep your noses clean, you still have a chance to graduate with the rest of your company. Dismissed!"

There was a collective sign of relief from the renegades. They were marched back to Company 54. It was late in the afternoon and they joined the company in a technical class learning how to breath through their noses so they wouldn't disturb others when they were trying to sleep on the ship. It was a very important class and they were relieved that they hadn't had to miss it. There were a lot of flared nostrils and wide eyes when the renegades entered the classroom. After class, they assembled to march to the Mess Hall for supper. New recruit leaders had already been assigned, and a new Chief glared at them as they lined up. Chief Crane was gone, replaced by a new chief who was precise, professional and seemed to be very sure of himself. He was a big motherfucker too, thought Andy. They moved out for the Mess Hall.

Chapter 7: <u>The Making of a Sailor</u>

One week to go until Christmas. 1969 was rapidly drawing to a close. The sixties were almost over. Ten years of protests, rock concerts, riots, rallies, drugs, sex, peace and love was soon to be another chapter in a history book. If there was a theme of the sixties, it had to be freedom.

"What better way to close out the decade of freedom than in the ultra-conservative fascism of Boot Camp," Jay bitched to Howard. "You know that fascism is defined as belligerent nationalism. Doesn't that hit the nail on the head!"

They were in their seventh week of Boot Camp and not in the best of spirits. It had been made clear that all recruit training would continue straight through Christmas; no home visits, no Christmas vacation, no Santa Claus.

"What better way to celebrate Christ's birthday than training with an outdated rifle?" Jay continued to bitch.

"Yeah, I guess if it was updated, really did shoot, and you had a commie in front of you. You shoot the commie for a birthday present. Christ could go for that. 'Shoot a Commie for Christ'. Go Jay! Go!" Howard was on a roll.

"Fuck you. You know what I mean." Jay wasn't religious, but he figured there was something sacrilegious about military training over the holidays. Besides, he really wanted to get out of the barracks.

To say that the first seven weeks had been different was an understatement. The first round of trauma had been the haircuts. A haircut was usually not a big deal, but in 1969, in the Navy, it was a different story. The youth of the free world had long hair. Long hair was a symbol of defiance, rebellion and freedom. And it didn't hurt that the girls thought it was sexy. The Navy haircut was more than a simple haircut, it was a statement. It was demoralizing and said, "...we've got you by the balls and we can do anything we want with you without even batting an eye."

That didn't feel good to Jay. He began noticing the size of people's ears. He had never realized ears were so big. The barber was the first stop on the Boot Camp assembly line of demoralization and intimidation. It immediately transformed a group of normal (or somewhat normal) looking teenagers into a bunch of prematurely bald headed misfits. Once they looked like misfits, they started to act like misfits. They were expected to. And they looked alike. Once they looked alike, they were expected to act alike and think alike. They were on the road to being mindless misfits, with no individual identity.

Second stop was the wardrobe department. Everyone was presented with a pile of mothballs that resembled clothes. Once separated, the pile included shirts, pants, boxer shorts, shoes, coats, and even a cute little neckerchief. "That must be to keep our hair from getting mussed in the wind," Jay told Howard.

Everything (especially the boxer shorts) was too big. Once in uniform, with their freshly shaved heads and baggy clothes, the group looked like a collection of Dopeys from the set of Snow White and the Seven Dwarfs.

"Look at this!" Jay said. "Some lean, mean fighting machines we are! How in the hell do they expect us to fight anybody looking like this?"

"Any enemy will be too busy laughing to fight," Howard observed. "Maybe they'll feel so sorry for us, they won't fuck with us."

"I look like the village idiot. Look at us, we're a rock band: Dopey and the Village Idiots!"

After they received their clothes, they were confronted by a tall, lanky Engineman Chief with graying hair who introduced himself as their Company Commander. Their new home was Company 53 and their new leader was Chief Slinde. A stocky, First Class Machinist Mate with a crewcut, standing next to the Chief, was Petty Officer Dobber. He was the Assistant Company Commander. Chief Slinde had told them in no uncertain terms that they had ten weeks to become the men of which the Navy would be proud. For ten weeks they were to behave themselves, apply themselves, drive themselves, prove themselves, and make it through Boot Camp with flying colors. He didn't want any fucking up. He wouldn't tolerate any fucking up. This was his last fucking duty in the Navy. He was going to retire in three months and nobody, but nobody, was going to fuck up and make him look bad. He intended to go out with a spotless fucking record. Dobber nodded in accompaniment to Chief Slinde's speech.

Engineman Chief Slinde then appointed an RPOC (Recruit Petty Officer, Chief) and other assorted *recruit* officers. Neither Jay nor Howard were chosen for any of these special positions. Apparently they weren't officer material. He also appointed a flag boy, Apprentice Recruit Seaman Crolinelli (ARSe), who went by the nickname of Crow.

Every company had a flag boy. The flag boy was typically the smallest, mentally slowest or cutest recruit. He was the company mascot. Flag boy Crow was small but not cute. He was an eighteen-year-old replica of Don Knotts. His job was to carry the company flag and march at the forefront of the company of marching Dopeys.

They marched everywhere they went. They always traveled in a group. No one could go anywhere alone, at least in the early weeks. Jay figured a group of 100 marching Dopeys must have looked more impressive to any enemy spies than one or two individual Dopeys out for an afternoon stroll. In reality, there was nothing very impressive about Company 53's marching skills.

During marching exercises, everyone had a job. The RPOC led the Company everywhere they marched. Engineman Chief marched alongside, yelling encouragement and keeping them in line. Dobber stayed back, performing the daring double duty of smoking and guarding the barracks. Flag boy Crow marched out front with the flag; a warning to all that Company 53 was on the move. Whenever the company would come to a street, he'd run out in front and block traffic so the company could cross the street and continue on with their very important mission. No doubt a mission vital to the national security. Jay wasn't sure about the need for a crossing guard. They weren't in third grade anymore. Besides, a lot of the marching took place during weird hours (5am or 7 pm for example) when little traffic was around. Besides, since Great Lakes was a Recruit training Navy Base, everyone on base should expect to see several large groups of Dopeys marching around. Any sane driver on the road should be able to avoid a group of 100 young recruits without any problem.

However, there was a good reason for having the crossing guard. It wasn't wise to try to stop a marching company on short notice. It was not a pretty sight. It resembled a freight train that had just slammed on the air brakes. All the cars (or men) would be bumping and crashing into each other. Then the Company Commander would get embarrassed and pissed off and demand pushups.

By mid November, the weather turned extremely windy and freezing cold, and all of the outside physical training had been moved indoors. For a while, sanity prevailed and marches and other activities were called off because it was too cold to venture outside without severe risk of frostbite. The severe wind off Lake Michigan had become the recruits' friend.

When Jay enlisted, he assumed that shooting guns would be a major part of military life. He had been a target shooter and hunted a lot. He'd even been a member of the NRA. Then he realized that his political views did not match theirs (plus they wanted too much money for membership dues) and he quit. One of Jay's claims to fame had been to fire a double barrel shotgun (up to a 12 gauge)-both barrels at the same time-from his shoulder. Either shoulder, it didn't matter. Although one or both shoulders was usually sore, he was respected by the guys. But the girls thought he was crazy. He'd hoped it would've been the other way around. When the day came for firearm training, it turned out to be firing five shots from an ancient .22 toward an unseen target. The company then marched back to the barracks. That was the end of firearms training.

Jay also assumed that swimming would be a big part of Navy training. He wasn't a good swimmer, but could usually get around in the water without drowning. Swimming wasn't one of his favorite pastimes. Howard, on the other hand, loved to swim. He'd been a star on their high school swim team. He had been so dedicated that whenever he and Jay skipped school, he made it a point to be back for the 3:30 swim team practice. Jay had hoped that the swim training would be done in Lake Michigan and it would also be called off since it was so cold. No such luck. It was just moved indoors. On a cold December day, Company 53 marched to the indoor swimming pool. It was a successful march. Crow had done his job and the group made it without being hit by any cars. It seemed that Company 53 was getting good at sneaking up on people. When they arrived at the pool, the Chief in charge of the pool was taken totally by surprise. He jumped to his feet, dropped his girlie magazine and spilled a whole cup of steaming coffee down his crotch. After he recovered from his embarrassment, he got pissed off.

Christ, thought Jay, if these guys aren't yelling about something, they're always pissed off about something.

Engineman Chief left them in the hands of the Pool Chief and headed back to the barracks to join Dobber, a true example of a wanna' be Chief.

The Pool Chief was wet and primed. His crotch burnt. His girlie magazine had gotten ripped. He had been surprised by scumbags. Scumbags who didn't have their Company Commander with them. This was going to be fun. Maybe he could accidentally drown a couple of them.

He grabbed Crow and blamed him for the surprise on his peaceful afternoon. Crow was at attention, his eyes wide, awaiting certain torture. The Pool Chief continued to yell at him while eyeing up the rest of the Company before him. The Pool Chief then turned to Crow and kicked him square in the ass. Crow flew into the pool.

Pool Chief turned to the rest. "Alright, ladies! Get down out of your uniforms and into your swimming trunks!" They complied.

"Now! Get your stinkin' scumbag asses into the pool! I mean NOW! On the double!"

Everyone jumped in without thinking. It was a big pool, but fifty recruits jumping in the poll at the same time set off a small tidal wave that threatened to engulf the water treading Crow. They looked like the rats of Hamlin town, piped into the river by the Pied Piper, Chief Pool.

The rest of the swimming class was fairly standard and about as intense as the firearm training had been. It was divided into two parts: jumping into the water, and life saving techniques.

Everyone had to jump in the water. First, from a low diving board and then from a higher one. A much higher one. A twenty five foot higher one. Jay had a little problem with the high one. He was afraid of heights. Howard helped him out. He was behind Jay and nonchalantly nudged him over the end of the board.

"Howard you coc......", SPLAT. Jay did a perfect belly flop. Pool Chief thought it was the funniest thing he had ever seen.

The life saving techniques started with everyone jumping into the pool fully clothed. They were then told to remove their pants and shirts and tie knots in the legs and sleeves. They were then told to whip each piece of clothing over their head to trap air inside, then place the semi inflated shirt or pants under their armpit to keep them afloat. Instant life preservers! Jay was impressed. It actually worked. However, the problem was it only worked for a short time, several minutes, then they had to repeat the process all over again. They'd taken their boots off. Pool Chief decided that it'd be fun to kick all their boots into the water and make them dive for them, not stopping until they had retrieved their own pair. Pool Chief must have been a submariner; all he kept screaming was, "Dive! Dive! Dive!"

Finally, after what seemed like hours, they were back in formation. The wet clothes and boots collected, and put on. "What did you goddamn sissies learn today?" He screamed at them.

Obviously that swimming in your clothes makes more sense than swimming in a bathing suit, Jay thought. But he decided that the thought was best kept to himself under the circumstances. He didn't want to be booted back into the pool.

They headed out into the 10 degree temperatures in their dripping uniforms and sloshing boots. The only dry things they had were their gloves, hats and coats. Jay figured they were becoming men of the sort the Navy could be proud. That is, unless they caught pneumonia first and died.

Now that the Navy had them, it needed to decide what to do with them. They were to forget what the recruiter had promised. All recruits had to take a battery of tests to determine where they would be best suited to serve their Uncle Sam. The tests would decide their life, their job, and their status for the duration of their enlistment. They had no choice in the matter.

Company 53 was marched to a classroom where they met the 'Officer in charge of job (rate) assignments'. He addressed the assembled Dopeys, "It doesn't matter what you want to do. We're going to decide where you can best serve the Navy. You'll be thoroughly tested and assigned to where we think you're best suited. If you get a rate (job) you can't do, no problem. We will teach you to do the rate to which you've been assigned. We will teach you to do the impossible because we have been teaching impossible people to do what they can't do for years. We're better at it that anyone else, because we do the impossible with the impossible in every impossible way possible. We wrote the book on forcing square pegs unto round holes and each of you will be thoroughly trained in your new rate whether you like it or not. You are the round pegs that will be forced into the square holes. We will make you fit because you can't."

"I'm confused," Jay whispered to Howard, who was sitting next to him. "What the hell is he talking about?"

Howard told Jay to just fake it. No one would really know if he was round or square or, impossible or just plain irascible. "And really Jay, no one cares because he said he can make you do anything." Howard made out pretty good in the job placement process. He wanted to be a submariner and the Navy wanted him to be a submariner. They had a shortage of submariners, so he was welcomed like a long lost rich uncle.

Jay was a different story. He had signed up for the Sea Bees, but had changed his mind when he realized it was a one-way ticket to Viet Nam. It didn't matter anyway; the billets were all filled. So he was tested and retested and tested and retested until they decided he had an aptitude for foreign languages. This surprised Jay, who had single-handedly flunked two years of high school French, two years in a row without even trying. In the course of two years, he had learned a grand total of five French words, but he was always forgetting what those words meant. But the Navy decided he was good in foreign languages and would be a good interpreter. With a little training, he could become a top-notch Communications Technician-Interpreter.

Sounds impressive, thought Jay, who was envisioning spending the rest of his enlistment translating French love letters into English. It never occurred to him at that time that it would mean sitting in Viet Nam, translating messages between the Viet Cong and the North Vietnamese.

Every would-be interpreter had to pass a security clearance by the CIA, the FBI, the OSS, the DAR, Naval Intelligence, and god knows who else. No sweat, thought Jay, this is obviously big time stuff so I'll be totally honest, no matter what they ask. I don't have anything to hide. After all, I'm an all right guy and never hurt anyone that I know of. Honesty will impress them.

Things went well at first. Jay was questioned by lifers in uniform, lifers in civvies, civilians in uniform, and civilians in civvies and answered everything truthfully.

"Police record?"

"No sir!" Jay proudly answered. He remembered that someone had told him that a juvenile record was erased at eighteen, so he was telling the truth.

"Member of the SDS, of the Communist party, etc.?"

"No sir!"

"Member of the NRA?"

"Yes sir, used to be." Jay left it at that.

"Excellent." They really, really liked that answer.

On and on it went until Jay was left with one last question. The last interview with a uniformed lifer.

"Have you ever used drugs?"

"No sir!"

"Ever smoked marijuana?"

"Sure thing."

"WHAT?!?"

Oh, oh, Jay thought, too late. "I mean yes, but only once, sir."

"WHAT?"

"Just once and only a little bit." Jay was trying to think fast. "Just one time. It was a mistake."

"How SO?!?!?"

"Well, one time when I was drunk, real drunk, someone put some into my beer or at least they said they did the next day. I never realized it at the time. I'd never do it if I knew what I was doing, sir."

"You mean you don't always know what you're doing?"

"No sir, I always know what I'm doing." Jay answered. "Usually. Most of the time, Kinda'."

"Let me get this straight. You smoked marijuana but didn't know what you were doing?"

"Right, sir. But I didn't really smoke OR inhale it. I think I drank it but it may have really been a joke. That doesn't count for anything, does it?" Jay was getting nervous.

"Marijuana is no joke!'

"Yessir. I know that. Remember, I was in the NRA." Jay was grasping at straws.

"Well, we have us a problem here. Let's see what we can do about it." The lifer had an idea. "I know." He had his pencil poised over a paper in front of him. He put the tip in his mouth and licked it real good. He then erased the letter "C" that was in "CT" by Jay's name and wrote in "B." He showed it to Jay. It was now "BT".

"What's that?"

"That's your new job. Obviously you aren't trustworthy enough to be a CT; you failed the security clearance. Now you're a BT. Close enough."

"Close enough? What's a BT?"

"Boiler Technician, boy. " Don't worry, you'll love it." The lifer laughed but Jay didn't get the joke.

Four days before Christmas, Chief Slinde announced that they were getting a week off for Christmas. "You pussies have a present from Santa Claus. But when you get back you'll have to work twice as hard to make up for lost time. Things'll be rough for the rest of your time here. Don't think you're getting out of anything."

Just to make sure they didn't think they were getting away with anything, on the day they were set to leave, they were marched to the barbers and had their heads shaved once again. They were told how lucky they were to be going home. All the other companies were going home except for one that was so far behind that they had to stay to make up their time.

"They're a bunch of real fuckups," Chief Slinde told them.

So, just before Christmas, at the very last minute, Chief Slinde's announcement that they would be allowed to go home for Christmas, sent Jay and Howard heading back to Milwaukee in record time.

"This hasn't really been all that bad so far," Howard said. "We're over half done and already we get a week off."

"Yeah, but they added another week to our sentence so now we don't get out until God knows when."

They were sitting in a bar on Madison Street. Earlier that day, they'd taken the train to Milwaukee and caught a bus to Mendota. After all the hoopla and family fuss, they retreated to the bar. It was cold out so they had an excuse to wear their caps over their very bald heads.

"I never realized your ears were so big," Jay said.

"Yeah? Yours too, asshole." Howard looked around him. "Do you think anyone notices?"

"Of course not," Jay answered sarcastically. "We're only sitting in a bar in Mendota in December of 1969 and there isn't anyone within 100 miles with hair as short as ours. Except maybe Larry, the asshole recruiter." Jay added. He suddenly remembered they were just down the block from the guy who had sold them into military slavery. "Let's go pay him a visit. I have a few things to say to him."

"Oh no you don't! You're forgetting something. You may be sitting here pretending you're a free man, but your ass belongs to

79

Uncle Sam. Larry's a Chief; you're a Seaman Recruit. In the Navy, he's God; you're a piece of shit. He's right; you're wrong. You even raise your voice to Larry-hell, you even walk in there-and he'll have your ass hauled out and you'll be in shit so deep you'll never see the sky."

"You sure have a way with words. Thanks for reminding me. That pretty much wipes out any good mood I may have thought about having for the rest of the day."

"Look, if we drink enough, maybe we won't think about it."

"I don't think that's possible, but I hear you. Fuck it. I don't give a shit. I had short hair for over half my life; I can live through this." Jay tried to come up with a positive thought. "At least we're out for a week."

Two days later, Jay found himself having trouble adjusting to living at home, even if it was temporary. Over the past two months, he'd been told he was an adult. He'd been lectured that he was no longer a momma's boy and he had to think for himself. He was an adult. He was a Sailor.

This made being back at home a little tricky. The parents still thought in terms of curfews and frowned on smoking in the house.

"So the smoking lamp is out?" Jay asked.

"What on earth are you talking about?" his mother replied. "Its a filthy habit."

"Yeah but I'm an adult now."

"So you think. By the way, you came in pretty late last night. Don't plan on going out again tonight. Your dad needs the car tonight."

I have got to get out of here, Jay thought. The house seemed a lot smaller than usual. The walls were closing in. He called Howard.

"I've got to get out of here. I'm getting desperate. Let's go somewhere for a few days. Anywhere!"

"I'd love to, but I've got no wheels."

"Me neither." For the hundredth time, Jay wished he hadn't sold his car before he headed off to Boot Camp. But how was he to know? Last October 31, the last thing he would've expected was to be back in Mendota so soon, even though it was only temporary. "Let's buy a car."

"Have any money?"

"A little." Jay thought a minute. "But not enough." He thought a minute. "Let's rent one."

That afternoon, they were at the Ford dealer, looking over the rental cars. A fairly new three quarter ton pickup caught Jay's eye. "That's it! Its perfect!"

"You're nuts! What he hell do we want a truck for? We won't get any chicks in a truck. Let's get that Mustang over there."

"No way! Everyone and their mother has a Mustang. All the rich kids drive momma's Mustang. Think how cool a truck will be."

"Absolutely not!" Howard put his foot down. "No fucking way!"

Three hours later they were heading north. The cab was not as small as Howard had thought. "Pickups have plenty of room," Jay observed.

Howard grunted a reply. He had been a little pissed at first, but after they added a few options: a portable radio and a mini keg of beer, Howard finally relaxed and conceded that maybe this hadn't been the worst idea.

"No," Jay responded. "I can think of one idea that you had last summer that took the prize for bad ideas."

For three days, they toured the state in the new truck, putting on hundreds of miles. "This could get expensive," Howard said.

"Maybe, but we don't have anything else to spend our money on these days. We haven't had to pay for clothes, food or housing."

"Or haircuts."

"Yeah, I know." Jay eyed himself in the mirror. He didn't like what he saw.

Things went well. They connected with old friends and were asked a lot of questions.

"What's it like?"

"What do you do in boot camp?"

"Are you going to Nam?"

"You had any whores?"

"Screwed any Waves? Aren't they all nymphos?"

"Are you guys nuts?"

And on and on and on until Jay was tired of being the center of attention. He felt like a freak. Pretty soon, though, he began to feel less self conscious about the short hair. The later at night it got, the less Jay thought about it.

The night before heading back to Mendota Jay tried to prove that four could comfortably ride in the cab. Visibility became a problem and he deftly sideswiped a hospital ahead sign in the small Wisconsin town they were going through.

"How'd that happen?" Jay couldn't believe it. He was normally a good driver.

"It may have had something to do with that girl on your lap who was helping you steer."

"Nah, I could see around her. I think it was the ice on the road."

"No way," said Howard, "her hands weren't on the truck shifter, shithead."

Red lights flashed behind them. The two girls remembered they had to be somewhere else and bolted from the truck. Jay could see two officers approaching them in the mirror.

Oh shit, he thought. He was out of the truck, surveying the dent. "Look at this! Here comes a big ticket."

"No sweat," Howard assured him. "It's just a scratch and you can hardly see it. Besides, the cops'll probably be impressed because we're in the Navy."

Sure enough, after initially gawking at their hair, the first officer asked for Jay's license. Jay accidentally pulled out his brand new military ID.

"So, you're in the Navy, huh?"

"Yep."

"What do you do?"

"Well, we're in boot camp right now," Jay said. "But I'm going into Sea Bees and he's going into Subs."

"You going to Nam?"

"Yep. Volunteered for it."

"No shit! You guys are ok. There really isn't much damage here at all and the road is too goddamned icy anyway. No harm done, just take it easy and have a good night."

"And so," Howard said, "that is that."

"But the sign is smashed up," Jay said.

"What?" The second cop turned back.

"Shut up," Howard advised under his breath.

"Nothing," said Jay.

"Take care, sailors!" The first cop waved as he got into the squad. "Kill a commie for me."

"Sure thing," Jay answered.

Things went well until they got back to Mendota. They turned the truck in and the bill was added up. Jay was on the phone. "Say Pop, I've got a little problem here. Yeah. Right. Yeah, a lot. 600 bucks. A little dent. Yeah. They say 1500 miles, but I think the odometer is wrong. Yeah, just a loan. I'll pay you back. Really. I've got nothing else to spend it on. I'm not doing anything for the next several years that'll cost anything. I can pay you back real fast; food, clothes, housing and haircuts are all paid for. Yeah, I'm sorry . Yeah, I'll stay home tonight. I need the sleep anyway. Huh? Oh hi, Mom. Yeah. I'll quit smoking. Thanks. So you're coming soon?"

By noon the next day, Howard and Jay were on the train back to Great Lakes. "I feel like shit," Jay announced. "Maybe we should have stayed in last night."

"Nah, it was our last night of freedom for a while. It was our duty to go out. Besides, its your own fault you're all bruised up. You didn't have to get in that fight."

"Hey, that guy said my ears were big and I looked like a monkey. I didn't like that."

"Well you kind of do. And now you have two black eyes to boot."

"I wonder why we didn't get any girls?"

"It may have had something to do with you spilling beer on everyone you came into contact with."

"At least I didn't puke down that girl's blouse. What were you looking for down there, anyway?"

"Jeez, I wonder. At least I didn't pass out on the dance floor."

"Things could've been worse. At least we didn't get arrested for that fight."

"Yeah, the cops were impressed we were in the Navy. Especially when you told them we were in SEAL training. Cops really seem to be impressed with this Navy stuff." Howard looked at Jay.

Jay was asleep in the seat.

They stumbled off the train and made their way back through the gates of their temporary home. Back in hell.

A lifer passed them on the sidewalk. "Hey scumbags! Salute your superior!"

"Yessir, your superiorship." Jay mumbled.

"What?"

"Nothing sir. I said I was hoping to get a superior ship, sir!" Jay decided he better try to salute. His hand wandered to a spot above his bruised eye.

"You asshole scumbags look like shit! You stink too. You smell like stale beer."

"Yessir. We're back from Christmas vacation."

"What??"

"He means leave, sir." Howard corrected the error.

"You look like you had a good time." The lifer eyed Jay's black eyes. "What happened? Some long haired queer insult the Navy?"

That sounds good, thought Jay. "Yes sir!"

"You win?"

"Yessir."

"Outfuckingstanding! Goodfuckingjob, sailor! Carry on!"

"Yessir!" Jay tried saluting again.

They moved on. "Home sweet home," Howard said grimly. "Anchors await."

"My head hurts." Jay felt like an anchor was dragging him down.

Several days later, Jay decided he had given Karla enough time to write him back. She had never responded to his letter.

Jan. 5, 1970

Karla Frazoli
Milwaukee, Wisc.

Dear Karla:

I haven't received any letters from you. They must be censoring my mail here so I hope this gets to you. What have you been up to these days?

Howard and I were home at Christmas. I called your house and your Dad said you'd moved to Duluth. I thought that was weird. I mean, moving to Duluth in December and all. Anyway, he must have been wrong, because Howard and I saw you on Madison Street that week after Christmas. I yelled at you, but I guess you didn't hear me. I guess you didn't recognize me either. You and your friend looked our way but you must have been telling a joke or something-the way you both were laughing so hard. In case you heard Howard that day, instead of me, well, he apologizes for calling you a slut and a bitch-again. If you didn't hear him then forget it because he might not have said it after all.

We have four weeks to go before we graduate. Its been colder than the virgin mother's vagina here on the lake, but it keeps us inside so we don't do much physical training. We still march wherever we go, and we still have to sing a Navy song called "Anchors Aweigh" every time we march somewhere. Its weird around here with all these groups of singing guys with big ears and oversized clothes marching around with no particular place to go. Its been so cold that we spend most of our time marching in the field house, around and around and around, going nowhere.

We just finished two weeks of what they call Service Week. Our company was assigned to the bakery. It was pure hell. We had to work like twenty hours a day and couldn't sit down or anything. A radio blared out Jackson 5 and Osmond songs like some kind of bizarre torture. (Oops, I forgot you like the Jackson 5, don't you?) Anyway, I used to think that bakeries were run by grandmotherly old ladies who specialized in cookies and milk. Wrong! This outfit was run by overstuffed lifers with bad attitudes as big as their beer guts. I thought fat people were supposed to be jolly. To cope, some guys came up with innovative ways to amuse themselves in the kitchen from hell. Spitting in the dough was real popular. I won't mention what some of them did while making frosting. I myself discovered that cigarette ashes mix well with cinnamon. After two weeks of hardly any sleep, I'm real glad to be done with that, but I think I'm going to have a thing about bakeries for the rest of my life. A permanent psychological scar.

We still stand watch in the barracks. We struggle to keep our eyes open, because if we get caught sleeping, we get shot or something. I play mind games to stay awake, pretending to be somewhere else, light years away. They take the sentry work real seriously around here. I'm not sure if its meant to keep us in or keep the commies out. They say its to watch for fires in the barracks. I don't know, but with all the gas that's passed during the night in the building, we wouldn't have to worry about a fire; the explosion would wipe out all life for miles around. I suspect the real reason for the sentries is to keep the commies from getting in here in the wee hours of the morning and stealing our military secrets (like the words to Anchors Aweigh, our shoe shining techniques, sock folding procedures, or toilet scrubbing protocols). I haven't seen any commies around here, so we must be doing a good job.

Our social life is improving. We now get to watch movies every Saturday. They're mostly old shitkickers (westerns) that star John Wayne or Ronald Reagan. There was talk of showing Easy Rider but that was quickly censored by the Chief-in-charge-of-censorship-or-something.

Our Company Commander keeps telling us that we're getting him in trouble because we keep screwing up. We have real low scores in all of the competition events. Everything we do: shoe shining, cleaning barracks, inspections, physical activities, etc is scored and compared with other companies. Its kind of like the Olympics of useless activities. We don't do very well. The Engineman Chief is pissed at us because he wants to retire and they won't let him until we graduate. He sits in his office a lot, with the door shut. From time to time, I think I get a whiff of what smells like booze, but Howard says I'm hallucinating.

We've been hearing talk about this other boot camp company who they say is in real deep shit. They say its infiltrated by commies and hippies who will probably be shot for treason because they violated the constitution or something. They're probably misunderstood, and are really nice guys who are just trying to adjust. Any bunch that can stir things up that much can't be all bad.

I've got to go. I probably won't be back to Wisconsin for that matter, for a long time. Next month we get our orders and nobody has any idea where he is going. I'll probably be sent overseas and you may never see me again. It'd be nice if you'd write, but if you don't, I'll understand. I'll get along. Somehow. Probably.

Regards,

Jay

P.S. If you're not going to write, would you please send back those stamps I sent you in December?

Chapter 8: <u>Assholes and Elbows</u>

As Andy ate chow that night, he asked some of the guys what happened to Chief Crane. He was told that the Navy had decided they were going to make an example out of Company 54. The Navy didn't feel that Crane was up to the job so they'd brought in not one, not two, but three chiefs to share the job of kicking Company 54's collective ass and whipping everyone of the recruits into shape. Andy didn't like the sound of that.

The three Chiefs were three of the hardest Chiefs the Navy had available. Supposedly three experts in various techniques of recruit training. Each had led previous companies through boot camp with multiple honors (and multiple recruit wounds, no doubt). Company 54 was being worked overtime to catch up to the rest of the companies on the base. The good news was that the Navy wanted Andy to graduate on time; the bad news was that they were planning on breaking his ass to do it. The company was up every morning at 0400 and they didn't stop drilling until 2200 (sometimes later). The Big Three said they would continue with the 18 hour a day schedule until they felt that Company 54 was properly prepared. The Big Three didn't care about 18 hour days. They could relieve one another any time they pleased or they would ride them en masse.

It was obvious from the start that the unholy trinity was dead serious and would tolerate no bullshit. They made that clear each morning at 0400. At least two of the three would be in the barracks

a certain familiarity and warmth to it. At least you knew how to feel and what to expect when they called you scumbag. When they didn't and were nice to you, you knew you were heading for a screwing of some sort.

The ASSO looked at a clipboard. "Ah! That's it! Here you go! BT, yeah, not NT, but BT! It's all we have left." He smiled evilly at Andy. "You're going to be a BT-a boiler technician, scumbag. You'll love it."

From Nuclear technician to Boiler technician in ten minutes. What's this mean. What the hell am I in for? What's a boiler?

Boot Camp was really starting to get to Andy. He had barely started with it and he was already demoted. He had gotten crabs, and all the ridicule that breeds. Every fucking Chief or Petty officer he had met so far had abused him. At best, screaming at him. At worst, kicking his ass and standing on his back, ripping his locker apart, his bunk and his clothes apart, for psychotic inspections at all hours of day and night. Now they just unilaterally changed his career for the next four years in a matter of minutes. And, just to pile on, the base commander had given all other companies time off for a Christmas break. Not true for Company 54, they were behind. They had to stay and drill. Andy really wanted to survive this whole experience with his sanity intact, but he was having his doubts.

The clothes. They didn't fit. The shirts were too big. The dungaree pants were too short. The dress uniforms had no shape. They were straight up and down, not like the chic-looking uniforms in the recruiting posters. They were heavy, baggy and hot-even in Winter. The boxer shorts were also baggy and chaffed Andy raw when he walked. The boots were Lil' Abner rejects and the socks were too thin for the arctic climate of Great Lakes. The socks were actually thin dress socks for chrissakes. However, the peacoat, wool watch cap, and gloves fit perfectly and were a godsend in dealing with the coldest weather Great Lakes Training Camp had seen for many years.

They had to stamp their names on all of their clothes, including socks and skivvies. They each were issued a stamp which they personalized, and two inkpads-one black, one white. Personalized clothes kept thievery down among the ranks. Nobody would be caught dead wearing skivvies with another man's name on them. That'd look real bad to the homophobic Chiefs and then they'd kick the offender's ass. Washing clothes was an experience: there were no laundromats so they did it in a two-gallon bucket with hand soap, and a brush. The rinse and spin cycle was manual; they'd wring the clothes out and have to hang them outside in minus ten degree temperature. They never would dry; they just kind of froze up and looked dry. They'd bring the clothes in, the clothes would thaw but never really dry. They had to put them on anyway, then march outside in the same subzero temps from which the stiff cloths had come. Everyone seemed to march straighter with frozen uniforms.

Every village has a village idiot, Andy remembered reading once. Even if he wasn't a true idiot, the fact that he was a little different, in some way, made him a target. He tried to make good, but just couldn't cut it. Comapny 54 was no different. They had recruit DeFoose, Dufus, as he came to be known. Andy felt a little sorry for him, but kept his distance. If anyone tried to befriend him, they came to the attention of the Chiefs and ended up in a world of shit. So for self preservation, Andy kept his distance and watched Dufus become the butt of everything. Even the other recruits reacted like a bunch of chickens, going after the one who looked a little different. Dufus really didn't know which end was up, but he tried, hard sometimes.

Once upon a time Dufus played Christopher Columbus and claimed territory that wasn't his. He took his personalized stamp and marked his bunk, his sheets, his pillow and the floor around his bunk.

Dufus was almost done marking his territory when Chief One came in. Someone yelled, "Officer on deck." Everyone snapped to attention, as they had been trained to do. Most were in their underwear because it was getting late and they were wiling away the last few minutes before taps shining their shoes or refolding their clothes or combing their bald heads. Chief One stopped dead in his tracks when he saw the work Dufus was trying to finish. Names stamped everywhere. All in the wrong places. The

Chief could spot something like that real quickly. He was trained to notice mistakes. Dufus had made a big mistake by trying to personalize his own collection of linen.

Chief One was not impressed with the work of Dufus. "We're not developing a goddamned dowry for you bunch of fairies! What the fuck are you doing Recruit DeFoose? These are not yours! You are just renting them! The sheets are the Navy's! The pillow is the Navy's! The floor is the Navy's! The bunk is the Navy's! Your stupid ugly ass is the Navy's! What are you stamping your name on your arm for? Are you a natural idiot or do you have to work at being an idiot, DeFoose?"

"Yes sir, sir!"

"Yes sir, what? You're natural fucking idiot or you have to work at it." Which is it, idiot?"

"Sir, I'm a fucking idiot, sir!"

"So, do you work at it or is it natural, scumbag?"

"Sir, I work at it, sir!"

"Are you telling me that you are trying to make my life miserable, on purpose, by working at being a fucking idiot DeFoose? Cuz if you are, I'm going to kick that dumb ass of yours right up between your shoulder blades."

"No sir. Its hard, sir. I work real hard at trying to be.....uh...... right, sir."

"Well, you're not right, DeFoose. You really work harder than anybody at not being right. But, you are going to be right. Aren't you, DeFoose?"

"Yes sir. I'm going to be right, sir!"

Recruit DeFoose was real, real nervous; he sensed something wasn't quite right in his world and maybe Chief One thought it was him. He began sweating all over his shaved head; sweat began running in his eyes, making him twitch because it tickled and burned. He stood there, a big shaved head, doe-eyed, lump of nervousness, sweating and shaking, blinking and twitching in his skivvies. Then he began to fart. Just a little squirting fart, wet and stinky. Then another, and another. Some of the other recruits began to snicker. That sent Chief One to another level of pissed-offness.

"Jesus Christ, DeFoose! What are you doing now? Shitting yourself in front of everybody? Are you trying to shit on me?"

"No sir! I'm sorry, Sir..."

"Shut your fucking mouth, DeFoose! I didn't ask you for an answer. When I ask you for an answer, then you can talk to me. You big piece of shit. That's it! You're a goddamned big piece of stinking-shit-idiot-recruit, aren't you?"

"No sir, I don't think so, Sir! I think..."

"Shut up, scumbag. I can smell you. You are a piece of shit and I don't care what shit thinks. Shit stinks, it doesn't think! You shit! I smell it! You fucking stink, goddamn it! I told you you're a fucking piece of shit, didn't I? And if that's what I say you are, then that's what you are, right shit bag?"

"Yessir! You're right sir! I am a fucking piece of shit SIR!"

Recruit DeFoose then actually began shitting himself, not exactly solid, but oozing, moist, shapeless shit. His face turned white, he was so scared. His skivvies turned brown and shit ran down his leg. The other recruits watched in silence. Some were in shock; they'd never seen anything like this. Others were trying real hard to ignore what was happening. Still others were hurting on the inside from trying not to laugh out loud. Nobody dared laugh again. It would've been the kiss of death if Chief One was to focus his attention on anyone else. They were all content to let Dufus be the target; no one else wanted it. This is a real sick situation, Andy thought to himself. And, a stinky one too.

"You really are shitting yourself!" the Chief continued. "What the fuck are you going to do-dump the whole load on the floor right here? In my fucking barracks? You goddamn asshole! Get your dumb ass to the head right fucking now! Then get back here and clean this goddamn floor and the goddamn bunk and the goddamn sheets!"

Chief One was obviously worried that Dufus wouldn't make it to the head in time, so he kicked him in the ass, real hard. That didn't have the effect he expected. Instead of moving faster, Dufus stopped, let out a bellow of pain and dropped a couple of loose, slimy road apples on the floor. Chief One was close to losing what little control he had left. He was real disgusted by the whole affair. His face was bright red. His jaw muscles were so tight, Andy thought they may snap and spring loose.

Chief One looked like he was ready to explode. He moved to the nearby bunks and began ripping off sheets. He worked his way through the barracks, stripping each bunk and tossing the bedding on the floor. He kicked at the clothes lockers, sending many of them crashing to the floor. Chief One was having a full blown tantrum. Meanwhile, Dufus was limping to the head yelling, "Sir, I'm a shitbag, sir! Sir, I'm a shitbag, sir!'

"Shut the fuck up SHITBAG!!" screamed Chief One.

Andy surveyed his locker area. As much as he didn't like refolding all his clothes and remaking his bed minutes before going to bed, he really wanted to laugh out loud at the absurdity that was taking place. He had to bite his lip-hard- to keep from bursting out. What else could you do but laugh at the insanity of boot camp and the bullshit that was involved?

Chief One then informed the company that they would be mopping the barracks. The entire barracks. He was leaving for a while and it had better be spotless before he came back. Still red faced, but in better control of himself, Chief One stormed out of the barracks.

He won't be back Andy thought. He won't return until morning. They would do that. Say they'd be back and then never show up. Or sometimes they'd show up unexpected at ungodly hours. Andy had learned never to trust a Chief at his word; they were full of shit.

Dufus wasn't real popular because he had a history of bringing the attention and subsequent wrath of the Chiefs down on the rest of the company. Dufus would invariably screw up and the rest of the company would pay for it. Andy had learned to come to expect it. Sooner or later, they all ended up paying for Dufus's goofy shit. About a week after the shitting in the skivvies incident, he began collecting others' frozen shirts off the clothes line. Andy figured Dufus had run out of clean shirts. Then Dufus started wearing them, not bothering to stamp them with his name-partly because of the trouble a week earlier, but also because someone else's name was already on the shirt. That didn't stop Dufus.

Company 54 was drilling in the field house when the shit hit the Dufus' fan, again. It was warm in the field house so they didn't have to wear their coats. The company was ordered to stand for inspection and Chief Two started down the line. He got to Recruit Pielson and eyed him up and down. Satisfied that everything in Pielson's world was ship shape, he moved on to the next sailor, Recruit DeFoose. Unfortunately, Dufus's shirt also said Pielson on it. Chief Two eyed Dufus up and down and stopped in his tracks. Dufus was not the Navy poster child that day. His shoes were scuffed and his shirttail stuck out from the side of his waist. Chief Two didn't like what he was seeing. He eyed the name on the shirt. He needed to know who he was yelling at. "Pielson! Who the fuck dressed you today? Your momma?"

"No sir!"

The Chief spun to his right. The recruit next to the one he had addressed had answered. "I wasn't talking to you, dumb shit! I was talking to Pielson!"

"I am Pielson, Sir!'

Chief Two spun back to Dufus. He looked at the name on the shirt again. Pielson. He turned back to the real Pielson. Then back to Dufus. Sure as shit. They both had Pielson on their shirts. "What the fuck is this?" The Chief screamed, "Which one of you two dipshits is the real Pielson?"

"I am, Sir!" the real Pielson replied.

"Then who the fuck are you?" The Chief's face was an inch away from Dufus's. "Are you Mrs. Pielson? Are you two fudge-packing fagnet assholes married?"

He didn't wait for an answer. "You! Why do you have Pielson's shirt on?"

Dufus couldn't answer to the satisfaction of Chief Two, so he made him scrub the entire barracks head including urinals, sinks and toilets with a toothbrush. He worked almost all night.

The next day, Dufus was so tired that he was worse than ever on the drill field. He messed up so much that the Three Chiefs wouldn't let the company go for chow that night. They kept them marching and marching. When they were done marching, they did a marathon of situps, then push ups. Finally at 2200 hours,

Company 54 was marched back to the barracks for a field day exercise of cleaning the entire barracks, again.

By midnight, everyone was both dead tired and pissed off. Dufus was the target of all anger. Shortly after lights out, several of them snuck out of their bunks, went to Dufus's bunk and pulled the blanket tight over his head. While four guys held the blanket tight, the others beat him with soap wrapped in socks, fists wrapped in towels or anything else they could improvise.

It was not a pretty sight. Andy didn't participate and as pissed as he was at Dufus, he couldn't help but feel sorry for him. It wasn't right to give Dufus a blanket party. He didn't do the stuff he did on purpose. He tried to do right, but just couldn't. Andy figured that it would be more productive for some of them to take Dufus under their wing and help straighten him out. Over the next few days, several of them had decided to help Dufus out. If Dufus could improve, the Chiefs would be off everyone's ass. If Dufus looked good, they all benefited.

It worked. Dufus got better. Their lives got better. They worked harder; mostly driven by the threat of remaining in Boot Camp after the rest of the companies graduated. The Three Chiefs started telling them they were getting a little better, and they actually were getting better. As time went on, the Chiefs started saying they were not only doing good, Company 54 was better than any of the others. They were the best. Company 54 began to believe the Three Chiefs. A week before the graduation ceremonies, all of the companies were scheduled to meet in a big competition to see who was best in marching, drill, appearance and general all around Naviness. The Companies that won were given fancy pennants made of silk with gold trimming. The winner Companies got to attach their pennants to their company flags and strut around with them at the graduation ceremony. And also, receive the nods of approval from Admirals, Captains, and parents (who had no idea what any of it meant). The Three Chiefs had sent Dufus to sick bay that morning. He tried to protest because he sensed, more than knew, why.

It worked. The Three Chiefs knew what they were doing. Company 54 not only made it to the final competition, after an entire day of marching, drilling, strutting and everything else, they lined up with the rest to learn the outcome. There were twelve categories. Company 54 ended up winning all categories, except three. Company 54-the original F Troop, the misfits, the fuckups, the losers, had rebounded to become the best. Even Andy was proud of himself. He didn't know why and was not really buying into it, but since they had improved, the Chiefs had backed off and things were a lot easier.

Following the graduation, Andy received his orders. Boiler Technician 'A' School. At Great Lakes. So much for seeing the world, he thought. He was supposed to report in three days, right across the road, past the high fence of Boot Camp. Oh, boy, he thought. Here we go. Boiler Technician. How much brighter could the future be? Anchors await.

Chapter 9: Out of the Frying Pan…

"This didn't get over fast enough for me," Jay muttered to Howard. They were standing in the Great Lakes Field House Auditorium amid an ocean of blue sailor suits. Dress blues, the Navy called them. The air stank of the usual smells when thousands of people are crammed into quarters that are too small. "How many people do you think are here?" He asked quietly.

Howard did some quick math in his head. "Lots," he responded.

The rows of blue clad young swabbies, salts, and tars seemed to stretch forever. The audience seemed to number in the hundreds and consisted of proud parents, spoiled little kids and girlfriends in mini-skirts. The Lifers were decked out in what lifers get decked out in at ceremonies: shined shoes and lots of hash marks. All those nights of being on watch in the barracks had paid off, Jay thought, looking around. Not a commie in sight.

To ward off the considerable boredom, Jay considered the uniform for the zillionth time. Uniforms actually, as they each possessed several sets of monkey suits. First you had the blues. Very chic and functional if you lived in Siberia, never had to take a piss, and didn't care how foolish you looked. The woolen suits were hot and itchy. The pants were baggy with wide legs; bell bottoms the Navy called them. What they had to do with bells was beyond Jay. There were eighteen buttons on the front flap, which was fine until nature called. The shirt had a big flap on the back for God knew what. The blues were divided into dress blues and working blues. The dress blues were fancier, with white trim.

Then there were the whites. Dress whites and working whites. The working whites reminded Jay of pajamas. White, now there was a logical color, especially for BTs like Jay would soon become. He could understand blue, the deep blue sea and all that, but white? Jay wasn't sure what BTs did, but he suspected that it was dirty work and involved oil, grease, soot, and other messy stuff. White uniforms didn't make any sense to Jay.

The dungarees were for informal occasions like scrubbing toilets, cleaning sewers and generally hanging around where the public couldn't see them. The Navy had a phobia about allowing sailors to appear in public in dungarees. Dungarees looked suspiciously like blue jeans and work shirts except the pants had bell bottoms and were baggy. Jay could relate; jeans and blue work shirts had been the attire of choice in his previous life of classrooms and bars. He'd been told that the difference between jeans and dungarees was that jeans were worn by draft dodging pinkos infiltrating the colleges, and that dungarees were worn by god-fearing patriotic sailors.

The hats were something else again. They defied description. Nobody wore hats. They weren't cool, so hats were weird to begin with. The Navy forced them to wear white beanie like hats atop their shaved heads. The hats looked like they were missing a propeller. In an effort to salvage some sense of individuality, some recruits had taken to modify their hat with a personal touch. Some squared their hats, some flared them. Some tried to mold them into other shapes, usually without success. The Company Commanders kept a close eye on that and censored anything that seemed too radical.

Jay had come to realize that the manner in which a hat perched upon someone's head could signal the wearer's personality or mood. For example, gung ho jerks wore it squarely on their head in a manual-perfect fashion. Real gung-ho jerks wore it low on their foreheads, touching or covering their eyebrows. Cocky, real gung-ho jerks wore it low and at an angle, just over one eye. Tired gung-ho jerks wore the hat back on their heads when no lifers were present. The latter group was sometimes confused with the "don't give a shit" group who also wore their hat back on their heads, but didn't care if a lifer saw it or not. The hard core, "Don't give a shit" group always seemed to be losing or forgetting to wear their hat altogether. Jay had lost six hats during his stint in Boot Camp. The Navy's 11th Commandment stated that "Thou shall never go outside without your hat." Or "thou shall always wear thy cover." So the hat was actually a cover. Wearing the cover outside made some sense to Jay. It protected the shaved head from sunburn and the shit of seagulls. It also provided a distraction for the short, short hair. However, Jay didn't like wearing the hat. He didn't like being covered. He felt stupid.

Jay came out of his reverie when the crowd around him started marching. They were heading past a reviewing stand. The chiefs were strategically placed to ensure that all eyes were to the front, a formidable task especially with the miniskirts on the sidelines.

Then the daydreaming began again. It was hot in here........ the past ten weeks had been terrible. Unlike anything Jay had ever imagined, let alone experienced before. It had taken Company 53 a little time to readjust to the routine after the week off for Christmas. The combination of mind games, monotony, boredom, brow-beating and physical exertion had taken its toll. Tempers had been shortened. In the nick of time, in the past month of training, liberty had become available. They were granted a twelve hour liberty. 12 hours. A weird time allotment. They could leave at 1200 hours (noon) and had to be back at 2400 hours (midnight).

Their first mini-liberty occurred on a Saturday in early February. Jay and Howard decided to go to Chicago with two of their fellow recruits: John and Wayne. John was a big city boy and knew his way around Chicago. Early that morning, they were up early, ironing their thick woolen uniforms with their small plastic soap boxes and lighting up, burning and polishing their shoes. Before they could be let off the Base, they each had to go through a rigorous inspection by both the Company Commander and by the Chief -in Charge-of-the Main-Gate. The Navy wanted to make sure that they each looked impeccable and would be a picture perfect representative of the U.S. Navy. Hair length was scrutinized, shoes closely inspected, money and cigarettes had to be stowed in their socks. The Navy's 12th Commandment disallowed the use of pockets for anything.

It was better to put dollar bills and cigarettes in socks so they could get sweaty, stinky and have that athlete's foot feel and smell to them.

The four of them finally passed the lengthy inspection and caught the train to the Windy City. "Act like Sailors!" the Chief-in-Charge-of- the-Main-Gate had ordered them.

Once off the train, they searched for a cab. Not just any cab. They were looking for one with a particularly shady looking driver who could possibly direct them to booze and women. It didn't take long to find one. They picked a driver with two days of gray stubble, an ever-present cigarette dangling from his lip, yellow fingers and a watery left eye. He had enough grease in his hair to fry a dozen eggs sunnyside up. Tattoos covered both arms. His name was Fly. Jay figured it was his Christian name. It had to be more than just a nickname.

They stopped for whiskey. The three bottles they bought included a 100% surcharge for the cabby. Fly then dropped them off in front of a run down hotel in a seedy looking neighborhood. They went into the lobby of the Northern Hotel, signed in and got into the elevator. A skinny old man with jaundiced skin closed the door behind them .

"Fly sent us," John announced to the dead looking elevator man.

"Dunno no Fly," the dead elevator man cackled.

"Fly, the cabby," John persisted. "He said you could set us up with some women."

"Dunno no Fly. Dunno no wimmin. Here's your floor."

"You know anything?" Wayne asked.

"Nope. Dunno nuthin'. Here's yer room."

It wasn't the Hilton, but it was better than the barracks. At least they were free. For a few more hours anyway. They sprawled out on the two beds and on the floor and went to work on the whiskey. The bottles went from one to another so that everyone got their fair share. They drank a lot of alcohol in a short time.

"After we're done with this, lets go find some women, "Howard said.

"Yeah, and get some more booze." Wayne took a hearty swig from the bottle. He had bought cigars and they sat in the crowded room, smoking Dutchmasters, drinking Ten High, and watching a black and white 14 inch RCA. "Ain't this living?" he asked.

"No, it's not living!" Jay snapped. He was impatient and feeling more than a little claustrophobic. The whiskey had amplified his need to do something. Anything, instead of sitting around. "There's nothing on TV. I don't want to sit in here all day watching you jerks. We rushed out for liberty, rushed over here, rushed to get drunk. Now what? It's wait, wait. For what? What the fuck are we waiting for? Nothing. We're waiting for nothing. Hurry up and wait is too much like what we've been doing for ten fucking weeks. Let's go do something! Something big!"

They looked at each other. "Let's finish the booze first," Howard suggested.

There was a knock at the door and in strolled the dead elevator man with a woman on his arm. "You guys still looking for wimmin?" He cackled.

They stared for a good twenty seconds. "Uh, yeah. Sure." Wayne was the first to speak.

"You only have one?" John asked. "We all want one."

"One's all there is. Ya'll can have one. One at a time. That's all." The dead elevator man cackled as he headed for the door.

Wayne was from a small farm town in the Midwest. "What good is one woman going to do us?"

"She's a whore, stupid," Jay informed him.

"Oh. Ya' mean, we have to pay?"

"Fifteen bucks apiece," the dead elevator man said from the doorway.

"Fifteen bucks?" They looked at each other. "Sure," John spoke up. "Fifteen sounds good to us."

"Hey," Jay asked. "Why didn't you tell us about this before, in the elevator?"

"Can't be too careful," the dead elevator man said. "They let anyone in here, but I figured I could trust you gennelmen." He laughed hard. Jay didn't get the joke.

The hooker, who had been quiet, suddenly came to life. "Okay, boys. What'll it be? One at a time? Two at a time? No more than two." She laughed and started humming the theme song from the Stripper as she headed for the door to an adjoining room.

An hour later, the whiskey was almost gone and the hooker was almost done with her job. Jay never did remember what she looked like, except that she had frizzy red hair, nipples that couldn't be concealed through her bra, and wore high black boots. There was very little left to the imagination.

Jay was laying in the bed, watching "McHale's Navy" on the small black and white screen. The cigars and whiskey had put him in a philosophical mood. "It's not right to pay for it," he lectured the rest. "It's just not right."

"You're just cheap," Wayne said.

"No, I'm not. Why buy milk when you have free cows?"

"I think you have something mixed up there," Howard said. "Besides, its only fifteen bucks."

"Still, isn't right, Howard." Jay had spent too many hours at the gas station listening to the older pump jockeys, self-proclaimed experts in the ways of the world, expounding on free sex and how real men didn't pay for it. Jay had always figured that they were bullshitting about never paying for it, he agreed with the concept. But, maybe he was just cheap.

Jay turned his attention to the TV. There was something ironic about all this. Something about McHale's Navy on TV at this time. In this place. Sometime later, shortly after Ernest Borgnine pushed a wimpy Captain overboard, Jay laughed and promptly passed out. There were only a few drops of whiskey left in the bottle.

"Come on! Get up! We're gonna' be late for the train!" The others shook Jay awake, dragging him off the bed. Soon everyone was back in full uniform, in a half-assed way. They stumbled, staggered and swaggered to the elevator. The hooker wobbled on board with them and the dead elevator man.

They all eyed up each other on the way down. Jay started snickering. This was too much. She looked like a horse in boots. The hooker figured she was being offended. She leered at Jay. "I don't remember you, little boy. You ain't man enough?"

"Neigh. I was busy. Besides maybe you had me and didn't know it. I wouldn't have hurt you anyway. Maybe I never paid you for it. We all look alike anyway." That was all Jay could think to say.

She gave Jay the finger as they left and said, "Merry fuckin' Christmas you teeny weeny of a scumbag!"

Gee, thought Jay, she knows my name too.

They caught a cab and then took the train back to the base, arguing among themselves about who the hooker liked better. Howard abstained from the discussion because he knew better. Besides, he didn't care if the hooker liked him or not. Jay abstained for other reasons, plus he had fallen asleep again. Watching all that TV and hurrying up and waiting was tiring.

The returning cocksmen were greeted at the Main Gate by a new Chief-in-Charge-of-the-Main-Gate. "You all look like shit!" He greeted them. "What sewer did you spend your liberty in?"

"The Northland Hotel," Jay answered. "In Chicago. And its a dump."

"No shit. Thanks for the travel guide recommendation. "I'll make sure I stay at some puke palace that some fresh virgin Boots hang out at," he said sarcastically.

"We drank whiskey, Sir." John bragged, figuring that would impress him.

"No shit! I'd never have guessed that you pukes were drinking. Did you get into any fights?"

"No sir."

"You bunch of scumbag pansy asses, you should all be written up!'

"But we got us a whore," Wayne offered.

"Oh yeah?" The Chief was suddenly interested. "You babies pay big bucks?"

"Oh, no, Sir! Fifteen dollars, Sir!"

"Fifteen?" The Chief rubbed his chin.

"Uh, no, I mean, Sir, uh five bucks. We talked her down."

"No shit." The Chief was truly interested. "Outfuckingstanding!" He eyed Jay, who was having trouble keeping his eyes open. "How about you, Sleeping Beauty? You pay to fuck too?"

"No, Sir!" Jay's eyes shot open. "No way. Real men don't pay for it!"

"Fucking right! Real men don't have to. So you got it for free. Outfuckingstanding!"

Oh, oh, Jay thought. "Yessir!"

"That's a bunch of shit, Sir!" This came from Wayne. "He passed out."

"Shut up asshole," the Chief said. He's the only one with any balls and the sense not to pay for it."

"Yessir!" Jay couldn't help but agree. He wasn't sure what was going on, but things seemed to be in his favor at the moment.

"Bullshit!" For some reason, Wayne was getting worked up. "He didn't do anything with any whore. We did."

"Yeah, yeah, yeah and you pansies had to pay for it." Jay couldn't resist adding his two cents to the discussion, "besides, what happened when you passed out and pissed your pants, studley?"

The Chief stared at Wayne. He'd had enough. "Listen, you snot nosed little bastard! You can't yell at me like that! I'm the Quarterdeck Officer in charge and you're nothing but a tiny little shitball! I'll write you up just for spite!"

John jumped into the fray. "We were there! You weren't!" The alcohol had clouded whatever sense they once had.

The Chief eyed his new target. "And I'm here, you little shitballs. I'm standing on my fucking Quarterdeck staring at a bunch of smartass Boots who are about to get their asses kicked and their asses written up, in that order."

John didn't have sense enough to shut up. "Sir, we were with the whore. He wasn't!"

"Yeah, I know scumbags. You paid and he didn't. I've had it with this shit!" The Chief was royally pissed.

Then the fun started. Everyone started yelling at each other. Howard and Jay were able to slink past the gate into the shadows. They followed the fence for 50 feet, then moved back onto the sidewalk. They made a block before they met two guards heading for the gate at a dead run. They were both armed with night sticks and looked like they fully enjoyed their work.

They stopped by Jay and Howard. "Are you with that mess over there?" They pointed at the Main Gate. By now a crowd had gathered. Other recruits were coming back from Liberty. A lot of them. They stood in silence, watching the show. The extremely angry Chief-in-Charge-of-the-Main-Gate had Wayne by the throat up against the fence. His feet were off the ground. Other boots had stopped dead in their tracks, staring at the scene like deer caught in headlights.

"No, Sir!" Howard was quick to respond. "We're just coming back from Liberty. That must've started after we went through."

"Carry on, Sailors." The guards rushed on their way, nightsticks out, waving in the air.

Jay and Howard continued their walk back to the barracks. "I've got a headache," Jay complained.

"Cheer up," Howard advised, pointing at the deer back at the gate. "Things could be worse."

They were lined up at attention. Some Admiral was droning on about "...in these times of strife, in this time of war, the sense of a strong naval tradition, the immediate need for national security, the red menace, internal and external conflict, our personal patriotic duty, for the collective pride and honor of the nation and all nations and people and all peoples and blah, blah, blah..." and anything else that came to his mind. The lines of dress blues were wavering. This was taking a long time. It was hot. The recruits were hot. And getting tired of the flag waving. The heat was getting to some of them.

Blow the man down, Jay thought, looking around. Christ, he thought, I sound like Popeye. I wonder if he ever went to Boot Camp? And was Brutus in the Navy? If he was, he must have been a BT. Was Olive Oyl a whore? If she was she couldn't have been a prick tease. And was Wimpy really in the CIA? I hope we don't have to sing Anchors Aweigh, again.

But of course they did, and on went the reverie........Jay and Howard had been lucky. The other two had been written up for unspeakable crimes against the Navy, but Jay and Howard emerged unscathed. Two weeks later, they were allowed another twelve hour liberty.

The two self-professed cocksmen, John and Wayne decided they wanted to go to Milwaukee for booze and women. Jay and Howard, sensing a repeat of two weeks ago, decided instead to go to Chicago again and try a different approach to liberty. Jay had heard from someone that the Museum of Science and Industry was crawling with young women.

Howard was skeptical. "Going to a bar would make more sense," he argued.

"Come on, give it a try. We can go to the museum, pick up some girls and then go to a bar. The best of all worlds."

They again took the train to Chicago and caught a cab to the museum. After an hour of wandering around, Jay noticed there were a lot of uniformed sailors also wandering around aimlessly. "Where are the girls?" he wondered.

"At the bars, you dumb shit."

They wandered through the museum for an hour before Jay finally admitted defeat and agreed to find a bar. The few girls they did talk to were less than impressed and seemed amused at the thought of sailors trying to pick them up. It was the same old conversation.

"Do you guys have a car?"

"Uh, no."

"Have an apartment?"

"Uh, no."

"Have any grass?"

"Uh, no."

"Have any other clothes besides those monkey suits?"

"Uh, no."

"Have any money?"

"Some. Not much."

The girls would invariably start to laugh and then leave abruptly.

No one else was having much luck either. Another pair of sailors came up to them and asked if they'd had any luck.

"You sound like fisherman. We sound like fishermen," Jay responded. "Two boatloads passing in the channel. Have any luck? Nope, not much, but you should've seen the one that got away."

Howard was less amused. He wanted to go to a bar, but not with a crowd of other guys and definitely not with other sailors. "You guys trying to pick us up? What are ya', queer? Fuck off!"

The two sailors, also Boots, scampered off.

"Ok. We'll go to a bar," Jay conceded. "But remember, we're not 21. We need an understanding bartender."

"We'll just ask a cabby."

They hailed a cab and the driver was more than happy to help them out. He took them to his personal favorite spot, dropped them off and wished them well.

"Why'd he wish us well?" Jay wondered.

"Nice enough looking place," Howard observed, stepping in the door.

Inside, all talk instantly stopped the second they came through the door. Oh, oh, Jay thought. These guys aren't talking English.

Howard bent over and whispered to him. "It just hit me. The cabby was Puerto Rican, so it only makes sense that this is a Puerto Rican bar." He looked around. "An exclusively Puerto Rican bar. "

"We're dead meat," Jay whispered back.

Two hours later, things were looking up. Howard had befriended an elderly guy who appeared to be someone important and almost immediately tried to talk Howard into marrying his daughter. Apparently the rest of the bar thought that if this guy thought enough of Howard to let him marry his daughter, then the young sailors were ok. A good time was had by all.

It seemed that, only the old guy spoke English, but he translated for them to the rest of the bar. Whatever he was saying to the rest kept them happy and in a good mood. He'd point to Jay and Howard and say something. Then everyone else would laugh. This went on for a while. Finally, they called Jay and Howard a cab, stuffed them into it and told the cabby to take them to the train station.

"Adios gringos, su madre es puta grande (translation: your mother's a big whore)."

Jay and Howard laughed and waved goodbye.

They pulled up to the station. It was crowded with cabs and drunken sailors all trying to get back to the base on time. The cabby wheeled his way to the front entrance. Howard jumped out. "I've gotta' piss. I've gotta' piss! Pay the guy, I gotta' go. See you inside!" Howard stumbled through the doors of the station and was gone.

Jay reached for his wallet. Fuck! No wallet! What the hell?

"Eight buck, the cabby turned to the back seat.

"Uh, I lost my wallet."

"Bullshit! Conyo! Gimme eight buck!"

"Can't. I'll get it from my buddy. I'll be right back."

"No you don't, sengal, tu pinga. You ain't go nowhere! Eight buck or I call cop here, now! Arancalo los pelos del bollo!"

Desperate times call for desperate measures, thought Jay. He jumped out of the cab and ran into the station.

The cabby was right on his tail. "You thief bastard! Come back with my goddamn money! Chupa la pinga tu gringo!"

Thousands of sailors were in front of Jay. He jumped into the middle of the biggest crowd. All sailors. All drunk and all looking alike. He inched to the middle of the group and stood still. He watched the cabby walk into the station, looking left and right. Looking for the needle in the haystack. The cabby walked around the edge of the group for a few minutes. Then he threw up his hands in disgust and stormed out of the station, his curses lost among the loud and discordant babbling of the sailors.

Jay saw Howard come out of the bathroom. "Hey! I don't have any money. I lost my wallet," he told him.

"Lost? I don't think so. More likely lifted by one of your new friends at the bar."

Jay hadn't thought of that. He was disgusted. "Stuck in the middle of goddamn Chicago with no money. Fucking cabbie, cops, and the Navy breathing down our necks with a have-to-be-in-by-midnight-teaser-pass and no goddamn money. Son of a bitch! Now what?"

Howard found his wallet intact, with money still in it. "No sweat, man. I've got money. Let's get outta here."

On the train, Howard tried to console Jay. "It can't be that bad. What was in it?"

"About twenty bucks."

"That's ok, you don't have anything to spend money on these days."

"My driver's license."

"No loss, You aren't driving much these days."

"A rubber."

"Right. As if you ever get a chance to use one. I know, we could go back to the museum, I hear there's lots of women there."

Jay ignored him. "What else?" He tried to remember. "Oh, yeah, my military ID".

"No sweat. They'll give you new one."

Jay thought about that for a second. Outside of the twenty bucks, he hadn't lost that much. "You're right, things could be worse." Anchors await.

"Let's see your ID!" The Chief-in-charge-of-the-gate ordered Jay.

"I don't have it. Someone stole my wallet, Sir," Jay responded obediently.

"What? Someone stole your wallet?" the Chief said incredulously. Jay couldn't tell if the Chief was really incredulous or merely mocking him.

Jay confirmed. "Yessir, my wallet was stolen."

"And your ID? Did they get your ID, too?"

"Yessir. My ID too. And my wallet was stolen, both of them."

"You have two IDs, sailor?"

Jay wasn't sure where this exchange was heading, but he was sure it wasn't going to be good. "No sir. I meant my ID was stolen *also*. In addition to my wallet."

"Well, you can't enter the Base without an ID!"

"Huh?" That struck Jay as really weird. "Sir, I have to enter. My liberty expires in half an hour and if I'm not checked in, I'm AWOL and in all kinds of trouble."

"That right? Well, I'll tell you what. You try to enter without proper identification, I'll write your ass up. I need an ID."

"Look. I'm in uniform. My head is bald. Why else would I be here at this hour, trying to get on a Navy Base unless I had to?" Jay hoped that logic would prevail. It didn't.

"The uniform doesn't mean anything to me. How do I know you are who you really are and not some infiltrator, some impostor in a uniform? I need a fucking ID!" The Chief -in-charge-of-the-gate was getting confused. When a Chief-in-charge-of-anything got confused, trouble was never very far behind.

"Look," Jay tried to reason. "I'm really me. I can show you my name stenciled in my underwear."

"Are you getting smart with me, Boot?"

"No sir. But look, I've even got these dogtag license things that say I'm me."

"I need an ID!" The Chief held his ground.

Jay looked at the clock. If he wasn't checked in in ten minutes, he'd be written up as AWOL. He weighed his options. None looked good. If he came on base, he'd be written up. If he didn't, he'd be written up. "I'm coming on base," he announced, darting past the Chief. "Write me up if you have to."

Jay wasn't a hundred yards past the gate when the reinforcements arrived. Two Marines grabbed them and escorted them to the Base Sergeant at Arms Office.

In the office, they were face to face with the Sergeant at Arms himself: a kind of Super-navy-cop. The Chief-in-charge-of-law-and-order.

"So why are you trying to sneak on base?" He asked, looking as intimidating as possible.

"I didn't sneak on Base. I came on Base because my liberty was going to expire and I didn't want to get written AWOL. "

"You tried to come on base without a valid ID. I'm going to write your asses up for that."

"Someone stole my wallet, sir. With my ID in it."

Super-navy-cop looked thoughtful for a minute. "Oh. Why didn't you say so? That's different. Now I'll also write you up for destroying military property."

"What?" Jay forgot himself for a minute. "What the hell...?"

"Careful! Watch your step, sailor! Yeah, I'll write you up. You destroyed your ID, which is military property."

"Someone stole it. I didn't destroy anything!"

"Yes you did, Boot. By being irresponsible, you destroyed military property, namely your ID. And listen punk," Super-navy-cop was getting fired up. "Even if the ID belonged to you which it didn't, but even if it did, you belong to the Navy so everything that belongs to you belongs to the Navy. So you do anything with anything, you answer to the Navy."

"Huh?" Jay glanced at Howard, who shrugged.

"Here's the deal," Super-navy-cop said. "I'll write you up for destroying military property and I will drop the charges on entering the base without an ID."

"Don't I get lawyer?" Jay muttered.

"WHAT?", screamed Super-navy-cop. He was losing his cool.

Howard elbowed Jay in the ribs. Jay got the message. "Sounds fair, sounds fair," he stammered.

"What am I being written up for?" Howard wanted to know.

"Same thing."

"But my wallet wasn't stolen. I have my ID right here."

"So? You were there, weren't you? You could've stopped this irresponsible excuse for a sailor from destroying his ID."

"No way, I didn't know anything about it."

"Yeah? Maybe you stole it." Super-navy-cop eyed Howard suspiciously.

"Why would I steal it? I had to pay for his train fare back here as it was. You know," he confided to Super-navy-cop," he really is irresponsible. He should learn to stop screwing up." Howard smiled at Jay.

Fuck you, Howard, Jay thought.

Super-navy-cop considered that for a minute. "You've got the right idea, sailor. You're free to go. You can too." He motioned to Jay. "But stick close to your company so we can get back to you with the violation and collect our fine. And listen to your buddy. At least he knows his ass from a hole in the ground. Maybe some of him will rub off on you!"

"Yessir, I'll make it a point not to go anywhere. By the way, I can't pay the fine right away," Jay said. "Someone stole my wallet."

As they were leaving, and out of ear shot of Super-navy-cop, Howard whispered, "Yeah, stick with me scumbag, and maybe something near my ass will rub off on you."

"Fuck you again Howard!"

One week later, Jay was fined fifty dollars for destroying military property. He was also informed that the offense had been recorded on his permanent military record. At first Jay thought maybe he should be concerned. He reconsidered. So what? He thought to himself.

Jay was brought back to the present. The speeches had finally ended and the companies were being dismissed. Graduation was over. They were granted a weekend liberty and were heading back home to Mendota temporarily.

Earlier in the week, they'd received their assignment orders. On Monday, Howard was expected to report to the Electric Boat Company in Groton, Connecticut. It was there where he'd begin his submarine 'A' school.

Jay, expecting to be assigned to whatever distant and exotic port where a BT may be needed, was surprised to discover that, come Monday morning, he was to report right back to Great Lakes. This time, he'd be a real sailor and stay on the real base. He'd been assigned to Boiler Technician 'A' School for the next twelve weeks. This ought to be good, he told himself. I'm heading off to Boiler College. Anchors await.

Chapter 10: School? No One Told Me...

Andy didn't know the first thing about boilers. And he wasn't sure he wanted to learn anything about boilers either. But, after just barely graduating from boot camp and not getting Christmas leave like all the other companies, he and some of his new found friends had to go to the school anyway. Andy wasn't too enthused about staying in Great Lakes for "A" School. It was still too cold. He wanted to go to warm exotic ports. There were no 'identifiable' women at Great Lakes. What happened to women in every port? All the classes were filled with fresh boots like Andy, and Vietnamese sailors. Vietnamese officers, too. Andy wasn't prejudiced, but most of them looked too young to know too much. They looked like little kids. They didn't talk much in class, probably because they didn't understand the language. If they didn't understand English how could they understand boilers. Andy knew English and he didn't understand boilers. Andy could relate to that. After a couple weeks, he didn't understand most of what was being said, and he knew he understood English.

The school was the most boring experience Andy had ever been exposed to. Some of the instructors were really uncomfortable in their job. They read from manuals and drew pictures on the blackboard. Pictures that made no sense to Andy. 600 psi? Pounds per square inch? 'M' type boilers. 'D' type boilers. Some ships had superheated steam, Andy was told. That sounded different. Steam that wasn't hot or dry enough for the Navy's turbines had to be reheated under extreme pressure. The reheating removed all moisture and raised the temperature, hence 'superheated'.

During this particular lecture, the instructor came somewhat alive. He was almost preaching to the class. "Superheated steam! A killer if you 're not careful!" He rolled up a sleeve and exposed an arm with scars from hand to elbow. No hair, tight skin and ugly gaps where muscle used to be. His forearm.

"You have to be careful when you're around boilers that have superheated steam," he lectured. "The process makes the stream invisible at the point of release."

Point of release? Andy's ears perked up. What's that, he wondered?

"On board the ship," the scarred instructor continued, "steam lines will leak from time to time. Most of the time, they leak at the joints because a gasket wears out. These leaks are easy to spot because first you hear the noise of 600 psi steam hissing and screaming out of holes where the gasket used to be. Then you see the steam as it shoots at the cooler outside air and condenses at about 212 degrees Fahrenheit. The BIG problem arises when *superheated* steam blows a gasket, because all the moisture has already been removed. Without moisture, you can't see it. You only hear it. Its hot, too. 1400 degrees of extremely hot shit that can cut you in half, just like a cutting torch. When it blows out in the middle of a steam line and not at the gasket, it's really hard to determine where it is. Parts of my arm found the leak before the rest of my body. I'm just lucky it wasn't worse."

The instructor had every student's attention now. He continued, "We had a boiler blow up on another ship in my port just before I was transferred here. The superheated steam did an instant boil on the lungs of everyone in the fire room. Then it cut through the upper decks and cooked a corpsman and his patient. It continued upward until it fried an Ensign in his stateroom. Then the heat and pressure died down. This is serious stuff and I want you to learn what I know about it so the odds of you hurting yourselves or your shipmates are reduced."

Now Andy was listening intently. I'm all ears for this, he thought. He had a reason for staying awake in this class. He was thinking about survival and he needed to learn all he could about the basics so he could survive the next four years with little or no scar tissue, souvenirs. Superheated steam is some bad shit, he thought. Look at those poor Vietnamese, at least I understand English. What are they getting themselves into?

There was a mix up with Andy's paycheck. Actually there was a mix-up with everyone's check. Andy was supposed to have gotten paid as soon as he was out of Boot Camp, but two weeks after graduation there was still no check. Andy received a few advances on his pay, but it wasn't enough to actually go anywhere. It did allow for cokes and chips and a few friendly games of pool on the base. It was in cash. They paid in cash, not a check.

The base pool hall was the coolest pool hall Andy had ever seen. It was definitely the biggest. It had over forty old green felt pool tables, regulation and heavily slated with netted pockets. The white decorative 14 foot high metal ceiling had huge Casablanca type fans with twenty years of grease and dust stuck to the blades. Each table had a low overhead old-fashioned light with a banker green shade lending just the right amount of eerie dimness for the perfect gloomy, smoky pool hall aura. The light shade also had many years buildup of dust and grease: so unlike the Navy. Someone must have pulled some easy cleaning duty over a number of years. The pool hall was so big that it had four juke boxes. There were enough pool cues to outfit 100 tables and plenty of chalk and hand powder. It was a pool shooter's paradise.

It was somewhat wasted on Andy. He wasn't exactly Minnesota Fats; he couldn't shoot his way out of a rain barrel. But he liked to play the game. And Mazon, his friend and ex-partner in Naval crime had been assigned the same 'A' school. Mazon and pool halls were another matter all together.

Andy had first discovered the pool hall and had asked Mazon to go along with him one night. Mazon innocently agreed. Upon reaching the hall, Mazon reached under his peacoat and produced a smooth, black and blue hand-finished case. Inside was a stick that was perfectly weighted and had a Jimmy Carras signature on it.

Mazon could shoot pool. Nobody was anywhere near as good as he was. Andy could tell that Mazon played just good enough to win, though, and didn't flaunt it. A crowd had gathered and someone put his money up. Mazon beat the first challenger easily. He started shooting better and the bets on each game started going a little higher. Pretty soon, he was winning tens bucks a game.

Mazon had played about fifteen games when Andy noticed something had changed. Mazon was tired or bored or something. He seemed to be tired of playing and had started missing shots. So far, he'd gotten almost forty bucks from the sailor he was playing. And that didn't count the other games he had won earlier.

Mazon ended up losing the last two games and begged out, wanting to call it a night.

"What the hell are you doing?" Andy asked. "Those were easy shots you missed. Why'd you do that? You'd been making those shots all night. What are you doing?"

"What would you have me do, Andy?" Mazon asked. "Embarrass the poor guy and get him really pissed off at me? I gave him back a little of his money and saved him a little face. Now the dude thinks he's my friend and he has respect for me. Besides, I made enough money tonight for all of us to go to Chicago for the weekend whether we get our paychecks or not."

"Well, I would've just kept his money and when I got tired of playing, I'd just say I was quitting and leave. That's it. And I'd have more money than you do now."

"Yeah, but you don't have more money than me and you would have pissed him off."

"So what?" Andy said. "Fuck him."

"Fuck him for sure, but fuck him slowly. Another thing: he may have some real big friends. There's no need to find out if his friends want to get into a fighting frenzy over a pool game, once he lost all his money. This way we can always get more money out of him, or his friends, or anyone else who thinks they play well. There's no need to kill the goose that's laying the golden egg. Patience, Andy. Patience, perseverance, and personality. That's what it's all about."

Andy couldn't look any further than the moment. "Fuck him. I'd just take what I could get."

"Andy, Andy, Andy," Mazon shook his head. "You really are a common motherfucker."

They came back to the pool hall two or three more times and Mazon won more money. Not quite as much as before as word had gotten out. But he won enough money to take Andy and a couple others to the big city. Not Chicago, like they originally planned, but to Milwaukee. Neither Mazon, Andy, Big Lip Wayne, or Bill had ever been to Milwaukee. This would be a first ever adventure. They caught the train north out of Great Lakes. All recently graduated boots left Great Lakes by train because no one had a car. The train was fine. It was a quick trip to Milwaukee. They hit town and were directed to the Antlers Hotel by a helpful cabbie. It was seedy but right in the middle of downtown.

"So, what do we want to do first?" Andy asked.

"Lets get something to drink," Wayne suggested.

It was eleven in the morning and Andy thought it was too early to start drinking. "Lets get something to eat and ask a waitress what's happening. Maybe we could go to a movie, and then go check out a bar." Andy was hungry and he hadn't seen good movie in quite a while.

Everyone else agreed. They found a diner. The waitress was pretty and about their age. They tried to be cool. They ended up looking like love struck puppy dogs in heat. She didn't have much patience with them, but did suggest that after they took cold showers, they check out a flick down the street. Butch Cassidy and The Sundance Kid was playing. Big Lip Wayne didn't want to see a cowboy movie with 'jiveass white men in it. He wanted a bottle of Wild Turkey and if there was any movie that he had to sit through, he wanted it to be "Debbie Does Dallas."

They compromised. They bought two bottles of Wild Turkey and went to see the 'jive-ass' white men.

After the movie, they walked around for a while, but it was snowing and they needed to get somewhere warm. Somewhere where there were women and somewhere where there was booze. They flagged down a taxi and explained their situation to the cabby. He spoke in broken English with a Spanish accent. "I know. I know thee place. Eet ees called Chico's. You go? Si?"

Si. Chico's it was. It looked like a typical neighborhood bar. The Schlitz Brewery was right across the street. The street lights were not too bright, but bright enough to see the corner stop sign, the street sign and a few nearby bungalows. Once inside Chico's, things changed. It was a small bar. It was little Mexico, with marachis and Mexican songs coming from the juke box. Everything and everybody stopped when the four of them stepped in. All eyes turned to the boys in blue. Nobody spoke for what seemed to be a few long seconds. But then, thankfully, the patrons turned back to their drinks, resumed their lives and ignored the young sailors.

The pool table had a game in progress and quarter on the rail. Mazon immediately added his quarter. Although he had taken Spanish in High School, Andy couldn't understand much of it. He tried to remember some key words. Cerveza was a key word. Cerveza meant something... beer. That's it! Through the fog of Wild Turkey, Andy knew Cerveza meant beer.

Andy turned to the grinning bartender. "Cerveza, quatro, por favor."

"Hey," asked Bill. "what did you say to him?"

"I said beer, four, please."

"Well, it didn't work," said Mazon. "He's still looking at you."

He was right. The smiling bartender was still looking at Andy. "Que typo?"

Andy looked out the window, pointed to the Schlitz brewery and said in his best Spanish: "Schlitz!"

Success. The bartender produced four Schlitz. Mazon mumbled something about Andy at least being good for something. They paid and sipped the beer. Everyone began to feel better. Warmer. The bartender seemed impressed with Andy's attempt with the Spanish language and kept trying to talk to him. But he soon realized how weak Andy's Spanish was and went back to washing glasses.

Andy looked around. He felt good. In fact, the best he'd felt in a couple of months, maybe longer. Everyone was real friendly. They nodded every time Andy looked at them. He smiled. They smiled back. They smiled constantly. Maybe it was the uniforms or maybe they were just nice polite people. Maybe they were all drunk. They didn't seem like it. No one was acting drunk. Anyway, it was refreshing to be in a place where everyone was friendly. Andy felt relaxed. These were good, trusting people, polite and full of approving nods.

Mazon began playing pool and winning free beers. Andy didn't have to buy a beer the rest of the night. But ol' Big Lip and Bill kept up with the whiskey, and they would pay for that later, in more ways than one. The locals didn't seem to mind losing to Mazon. He was cool about it, and modest, and not beating anyone too badly. They seemed contented to just watch his game.

Bill rolled dice and lost constantly. The locals didn't mind taking his money. Big Lip drank the hooch, and you could tell he liked where he was. Andy headed over to the jukebox. He'd play a selection and the people at the tables would all nod their approval.

Man, this is too much, he thought. These people don't even know me and they're accepting me straight up-no questions asked.

There weren't any ladies that were free. They all seemed to be with someone, but that was okay. Andy figured that even though there was no English being spoken, more than a few patrons probably understood it well enough. This was their place and they come in here to shut out of the rest of the other world. A world where everyone else told them what to do, when to do it, how wrong they did it or how worthless they were. All this in English no doubt.

A group motioned Andy over to their table. Big Lip Wayne joined him and they sat down. Andy found himself next to an attractive woman. Not too young but not too old: probably about thirty. And a looker. She was the bar waitress, on break, sitting with her family. Her family consisted of 6 Mexicans, between 20 and 60 years of age, four males, two females, and all smiling and nodding at Andy.

Andy smiled and nodded back. He could really get into this. The waitress asked him if he wanted to dance and he was taken aback. "Uh, no thanks, I really don't know how."

She laughed. "Senor, Eet really doesn't matter. I can show you. Its easy." She got up. Andy got up.

God, thought Andy. She's talking to me like I'm human. I haven't heard anything like this since I joined the Navy and was renamed scumbag. She's also speaking the first English I've heard since we came in here. I must be in paradise man. She had that low husky voice with a touch of innocence that made Andy feel more special than the next gringo.

She pulled Andy close and placed his hands in exactly the right place, on her very shapely hips. Andy felt nervous at first, but soon relaxed. Then she took his left hand and started leading him in a dance around the bar. Andy was awkward and trying to listen to her: Something about two steps forward and four back, or three steps somewhere. Andy realized this was the first woman he'd been with in nearly three months.

He thought he might impress her by asking her name. "Como se llama?"

"Maria Theresa. Y, tu?"

"Andy." She laughed. What a cute laugh, Andy thought. He was falling in love. Andy was getting excited, he was too easy. Two steps: then two more. He didn't know what he was doing. She was pulling Andy around the floor, laughing at his missteps. But Andy was having more fun than he'd had in a long time.

Then Maria had to go back to work. She playfully shoved Andy away with a laugh. It was light shove, but Andy was a little unsteady and fell against a nearby table, knocking two full beer bottles to the floor. He ended up falling over a chair and landing on his ass. He looked around, embarrassed. The locals at the tables were laughing. The whole bar started laughing at the gringo sailor on the floor, pushed by the dark eyed, saucy dance instructor. She stood over him at his feet, long legs spread as wide as her skirt would allow. She didn't look amused. She looked pissed off, as if Andy had done it on purpose to make her look bad. She looked even more beautiful pissed off.

Andy got up and immediately tried to apologize to her. "Lo siento Senorita Maria, yo soy estupido. Por favor." Her hurt feelings somewhat restored, she accepted his apology, tossed her curly brown hair toward Andy, and returned to work.

Mazon didn't win much more than a few beers for his amigos. This sat real well with his opponents. Bill lost about 40 dollars in dice, which sat real well with his opponents. Big Lip Wayne was quiet and stayed mellow with his Wild Turkey.

On the way back to the base, Andy thought about the night. He'd enjoyed the company of a woman for the first time in awhile. The locals all seemed to enjoy them stopping in and everyone got along. There were no loud assholes picking fights; no hassles and no trouble. It had been a perfect spot to relax and unwind. It was almost like they'd been on vacation in a distant land; nobody spoke English and they didn't speak Spanish very well. The music was all Spanish. The locals hadn't known them and they didn't know anyone else in the bar, but everyone got along and enjoyed each other's company. They'd been far enough away from the regular sailor haunts, and this had served to make them celebrities, in a way. Not a patriotic-type of celebrity, but more of a celebrity status of being someone different, someone new. There'd been no other loud-mouthed, belligerent sailors in the place. None in the whole area, as a matter of fact. They had all been real people, friendly, always polite and smiling.

Once back on the base, and in the barracks, Andy, feeling lighter than he had for a long time, immediately fell asleep, more at peace with himself and the world than he had been for months. Anchors await.

Two weeks later, Andy drew guard duty for the weekend. Everyone else went on leave to parts unknown (typically Milwaukee or Chicago), but Andy was left behind to do his duty. At 2000 hours, Friday night, he was on watch, guarding a building. From what, he didn't know, maybe from commies. Guarding it, but he had a gun that couldn't shoot, and he had to make rounds and fill out logs and turn keys, checking to make sure that locks were locked and no commies were trying to get in or trying to get out.

Andy considered the building he was guarding. It was just a run of the mill, regular building in the middle of the base. It didn't house rockets, prisoners or military secrets. It was simply used for classrooms. It had locks. The Navy could just as easily lock all the doors, send the sailors on watch to bed or on liberty, and their building would be just as secure as ever from any perverted trespassing sailors wandering around on base, or any commies that might be lurking, trying to get in and do god knows what.

If anyone wants this building, they're welcome to it, Andy thought for the 100th time that night. He was so bored, he had been pretending he was the Rifleman, spinning and rapid firing his old gun from his hip. The gun wasn't for real. It didn't shoot, but Andy would have amused Lucas McCain. Did he get off thirteen shots or twelve?

I'm not going to get killed protecting this pile of concrete, he thought. It's not my building. Besides, who cares? Any commie spy worth his salt would know that the gun doesn't shoot and the guard doesn't give a shit. All this is just for looks. Everything around here is just for looks. Damn, is everything just posturing? Is anything here for real?

The next night, Andy was off of watch earlier and he wanted to go out. The problem was, nearly everyone else had left for the weekend. With no one around to "go over" (go off the base) with, Andy decided to head out by himself. He took his newly acquired cue stick (a Japanese Dragon stick from his Uncle Glen) and headed into Waukegan to find a pool hall. Although he wasn't old enough to legally drink in Illinois (Illinois was 21; Wisconsin was 18), he figured he'd find someone to buy him a pint or so of Southern Comfort.

He headed for a pool hall he'd heard about. It wasn't as nice as the one on the base, but at least he was out in the free world. Andy found an older sailor who willingly bought him a bottle for a hefty commission. Andy stuck the bottle into his peacoat and headed into the pool hall.

The hall was upstairs and was busy. Unfortunately, there were a lot of other sailors at the tables. Many of them already drunk. After all, Andy reminded himself, it was Saturday night. It wasn't too long ago that Saturday night really meant something: dates, parties with friends, good times. "LETS PARTY NAKED!" Lately, the weekend had become a time to escape from the routine of the base. Something had been lost. But Andy actually looked forward to weekends just as much, or more than he used to, especially when he didn't pull duty (stand watch).

Andy spent some time shooting pool by himself, enjoying the music from the jukebox, practicing shots, and taking an occasional pull from the 'Comfort' bottle. He was having a good time and feeling pretty relaxed. The bottle was almost gone when a loudmouthed sailor at the next table hit him in the back with his cue. Andy knew he didn't do it accidentally; he could tell by the pressure that it wasn't an "Oops, sorry I hit you" kind of bump", but rather one that had more of the "move it" or "fuck you" oomph behind it. Andy, giving the obnoxious sailor the benefit of the doubt, mumbled an apology and moved out of the way. The sailor hit him again as soon as Andy had turned away. Goddamn it! Andy thought.

The months of being cooped up, having to take all kinds of shit from everyone around him, plus the booze he had drank, pushed Andy to the brink. Here we go, he thought.

"Hey asshole!" Andy gave him a split second warning. What's fair is fair, he thought. Andy didn't even look at him; he swung around and hit the obnoxious sailor in the head with his cue. The cue was made in Japan and was weighted with a 1/2 round piece of ivory in the end. A loud crack filled the room and blood quickly appeared on the obnoxious sailor's forehead. Lots of blood.

Tough shit, Andy thought, you had it coming, jerk! I didn't start the trouble, but I might end it. He was also thinking about his pool cue. His uncle had given it to him, having brought it all the way from Japan years and years ago, during WW II. The stick had good balance and was a straight as an arrow. It had red and green dragons carved on its sides. It even broke down into a walking cane with a brass tip and the etched ivory ball for the top. Andy didn't feel he deserved the stick because he couldn't shoot pool very well. It should be proudly displayed on a wall, not breaking some drunk sailor's head in a run down pool hall in Waukegan. Andy regretted not thinking before he impulsively swung it at the obnoxious sailor. The stick was broken at one of the joints.

The obnoxious sailor was bleeding and mad as hell. Andy took a good look at him and didn't like what he saw. He wasn't real big, but he had broad shoulders and looked muscular. He was definitely not a skinny stickman; he no doubt worked out with weights. The sailor was up and coming after Andy. Andy grabbed him by the neck, like he was wrestling a mad bull. They crashed to the floor. Damn, this guy is strong, Andy thought.

The bull slammed Andy to the ground and was on top of him. Andy tried swinging, but the punches didn't have much behind them, coming from the bottom up. Andy was pinned to the ground. He took several hits to the face and tasted blood. The whiskey was deadening his immediate pain. Man, he thought, I bet I'm really going to feel like shit in the morning.

Somebody had called the Shore Patrol. Thank God, thought Andy. He was tired of being the punching bag. The SPs collared the bull and pulled him off Andy.

Andy tried to explain that the sailor had kept hitting him in the back and he was just protecting himself. But they didn't want to hear any of it. They hauled Andy off to the paddy wagon.

The paddy wagon was an oversized white Ford Econoline with a locked cell-type area in the back. It had locked doors, no windows and small, narrow benches against the side of the van. It also had U.S. Navy stenciled on the doors to remind everyone that it was a "for official business only" vehicle. This particular paddy wagon was full of extremely drunken sailors: the pride of the fleet. Two were sprawled on the floor, passed out. One was in a corner on a bad trip or something; he was muttering unintelligible things. In another corner was, predictably, a puker. There was no fighting in the paddy wagon; not that anyone was in any shape to fight. But if even they had been, the SP's were more than prepared to keep the peace. They looked like they thoroughly enjoyed their work.

The contents of the van were unceremoniously delivered to the base Sergeant at Arms. He collected everyone's name and service number. The two passed out sailors were tossed into a drunk tank in the building. They never woke up. The puker was escorted out of the van and locked in the head (bathroom).

"You'll get out when you're done barkin' and the head is spotless," he was told. "And you'd better be quick, because any punk that has to piss will be let in to hose you down, yaheah?!" That sounded pretty rough to Andy. These guys weren't fooling around.

Because he was able to exhibit signs of coherency and civility, Andy was allowed to return to his barracks. Before he was allowed to leave however, the Sergeant at Arms admonished him: "The Cap'n will be calling on you assholes pretty soon. Ya'll be getting a Cap'ns Mast notice real quick and you'd be wise to appear before the Cap'n at Cap'ns Mast looking sharper than ya'll ever looked before. Yaheah?"

Two weeks later, Andy got notice to appear before an Admiral Somebody for a Captain's Mast; one of the Navy's official judicial proceedings. An Admiral running a Captain's Mast, Andy thought. That's weird. This must be some serious shit.

The closer time got to the date of the Captain's Mast, the more nervous Andy got. He didn't know anyone who had ever been to one before. He was the first. He didn't like not knowing what to expect; the unknown was worse than the known. Others gave him helpful opinions on the outcome of his day in court: you'll go to the brig; you'll get busted; you'll pull K-P, you'll be shot; you'll have to walk the plank; you'll be restricted to the base; you'll get a fine (all fines go to the Officer's Club, he was told). They also suggested ways to act at Mast: act humble; act fearless; look like you don't know what's going on; act like you don't give a shit. The advice was endless.

The day of Mast, Andy was scared to death. Everyone there was real stern and formal in spotless tailored dress whites. Andy stood out like a sore thumb. His dress whites were regular government issue: jersey too small, pants too big and a six inch cinch was necessary for his Navy-issue web belt to keep his pants up. Everyone else had tailored dress uniforms: all of them, sinners and convicts waiting in line for the terrible swift sword. Andy Mathers, no more than a misfit recruit, reporting for duty on the chopping block, Andy thought to himself. It was assembly line justice and he was fifth in line.

The first convict, a Third Class BT named Blowke, was there because of insubordination to a Chief. The Admiral read the report aloud. He read that BT3 Blowke came back to his barracks at 2400 hours and refused to quiet down and get into his bunk.

"That's BLOKE admiral, not BLOWKEY, admiral sir."

"Very well sailor, BLOKE it is."

The Chief was summoned and told him to get to his rack and shut up. At that point, BT3 Blowke replied "that the Chief could kiss his sweet ass because he was used to getting a kiss goodnight and he couldn't sleep without a kiss and furthermore, he wasn't going to bed without a kiss and his ass was the only place that the sawed off little bastard of a Chief could reach." The Admiral read the report verbatim.

The Chief had requested help from others in the barracks, but all were sleeping too soundly to hear his orders to assist him. Then BT3 Blowke began screaming to the Chief to "pucker up or there'd be hell to pay". The SP's were immediately summoned. When they arrived, they witnessed BT3 Blowke pissing on the Chief's shoes, while the Chief was standing on a chair, inspecting Blowke's bunk for something. The Chief was startled and slipped off the chair, fell into the urine and broke his arm. This amused BT3 Blowke to no end. The SP's gained control of Blowke and led him away. While leaving the barracks, he stated "he should have kissed my ass and none of this would have happened." He then started singing, 'Don't want no baldheaded woman to be my wife.' And that is exactly how it was read at the mast.

Andy was no longer so afraid of the terrible swift sword. He was more afraid that he was going to burst out laughing if Blowke's story got anymore bizarre. Everyone else had a straight face as the report was being read. How do they do that? Andy wondered. They either have tremendous self control or the Navy stole their sense of humor. He suspected the latter.

BT3 Blowke received a stern look from the Admiral and was sentenced to pay a $350 fine. He also lost a stripe, which meant he was busted down to regular Fireman (E-3). He was no longer a Petty Officer and had to pay his fine at the lower salary. Man, Andy thought, What some men will do for a goodnight kiss.

The next criminal was an E-2, a lowly Seaman Apprentice, who was caught urinating on a flower bed in front of some officer's house on base. When the SPs arrived, he was yelling, "Fire in the hole! Fire in the hole!" He'd obviously seen too many John Wayne movies. He continued that line from the movie all the way back to the base Master at Arms office. The Admiral couldn't really bust him a rank as he was already as low on the Navy pecking order as one could get, so he fined him $200 and gave him a lecture on the proper etiquette of addressing an officer.

The third sailor was picked up for exposing his sexual organ to several ladies on the strip and then passing out, with his organ still very much exposed. This final exposure created a lot of attention, as he was on the sidewalk and was noticed by some passing teenagers who reported him to the SPs. He was referred to the base Psychiatrist for questioning and evaluation.

The last sailor before Andy was also sent to the base shrink. He was a young Airman Apprentice who had passed out in the doorway of a church and refused to leave after the SPs arrived and rousted him. He had claimed that he had permission from his father to rest there. The SPs requested his name and he responded that it was Jesus Christ and that it was ok because it was his father's home. As the SPs dragged him away, he screamed, "Father's not going to be happy with this, he could make it hard on you guys!"

Wow, thought Andy. Either this guy found some dynamite drugs, or he snuck past the psychological screening in Boot Camp or he was trying his damnedest to get out. Andy had an after thought, man, wouldn't that be something, if he was telling the truth? Wow. Think about it. He felt himself smiling. Oh, oh. Can't have that. He reverted to the best poker face he could put together. The whole situation was getting to be too heavy for Andy. If he didn't laugh soon, he was going to explode. What the hell was going on here? Was everyone crazy?

He was brought abruptly back to his own little reality when he heard the Admiral's' voice addressing him. Whoa, he thought, he's talking to me. Here we go. My turn. Stand tall. "...and fine you $75 and two weeks restriction to the base. Son, you stay out of trouble." The Admiral paused for effect. "Do you understand me, sailor?"

What? That's it? What happened? I missed the whole fucking thing thought Andy. "Yessir!" he managed to reply. Man, talk about swift justice, he thought. He'd made out ok considering the various alternatives.

The next two weeks went by SLOWLY. Life was simple. Eat, sleep and go to class. Actually, it was boring, but Andy immersed himself in several books. He also played a lot of pool at the base pool hall. Life was ok. Not real exciting or fun, but it was ok. Anchors await.

When Andy got off of restriction, life became more complicated. More fun, but more complicated. They all decided to forego Milwaukee for their next Liberty and see what Chicago was like. The train ride was pretty much the same as the previous one to Milwaukee. Andy had been to Chicago several times before, but never by train and never in the type of monkey suit he had on. They still looked like boot sailors with their ill fitting clothes. Big Lip Wayne suggested that they'd forget how stupid they looked if they bought a couple bottles of whiskey and start looking for girls. They hopped in a cab and the driver obliged them with two bottles of Wild Turkey that ended up costing them twice as much as it should have because of the cabby's ability to legally buy what they couldn't. The four sailors, Andy, Big lip Wayne, Bill and Mazon walked around the streets of Chicago, slobbering and ogling every girl that went by them. Then they would stop at every back alley to drink out of their two brown bags.

"Just like common winos," remarked Mazon.

"But we're military winos," Andy said. "How many winos do you see in uniform?"

"How many normal people do you see in uniform?" Mazon wanted to know. "As a matter of fact, "do you see anyone else in uniform around here that actually looks normal?"

Andy couldn't say that he did. Nobody could.

Soon they had to fight off real winos who wanted some of the whiskey. "This is just great!" Andy complained. "The girls run from us like we stink and the winos are attracted to us like stink on shit."

Bill suggested they see a movie, but nobody wanted to spend the money. Bill persisted. "We could save money if we eat at the mission we passed a couple blocks ago. Then we'd have enough to see the movie." It seemed to make some sense, as long as they could sneak the whiskey in and drink in the comfort of the theater seats.

They went back to the Solid Rock Mission. There were several winos out front in different stages of consciousness. Most had the same brown bags the sailors had. Some were standing drinking, some were sitting drinking and some were laying down, not drinking. Down drunk for the count.

As they entered the Solid Rock, the smell of sloppy joe sandwiches and institutional corn was mixed with a musty odor of the men at the tables. There were twelve tables; each sat twelve people. The tables were about a third full. Many of the men (no women) at each table stared blankly at the food in front of them. Some ate like they hadn't eaten in years. Others picked at their food. Others just talked to it. All were listening to a would-be soul saver who presided over the crowd at the tables. In order to eat the free meal, they were required to sit through a bible reading and a short sermon of hellfire and brimstone.

"Goddamn it, Bill, this place stinks," Andy said.

"It's free food."

"Look, we're going to get subjected to some serious bible beating here. Just shut up and don't say anything. Eat your food and nod your head once in a while," Mazon advised. "This will only cost us a little listening time. And don't start any discussions!" He looked pointedly at Andy.

"I hear you. I'll be quiet." Andy promised.

"Can I drink my whiskey in a cup?" Wayne asked.

"No! Just drink water, eat fast, we'll get the fuck out of here, and then you can drink your fucking whiskey." Mazon was a born leader.

They went through the line and got their food served on metal trays that looked like the same ones they'd been eating on for the past several months. They headed for a table in the corner, as far away from the others as they could get. They hoped they'd escape the religion class. They didn't.

Before long, they were approached by a self-anointed man of the cloth. He had the Bible to prove it. He looked them over with

133

rheumy eyes for a few moments and then launched into a sermon about being deserving, of being worthy, and being thankful. Andy wasn't sure he was that thankful for the situation they were in. The preacher looked like he really believed what he was saying; he looked more than a little fanatical. A fucking lunatic. He preached to them about sharing what they had: they were receiving a government living and wealth. *They* should be here, in the mission, to share their bounties and spread God's word. He launched into a sermon about the whipping Jesus gave the money changers.

"Holy shit. Ain't nothing worse than a reformed whore," Andy commented.

"Shut the fuck up," Mazon muttered. "Don't get him going any faster than he already is. Just eat so we can get out of here."

Fifteen minutes later, the story of the whipping ended and they escaped.

"That was a good story," Bill offered. "Jesus kicked those guys' asses."

"Fuck you," said Wayne, "I couldn't get out of there fast enough."

"Hey, the guy was just doing his job," Andy added. "Besides, do you believe that Jesus actually whipped those guys? I mean, he beat those bankers with a whip? I didn't know he was violent."

"Mazon looked over at the three of them. "You are three common motherfuckers," he said.

They got to a theater and stood in line to pay their money to see *Bob, Ted, Carol and Alice.*

"This'll be as close to good looking babes as we're going to get", Mazon offered. "Lets get some cokes and mix this nasty shit with something drinkable."

"It tastes just fine," Big Lip said. "You Northerners are going to fuck up a good, natural taste."

"You're crazy, Wayne. "This shit stinks. I've gotta mix it with something so I don't puke," Andy said.

"Me too," added Bill." When I find a girl, I don't want to puke on her."

"Yeah, right! The only girl you'll find tonight will be in your right or left hand."

"Maybe I could wash that shitty food down with something else," Wayne conceded.

"Hey, it was free!" Bill said, "What do you expect for nothing?"

"Any girls we find tonight won't care if you puke. Let's get some sodas," Andy suggested. "We can hide the booze easier in Coke cups.

The theater wasn't very crowded and there were plenty of seats in the back rows. About halfway through the movie, Bill decided to move closer to get a better look at Ann Margaret. The whole time he was moving closer, he made comments about how good looking her big tits were. He was getting louder and he kept switching seats, moving closer in his quest to sneak up to the screen. He was bound and determined to get as close as he could to those big tits.

Mazon and Andy were getting a little concerned about Bill and his loud comments. Wayne didn't have a care in the world. Bill was getting closer, and louder. Although the theater wasn't crowded, there were the regular mix of movie-goers: young couples, middle aged couples, little old ladies, little old men; all in all, a fairly conservative bunch. Two ushers were moving in on Bill, who was in the front row, telling the whole theater how much bigger Ann Margaret's tits were in the front row than they had been in the back row. He invited the whole theater down to share his discovery.

Andy reached Bill just before the ushers did. "Bill! We have to get going. Now!"

"Huh?" Bill never took his eyes off of the screen. "Hey, look at the size of them! Man, they must be two feet across."

"Come on, big guy. We have to leave!"

"Why? I want to see if she takes..."

"She won't. Shut up! Lets go!"

"Why?"

"Mazon found us some girls," Andy lied.

"Alright! Why didn't you say so? Let's go!"

Andy grabbed Bill's arm and steered him past the ushers who had just arrived. Andy tried to apologize, "They don't let my friend out much." The ushers followed them to make sure they really left the theater.

It was now dark outside. Mazon grabbed Bill. "Thanks a lot, you pervert. I was just getting into the story!"

"Hey. It was free," Bill reminded him, "what are ya', a queer?"

"Don't start that shit! No, stupid, the shitty food was free. We paid good money for a movie we couldn't finish seeing because of you."

"You cost us good money, asshole!" Wayne joined in.

Bill remembered something important. "Where are the girls?"

"There aren't any, asshole."

"You guys are something else. Why'd you do that? I wanted to see if Ann Margaret was going show me those big tits."

A young woman with long legs and a very short dress with a fish net, see through blouse had been watching them argue. The blouse exposed everything, and everything looked pretty good to Andy. She moved up behind them and, in a husky whiskey-laced voice, asked if there was anything she could do to keep the peace.

Wayne replied,"if you want to give us a peace, we'll take it".

Bill said, 'Huh?"

Mazon and Andy wanted to know where, when and, most importantly, how much it would cost to obtain the piece.

She told them to follow her and headed down an alley. They followed. She was walking ahead with Bill and Andy on each side. They were fondling the hooker and she was trying to fend them off. Wayne and Mazon were guarding the rear. Wayne took his wallet out of his pocket, figuring he'd better hide it somewhere. He'd heard too many stories about hookers ripping off wallets. Suddenly he felt someone grab his hand and his wallet was ripped from his grip. He swung around to see a little bum in a large coat running back down the alley.

"Hey! The son of a bitch stole my wallet. Stop, you mother fucker!" Wayne took off after him. The others turned and, forgetting the hooker, followed Wayne. They chased the bum for a good four blocks before he ducked into a fleabag hotel. They followed him in.

A desk clerk behind a wire mesh cage eyed them as they ran in, then went back to the shit kicker he was reading. They headed up the stairs.

After three floors, Andy was getting winded. All that Jack Daniel's was taking effect. They came to a big room with at least 50 other bums in it, all on bleachers watching a small black and white TV. Wayne never broke stride; he knew who he was after. The bum in the large coat was trying his best to hide, but Wayne caught him in the corner and retrieved his wallet without a problem. All 50 bums were watching, but no one made a move. The little bum made no protest. Easy come, easy go. He sat down on a bench like nothing happened and turned his attention to the TV, hoping nobody would seek retribution.

Holy shit, Andy thought. What's with these bums? They give it their best shot and if they make it-ok. If they don't, there's always tomorrow? I guess if you've got nothing to lose, life could be simple, freer...easier?

They left the hotel, the whore was gone, they wandered around aimlessly, and then they headed back to the train station. They found a cab right away and they were back at the station in twenty minutes. Meanwhile, Andy had finished up the rest of the Jack Daniel's.

At the station, they met four girls who were also waiting for the train. College girls: a welcome relief from hookers. Andy and Mazon did most of the talking and things were looking good until three other sailors wandered by. One, a loud mouthed drunk, came up to introduce himself. He was obnoxious. Real obnoxious. A Third Class who looked down his nose at Andy. "Beat it, squirrel, a real man is here to take over," he sneered.

Andy wasn't impressed. The 3rd Class Petty Officer was also drunk. Without a second thought, Andy went around behind the loudmouth, grabbed the sailor flap-collar of his uniform and jerked him to the ground. The loudmouth hit hard, losing his wind. Then he puked. He was down for the count. His two friends looked at Mazon, Bill and Wayne and took off. Andy exchanged phone numbers with the girls (his was the general base information number at Great Lakes) and then noticed a guy in the corner who was watching him. The guy was in a civilian suit, looked official, and was definitely watching him.

Andy headed for his train with the others, watching the suited guy. The suited guy followed him. Definitely following, and watching Andy. Oh shit, Andy thought. What is this? FBI, CIA? What?

Andy boarded the train. It was full of sailors, most of them drunk; all of them looking alike. Andy figured he could hide there with no problem. To be safe, he moved through three cars before he decided he was home free. Safe at last, he thought. He turned around. The suited guy was right behind him.

"What the fuck do you want?" Andy demanded.

The suited guy flashed a badge that Andy couldn't read. "I'm the railroad dick. I was watching you. You committed a crime, a battery, on railroad property. You got a problem, sailor?"

Andy, without a clue as to why he responded the way he did. Said, "Yeah. I'm a sailor prick and I do have a problem. The problem I have is trying to figure out which way you're going to fall when I put your lights out." He swung at the little guy in the suit and missed.

The little guy in the suit grabbed Andy and slapped handcuffs on him. Damn, Andy thought, he's good and he's quick, and I'm drunk.

Andy was dragged off the train. They headed back into the station. Well, Andy thought, he's got a ways to go to get me back into the station. There were twelve inch metal stanchions in the terminal, running from floor to ceiling, spaced about 25 to 30 feet apart. The stanchions were in the middle of the loading area between the trains, splitting a boarding walk that was about fifteen feet wide.

Andy let the first one go by. He walked faster. The little guy in the suit liked the cooperation and moved to match Andy's gait. Andy moved faster and faster. Then he was running. They were moving at a pretty good clip when they split the next stanchion. It was a good aim; the force spun the little man in the suit down to the ground and the stanchion caught the handcuffs on the side. He yelled in pain. Andy was sure that his own wrist hurt, but he didn't feel it. The handcuffs flew apart. The connecting chain had broken. The little suited guy was on the ground writhing in pain.

Andy took off running and hopped on the last car of the train he had just been removed from. The train was just leaving. Andy looked back. The little guy in the suit was still on the ground, rubbing his hand and cursing. Andy moved as fast as he could through the cars. The fourth car had an observation deck. Andy had never been on one of those. He climbed up to the upper level as the train pulled out. He could see the little man in the suit back on the platform, looking at the train, but making no move to board it. He didn't even look up at the observation car. The train was moving away. Slowly, but moving away.

Before he knew it, Andy had finished "A" School. Graduated, hardly with honors, but with enough knowledge (at least as far as the Navy was concerned) to handle whatever a ship's boiler would throw at him. Andy wasn't so confident. He wasn't sure what he had learned, let alone how he could manage superheated steam, check valves and fuel pumps. All he wanted to do was survive the next three and a half years with all his fingers, toes, and sanity intact.

Andy rode a Greyhound home for a three-day leave before he was to report to his first real duty station: Charleston, SC, @ 1500 hours, 06/01/70. Finally, Anchors Aweigh?

Chapter 11: Permission to Come Aboard?

Jay was ordered to report to the Charleston Naval Base no later than 1500 hours on 7 June 1970. His orders had told him he was assigned to a destroyer, the U.S.S. Jetsomn DD 821. The good ship Jetsomn had just returned from Cuba when Jay hit Charleston. They had been keeping Fidel at bay.

The flight from Wisconsin had been broken by a stop at O'Hare to change flights. It was uneventful. Jay had tried to sleep, trying his best to pretend that he was someone else, somewhere else, doing something else. It hadn't worked. He got off the plane in Charleston in bad mood. He was still Jay and here he was, like it or not. The only saving grace was that he liked the South and usually appreciated seeing new places. This place was certainly the South and certainly new.

So this is home for while, he thought. The sun was bright, the air hot and very muggy. Jay was sweating immediately after stepping off the jet. The airport was full of sailors; some coming, some going, some waiting. Waiting for what? Jay wondered. Other sailors? Their ship to come in? Salvation? The second coming?

The summer dress whites appeared to be the latest Charleston fashion. Jay was in his heavy dress blues. It had been cool when he left Wisconsin and he hadn't given it a second thought. But now the heavy uniform not only stood out like a sore thumb, it was like a sauna. Jay hadn't planned on wearing any uniform but he had been told he had to in order to get the reduced military airfare.

Plus he had to wear it "just because he had to." It seemed that the reason behind most everything that Jay did these days was "just because he had to."

After waiting forever for his seabag to show up at the baggage claim area, he made a stop at a nearby men's room. Before anything else, he had to go through the ritual of undoing 18 buttons on the front flap in the front of his heavy, baggy dress blue pants.

"This crotch fly design is sure a fucking good idea," he said out loud to no one in particular. An old man sweeping the floor looked at him strangely.

"Yeah, I'm talking to myself," Jay smiled. "I'm fucking nuts you know. Why else would I be here in hot, humid South Carolina in June in a fucking heavy woolen dress uniform?" He rummaged in his seabag and retrieved his dress whites. They were wrinkled, but a few minutes of the heat and humidity would straighten them out in no time. He switched uniforms, then eyed himself in the mirror.

"Now look at the fucking wrinkled ice cream man," he sneered at himself. "And what flavor would you like?" He turned to the old man, but the old man turned away, ignoring him.

Jay was chauffeured to the base by a surly bald headed cabby who sucked a can of beer from a paper bag as he wheeled his '65 Ford station wagon through the Charleston highways and streets. Five sailors were packed into the car. All seemed to be having the time of their life, yelling at girls on the sidewalk as they passed. The wagon turned onto Dixie Boulevard, a long street full of activity.

"Welcome to yer new home, gennelmen," laughed the cabby. "This here's your new playground. Home of life, liberty and the pursuit of whores."

"What's all this?" Jay wanted to know.

"The strip. Everything you'll need. All in one place."

For over a mile, bars, massage parlors, liquor stores, greasy spoons, adult bookstores, and pawn shops lined both sides of the street. A couple of sleazy motels (rooms by the hour), a 7-11 store, and several vacant but very littered lots completed the landscape. A couple of Charleston PD squad cars and a Shore Patrol Paddy Wagon were parked in the only shaded areas on the street. Jay looked the scene over and thought about the carnival he had worked at only a year earlier.

"Lookit there!" The boy next to Jay yelled. "She waved at me!" He pointed to a female of indeterminable age in a mini skirt who was standing in a doorway of the Office bar.

"She's a whore, for chrissakes,' Jay said. She waves at everybody, as long as they have money."

"She wants me."

"She wants your money, stupid."

The crowded Ford pulled up at the main gate. Two muscular Marines and a middle aged rent-a-cop security guard were all trying to sit in front of a big fan in a small guardhouse. Beyond the gate, and as far as Jay could see, were buildings. Stores, houses, garages, workshops, warehouses, even a church. It was a self-sufficient city. And ships. Stretching out into the distance, ships' masts, cranes and towers of all sorts stood out against the skyline.

"Man, what a big place," Jay said to no one in particular. He wasn't sure if he was awed or not, but it was the closest he'd come to it since the whole fiasco had started.

"As far as I go, boys." That'll be 10 bucks each."

"Ten bucks? You're kidding!" Jay was no longer in awe.

"Yep. Gotta problem, boy?"

Jay eyed the big Marine Guard approaching their group. He silently gave Baldy a ten.

After showing their orders and IDs, they were directed to their assigned ships. Jay was sent to Pier L to be introduced to his new home: the USS Jetsomn. It was a two mile walk to the pier. It seemed longer in the heat and humidity. Jay was definitely no longer awed by anything around him. Hot, tired and sweating like a waterfall, this was exactly what he had pictured hell to be like.

The Jetsomn was a thirty-year-old veteran of World War II. It sat among four other destroyers tied up to Pier L, waiting to wage war on evil dogs. Jay looked again at the Jetsomn and decided that maybe the U.S. wasn't as safe from invaders as he had been led to believe.

There was a lot of activity on the ship. Lines of men, dressed in tee shirts and blue jeans (dungarees, Jay reminded himself), were carrying crates and boxes. He was surprised to see that several sported beards. Closely trimmed and neat, but beards nonetheless. Jay started across the ramp (gangplank) that connected the ship with the pier. Just as he was stepping onto the ship, a mean looking Chief in dress whites and mirrored sunglasses stopped him short.

"Where the fuck do you think you're going?"

"Huh?" was Jay's intelligent response.

"Salute the flag!" the Chief was mad. "What's wrong with you?"

"Oh. Ok, Sorry." Jay turned to the flag and threw a salute at it. This saluting thing was really a big deal, he thought. We salute everything. I wonder why?

"Hold it!" the Chief screamed. His assistant, a relatively normal looking guy in dress whites (a Seaman Signalman, Jay figured from his insignia) was smiling and obviously enjoying the show.

"Yessir?" Jay thought he better be polite although he had no idea why.

"I ain't no sir! I'm a CHIEF, you got that? A mother fucking Chief! Not no officer. What the hell did you learn in Boot Camp?"

I learned to keep most of my thoughts to myself when confronted by big mouthed assholes like you, Jay thought to himself.

"Ask permission to come aboard!"

"What? I've got to ask permission to come aboard? My orders tell me to be here, on this ship today." Jay couldn't help but add, "and I figure whoever told me to be here also wanted me to come aboard this ship that they told me to come to."

"You have to ask permission before your cross MY quarterdeck and I let you aboard!" The Chief insisted.

"What if I don't?"

"You don't get aboard this ship!"

"So where do I go then?"

"I don't give a righteous shit."

"But the Navy says I have to be here; here on this ship, right? And you're part of the Navy, right?"

"That's right, asshole. You gotta be here."

"But I can't come aboard, right?'

"Right. Unless you ask permission."

"And if I don't come aboard...?"

"Then you're AWOL, maybe even a deserter. And in a world of shit."

As if I'm not already, Jay thought. "Let me see if I've got this straight. I'm ordered to be here without any say in the matter, but you and the Navy want me to ask to be able to come aboard this ship that I'm already ordered to be on. So even though I'm ordered to be here, I can't really be here until I ask permission. They didn't ask my permission to be able to send me here. This doesn't make sense. The normal looking Seaman behind the Chief caught Jay's eye and rolled his eyes in a so-what-else-is-new look.

An important looking officer was heading toward the quarterdeck. He had gold trim (scrambled eggs) on his cap, a perfectly crisp white uniform and, of all things, a beard. The Chief spotted the Captain of the Jetsomn out of the corner of his eye and snapped to attention.

Man, he's one well-trained puppy, Jay thought. But he also struck a pose of attention, ready to snap off a salute when the situation would require it.

"Attention on deck!" The Chief screamed.

"At ease. Good afternoon, Chief. How's the watch?"

"A-one, sir!"

The Captain looked at Jay, who fumbled with a salute. "Request permission to come aboard, sir." Jay said. He decided he'd better follow the book. He handed over his orders.

"Permission granted." The Captain returned the salute, scanned the orders and eyed Jay's new-looking uniform and the seabag in his hand. "Welcome aboard, sailor." He turned to the Seaman who was now looking very business like. "Take BTFN West to the Engineering Office."

"Yes Sir!"

The Captain went on his way, saluting the flag as he crossed the gangplank. The Chief grabbed a microphone attached to the squawk-box. He hit something that let out three gongs and then announced: "Jetsomn, departing!"

Jay followed the seaman into the ship. This is pretty weird, he thought.

Within the hour, Jay was an official member of the Jetsomn crew. A BT-a snipe, he was told. "Why a snipe?' he asked Lt. Haurry, the Engineering Officer.

"Just because. Its an old Navy tradition."

Jay was assigned to the forward fire room and his name was added to the list of the Engineering crew. Haurry decided a speech was in order. "Welcome aboard, Sailor! You'll enjoy working for me. My boys work hard and they play hard. We have the most important job on the ship. Without us, the Jetsomn would just sit at the pier. We make this baby move!" Haurry was really getting into his speech. "We're real men! No wimps, slackers or (he looked around and dropped his voice) pussies in my department! Welcome to my crew!" He grasped Jay's hand in a limp hand shake. "Blake here will show you to the compartment and then you will assemble on the main deck to go to work."

Assemble what? Jay wondered silently.

Blake, a stocky BT, had been standing wordlessly in the corner of the office. He was rough looking. Jay followed him out into the passageway. They got halfway to the compartment when Blake turned and faced Jay.

"Howdy," he extended a beefy hand. "Welcome to the Jetsomn." He was grinning. "Don't pay no never mind to Haurry. He's a simple asshole." Jay shook his hand.

"What was your name again?

"Elvin Blake. But everyone calls me Gritman."

"Gritman? Why?"

"Now why do you think, you dumb assed Yankee?"

Jay laughed.

"Born and raised in north South Carolina." Gritman continued.

"Huh? You mean North or South Carolina?"

I mean north South Carolina. Its in South Carolina just south of south North Carolina. Big moonshine country."

"No kidding. I thought all that moonshining ended years ago."

"Ya'll got a lot to learn," Gritman laughed. "I'll show you around. You'll like it down here in Dixie."

Jay was heartened. Counting the eye-rolling Seaman on the Quarterdeck, he had now met two somewhat normal guys in this weirdness. Gritman led him down the passageway to the hatch that served as the entrance to the BT compartment. They went down the ladder. The compartment was empty except for an acne-faced kid sitting on a bunk reading a comic book. He was so absorbed in the comic that he never heard them until they were almost in front of him.

"Gritman! Jeez! You scared the shit outta me! It could've been the chief or something!"

"This here's Mud Dog. Mud Dog, Jay. He's new. Just got in."

"Hiya." Mud Dog shook Jay's hand.

Jay would find out later that Mud Dog's given name of Jim Kowalski was lost the night he attempted to participate in a mud wrestling contest with two Amazon whores at a bar on the strip. He'd gotten the shit beaten out of him, but had earned a new name. This week he was the assigned compartment cleaner. Whenever the ship was in port, one BT was relieved of fireroom duties and assigned to scrub, mop and wax the compartment each week. The Navy looked at it as a shit detail, reserved for one of the newest, lowest ranking snipes, but it was actually a welcome respite from the hot firerooms.

Jay was given one of two remaining bunks. One that no one else wanted: a bottom one of a tier of three. Everyone wanted the top or middle bunks. The top ones had better light and air circulation. The middle one was easiest to get into. The bottom bunk produced claustrophobia, and eventually, all human produced methane settled in and around the noses of those in the bottom racks. The lockers were on the floor directly under the bunks. Three to a section, one for each man above them. In order to get into any of the lockers, the resident of the lower bunk had to get out of bed to allow the others access. He was disturbed constantly.

Jay changed out of his sweaty dress uniform into a tee shirt and blue jeans (dungarees, the voice in his head reminded him).

"Now we have to go topside and pretend to work. Actually this is an easy afternoon. They're loading food so we don't have to work in the fireroom."

Jay followed Gritman up the ladder and joined the line of men heading for a big truck on the pier. The ship was in the midst of a taking-on-provisions exercise: loading food off the truck and into compartments on the ship. Jay headed back off the gangplank he recently crossed onto the ship. The Chief barely gave him a glance. All salutes and permission to come aboard requests were on hold for the exercise; the line of men carrying crates of food would have been slowed down indefinitely if they had to comply with the coming aboard ritual. The truck driver, a civilian, leaned against the front of the truck, smoking a cigarette. He had long hair and looked normal in the sea of short-haired seamen. Each man in the line grabbed a box, crate or basket of fruit, vegetables or canned goods.

After three or four trips, Jay was wet with sweat. It seemed that most of the crates he was handed were the biggest and heaviest. It must be because he was the new guy. No one spoke much. Most looked at Jay and eyed his new dungarees. A few stared at him and some actually said hi.

"Where are the other guys, the snipes?" he asked Gritman.

"Shush." Gritman grinned. He dropped his voice to a whisper. "Not here, that's for damn sure, at least not the smart ones. I'll show ya in a little bit."

They carried boxes for another 10 minutes before Gritman grabbed Jay by the arm and pointed to an open hatch on the main deck. They had been walking slower than the others and were temporarily by themselves, by an open hatch that went down to the lower most bowels of the ship.

"Quick! Down there!"

Jay headed down a steep ladder into the forward fireroom. They stopped at the upper level.

Jay looked around. So this would be home for awhile. He eyed the deckplates, valves, gauges, pumps, steam lines and two huge boilers. Each boiler was two stories high. The ladder extended down to the lower level, visible through the semi-open catwalk they stood on. They seemed to be alone. Jay had expected noise, heat, smoke and dirt to be part of the fireroom, but this was different. Everything was clean and some things looked to be freshly painted. And it was eerily quiet.

Gritman saw Jay looking around. "Of course its clean. What do ya think we do down here all day? That's our job you know. When we ain't running the boilers, we clean and paint and paint and clean and so on. As if anyone important ever comes down here or really gives a shit what this place looks like," he added sarcastically.

"Where is everyone?"

"All us low lifes are supposed to be toting groceries; all the lifers are probably on the beach."

"So we can hide here?" Jay asked. "No one'll know?" He was tired of carrying cabbage crates.

"Yeah, this's cool. Sides, if anyone comes down, I'll just tell 'em I'm showin' you around. What being a new guy and all. Come on, lets see who's around." Gritman headed down to the lower level. They crossed in front of the boilers, headed back to a far corner of the fireroom and started up a ladder.

"What's this?"

"This goes to the top of one of the fuel tanks. There're four of them down here, one in each corner of the fireroom. Its a great place. Non-snipes don't know about them and the lifers are too lazy to climb up here."

They got to the top of the ladder. A little three sided room was formed at the top of the tank. Three guys were playing cards. One more lay in the corner reading a book. All were smoking cigarettes.

"Hey, ya'll," Gritman greeted them.

"Hey yourself, Gritman. Who's that?"

"This here's Jay. New guy. Just got here." He turned to Jay. "This here's Thatcher, Maloni, and Hardin. And that there is Andy," he pointed at the reader in the corner. "He was the new guy until you got here. Another Yankee."

Andy grinned at Jay. "Welcome to gritland. You'll love it."

It didn't take Jay long to figure out the social order of the ship. It wasn't that he was a brilliant social scientist; the situation was just too obvious. The military exists and depends on a ranking system. It forces, enforces and flaunts it.

On his first day aboard, Jay became aware of his status in very short order. Not only was he the new guy, he was the newest member of the lowest social class on the ship: the subhuman Boiler Technicians, Snipes. Lower than the machinist Mates, snipes. The lowest. His uniform, clean and showing little abuse, identified him as a freshman, a virgin, a babe in the woods. Although he had been out of bootcamp for over four months, he was once again referred to as "boot."

Gritman consoled him. "Don't fret about it. The bad news is that you're the new guy. The good news is that its real temporary. Guys come and go around here a lot. In a week or so, they'll be used to you and a couple of more new guys will come along and you'll be old news."

Andy agreed. "Last week, I was the new guy. I ignored most of the bullshit they gave me. Told a bunch of them to fuck off. It doesn't mean shit. Most of them are real dickheads and too stupid to know any better."

"Yeah, that's a bad'n there. He's got a real attitude problem," said Gritman while staring hard at Andy.

"Hey you agreed with me Gritman. Those guys were laying it on a little heavy. They knew it. You knew it. Everybody did. Its okay now, so fuck it." Andy started to read again.

"What's he talking about Gritman?" Jay was interested in this. He sensed some relevance here.

"Aw, BT 1st Class Freeze was just funnin' Andy and Andy was fuckin' with Pappy Freeze. Freeze is fixin' to retire and he don't have to take no shit from anyone, least wise a smart ass boot fresh from 'A' school. And he knows it. Andy wasn't leavin' the ol' man any way out. Jes kept at 'em."

"Now wait a fucking minute, Gritman. That's my story, so if its told, let me do the telling," Andy started up again. "When I first came on the ship. Within the first fucking five minutes, this fucking old redneck…"

Gritman moved a little closer to Andy, "Whoa. Wait a little there, bad boy. Ever'ones got a little red on thar neck and you be better off rememberin' that."

"Okay, Okay, Gritman, calm down. Anyway Freeze is sitting on a chair with only the two back legs down, leaning against the outside bulkhead at the hatch that leads down to the aft fireroom."

Bulkhead thought Jay, what's that. The learning curve must shorten once you're on board

"Now remember its all new to me, and I had just stepped on the ship with pretty much the same greeting you probably received Jay. Confused? Disoriented? Sure I was. Anyway, I hear someone say. "Hey boy, cumheanghya!" I look in the opposite direction of which I was told to go, and this...um, old man is speaking to me. There are two or three other sailors standing there by him and others nearby. Anyway, he repeats the same gibberish. He's got a brown stain of tobacco juice in the corner of his mouth, so he's talkin' through a wad of tobacco. I don't know what he's saying. I mean, I have just had my whole fucking life completely changed: learning new terms, words, protocols, and various other catcalls, but I'm trying. I'm going to find out what he's saying. As I move toward him, I can see the guys standing near him are snickering a little. One's got a toothpick hanging from the corner of his mouth and his cigarette pack is rolled up in his t-shirt sleeve. The other's dangling a cigarette from his sneer. So I figure the old guy is fuckin' with me, but I figure 'boy' is better than 'scumbag'. The 'cumheanghya' part I don't know about. So I determine, in the interest of better communication...."

"Yeah right," interrupted Gritman.

"Whoah, wait a minute, let me continue. So I ask the old man if he could spell that 'cumheanghya' part because I can't understand it. As soon as I said that I knew I had made my first enemy on the ship. Without even trying I found an enemy and missed the friend part. I learned later that Freeze couldn't spell, that he wasn't very literate, just mechanically inclined. In his family he made quite a mark. He was soon to retire, he was still married, he was not an alcoholic, and to his credit he hadn't added to the gene pool.

When I asked him to spell it, there were others close enough to hear it and they wasted no time laughing. Freeze had a red face then. So, I asked again. More laughter. Freeze's face got redder. I got one more, 'Would you spell it please' and one more round laughter. Then Freeze got up from the chair letting it fall to the deck. He excavated his chewing tobacco from his mouth, threw it on the deck, pointed to the bow of the ship, and screamed, "Y'all shut yo' black pie hole fo' I stuff it wit' my rebel dick, and git' yo' fuckin' yankee ass to the fo'ward fireroom! Now, 'yaheanghya' me boy?"

"And Andy tucked tail, crept to the fireroom, and started blubberin' to me," finished Gritman.

"I don't remember the ending quite like that, but Gritman was able to explain that 'cumheanghya' was actually three separate words: 'come here you.' Gritman could spell and he was the first friendly soul I met," finished Andy.

"Anyway, you get the picture, Jay?"

"Yeah, pleased to be in gritland," said Jay as he looked around the dingy, smelly fireroom that was soon to become a major part of his life.

By late afternoon, the supply loading detail was finished. The living compartment filled up with men. Some showered, some started a card game. All were waiting for either liberty or the supper call. By now, Jay had moved his meager Uncle Sam-issued belongings into the compartment. He hadn't really noticed how small it was before, but once it started filling up with thirty or so guys, things got crowded.

The Jetsomn was, in many ways, both a city and a society within itself. The City of Jetsomn had its own diner (mess deck), barbershop, shopping center (the ship's store which was open at irregular, unpredictable hours, and rumored you could get a fat joint there too). There was also a medical center (sick bay, where the preferred treatment for many ailments was to find the patient capable to work, label him a slacker and send them back to the job), a library (with an inventory made up of dog eared paperbacks: shitkickers, spy novels, and old Navy manuals), a laundry, and even a movie theater (an ancient screen that showed even older movies on the mess decks). The employees of Jetsomn City included storekeepers, cooks, barbers, dishwashers, mechanics, janitors, and watchmen: just like a real city.

The Great Society consisted of a distinct social order: a true class system. As in most societies, there was an upper, a middle, and a lower class (the have-it-alls, the have-some-of-its, and the have-nothing-at-alls). This Great Society had its own methods of social control. Standards and norms were strictly enforced. The distinct classes were maintained by codes of acceptable behavior and dress.

The three major classes were separated into Officers, NCOs and enlisted men. Within the officer class there were three subclasses. In the NCO class, there were two.

The upper officer class consisted of the Captain and the Executive Officer (X-O). The middle class consisted of the department officers (Lieutenants and maybe a few Lt. JGs). The lower class consisted of the newest officers: Ensigns, mostly, fresh from ROTC or the Academy. Since many of the officers weren't much older than some of the enlisted men (younger in some cases), it was difficult, if not impossible, for many of the officers to project a credible image of a seasoned salt to their subordinates. This led to problems. In many cases, the less respect an officer was shown, the more he'd try to force the issue. The harder he forced it, the less he'd be respected and on and on it went.

The NCO's, at least on the ship, only had two classes. The upper class consisted of the Chiefs, who got to wear khaki and dress like officers, but without most of the medal decorations. A few First Class POs were also among the elite. The lower class consisted of some of the First and all of the Second Class Petty Officers. They either couldn't or wouldn't advance to the upper class status. It was common knowledge that the upper class NCO's, especially the Chiefs, knew more about things on the ship than the officers. As for the lower class NCO's, many had convinced themselves that they knew more than anybody about anything, even if they didn't.

The enlisted men class structure was split into a higher class (typically Third Class PO's well into their first enlistment), and the lower class, newer kids in town (usually Seamen or Fireman

Apprentices), and Seamen or Fireman, often fresh out of Navy 'A' School. More typically they were total screw-ups.

In addition, enlisted men were clustered as to job. Snipes and Machinist Mates were at the lower end of the social ladder, usually considered to be undesirable but also holding a reputation as being both crude and crazy. Closer to the bottom were the Boatswain's Mates or deck apes: the ship's janitors and overall maintenance men. They were considered to be the unskilled or semi skilled laborers of the ship's society.

A second group consisted of the sailors in the cleaner, more honorable jobs: signalmen, gunners' mates, radiomen and the like.

Several billets (jobs) held a fairly high status. The cooks usually held themselves above everyone else. The crew alternately loved and hated them, depending on what daily menu was and how it tasted. The mailman (a yeoman who ran the ship's store and post office part time) was loved by all. No one dared piss off the mailman. After all, where could you get mail, munchies, and panama red without ever leaving the ship? One stop shopping. The man was ahead of his time.

In general, the enlisted men were divided by seniority and job. Individual toughness and personality played a major role in determining where an individual fit on the food chain.

It didn't take long for Jay to figure where he ranked. He was the new Snipe. He couldn't get much lower, unless you were a new deck ape. But he wasn't too concerned; Gritman had said the social structure changed fairly quickly. Besides, he had trouble taking it real seriously. He had little to lose being in the situation he was in. He rationalized that things could only get better. What's the worst that can happen, he asked himself, make me a Snipe and put me in the bilges? He was already there, at least figuratively. He'd soon be there literally. Anchors await, and will they be heavier?

Chapter 12: Clothes, Cars, and College Girls

After several days of wandering around the strip in uniform, Jay was getting frustrated. "Liberty!" he spat the word out. "What the hell is liberating about being in a uniform that tells everyone within twenty miles that you're a sailor? They hate sailors down here. They make fun of us and try to hustle us out of our money. We walk down the street and we get hit on by everyone, from hookers to winos. Kids tease us. Girls laugh at us, so we can forget trying to get it on with college girls. Even the cops hate us. I may as well wear a big sign: Fuck me! I'm in the Navy. I'm a fucking loser. I have no brains and less money, but the money I have is all yours."

Navy regs didn't allow the peons (piss-ons Andy liked to say) from leaving the ship or base in civilian clothes.

"What ya need to do is get yourselves a locker at the Locker Club," advised Gritman. "Its right outside the main gate. You rent a locker and keep your civvies in it. Change out of your uniform after you leave the base and back into it before you return."

"Sounds like another rip off. What a deal! Rent a fucking locker to hide clothes in that I should be allowed to wear anyway."

"It's a racket, that it is," agreed Gritman, "but its your only option, unless you get yourselves a car or rent an apartment or house trailer off base."

"I'm all for it," Jay said. "I gotta get out of this uniform. It's like I have no identity anymore. Let's check it out. Get some normal clothes and no one will know we're in the Navy."

"Yeah right." Andy eyed Jay's short hair.

"Fuck you. It's growing. And its going to keep growing. When it gets longer, I'll grease it down and hide it under my hat. On the ship, no one will know the difference.:

"He's just a little sensitive about this hair," Andy said to Gritman.

"Aw, he'll get over it. I always had short hair. Doesn't really matter to me."

"Fuck you guys. I just don't like looking like some redneck lifer when the rest of the world, the real world, is into long hair and beards. But at least I'm not going bald." Jay pointedly eyed Andy's receding hairline.

"Don't mean shit," counseled Gritman. "Actually down here in Dixie, you're better off with short hair. This ain't exactly the land of bleeding heart liberals. Anyway, the red on your neck looks a little natural."

The Locker Club stood about 200 yards outside the Main Gate. It was a big, white building that had seen better days. Hundreds of lockers lined the walls, as did about 25 shower stalls (no soap, bring your own towels). Lockers went for 15 or 20 bucks a month, depending on size. Jay and Andy got a smaller one. The last one left, according to the man they gave their money to.

"Ya' pay the first of the month. Gotta' get yer own lock. If we don't get paid by the 5th, we cut yer lock and keep yer stuff. We ain't responsible fer yer valubles. Ya' can't keep drugs in the locker. You got any drugs?" He looked at Andy.

"Nope. Not us."

"Oh," the lockerman shrugged. He looked disappointed.

They paid him two months rent in advance. Now they needed clothes and a lock. They caught a bus and headed for the Palmetto Shopping Center. Jay sulked in a back seat and glared at a group of young girls who stared and giggled at him from a half dozen rows away. A couple ten year old juvenile delinquents behind them were making obscene references to Popeye.

"I hate this shit," he said to Andy.

"Relax. Its our last public trip in these monkey suits."

"We're taking a cab back to the strip, no matter what it costs."

"May be we've outgrown the strip Jay. We could…."

"Whatta' you talking about?"

"Never mind, maybe later."

Two hours later, they were back at the Locker Club. Jay was still bitching. "I don't believe you didn't let me change in the store."

"It wasn't a good idea. There weren't any changing rooms. They frown on people wandering around the aisles in their underwear. Especially Navy boxers with your name stenciled on them."

Their new wardrobes consisted of bluejeans, T-shirts, and tennis shoes. They had looked at other clothes: bellbottoms ("No way-we already have bellbottoms."), paisley shirts ("I don't' think so"), Nehru jackets ("Not in the summer") and assorted necklaces, beads and chains ("Too much"). Jeans, T's and sneakers were all they could afford. They still needed cab fare and enough for several beers back on the strip. Jay couldn't wait to get back to the Locker Club and put on the new clothes.

"Maybe we didn't get much." Andy commented, "but fashion wardrobes have to start somewhere. They're built one piece at a time."

"I don't care. At least I'll be out of this damned uniform."

Back at the Locker Club they rushed to change. A quick self appraisal followed in the cracked mirror that hung on the wall. I should have bought a comb," jay observed, rubbing the short hairs on his head.

"Knock it off, lets go." They headed for the nearest bar.

It was dank and dark inside the Office Lounge, and smelled of mold. Two sailors were playing pool. A couple of middle aged rednecks were arguing by the jukebox. From a pair of stereo speakers (of which only one was working), Charley Pride was singing about rain dripping off the brim of his hat. A bored B-girl sat at the bar smoking a cigarette and polishing her nails. She didn't even look up. The bartender was friendly enough. "Howdy boys. What'll ya'll have?"

"Two Schlitz."

"What ship ya on?"

Jay bristled.

"Jetsomn", Andy offered.

The B-girl had finished her nails and was now back in business. She sauntered over and eyed Jay. "You sailors want to buy a lady drink?"

"Maybe we aren't sailors and you sure ain't no lady." Jay snapped.

She shrugged. "Cheap asshole." She went back to her seat. "Nice haircut," came from over her shoulder.

Jay bristled again.

"Calm down," Andy counseled. "You know better. We're not hiding anything. We know we're sailors. They know we're sailors. We know they know we're sailors, and they suspect we know they're whores."

The pool shooters finished and left. Jay loved to play pool. Andy put a quarter in the table and racked the balls. The Office was unique to Andy. He liked the smell, sort of. It emanated from the empty peanut shells on the floor. At the Office there were four huge wooden barrels with salted peanuts in them. They were free, and you just threw the shells on the floor. The shells soaked up spilled beer, a little saliva, not much puke, and some of the boys' piss over at the bar. Every once in awhile the barkeep would sweep, and literally shovel the shells into a wheel barrow. Then dump all of it, several barrow loads, in his pick up truck. Back at his little place in the country he had some hogs, next to his trailer. He said his hogs couldn't get enough of those shells. "Lotsa' vitymins an minrals soaked up in them empty shells," he would relate, as he squirted a stream of brown 'tabackie' juice through the gap in his mouth left by the absence of his two front upper teeth "and later, after butcherin', they's the bess' tastin' pig meat anywhars'." And actually, the bar floor always seemed to clean up pretty well, after a good shoveling.

Jay eyed the pool table and was vigorously chalking up his stick. He hit the balls so hard that the queue ball went flying off the table, hit the wall, and fell to the floor, making a soft landing on some moist peanut shells. Andy picked the ball up, tapped the nearest sailor on the shoulder, with the hand that had the ball in it. He asked the sailor if he wanted the next game while he wiped the moisture from the ball on the back of the sailor's sleeve. The sailor politely declined, but thanked Andy for the offer. Jay was not amused or pacified. "That was real cute Andy. It's a good thing he's had a couple beers."

"No biggie Jay, everybody here has had at least a couple."

"What does it take to look like you're not in the Navy," bellyached Jay.

"Not being in the Navy is what it takes. Sitting in a bar in a college town with a head of long hair and a beard, drinking wine, smoking dope, and protesting the war. That would be what it takes. Face it, you can't hide from the fact that you are now what you are and are now where you are. Everyone who hangs out on the strip is either in the Navy or wishes they were. Or they used to be in the Navy, or is a hooker, or a wino, or is a generally fucked up all-around loser with serious mental problems. Or they could be any combination of any of those things, and more. You could come in here in a clown suit and they'd still figure you were in the Navy. You can't fool yourself and you can't fool these people. And why would you want to? What's the point? Fuck 'em. They've seen thousands of guys like us standing at the bar in stiff brand-new jeans, T-shirts with the price tag still on them, and short hair. All of them pretending not to be in the Navy. So either you're in the Navy and are here through no choice of your own, or if you're not, then you'd have to be a certified head case to be here."

Jay had to agree. "You're right, but I still don't like it."

"You don't' have to, but it really doesn't matter. As long as we are anywhere near the base, we are going to be recognized as sailors."

"So we need to go other places," Jay was thinking." This is a Navy town, but Charleston is a big city and there have to be a lot of places we can go. Lets check it out." Now Jay was on the same wave-length as Andy.

They left the bar. They didn't have to go far. They stopped at a sleazy magazine stand on the corner. They passed up the nudie magazines and fuck books; they were on an important quest. They picked up a Charleston newspaper, a city map, and a South Carolina state map. They headed down the street to the Ship's Inn. The Ship's Inn was the spitting image of the Office Lounge, but larger, dirtier and darker. It was deserted except for a bartender who was being entertained by a small television. They ordered two beers and pulled chairs up to a vacant table by the window.

"Look at this! There's a lot of stuff around here." Jay poked and pointed at the map. "Folly Beach, Isle of the Palms, Mount Pleasant, the Battery, North Charleston, there's a college downtown and everything. All kinds of places to go."

"Alright! But we need wheels."

"Yeah, the bus doesn't cut it." We need a car."

"How much money you got?"

"About a hundred fifty put away. And we get paid in a week. That's another 50 or so."

"Me too. We could probably get a car for a couple hundred. That's about all we can afford, what with license and gas and all."

"Yeah. Lets start looking around for one."

They had another beer. Jay asked the bartender if he knew of any cars for sale. He directed them to several cheap car lots in North Charleston.

"We can't do anything now, its Saturday night and everything's closed. Besides its getting dark. Lets go look around tomorrow. Being Sunday, we can look in peace, no salesmen to hassle us."

"Good idea. But we'll have to take the bus."

"I don't care." Jay was excited." I can take the bus one more time for something like this."

"Okay, now you realize we gotta' get away from the base. Let's try out your new clothes somewhere else. Maybe at the *Flying Dutchman*." The *Flying Dutchman* was a new dance place for young people. The radio wouldn't stop raving about it. It was even advertised as a discothèque, sometimes. It was a cavernous building with a huge rectangular bar. It had plenty of tables and two dance floors, a large pool room, and an arcade with old and new types of machines. There were cages hanging from the ceiling with go-go girls in them, and all of the areas were on different levels. The dance floors were lighted, multi-colored, and the colors flashed with the beat. In fact, there were lights everywhere. The place was too well lit up for Gritman. No pissing under the bar here.

"We can't go there. Its too far away. We don't have enough money. We'd have to ride the bus and its too early. They aren't even open yet."

"You're close on all accounts, but we ain't playin' horseshoes pardner. We want to go there <u>because</u> its far away. We do have enough money for the bus. We need to eat something first anyway, and then it'll be open. Why wait for a car? Lets live now."

Jay was still excited about the car talk, "Yeah, we could walk over to Shorty's. Get some cheap chili dogs, then catch a bus right there..."

"And by the time the bus gets to the *Flying Dutchman*, it will be open," Andy finished.

The boys were off! Greasy chili dogs, two buses and a transfer, and boom, there they were at the *Flying Dutchman*. It had just opened. When they entered they could tell they were early, but still, there were several people there already. This was it. These people were Jay and Andy's age. They didn't look like rednecks, and they didn't appear to be lifers. They had to remind each other to keep their mouths closed. They weren't here to catch flies. It was fantastic! They shot some pool and had a pitcher of cold Schlitz. When the music started playing they found a table close to the dance floor. And when the music began, the people really started coming in. They were streaming in! It was good they got here early because soon it would be standing room only. It was hard not to watch the dancers in the cages. They looked good. Real good. Yeah, they were easy on the eyes.

Then it happened. Not one, count 'em, not two, but five southern beauties sat down at the table next to Jay and Andy. "If you kick me in the shin one more time Jay I'm gonna' spill my beer on your crotch."

"Well son of a bitch man..."

"Well son of a bitch man, I saw 'em too. Do you think I'm fuckin' blind?"

Its funny how it happens, no one really knows, and it just happens. People gravitate toward one another, or they don't. First appearances or impressions or whatever, it has to be gravitational.

The girls didn't seem to be put off by haircuts, or clothes, or accents. Without much conversation Jay gravitated toward the petite blonde with little make up. She didn't need it. She laughed at everything he said and they danced to many songs. Slow ones. Fast ones. It didn't matter. They really hit it off.

Andy didn't even know Jay could dance, and Jay was surprised that Andy's feet didn't get tangled up with his mouth. Andy couldn't leave the sophisticated dark brunette alone, and she wanted to hear more. She was taller than the blonde, but neither were much more than five feet, if that. They were small, cute, and intelligent: just naturally beautiful.

Jay and Elizabeth did more dancing than talking. Jay was sweating, unbelievable, he thought, she doesn't care.

Andy and Caroline did more talking than dancing. Both of these fine ladies were in college doing what Andy and Jay should have been doing: studying and moving toward graduation. Elizabeth was going to be a teacher and Caroline was on a fast track: double major in three years. Whew she was hot, in more ways than one. Andy hoped he wasn't slobbering as much as Jay was sweating.

"Can they be cute and beautiful," Jay asked at some point.

"Yeah," said Andy, "they are anything we want 'em to be."

Each of those southern beauties had eyes that sparkled that innocent glitter that gets lost after the first touch of some real heartbreak or misery sets in. They bubbled, they were full of energy. They had just a touch of a southern accent. Just enough accent to cross the boys' eyes. Yes, they were star struck, they were full of the moment and didn't know it.

"Yeah, cool, so lets...you uh, I mean, Caroline...er..." it wasn't often that you'd see Andy's mouth without words. It wasn't working.

Jay was quick though, "er...yeah we got a bus right outside. Wanna' go for a bus ride with us Elizabeth?"

Andy snapped out of it just long enough to realize Jay's quickness, under these circumstances, could backfire. End a relationship before it had a chance to get started. They didn't have a bus. The city of Charleston had a bus, and it wasn't running at this hour. And besides, they couldn't tell them anything near the truth. "Uh,…yeah, but the mini bus is dirty, and uh…real full."

"Full of what?" purred Caroline.

"Er,.. I mean…."

Jay's quickness returned, "They're full of our gear."

"What gear do you have? What's gear?" said Elizabeth.

"Well we can't talk much about it, but we just got in from South America. We're Special Forces and its just stuff we use, but its so much its practically falling out of the mini-bus."

Jesus fucking god thought Andy. Jay has had way too much Ten High. Where did he get that shit anyway? I hope he doesn't get out one of those fucking cigars. What the shit? Special Forces? Why doesn't he just tell them we're goddamn Martians? I need to pay closer attention to what this fucker is reading.

It was obvious to Andy that Jay hadn't thought too far ahead on this one. "Well what Jay means is that we're in between duty stations, uh, assignments. And we have to report to some *special* training tomorrow. It's a ten week *special* crash course to orient ourselves to our new assignment or duty station. That way we won't have to *force* ourselves to get used to the new assignment."

"Yeah," said Jay cutting in, "Its real dangerous. We could get killed or something. You know, we're young, and haven't really experienced life too much. Sorta' not too much ya' know, uh. And you know we need…"

Andy cut in, "Well walking across the street could be dangerous, you know. Hell, everybody here is young." He went on to explain that the bus was just crammed full and they had just stopped in on their way to the new station and, "do you girls come here often?' Andy wanted to get the conversation away from Jay and himself and back to the girls.

Elizabeth wanted to tell them everything. She was real talkative. And for having a southern accent she could move right through her declarations very fast. Yes, they came here almost every weekend since there wasn't any other place to go. Sometimes she couldn't get Caroline to go because she had to read something.

Andy was watching Caroline and she was kind of dancing in her seat, eyes sparkling, sweet red lips sort of mouthing the words of the song, and her long brown hair was moving back and forth. She was content to let her friend do the talking, and Andy was content to watch. He didn't know he was in the Navy, let alone the Special Forces.

It was good that Elizabeth took over the conversation. Jay couldn't get a slurred drunken word in edgewise. They were going to "....have to leave soon because their dorm mother had a curfew on all her girls. But here's our dorm phone number and we'll be back here next Saturday. Caroline has her parent's station wagon so we'll just leave in it. Will you guys be back? Sure you will won't you? Well..."

"It is getting close to our curfew. So will you call me Andy, and let me know what you two *special* types are up to?"

"Yeah, I won't forget."

"Okay. Good. Come on Lizzie honey we have to go now."

They both slid out of the booth and Jay and Andy watched their cute little asses wiggle all the way out the door.

"Okay, Mr. Special Forces dickhead. What the fuck were you thinking of? Don't tell me. All the blood went to your little head and you were not able to use that fat lump of shit on your shoulders, that sometimes passes for a cranium. And where did you get that whiskey?"

"Hey, easy man. I was just making us exciting. And yeah, it was kind of hard to think in here. You know, all the smoke, beer, cigarettes,..."

"Whiskey!"

"Yeah, that too. I don't know. You remember when we volunteered for PBR assignment in Nam?"

"Yes I do. It was a good thing we found out it was Patrol Boat Rivercraft and not Pabst Blue Ribbon, or else we probably would have had our dumb asses shot off by now."

"Okay, okay, Andy. Look, those girls are real, not strippers or barhogs. They *are* good looking and intelligent, not some shit for brains teeny bopper. They are the first decent thing that's happened t us since we've been in this fucking outfit. Besides, you got to say, we did it. New clothes. New bar. Far away from the ship. Mission accomplished."

"Yeah, you're right. I haven't had this much fun for a long time. But Special Forces? Mission accomplished? I say no more *I Spy* reruns for you. You have to quit listening to Barry Sadler. And we have to broaden your library beyond detective stuff."

"Okay, go easy now. We had a good time. Its gonna' happen again real soon. All we have to do is get back to the ship. I'll call a cab."

"Call me broke Jay."

"Shit me too!"

"What now 007?"

The whiskey cloud was drifting away from Jay's brain and the blood had also returned, and he was ruminating. You could see it in Jay's eyes when he was like this. Some would think he was going blank, but he wasn't, it was a deep pondering. Then,..."Okay, I remember my mom telling my dad, 'Gearhardt, why do you have to have all those things bulging in your pockets? Can't you at least leave your keys on the visor so they won't jangle and tell everyone our every move?' Alright, that's it, we go to the parking lot and check cars for keys. On the visor, under the floor mat, in the ashtray..."

"Oh shit, now we're car thieves. How much whiskey have you had Jay?"

"Not thieves. We're just going to borrow the car until we get back to the base. Park it a couple of blocks from the main gate. Then bingo, change clothes and just walk through the gate and on to the ship. Remember, borrow."

"Whew man. That's a stretch. But what else are we going to do? Flat fucking broke. We have to get back. Its too far to walk. Shit, it must be seven or more miles back. Goddamn it!! Oh well, you know what we always say in a tight situation. FUCK IT!! We gotta' do it now though because this place is gonna' shut down in less than an hour."

The boys went outside, and, trying to be nonchalant, separated so each could look. They didn't need to go far. Jay found the keys of a Plymouth Valiant in the ashtray. Second car he looked in.

"Hey! Psssst! Andy come on."

Jay had the car already started by the time Andy got there. Damn, the muffler sounded loud to Andy. This was spooky he thought. Jay was into the driving. He wished it was a Duster or a Camaro. There was plenty of gas. Andy had checked because he thought it would suck if they stole the damn thing, went a little ways, ran out of gas, and still had to walk back to the base. It was a nice ride back. The radio was decent. It was preset to rock and roll stations. Jay seemed to have no problem getting back to the base. Andy didn't have the same inherent sense of direction that Jay had. He couldn't have done it this time. The cool night air streaming through the open windows, good music, and the afterglow from the girls had Andy feeling on cloud nine, light as a feather. CCR and their "...rollin' on the river'..." seemed to put the final touch on an excellent evening. Anchors Await.

The boys did the same routine four more times. Then the girls went home for the holidays. Then the Jetsomn pulled out for six weeks of unannounced-at-sea-training down below Cuba, somewhere. They made only one stop in St. Thomas so everybody could buy a gallon of untaxed liquor.

When they returned to port, and ultimately, to the Flying Dutchman, the girls weren't there. Then the next time Maloni and, even Gritman had to go along. It was just as well because it was obvious this time that both Caroline and Elizabeth had new interests. The Dutchman had lost its appeal. Oh well thought Andy, easy come, easy go.

The four sailors, usually minus Gritman, began to make it a regular part of their routine. However, the car borrowing, even though it had gone smoothly up to this point, could get a little more complicated at some point.

It was just another Saturday night on the Jetsomn. Jay and Andy sat with a few others on the fantail. It was a quiet, lazy night. Most of the crew were on liberty. Andy was reading Marx's Communist Manifesto. Maloni, Gritman, and Jay were playing cards. Jay was extremely bored.

"Enough is enough!' Jay announced. "I have to do something! I can only take only so much of this quietness. Its been way too quiet since we got back from shitmo, or shit fuck, or whatever that training shit was called!"

Andy looked up from his book. "The assholes called it Gitmo. What do you want to do?"

"Oh, I don't know. The options are endless when you get lazy. We could go to the strip and pick up girls and get drunk. Or pick up girls and get drunk and go to the strip. Or get drunk and go to the strip and pick up girls."

Andy had heard all this before. "Yeah. Endless options. The strip or the Enlisted Mens" Club. Barhogs or other sailors. What a choice!"

Maloni looked up from a losing hand. "Let's go dancing again at the Dutchman."

"You're shitting me!" Jay remembered he didn't like to dance, unless it was with Lizzie, and she didn't know if he still existed.

"No, really. If you want to pick up real girls, you have to go to a place where they go to dance. All girls like to dance."

"He's right, we know the Dutchman is the only place to go," Andy agreed.

"Disco? Again?!? No way!" Gritman stated.

"Listen, you hick," Maloni continued. "You aren't getting any girls in those redneck bars on the strip, are ya? Just the same fucking rip-you-off barhogs, and maybe a sympathy fuck from some ancient 40-year-old woman. If you're lucky."

"Maybe we should give the Dutchman one more try," Andy suggested. "What have we got to lose? Its gotta' be better than sitting here with a bunch of losers who haven't anything better to do with their lives. But Gritman, this time don't kick the go-go dancer out of her cage and take her spot. These people aren't interested in your mule stomp. They all want to see tits and ass."

An hour later, the four of them headed out. They changed into their civilian disguises at the locker club and stopped at the Fleets Inn for hamburgers and beers to get the night started. At about 8:00 they caught a cab and headed for the hip Dutchman.

"Christ! It sounds like the Jackson 5," said Jay. "I hate them. I don't need this. I hope they get back to CCR or Janis Joplin, or the fucking Doors."

"Yeah, " agreed Gritman. "What the hell are we doing here? At least the strip is predictable"

"Come on!" Maloni urged. "You know there're millions of girls inside. You'll get in the mood, bitch. Let's go!"

After paying the steep two dollar cover charge, they were let in. The building's giant dance floor and two bars strategically placed at each end lifted Gritman's spirits. The dance floor was crowded as usual, and the bar area was relatively empty. Gritman headed off in the direction of the bar. In a few minutes, he returned with an armful of Schlitz bottles.

There were still a lot of girls here, Jay had to admit. They all ended up dancing, even Jay who didn't seem to mind even though it wasn't Lizzie. The more he drank, the more he danced. Before too long however, it became apparent they had the same old problem.

"How are we going to pick up girls if we don't have any wheels and no apartment to take them too?" Andy wanted to know.

"Its not that bad." Jay said. "All we have to do is meet some girls who have a car and an apartment and want to take us home with them. We, stupidly, haven't looked at it like that."

The others pondered this. Their wheels consisted of a 'borrowed car' and their home was a ship with 200 other roommates, all male.

Things ended up working out for two of them. Maloni and Gritman met two girls, with both a car and an apartment. Around midnight, Gritman waved goodbye to Andy and Jay, wrapped his arm round a hefty, well fed red headed young lady and headed out the door. "That was a good idea we all had. Don't wait up for us. See ya'll tomorrow," he said over his shoulder.

An hour later, the crowd started thinning out. Andy and Jay had been unsuccessful in their quest for female companionship. They had met several nice girls, had gotten some names and numbers, but all the girls were without cars and were riding with someone else. None seemed to have apartments either. They were surprised at all the girls who said they were still living with their parents. Before too long, they left the bar and found themselves in the parking lot.

"All *revved* up and nowhere to go, or at least any cool way to get there." Jay observed, "I guess we can find a ride easy enough, as usual. Help me look for a car with keys in it."

"You're shitting me. We're gonna' get caught, just you wait and see."

"No. It'll be ok."

"Had you ever done this before, back home?"

"Kind of. I borrowed a couple of trucks. Never really stole them. Just borrowed them. Didn't hurt them. Took a ride to where I was going and then left them for the owner to find them. No harm done. Just like we do here."

"Ever been caught?"

"Not yet."

"That's real reassuring. But what the hell." Andy shrugged. "I'm tired of thinking about it and you're right we haven't got caught yet. But it seems like the odds are getting more against us every time we do it."

"Yeah, but its really just the opposite," said Jay, "as I found out in a statistics class I took once."

They found a car in less than 5 tries. A green '59 Ford, the keys were over the driver's visor.

"People think they're so clever. That's the first place to look." Jay pulled out of the exit. "That's exactly where Gearhardt always put them. We'll leave this outside the base, on a side street, just like we always do. No worse for wear. No damage done."

"But I'm sure someone, like the owner, is always pissed off," Andy said.

They got to the strip without incident. Jay parked on a side street off of the main drag. "We'll leave it here. There're enough cops around that they'll find it quick and the guy will have his car back before he knows it."

"Let's stop at the Dixie Bar for one last one before going back to the ship," Andy suggested. They walked a block before Jay noticed the large portable radio/tape player that Andy was carrying. "Where'd that come from?"

"The car. I'll give it back as soon as I'm done with it."

"Jesus Christ!"

"The guy shouldn't have left his keys in the car."

"You shouldn't have kept it. This radio is different. You stole it. It could get us in trouble."

"I don't think so, be cool. Remember, its not a car, just a little ol' radio."

The Dixie Tap was quiet. There were a handful of drunken sailors there, but they kept to themselves in a corner. Jay and Andy each ordered a beer. The bartender announced that they had to drink fast, he was closing up real soon. A half an hour later, they stopped at the locker club, changed into their uniforms and headed back to pier L, and home to the Jetsomn.

As they walked down the main drag of the base, Andy turned on the radio and was getting into the music. Grand Funk sang about being an American band.

Suddenly a car drove by them. A green 1959 Ford. It slowed as it passed by. Jay glanced at it. Hmm, he thought. It looked just like the one they had just left outside of the strip, on the side street... "Holy Shit!" He grabbed Andy's arm. "We have big trouble."

Andy had seen the car. They watched it slow to a stop about half a block ahead of them. It turned slowly around. As it passed under a street light, Jay could see what looked like four guys in the car four big motherfuckers. "We're dead."

Andy was thinking fast. He switched off the radio and tossed it into a trashcan behind his back. They were on a stretch of sidewalk that was between streetlights and Andy was counting on the darkness covering the tossing of the radio. "Act real drunk," he whispered to Jay. "Real drunk."

The two of them started staggering down the sidewalk toward the oncoming Ford, singing "We're an American Band" at the top of their lungs. The Ford pulled alongside them. Jay confirmed that there were indeed four guys in it, four big football types who got out and walked over to them on the sidewalk. They had long hair and one had a beard. No Navy punks here, Jay thought. Two wore caps, one was Cat-diesel powered and the other advertised the NRA. We're in deep shit, thought Jay.

"Remember to act real drunk." Andy whispered. "Ahoy mates," he yelled to the approaching four. "Howdafuckareya?"

169

The driver came up to Andy and eyed him up. He glanced at Jay. "Fucking sailorboys," he observed."

"Fuckin' A, Jack. Fightin' the commies for ya'll," Andy slurred.

"Where ya'll been tonight?" One of the rednecks demanded.

"On the strip. Got myself fucked and fucked up in one night," Jay bragged.

"Fuckin A," Andy added.

"Ya'll weren't at the Dutchman?"

"The what?" Andy asked.

"The Dutchman, you idiot," the driver answered.

"Naw, I'm not into dancing," Jay added his two cents worth.

"Oh listen here, he's not 'into it'. What are ya, some fucking hippie in a sailor costume?"

Fuck you, Jay thought. He was getting mad and was about to respond, but Andy saw it coming and kicked his foot, hard. Jay held his tongue. Four against two was not good odds.

The driver spoke. "Well boys, we got us a problem. Seems my car was ripped off at the Dutchman and showed up on the strip. Figured some sailor boys took it and took the radio that was in my back seat."

"Yeah," one of the others added. "We was driving by and saw ya'll walking. Thought we saw, and heard, a big radio like what we had stole from us."

"Hey!" Jay thought of something. "S'ow did you get on base? You aren't shupposed to be here."

"I work in the yards and I gotta pass. I can go anywhere I like," the driver responded. "What's it to you, asshole? Got something to hide?"

"Fuck you. I don't know what you're talking about." Jay tried to remember to slur his words but somehow he thought it didn't matter anymore. "We don't have your fucking radio." He opened his arms wide. "See? No fucking' radio. We're all fucked up and were just singing."

"Wish we could help you, but we don't know anything," Andy added. He glanced at the trash can which was a little closer than he would have liked it to have been. He turned to Jay. "Come on man, we gotta get back to the ship..."

"Good luck, boys," Jay slurred. They started down the sidewalk once again. "Sweet, sweet Connie was doing her act-had the whole show and that's a natural fact....," they sang. Jay glanced over his shoulder. The four rednecks were still there watching them.

"What do you think?" he whispered to Andy.

"I don't know. So far so good. Oh shit! One of them is heading for the trashcan. I think the jig is up!"

They started running. Suddenly, they heard shouting behind them. They looked back and saw the four piling into the Ford. One held the radio he had retrieved out of the trashcan.

"I told you that'd get us in trouble," Jay said. He looked around. "Shit! We have to get off this lit up street. Over there!" He pointed to the nearest buildings. They darted across the street, across a field, to several buildings. Using the buildings as cover, they came to Pier C. They had a long way to go to get to Pier L. They could see the Ford out on the road. It headed slowly down the road toward Pier D, where it stopped.

"I think its going to take us a while to get back the ship," Andy said. "We just have to think this out, take our time and keep out of sight."

"No argument here." They waited for what seemed like forever. Finally, the Ford moved on, stopping at Pier E.

"We'll let them stay a ways ahead of us. Sooner or later, they'll get tired and leave," Andy commented. They watched as two guys got out of the Ford and started walking among the buildings on Pier E. After a few minutes, they got back in the car and headed down to the next pier.

"That doesn't look good," Jay whispered.

"I don't think we have much to worry about." Andy didn't seem too concerned.

"These guys won't stray too far from the car. They'll stick together. They may be pissed at us, but they don't know what to expect. They've also figured out that we're not as drunk as we pretended to be."

The cat and mouse game went on for what seemed to be over an hour. Andy and Jay finally made their way to Pier K, moving a little closer to L, and then waited in the shadows, watching the Ford which was now parked at the head of Pier M.

"They're a little too close," Jay whispered to Andy. "If they spot us from here on, it'll be easy for them to figure what ship we're on."

"Yeah. And don't forget, even though they're assholes, they have the law on their side. Lucky for us, they haven't called the cops"

Suddenly, two of the rednecks stepped out of the shadows and stood next to the Ford. Jay could hear some discussion, but couldn't make out the words. Then they got into the car and suddenly took off, tires squealing. The green Ford headed back down the road toward the main gate.

"Finally! They gave up." Jay was relieved.

"Maybe. Let's get on the ship quick, just to be safe."

As soon as the Ford was out of sight, they raced across the 100 yards to Pier L. Out of breath they crossed the Quarterdeck, tossed the mandatory salutes to the flag and a tired looking Second Class. They sat down on the fantail.

"Man. I need a cigarette," Jay said.

They had just lit up when Andy grabbed Jay's arm. "Look!" He pointed to toward the end of the pier. The Ford was back. It was about 50 yards from them, on the main road, cruising slowly past Pier L, heading toward Pier M and beyond.

"Christ!" Jay ducked.

"Don't worry. They can't see us here. They lost us but now they're making one last check to see if they can spot us."

The Ford kept going. Jay watched the taillights disappear. "Damn, that was close. Enough of this shit. It's bad enough to get the shit knocked out of you, but to get beat up and then face a felony auto theft rap is not my idea of a good time."

"Yeah," Andy agreed. "That was close." Anchors await my boys, anchors await.

Chapter 13: On the Beach

Andy and Jay settled into the work routine rather easily, but they had little choice. Chow at 0630, muster on the fantail at 0730, inspection, then the fireroom work for eight hours. Work in the fireroom consisted of washing, greasing, and oiling equipment, cleaning and painting the bilges, cleaning and painting the boiler and steam lines, and cleaning and painting the bulkheads (walls). A motto in the navy was 'If it doesn't move, paint it'. The more experienced firemen, E-3 thru E-5, actually did maintenance and repair on the fireroom's steam lines, boilers, and related equipment.

One job that was actually somewhat enjoyable was the everyday ritual of coffee making. It had to be done the first thing in the morning. Always one of the lowest class snipe had the duty. The upper class NCOs each had their own personal coffee cup hanging on the bulkhead next to the stainless steel 20-cup coffee maker. Lower class snipes / enlisted men used Styrofoam cups. Andy, and then Jay, learned the 'Joy of Coffee Making'. Gritman, Maloni, and any of the other low class snipes would race to their respective fireroom's hatch right after inspection and ship's orders. Down the ladder and to the coffee maker. Everything was normal except the added ingredients: sometimes it was lube oil; sometimes it was a few hockers; sometimes it was Borax, and yes, sometimes it was piss. "Not too much," Gritman would say, "we dasn't want 'em catchin' on, jes want em' drinkin' up dis evil potion."

Yes the joy of coffee making could make a low class snipe's day go a little easier as he heard the compliments from NCOs and watched them sip and gulp the brew. Once they had their fill they would usually pour themselves one to go, never wondering why the low class snipes didn't drink the brew. Gritman was now head low class snipe and he just loosely supervised the coffee making while he wiped the rim of each coffee cup with the head of his dick.

When Friday afternoon finally rolled around. Andy and Jay had washed the grime (oil, grease, asbestos fibers, bilge effluent, etc.) off and were sitting below the main deck on the boilermen's side of the sleeping compartment waiting for the call for supper chow. Some of the guys were playing poker. It seemed like there was a never ending game of poker going on whenever ships' work knocked off. There was always a blanket over the table on the machinist side of the compartment that served as the poker table. The blanket was necessary in case an officer ever wandered below deck into the compartment. Gambling was illegal. Way illegal. Especially with a Captain, almost ordained as a man of the cloth, as by the book as this one. If an officer did happen down then someone would grab the four corners of the blanket and shove the whole bundle under a mattress, or into an empty locker. Andy, who was a regular at the table, only saw this happen once. No one got in trouble, but when the officer left, all hell broke loose. Each player claiming to have more chips than what any other player believed was the truth. A small fight had broken out, and Gritman, because of his bulk, helped to quell the disturbance before anyone above deck heard the struggle. Six players were involved, all chips were divided equally. Half were happy and half were not. Equal justice according to Gritman. Case settled.

"Well now that the show's over and we're all dressed up and nowhere to go, what's next? Another weekend free from duty and nothing to do. We have to go somewhere. We have to do something different. I can't see sitting here all weekend. We're all tired of the strip, the base movies, and the Enlisted Mens' club. We need to go somewhere new," Jay was whining.

"Let's go on liberty. Let's hit the beach!" Andy offered sarcastically. "We'll visit the cultural fucking center of Charleston-

The-Strip one more time. I'm sure there's one bar there that we haven't been in a dozen times already. We could dress up in our spiffy clothes, drink warm Schlitz, pick up some girls with no brains and less morals and end the evening dining in style at Shorty"s, the only place guaranteed to give you heartburn and the shits. Its cheap, its warm, and you won't forget it in the morning. Let's live it up."

Jay rolled his eyes. "You're sick."

"I know, I like that about me," agreed Andy.

"Look, we got a little money. Let's go somewhere really different. Somewhere really cool." He opened his locker and pulled out a map of the Charleston area. After studying it a minute, he jabbed his finger on a spot. "Here we go! The ocean!"

"Great. We don't see enough of the ocean already."

"No. Look here. Isle of Palms. Sounds neat and we'll see the ocean from the shore. Surf, sun, sand, palm trees, girls in bikinis, no sailors. A perfect spot!"

Hmm, thought Andy, beach, bikini clad girls, beer. "Ok, different and cool. Good by me. Fuck chow. Fuck the ship. Let's go, but no car-borrowing. Okay?"

"I promise."

Andy was easy, you just had to know him.

After the necessary stop at the locker club to get into their civilian disguises, they left the base and caught a bus going downtown. They transferred to another bus that took them over the high bridge, through Mount Pleasant, over a series of smaller bridges and finally dropped them off in downtown Isle of Palms.

The village consisted of a row of businesses along a boardwalk which ran parallel to a long clean beach. A 7-11, a real estate office, and the city hall stood in front of them. Past them, they could see a few restaurants, a drug store, a run down souvenir shop and three bars. A couple of empty buildings and a large open air pavilion used for bingo, dances and whatever else, completed the business district. Past the other buildings, small houses could be seen as well as a couple of motels, which appeared to be full. The beach was full of people. Mostly real young or real old.

"So where are the girls?" Andy wanted to know after a trip up the beach and half of one back.

"Beats me. Let's try the bars."

Two hours later, they had hit all three bars on the island and were sitting in a small restaurant eating fried shrimp. "At least this is better than the ship," Jay offered. "Food's good."

"Yeah," offered Andy, "so far its different. But not cool."

They bought a six-pack of beer and headed up the beach. As they passed one of the motels, a couple of girls called from an open window.

"What do they look like?" Jay wanted to know.

"Can't tell, too far way. Let's check it out."

They walked closer and Jay got a better look at them. "Jesus Christ! They're all of 14 or so. Teeny boppers. Damn our luck." They turned and continued heading down the beach.

"Hey! Where ya goin'? Come on back. Faggot sailors. Fuck you guys. Fuck your mommas!"

"Teeny boppers alright," Andy said. "Talking teeny bopper language."

The sun was beginning to go down and the air was getting a little cooler. They turned around and headed back toward the center of town. They went into the first bar they had stopped at several hours earlier. By now there were a lot less people on the beach and only a few in the bar.

"Now what?"

"I don't know. Not much else to see here today. We could head back to Charleston and check things out there."

"Yeah, I guess."

"Hey!" Jay yelled to the bartender. "When's the next bus back to Charleston?"

"Tomorrow morning at 9:00."

"You're shitting me, right?"

"Nope. Last bus left a half hour ago."

"Oh, great. Now what?"

"How much money you got?" Andy asked.

Jay dug through his pockets. "2...3...5...$5.75! Shit! I had a twenty here somewhere. Where the hell did that go?" He double-checked his pockets. "Its gone. Must have fallen out somewhere. That's just great! Damn!"

"I've got about 7 bucks left. That pretty much eliminates any hope of a motel room."

"Unless you want to stay with those teenyboppers. Maybe they have older sisters."

"Yeah, sure. Or mothers, and don't go any further with this Jay."

"Or grandmothers."

"Son of a bitch, and fuck me a runnin'! We can forget calling a cab. We must be 20 miles from Charleston. Its been different, but now I feel a chill coming on," grumbled Andy.

"Let's hang around and see if wee can hitch a ride with someone back to town. Too bad I can't borrow a..."

"Forget it!" demanded Andy

Two hours later, things didn't look any better. Half their money was gone, spent on beer and pool. They asked a number of people but no one was headed for Charleston, or so they said. "These assholes are prejudiced against us because we're sailors." Jay grumbled.

Even Andy, who usually had a knack for figuring ways to get what he wanted, was feeling stuck. "Well, it looks like we'll be staying here tonight."

"Here where?"

"Here, here. The great outdoors. On the beach. You know, really on the beach, at one with nature." Andy waved his arms expansively.

"Ok with me. But I'll feel better with a nightcap or two."

They counted out their remaining money. "Not much left," Jay observed, 'after we take out enough for tomorrow's bus fare. Can't lose that."

"Enough for a couple bottles of Boone's Farm or Ripple and some Schlitz. Nothing like a little fine wine for a nightcap to make you sleep like a baby."

They headed to the 7-11 and bought the wine and beer. Jay got the Boone's Farm and Andy bought a Ripple and a quart of Schlitz. Andy wanted to mix it up because it was the cheapest blitz he knew. Fully stocked, the two headed out to sit on the beach. The beach was deserted. The moon was hiding behind a bank of clouds. They opened their wine and beer. Sitting on the white sand, they could hear the waves pounding in front of them. The moon had come out for a second and the sand glistened like fresh snow.

Jay could also hear rustling sounds behind them. Out of the corner of his eye, Jay saw something moving. "What's that?"

"Crabs probably. Those big white ones that run sideways. Fiddler or something like that. They have one big claw and one small one. Fast little critters as Gritman would say."

"That's just great, sleeping with crabs. We sure know how to have a good time."

"I don't want to talk about crabs," said Andy, remembering his experience in boot camp. You could get crabs more than one way Andy thought. Jay didn't need to know about that. Nobody did. Boot camp was over and there wasn't anyone from that place to remember. Yes, Andy's crabs were on a need to know basis.

The wine helped mellow them out. They looked out over the ocean and talked wine induced talk and thought wine induced thoughts. They could hear the music coming from the closest bar behind them. After a short while the music stopped and the bar lights went dark. Andy turned around. "Last call. Closing time," he announced. But Jay was lying on his back in the sand, already asleep.

About three hours later, Jay sat bolt upright. He was soaking wet. Where the hell was he? Sitting on a beach. It's raining like hell. Soaking fucking wet. What the hell is going on? His mind was foggy. Wine. That's right, we drank wine. Shit! Come on, think straight.

Suddenly, Andy jumped to his feet. "Son of a bitch, motherfucker!" he yelled. He started running around. "Goddamn it! I'm soaking wet! Someone pissed on me! Who pissed on me? I find the cocksucker, I'll kill the son of a bitch!"

Jay had to laugh. "You looked like a drowned rat having a seizure."

Andy slowly realized it was raining and no one was pissing on him. "Jeez, I'm wet. What a fucking way to wake up. I'm fucking soaked. I've never been this wet and sandy. I'll never fucking dry out."

Jay was on his feet. His head hurt. His head really hurt! Thank you Mr. Boone! "Let's get out of here and find a dry place." They half ran, half stumbled toward the row of buildings along the main street. The rain was coming down in sheets. They found a dry area in the open air part of the nearest structure. Andy had managed to salvage a little of the Schlitz, and offered a slug to Jay. Jay politely refused, indicating he might spew the contents of his stomach all over the only remaining dry area if the bottle were thrust any closer. "Sorry," said Andy, "it is a little warm. However, my good friend, and keeper of the different and cool, it does help one to fall back into that..." Andy turned and saw that Jay didn't need any help crawling back into his slumber. He was already passed out in one of the only two dry corners. Andy stumbled to the other dry corner and thought how cold it was. If he could switch his cold to the remaining warm Schlitz, well that's not possible. But, he could take the last warmth of the beer and....that was all it took. He was out like light.

The rain had let up by morning, and by 8:00 it was only a slight drizzle or a fog. Whatever it was it was certainly dreary. A real depressing day. Jay opened his eyes. His eyes hurt. His head hurt. His whole body hurt. He was cold, wet, stiff and sore. He moved a little. It felt like he was lying on a concrete floor. He looked around. He was on a concrete floor alright, in the corner, against a wall in an open air part of a building. Once he was able to focus, he realized they were in the empty dance pavilion they had seen earlier last evening. Slowly, he remembered the wine, the beach, the rain, and seeking shelter in the pavilion several hours ago. Andy was curled up in another corner. He looked like a rat for the second time in just a few short hours of the same day: wet clothes, wet hair, and sleeping in the smallest of cracks. A long, smooth, hairless tail would complete the picture.

"Hey! Get up!" Jay yelled. "Get up asshole, and share the misery. Come on, I need some Schlitz or wine or something, jeez! Get up party boy!"

Andy groaned and stirred. He got up slowly, shaking slightly. He didn't say anything.

Jay stood up. His clothes were soaking wet too, and caked with sand. He hurt all over. "Are you alive?" he asked Andy.

"Barely. Where the hell are we? Never fucking mind, I know. I can't hardly see. Everything is blurry." He looked around, groaning, rubbing his eyes, and trying to focus. In the process he began to answer his own question. "Did I have fun?"

"Yeah, you were the life of the party."

They brushed sand from their clothes and hair the best they could. They headed out to the main street. Nothing was open yet. It was too early on a Sunday-go-to-bible-belt-church morning.

"What time is it?"

"8:20. The bus should be here at 9."

"Hope I can live that long. The way I feel, it'll be close." His head was throbbing. Andy, in some mysterious mode of concentration, had found a long dry cigarette butt in the corner of the building, fumbled for his matches and remembered they were still pretty wet. "Dammit, I need a smoke, oh my fuckin' head." Oh well, maybe the bus driver will have a light, thought Andy.

They sat at a picnic table outside of a closed restaurant. The fog and / or the drizzle gave the scene a surreal look and feel to it. The fog and the drizzle in their minds only heightened the surreal look and feel. The boys sure felt surreal this morning, once they got away from the initial pain of a huge hangover. There was no sign of anyone else around. The stillness was getting to Andy. "Maybe we're dead and this is hell. Yeah, hell, No Smoking. I bet they smoke for free in heaven."

"Maybe everyone else is dead. Maybe there was a war and we missed it. You know, I saw this Twilight Zone episode where this guy comes to a town and everything is all set up, normal like. Radios are playing, lights are on but no one's around. No one at all. And this guy doesn't know where everyone went. Maybe that's what we're up against here."

"So what happened to all the people? How did it end? Did he have any smokes?"

"I don't remember too much, but there was warm food on the table of one of the houses he went into. You could see the steam rise off the food. There just wasn't anyone around to eat it. I don't know, my brain isn't working at full capacity at the moment."

Suddenly two dogs ambled out of the fog, headed past the table and stopped at the corner of the building. They didn't seem to notice Andy or Jay at all. They started humping.

"Look at that. What a fitting touch to an otherwise dreary, unreal scene," Jay commented.

"Its great! Just what we needed for the weekend. We've now had it all: sun, surf, sand, and now sex." Andy laughed. "This couldn't be any more entertaining if they were elephants. They don't even care that we're here."

"That's only because we're so well camouflaged in our wet and sand covered clothes they can't see us. We're part of the beach to them." Jay put his head in his arms on the table. "Wake me when my limo arrives."

Andy idly watched the dogs. Sometimes it'd be nice to be a dog and not give a shit about things, he thought. "You know Jay, they say there is no bad sex. Only some sex is better than the others. Those dogs seem to be enjoying themselves. There's just different, uh, levels of sex."

"You thinking about having sex with the dog?"

"Fuck you Jay."

"Not today buddy." He looked out on the ocean, barely visible through the mist. "This is too weird, bottom level weird," he said aloud.

Eventually, they heard the sound of a vehicle and the bus emerged from the fog. They waved it down and the driver stopped. They were getting on when the driver stopped them.

"Hold it! Ya'll ain't comin' on my bus lookin' like that. No bums on my bus! Beat it you winos! You ain't messing up my bus."

"Jesus Christ!" Jay snapped. This was the last straw. "You son of a..."

Andy interrupted, the fog in his mind was clearing a little. "Listen, pal. We have an emergency here. We got mugged out here early this morning. Some guys took our car and all our money and knocked us out and left us to die on the beach. We've got to get back to Charleston and report it to the authorities."

The driver was skeptical. "Why not report it here to the local cops?"

Andy was ready for that. "Because we're in the Navy." He showed his dogtags. "We have to report this to the Shore Patrol. We're government property and the Navy needs to know when their property has been damaged. We really have to hurry back to the base. We probably need medical help too, but we have to get to the base to get it."

The driver bought it. "Ok, hop in. Ride's on the house. But try not to mess up the bus."

"You got a light?", Andy couldn't resist, shoving the cigarette butt in the driver's face, "my butt's dry enough."

Back at the locker club, they showered and packed their wet, sandy clothes into the locker. "Once they're dry, we can brush off the sand and wash them. They'll be good as new."

"Or else they'll get all rotten and moldy and we can shitcan them and buy new ones."

Back on the ship, they were greeted by the Officer of the Deck as they crossed the Quarterdeck. "Rough night boys? Ya'll look like shit."

They headed for the compartment and went straight to bed and no one bothered them, for a while. Then Gritman and Maloni got off watch and wanted to know about their adventure. Jay and Andy told them they had too much booze, way too much fun, and more sex than they could bear. That was good enough to lift the weight for Gritman and Maloni, for awhile.

Chapter 14: Helping Out Ratso

It was Friday afternoon. 1500 hours. Jay, Andy, and the other lowest class BTs were sitting in the bilges, cleaning up oil from a leaking fuel oil pump. Jay was daydreaming back to another time, another world, where Friday afternoons were something special. In school, the clock would inch at a snails pace to 3:30 when the bell would ring, signaling freedom until Monday morning. As he grew older, the clock moved just as slow on Friday afternoons at work, until quitting time would come and freedom would be granted until Monday morning. Friday afternoons were the first step to the football games, happy hours, and parties that Friday night brought. Undemanding Saturdays and Sundays would follow. That was the time necessary for the 'letting of your hair down' in order for one to enjoy the requisite of irresponsibility and fun. Jay came back to the present with a jolt. No goddamned hair to let down!! Things had changed.

The morning hadn't started out that bad. Up at 0600. Breakfast at 0630. At 0730 they assembled on the fantail. Then, the officers and chiefs could look them over, make sure they hadn't grown their hair past regulation length overnight, and provide them with a few words of inspiration. Words by which to inspire were inevitably: "trim that beard sailor; yer shoes look like three kinds of shit sailor, get 'em shined; or cut the hair sailor cuz' you're startin' to look like a girly boy, and blah, blah, blah." Ship announcements were announced, and work assignments made. They then filed down the ladder, to the bowels of the ship, the boiler room. At 0800 they began their work day. This routine occurred without fail five days a week whenever the ship was in port and seven days a week at sea. Today, the lowest class forward fire room (not to be confused with the aft fire room which was the same, only aft) BTs would spend the day cleaning and repainting the bilges. However, the boys never forgot the work day always began with the 'Joy of Coffee Making'. And Gritman continued to take the lead and, great pleasure, in meticulously wiping the outer and inner rims of all the coffee cups with his most prized possession.

The forward and aft firerooms were almost the same and each held two huge boilers and had three levels: upper, lower and bilges. The upper level housed toolboxes, a board for announcements and notices, four blower rooms and the check valves for the two boilers' water levels. It was also home to the all important 20-cup capacity coffee urn. The lower level housed fuel oil and water pumps and the boiler fireboxes. Numerous water, air, steam, and fuel lines crisscrossed the entire fire room, and numerous gauges and valves could be found everywhere. Each level had a couple of fresh air ducts which were supposed to bring cool fresh air down from the deck. These ducts were ineffective in their attempts to keep the heat at a tolerable temperature, especially when the temperature on the Charleston, South Carolina deck was over the 100 degree mark.

The bilges were the true basement of the ship, usually full of slimy water, fuel oil leakage, rags, cigarette butts, urine and other assorted trash. The bilges were covered by removable diamond plate deckplates. These deckplates and other see through metal gratings made up the fireroom walkways.

Jay was remembering an earlier morning, when he was the 'new guy'. It now occurred to him that he had been the 'new guy' for a longer time than others. He had guessed the ship had reached its capacity or the Navy wasn't able to recruit fast enough. Anyway, he remembered he was the 'new guy' for what seemed like an eternity. After descending the outboard ladder that morning, BT chief Bronski, full coffee cup in hand, stood on the upper level after greeting his crew. BT1 Freeze was at his side, also with a loaded coffee cup. NCOs were short staffed in the boilerman's rate and the chief had taken over personal responsibility for the forward fireroom. He often would get the men started then leave Freeze in charge of both firerooms. Back in the aft fireroom, Freeze knew he had enough suck asses and snitches to make sure everyone was doing what he wanted. Several senior enlisted men were assigned to preventative maintenance on two of the blowers. Two more were assigned to repack a leaking steam valve.

"You!" Bronski pointed at Jay, forgetting he had a full coffee cup in his hand. "Damn it!" he yelled as the coffee spilled onto his uniform. At least the coffee stain will match his khakis, Jay thought. "You!" he yelled again. "Stand fast!" The rest were herded to the lower level and the awaiting bilges.

"Can I have some coffee?" Jay asked. He figured Bronski had some disgusting idea of a job for him and maybe asking for coffee would distract him temporarily. Jay sure as hell wasn't going to drink it. Coffee seemed to be near and dear to the Chief's heart. That's a perversely comforting thought mused Jay.

"Cumheanghya and get it yo'sef,' Freeze answered for the Chief. He pointed to a pile of used, once-white, grease streaked, Styrofoam cups. Jay understood the language so he just poured his coffee into what looked to be the least greasy cup in the pile. The liquid was coal black and thick. Jay could just barely notice the little oily hints of some of the strangest coffee he had ever seen, and almost gagged just looking at it. This'd be a good time to quit drinking coffee, he thought. Please god, don't let me forget and take a sip.

"Whassa' matter, buds?" Freeze laughed. "Too strong for ya? Its purrfect. I like my coffee jes' like my wimmin': hot, strong, and black." Freeze cackled again.

Stupid redneck, Jay thought to himself. So you like your 'wimmin' oily and full of piss too, eh? Is that the best you can do? That's not only stupid, its older than hell. His thoughts were interrupted by Bronski.

"You're the 'new guy'. New guys make the coffee. From now on, its your job to make the coffee every morning before you turn to. Get down here and get it going by 0700. Its gotta be ready by 0730. If it ain't, you'll be in a world of shit."

Freeze nodded his head in somber agreement. "Don' ya'll fuck up," he advised.

Man, Jay thought, the same fucking speech, over and over. This is some serious shit. If they only knew what really happened to their coffee. It's a group effort and they don't know. What's the deal with these guys and their coffee? "How long do I get to do this?' he asked again, incredulously.

"Until you're not the new guy any more."

Bronski finally realized that Jay was stalling. "Listen up!" he roared. "Being new and all, Freeze here will orient you to the fire room. That won't take long seeing as you been to school for boilers and all. Pay attention. I don't want you fucking things up just because you don't know what you're doing."

So its ok to fuck up if you know what you're doing? Jay wondered to himself, not daring to say it aloud.

Bronski turned and filled his cup again. He started up the ladder to the deck. Freeze turned to Jay. He was now in charge and was prepared to prove it. "Cumheanghya 'new boy'. Foller me!" Jay dutifully followed Freeze around the fireroom. He looked at boilers, blowers, water level gauges, check valves, pumps, squawk boxes, burners, pipes, lines, deck plates, hatches, torches, tools and finally, the bilges. "Any questions ya'll wanna' ax?"

"No," Jay lied. It was pretty confusing, even though he had been to school at Great Lakes for this. The fire room was a lot different than the classroom with the mockup boilers. He was totally lost, but he was afraid if Freeze tried to explain anything to him, he'd get even more confused and piss Freeze off. He thought it best to keep his mouth shut for now.

"Thass good. Now git ya ass to work. Hey Ratso!"

Ratso, a big, muscular BT2 was lumbering down the inboard ladder, carrying a stack of ragged, stained, but freshly laundered green coveralls.

"Fix West here up and get him in the bilges with the others!"

"Sure thing. Here ya go, Boot." Ratso flung a pair of coveralls at Jay.

Freeze headed up to the upper level, topped off his cup and started climbing up to join Bronski on the deck. He looked down at

he now smiled when Bronski and Freeze called him Ratso. To him, it implied camaraderie. He was one of them. It had never occurred to him that it wasn't a compliment. As lacking as he seemed in most areas of his life, Ratso was a whiz with boilers and all that came with them. He had always been intrigued by mechanical things and had wanted to be a mechanic when he was younger. He was never able to pull it off. Rumor was that he had been kicked out of school in 10th grade and spent most of his teenage years on the wrong side of the law, in and out of juvenile detention facilities. The day he turned 18, he enlisted. He joined the Navy because the Navy recruiter was the first recruiter he saw. When Ratso told the recruiter he wanted to be a mechanic and working on boilers was fine with him, the recruiter couldn't sign him up fast enough. The recruiter knew a good thing when he saw it. Nobody volunteered for BT billets. Ratso came to love the Navy as much as he loved boilers and all that came with them.

Ratso ran the fire room. The chief would write up the daily job assignments and give them to Freeze. Freeze would glance at them, take a swig of coffee and hand them over to Ratso, and Ratso made the list happen. While Bronski and Freeze sat up on the deck, Ratso kept the forward fireroom shipshape.

Deep into his book, Ratso was temporarily oblivious to the men in the bilges below him. Andy and Jay had moved around a corner of #1 boiler, out of Ratso's immediate sight.

"Why should we help Ratso out?" Jay wanted to know. "He's a prick."

"I know, I know," Andy replied. "But he'd be easy to fuck with. He's getting shafted and doesn't even know it."

"Unlike those of us who are getting shafted and really know it."

"Look, life would be easier for us if Ratso decided he liked us. But I'm not talking about kissing ass. Its more like getting Ratso to start thinking differently. Get him to stop thinking about you and me as the enemy. And if we could get him to start doubting Freeze and Bronski, well, that would be something that could only do us some good."

At 1700, they were standing in the chow line. They hadn't finished the bilges. They had been let go at 1630 with orders that the bilges would be finished up tomorrow (Saturday) morning. Jay had thought back to another time, another world, when Saturday mornings were something special. No liberty until the bilges were clean.

They had gotten rid of their filthy coveralls, but their dungarees were still dirty and stunk. Other sailors standing in line, yeomen, clerks, and radiomen in their spotless and pressed working uniforms, kept a safe and sanitary distance from the bilge rats.

After a tasteless supper, they showered and sat on the fantail smoking cigarettes. A game of poker started.

"So how do you propose we help Ratso out?' Jay asked.

Maloni looked up from his cards. "What are you talking about? Helping that asshole?"

Andy ignored him. "You and I are going to be his friends," he said to Jay.

An hour later, Ratso showed up on the fantail. He hadn't showered but he didn't have to. He hadn't been in the bilges all day. He sat down, lit up a Camel and took out his book.

"Hey Ratso," Andy called." Come join the game."

Ratso looked surprised.

"Yeah, come on," Jay added, half heartedly. He still remembered the shove in the bilges. "Show us how the game is played." He choked the words out.

"I'm out of here," Maloni said under his breath. "You guys are fucked up ass kissers."

"Come on, Ratso, take Maloni's spot."

Ratso lumbered over and sat down. "Alright, boots, prepare to lose yer asses and yer money."

The remaining card players were surprised, but after a few hands it became obvious to them what was going on. Andy sounded so sincere when he asked Ratso about himself. Jay sounded so interested in mechanics and boilers when he asked Ratso about rpm's and psi's. After an hour of cards, Ratso was up by over 15 bucks: most of it from Jay and Andy.

"You know, Ratso, it's too bad that they make you do all the dirty work. With all you know, you should be a Chief or something. Wouldn't it be great to be really in charge? You'd make a hell of a lot more money and, you could wear khakis. Too bad they won't give you a chance. Bronski and Freeze don't want you to get ahead. They'd have to work then." ...and on and on and on.

Ratso bristled at some of the comments but he was having too good a time winning to get seriously mad. When the game finally ended, Ratso stood up and collected his winnings. He looked down at Andy. "That's all bullshit what you said about the Chief and Freeze. They're my buds. Nobody is stopping me from anything. You're full of shit."

"Maybe so. If that's what you want to think, go ahead. Its none of my business. Its just that every day I see them up on the main deck in the fresh air, drinking coffee, looking at the girls, bullshitting, and you're stuck down in the fire room with us. Hell, you even have to get dirty sometimes. I just don't think its fair. That's all."

Jay was having trouble controlling himself. He was afraid he'd either puke or laugh out loud at all this. He pulled himself together. "That's right, Ratso. I know I'm just a shit for brains boot, but I don't think you're getting a square deal. I don't like to see people get screwed."

"Bullshit," Ratso said, pocketing his winnings. "We'll have to do this again, boys." He lit a camel and walked to the mess decks to join Freeze for a cup of coffee (unadulterated).

"That was a waste of time and money," Jay commented.

"I don't think so." Andy wasn't concerned. "This may take a while but the seed has been planted. We will now practice patient persuasiveness."

The seed had indeed been planted and even though it took a while, it started to grow. Over the next few weeks, they started noticing a change in Ratso. It was subtle at first. Ratso started joining the card games more frequently: several times a week. Andy and Jay still let him win most of the time, but had started cutting back on the amounts they would lose.

"I can't afford this much longer," Jay complained more than once. "Ratso is becoming an expensive project."

Ratso started spending less time in the fire room. During the weekday, after Freeze and Bronski issued the daily assignments to him, he'd put the crew to work, and then disappear for a couple of hours at a time. No one was sure where he went. He was definitely getting less concerned with the fire room operation. He definitely didn't have the same drive as he had previously. Slowly, he stopped being an asshole. He was still hard to get along with, but he was mellowing out. He was talking less and less to Freeze and Bronski. Jay and Andy would encourage the new Ratso every chance they had. They even stopped trying to be subtle about it.

"How long are you gonna' put up with this shit? You need to take charge of your life. Stop letting them push you around. Go get yourself a girl. That's what you need. You need to get laid. Live a little, for Chrissakes."....and on and on and on.

Then they stopped calling him Ratso. Initially it was Russo but as time went by they began to address him as Eric: "a-rack". He liked it. This was not lost on Andy and Jay. "You know, when they came up with Ratso, it was to mock you. They love to make fun of you when you're not there. Ever see Midnight Cowboy? Dustin Hoffman is in it, he plays a con man, a fucked up loser, a real sleazebag. Named Ratso. How about that? So they call you Ratso? What's with that? How long are you gonna' take that shit?"...and on and on and on.

Ratso started spending more and more time off the ship. He started taking advantage of liberty. He took a bunch of money he'd been saving and bought a car: a three-year-old Camaro with all the goodies. His infatuation with the fire room was replaced by the Camaro. He started going to bars on the Strip. Word was, he met and was shacking up with a girl: an 18 year old dancer in one of the stripper bars. Jay and Andy had never seen her although they had made several visits to the Strip to see if they could spot Ratso in action. They never could find him.

"Whoever or whatever she is, she must exist. Someone's sure occupying Ratso's time and attention these days."

"Yeah, he's like a dog in heat. Got one thing on his mind, that's for sure, and it ain't the Navy."

A large, rusty cooler keeps the soda at a constant 62 degrees. 25 cents a bottle for either Coke or Pepsi. Scattered around three scarred and stained tables, a handful of folding chairs provide seating to those too drunk to stand at the counter. A large, faded American flag adorns one wall; several black and white photos of various unnamed ships adorn another. "America: Love it or Leave It" and "Sailors Have More Fun" signs are tacked under a grimy window. Shorty's is a truly patriotic place. Most patrons order their dogs to go.

Behind the counter, Shorty himself rules his roost. A short, enormously rotund, tattooed troll, snarling and swearing, he serves his wares 6 days a week. Even Shorty takes the Sabbath off. Claiming to be 45, he looks 20 years older. The aging process was obviously accelerated by daily mega-doses of bourbon. Shorty brags that he retired as a Chief Cook off a carrier out of Norfolk. As the evening wears on, and as he works on emptying the ever present bourbon bottle under the counter, he'll brag of the feasts he single-handedly created for Admirals, Diplomats, and even Presidents during his lengthy Navy stint. Actually, Navy records reveal that Shorty retired after 20 years as a Machinist Mate, an MM3 to be exact. Rumor has it that the parting of Shorty and the Navy was less than amiable; the result of numerous Captains Masts and, some say, problems Shorty experienced in getting through the engine room hatches due to his ever expanding girth. It is assumed that he receives a retirement pension of some sort. Contrary to Shorty's grandiose claims, it is difficult to believe anyone could make big money dishing out coney dogs, 25 cents at a time.

Shorty swears he won the business in poker game. However, more reliable sources will say that he actually inherited it from his since deceased mother. At one tine it was reportedly a respectable diner with good food that his mother personally made and served. However, that was before Shorty got his hands on it and things have since changed.

Shorty immediately streamlined the menu to specialize in Coney Dogs. All non-essential furnishings were sold off for booze money. "Too frilly," Shorty would snarl. "Don't want to attract no pussies or fudgepackers in here!" Proof of his shrewd business sense is reflected in his hours of operation. Opening whenever his hangover allows him, usually mid afternoon, he serves his dogs until the after bar crowd crawls home, often between 3 and 4 am. The business really booms between midnight and closing time. Shorty learned early on that he could make extra money by screwing over very drunk sailors who would often have no idea how much money they were paying for the dogs.

Strategically located next to the main gate, the faded sign serves as a beacon, beckoning hungry sailors in for a last, late night feast on their way back to their ship. Thousands upon thousands of bagged dogs have made the trek from gate to pier to ship with thousands of sailors over the years, alternately being eaten and spilled on clothes enroute to the ship. Many a hung over sailor awoke the next morning with a splitting headache, an empty wallet and the nausea that comes with a stomach full of slimy coney dogs. In addition, many a hung over sailor, during a hazy morning after, has had to face a once-white uniform now full of booze and coney dog stains.

In that summer of 1970, Andy and Jay discovered Shorty's. At 1 a.m., after a fairly uneventful night, Jay was hungry. He liked hotdogs, and that, combined with enough alcohol to impair what little judgment he once had, was more than enough to draw Jay to Shorty's, like a moth to a flame. Andy was thinking more about girls than hotdogs, but since there seemed to be a lack of the former on the Strip at this hour, he couldn't come up with a better idea. Into Shorty's they went.

The place was packed wall to wall with drunk young sailors, drunk old sailors and a handful of ugly bargirls, pretending to be drunk.

"We'll just get a couple and head back to the ship." Jay was hungry but he was also starting to feel claustrophobic in the sea of drunk people.

"Look at all the lifers," Andy observed. "No wonder they're so fat."

A bargirl sidled up to Andy and asked if he had a wiener to spare.

"I think there's a double meaning there," Jay commented.

"You're a real fucking genius," was the response. Andy laughed and suggested that she looked like she'd had her fill of a great many wieners. She retreated in a huff.

Perched like a fat old toad behind the counter, Shorty was unsuccessfully trying to come on to one of the bargirls. She didn't seem eager to take him up on his suggestions.

"Gimme three dogs," Jay ordered as he stepped up to the counter.

"I'll take two-no sauce," Andy added.

Shorty turned to them, irritated that his fantasy about the bargirl was interrupted. "No sauce? Ya' gotta' have the sauce."

"The sauce looks like shit."

"All dogs come with sauce. No special orders."

"Look, it's simple. Just put the dogs in a bun and don't add the sauce."

"Ok, but it'll cost you more."

"More? For no sauce?"

"Yup. Its a special order."

"What the hell?"

"Gimme my three dogs with his sauce," Jay tried to be helpful.

"What are you two assholes, assholes or something?" Shorty was getting really irritated

"Christ! Ok, ok. Just give us the five dogs with sauce," Andy conceded. "I'll just give my sauce to the cats."

"Coming up right away, Admiral," Shorty snarled sarcastically.

The dogs appeared on the counter with an unceremonious plop. "Buck and a quarter. Only one napkin per customer and we're outta mustard."

A drunk Lifer shouldered up to the counter, bumping Jay. "Gimme 6 dogs, Shorty! I'm just getting started." The Lifer glanced sideways at Jay, eyeing his three hotdogs. "What are ya' boy, some sorta' candyass?"

"Mgugh?" Jay's mouth was full.

"Three coneys all a little boy like you can handle, Slick?

"Huh?" Jay's mouth was emptying. "What the fuck you talking about?"

"I bet I could eat more hotdogs than you any day of the week, Slick," the lifer sneered.

"No doubt about that," Jay agreed, eyeing the lifer's big gut. "Looks like you've had a lot of practice."

Andy, never one to pass up any interesting situation sensed that this had the making of one. "Hey, man," he yelled at the lifer. "You know who this is?" He gestured toward Jay.

"Yeah, and I know what you both are. You're a couple of limp dicked boots."

"This here is the fucking grand champion hotdog eater of Wisconsin and probably the whole fucking world. Go up against him and he'll make you look like the wimpass pussy you are. You call yourself a man? You're all talk. Lets see you put your money where your mouth is, fatboy." Andy was definitely on a roll. Once he got started, he could talk as fast as an auctioneer, insult like Lenny Bruce, swear better than just about any sailor, and had the persistence of a mosquito when he found the target. He could get under people's skin when he wanted to and it seemed he enjoyed doing it.

Jay tensed at the mention of money. "A bet?" he whispered to Andy. "That's not a good idea."

"Fucking-A. A bet. Come on fat man, lets have us a bet," Andy yelled.

Jay was getting real tense. "Look," he whispered to Andy. "I don't have any more money."

"Me neither," Andy whispered back. "But don't worry about it, you're not going to lose."

Jay wasn't so sure about that. He was thinking about the beer he drank and the three dogs he had already eaten. He looked around the room. By now everyone in the place was listening and a big crowd was gathering behind the Lifer. Jay realized that he and Andy were noticeably alone.

"Ok, bigmouth!' the Lifer yelled back. "You're on. Fifty bucks says I can out eat your candyass friend."

Andy laughed. "Fifty? Make it a hundred and you're on!"

Holy shit, Jay thought. "Hey Andy, wait a minute..."

"You want to go more than a hundred?" The Lifer eyed Jay with a bleary-eyed unfocused glare.

"Uh, no."

"Ok, we're on."

"We're on," agreed Andy. "Plus loser pays for all the food."

They leaned closer to the counter. Jay took Andy aside while Shorty was lining up the coneys. "This is nuts! I can't do it. I'm already full."

"Listen to me. The lifer already ate more hotdogs, and, he's drunker than you. He's full of food, beer and," Andy added, "he's full of shit."

"Yeah, but he's also got a bigger, uh, storage area."

"Go puke and empty your storage area."

"What?" Jay stared at him. "You're nuts. I don't want to puke."

"Really. It'll help."

"No way."

"Can't you use fifty bucks?"

"What fifty bucks? Its a hundred."

"Fifty is your half. I get a cut for setting this up," spoke Andy the promoter.

"Oh, man! This is going from bad to worse. Let me remind you, I'm doing all the work here." Jay paused. "Oh, alright, well, uh, let's get to it." He shook his head and headed for the men's restroom.

"Hey! Where ya' goin?" demanded the lifer.

"None of your fucking business," Jay snapped. "If I'm not back soon, start without me," he added.

"He's gotta take a whiz. He'll be right back," Andy promised.

Jay returned looking somewhat pale and stood at the counter.

"Alright!" Shorty yelled. He had assumed the role as emcee, referee and overall man in charge. "Here's how it'll work. The man who eats the most hotdogs in ten minutes wins the bet."

"Let's make it five minutes," Jay said. He wanted to get this over quickly.

"Alright with me, candyass," sneered the lifer. "I can beat your ass in five minutes, ten minutes or two hours."

"Alright, five minutes it is," Shorty proclaimed.

The dogs were lined up in front of them.

201

"On your mark, get set, uh, er, go!" barked Shorty.

Jay and the lifer started shoveling dogs into their mouths. After the first ten, Jay slowed to pace himself. The lifer was stuffing dogs into his mouth two at a time. At the ten dog mark, he let out a huge belch and dropped a dog from his mouth to the floor.

This isn't looking too good, Andy thought to himself. I have to do something. He started needling and pimping the lifer mercilessly. "The dog on the floor doesn't count! Come on fatboy, you're slowing down. What's the matter-getting full? Come on fatboy, you're slowing down. Hey! Try stuffing four into your big ass mouth. You're losing, loser. You look like a beached whale, lard ass."

The Lifer stopped in mid bite and lunged for Andy. Andy dodged him and stepped behind Jay.

"Come on mate. Keep eating," Shorty urged the Lifer. But while the Lifer was distracted, Jay had taken a slight lead and the clock was quickly closing in on the five minute deadline. In final burst of speed, Jay plunged hotdogs number 25 and 26 into his mouth just before Shorty bellowed, "Time's up!"

The finish line was not a pretty sight. Coney sauce covered both their shirts. Bits of hotdogs and buns littered the floor. The cats were eating well tonight. The Lifer was bright red. He was angry and bloated. Jay, by contrast, was looking a little green.

"That's it!" Shorty announced. "The boot's the winner with 26 dogs." The Lifer had only eaten 22.

Jay sat down. He had never felt so full and was starting to feel real sick. He could hardly move. But Andy was on top of the world. "You did it! Great job! Way to go!" He was all over the place. The Lifer was leaning against the counter, looking like he'd just eaten a refrigerator.

"Ok, pay up!" Andy got right to the point.

"Fuck you. I ain't paying you pukes nothing!"

"What?"

"You heard me. You fucking cheated. No way I'm paying you shit. I should kick your ass. Both of your asses."

Andy looked at Jay for support. But Jay wasn't up for a fight at the moment. He had a war waging in his stomach and was not going to be much help.

"Son of a bitch!" Andy ranted. "Pay up!"

"Get lost, squirrel," sneered the lifer, who had now collected a group of friends around him.

"He ain't gonna' pay you boots," a voice from the crowd chimed in. "You better get outa' here."

"Yeah, get outa' here," added a guy who looked like a beer barrel with a crew cut.

"I didn't know beer kegs could talk." Jay was feeling a tiny bit better. He felt he should join in, even though it was a huge effort.

"What did you say, asshole?" said another guy who looked like he bench pressed pickup trucks for fun.

Jay looked around. He didn't like what he saw. He caught Andy's eye and nodded at the door. "Fuck it. We're leaving."

Andy had quickly reassessed the situation and decided that they didn't need the hundred bucks that bad and weren't going to get it anyway. "Yeah," he agreed. "We were just leaving."

"But we might be back, assholes," Jay muttered to himself.

"Hey, wait a minute! ' Shorty just realized that he hadn't been paid. 'Who's gonna' pay for the food?"

"I won, so I don't figure I should have to, right, sir?" Jay looked Shorty in the eye. "I mean, I've already been screwed out of the bet money."

Shorty eyed Jay for a full minute. "Damn if you ain't right!" he slapped the counter and turned to the lifer. "Now then mate, pay up. You owe me for 48 coneys."

"Fuck you, Shorty!" the Lifer snapped back.

"Mate, if I don't have the money in my hand in five seconds, I'm gonna' introduce you to my friend here." Shorty pulled a sawed off shotgun from under the counter. "And after the two of you have been properly introduced, I'm calling the cops. I ain't even going to fuck with your Shore Patrol buddies. I'm a businessman and as I figure it, you're robbing me."

The crowd was moving away form the Lifer and was inching toward the door.

"Aw, Shorty. I was just funnin' with ya'. Here's yer money." The Lifer dropped the bills on the counter.

Shorty smiled and put the shotgun back. The Lifer looked around for Andy and Jay, but they had snuck out with the crowd.

"Man, I am still dying," Jay groaned. He was leaning against the outside wall of a building a block away from Shorty's. He had puked for a long time and was now feeling a little better, although his stomach still ached. "I am never going to go along with anything like that again."

"It was a good night,' Andy consoled him. "You made a new friend in Shorty. Because of you, he sold more hotdogs in five minute than he ever does in an hour. Besides, look at it this way: you got a free meal."

"I'll never eat again," Jay vowed.

They headed to the nearest bar. Jay needed something to wash the rotten taste out of his mouth. They nursed a beer each and headed back to the locker club. As they passed an alleyway close to the main gate, they heard a loud crash and saw a large shadow reel against a wall and collapse against two trashcans. They walked past without stopping.

"What was that all about?" Jay wondered.

"Damned if I know. Should we look?"

"I suppose it wouldn't hurt."

They went back to the alley and came upon a body sprawled up against the wall, half sitting and half laying. In the dim light they could see it was the Lifer from Shorty's. He looked at the two blurry figures standing over him and began to mumble something which soon became a loud curse like screeching, "You're the two fucking boots that screwed me outta' my goddamn money, fucking ass holes. I'm gonna' kill you." He started fumbling around in his pockets, and finally came up with an old rusty pocket knife. He wasn't a threat. He couldn't even stand. He just half laid there slashing around wildly and cursing. Andy kicked the knife out of his hand. The drunken old sailor just slumped over, and his eyes closed. Then he came alive with a start and puked all over himself and finally passed out, laying in a heap amongst the trashcans.

"Well, look at what we have here."

to anyone we'll pound sand up your ass until you fucking sneeze sand! You understand that don't you, Oswald."

Oswald sputtered and stumbled up the ladder, "You guys leave me alone. I haven't done anything."

Andy called after him, "That's right, Oswald, you're okay. You do get it. None of us have done anything."

They walked the mile to the Club. "I hate this uniform," Jay complained. "I look like a real stooge in it. Do you think Oswald will say anything?"

"The stooges are cool; you're not, and Oswald is ignorant, and you're not. I really don't give a shit if he does say anything, but I don't think he will," Andy offered.

"Fuck you for everything, and I really don't think he will either. You did a number on him."

"Take it easy. There's no one around to impress, no one to see you in your nice uniform except other dorks like us in the same nice uniform. Besides, you have to wear it to get into the Club. No civvies allowed in this man's Navy. And, no matter what, it beats firing up the fucking boilers."

At the front door, two gorillas in Shore Patrol uniforms glared at them, paying special attention to their hair and shoes. They seemed to take their job very seriously.

"Ahoy mates," Andy greeted them "Keeping the officers out for us?'

"Watch your mouth, Slick," Ape number 1 growled. "I eat assholes like you for breakfast."

"So with milk and sugar or plain or what?" Jay asked, heading through the door.

Ape number 2 came to life. "Hey, come back here!" he yelled after them, but they had quickly disappeared into the crowd of identical while uniforms.

"You know, a benefit of conformity is anonymity", philosophized Jay.

"That's pretty heavy," Andy laughed. "I have to remember that."

A while later they were sitting at a table, an empty pitcher of beer in front of them, and another on the way. "This sucks. I can't get fired up in here."

"Yeah, it does, but try not to use the word fire." Andy agreed, "This is worse than an SIU Frat party. But at least there were girls and entertainment at those events. Even fights once in a while. And don't forget the idea was always to just avoid some ship bullshit, not to set the world on…, fuck it, FIRE!"

"This wouldn't be a good place for a fight," Jay gestured toward the two SP gorillas who periodically looked into the Club from their station at the front door. "Those two would love an excuse to use their night sticks."

"At least the beer's cheap."

"Its 3.2 beer."

"There's a jukebox."

"With shit for songs."

"There are actually two girls in here."

"Yeah, two haggy bag waitresses I wouldn't wish on my worst enemy."

"I give up," Andy conceded. "You win. It sucks."

"I'm almost out of money."

"Me too, but I don't; think we should go back yet."

"Me neither."

"I've got an idea," Andy announced.

Fifteen minutes later, Jay was sitting with his head in his hands, a number of empty beer bottles strategically placed around him. He bobbed and weaved, mumbling every once in awhile.

"Come on, its this guy's birthday. 21 years old today and he has to spend it here instead of back in Wisconsin with his wife and kids."

Wife and kids? Jay thought to himself. Man, Andy can really spread it on.

Andy was on a roll. "Buy him a beer and see how drunk he can get. Watch a sailor get drunk. Its free. How stupid will he be when he gets shit faced?" In less than an hour, Andy had gotten them four beers and a pitcher, which they discreetly shared.

"Come on," you're not acting drunk enough," Andy urged.

"I'm trying," Jay whispered. But no one else seemed to want to buy them any more beer so Andy gave it up.

Jay got up to go to the head. "Hey you! You don't look that drunk anymore," yelled a sailor who had been watching Jay for a while. He and two of his friends came over to the table.

Jay eyed him up. 'What are you talking about?"

"You. You're ripping guys off, pretending to be drunk."

"Fuck you."

"What'd you say?"

"You heard me. Fuck you. Fuck your loser buddies too. Now get out of my way. I have to piss. Remember, I'm the one who's drunk. So, fuck y'all very much!"

Andy jumped in. "Hey, man, take it easy. He seems sober because he's got a superfast metabolism. Drunk to hungover to sober in... bang!" He snapped his fingers. In only a matter of minutes."

"Is that so?" the sailor sneered.

"That's so," agreed Jay, "and now sober enough to kick your ass, except, this is your lucky day. I have to go piss."

"Actually," Andy added, "he's still drunk, hungover and ornery enough to want to kick your ass and sober enough to do it."

The sailor and his friends looked at Jay, looked at Andy, looked back at Jay then looked toward the front door. "Well, goddamn," said the sailor. "I guess its none of my business. I didn't fall for your shit so you didn't get no beer from me. But I gotta' admit that you guys are resourceful. That's a good trick. I gotta' try it sometime. Let us buy you guys a pitcher of beer." Jay sat down without going to the men's room. The line had begun to snake out the door. There was no line at the women's room.

They were nursing the newly donated beer. "I'm hungry," Andy said.

"Me too and I got to piss like a racehorse, but the fucking line is out the door at the men's room."

"Go piss in the women's room."

"Fuck you Andy."

"Hey, slow down hot stuff. You forget what Gritman taught us? The lights are low. Everybody's talking. Just piss where you are. Like you're in the woods."

"I'm not standing at a bar," said Jay, "I can't piss here like I was standing at the bar."

"Remember, anonymity is a benefit of conformity. There must be twenty tables here. All of them have the same sailors sitting at them. Just piss on the floor like it was the bar. Its better than a bar, we have carpeting here. That'll soften the noise."

"Damn Andy, I can't do that," said Jay.

"Look Jay, I know you're not drunk. When's the last time you saw me get up for the men's room? The lines been like that for awhile. I believe in Gritman. He has good ideas sometimes."

Jay looked under the table, "Shit, Andy don't piss on me."

"You're not takin' a dump, just a leisurely piss. When you gotta' go, you gotta' go. Relieve yourself Jay. Relax. You're anonymous. This could be the woods of Wisconsin."

Jay acquiesced, with ease.

"God, those hamburgers do look good, but no more money. Now what?" Jay had recovered from his full bladder and began to reflect on his empty stomach.

"I have an idea," Andy announced.

From their table, Andy had noticed that the door on the opposite wall went into the kitchen. The two waitresses went in and out, moving food to the tables. Andy had been quiet for a few minutes, planning his move.

"I'll be right back," he finally said. "Keep your head down."

Putting on his hat, he pulled it even with his eyebrows and nonchalantly strolled into the kitchen. Seconds later, he emerged from the same door, carrying two plates of food. He dodged, ducked and weaved through the sea of white uniforms, quickly ending up next to Jay. He handed a plate to Jay and sat down and took his hat off. "Hold the plate under the table for now, but up real high. Now, just drink your beer," he instructed. "Don't look obvious."

Suddenly, a heavy-set, cook, sweaty and hairy, in a stained white tee shirt and greasy apron burst through the kitchen door. He looked real mad. He looked left and right. Back and forth. Up and down. He yelled for the bartender. He yelled for the waitresses. He yelled for the gorillas at the front door. They all assembled around him. Jay couldn't hear what he was saying, but he was gesturing and pointing around the Club. The bartender shook his head. The waitresses looked bored. The gorillas started slapping the palms of their hands with their nightsticks, scanning the crowd.

"Don't catch their eye," Andy warned.

After a few minutes, the cook threw up his hands, hit the kitchen door in frustration and stormed back into the kitchen with the waitresses at his heels. Ape number 1 went back to the front door, while Ape number 2 stood guard by the kitchen door in case another attack occurred. The bartender went back to the bar, and a modicum of peace returned to the Club.

"Ok, now we can eat."

Out came the plates of hamburgers and french fries.

"How did you do that?" Jay was impressed.

"Simple. I saw that the cook faced the grill not the door. i walked in and saw these two plates of hamburgers. I asked if these were the hamburger orders. He said yeah without turning around. I said thank you and left. I didn't stick around to see what else happened in there."

"That was brilliant. Weren't you scared?"

"Not too much. I had heard that a benefit of conformity is anonymity. You and I look like everyone else in here. And besides, right now I *am* too drunk to give a shit. That's a benefit of beer drinking."

"Brilliant," Jay said again.

They slid the empty plates over to the end of the bar. No one pays attention to someone cleaning up. Andy and Jay seemed contented. Drinking and Pissing. Pissing and drinking. Pissing and eating. Eating and pissing. And pissing. And more pissing.

It was time to leave before their luck ran out. They waited until a large group of sailors headed for the door. They put on their hats, pulled them down level with their eyebrows and got up so they could leave in the middle of a group of white uniforms. When Andy slid his chair back and stood up his foot hit the floor. With a splash! He looked down at the low multi-colored shag carpet and could just barely make out some liquid.

"Damn Jay how much pissing have you been up to? The fucking carpet is soaked!"

213

"No more than you, piss for brains!" Jay was sloshing his way around the table too.

Andy started laughing. Jay began to laugh. They both went once around the table still managing to stay with the group of white uniforms. They all were sloshing, but no one noticed except Jay and Andy. Both were laughing uncontrollably, but the white uniforms were laughing too. The white uniforms laughed just enough. Why not? They had their stories too. Andy and Jay knew if they didn't escape the sloshing and splashing soon, they would also be puking from laughing so hard. They barely managed to stay with the white uniforms, escape the swamp around their table, and move out the door. The SP Ape guarding the door never gave them a second look.

On the way back to the ship, smoking and joking, they knew they had done it again. They felt like the weight had been lifted, even if it were a short-lived relief. It was relief, nonetheless. "Actually, that was relief in more ways than one," surmised Jay.

Back on the ship the boilers had been lit and several hapless BTs had been volunteered for watch duty. Andy and Jay came on board, warily watching for Freeze or Bronski. They weren't spotted.

"I just want to go to bed. I don't want to have to get up and stand watch in a couple of hours."

"Me neither."

Jay had an idea. "Look. They did this at the last minute so there's no schedule and they're taking whoever they can find. If they can't find us, there isn't anything to worry about."

They headed for the Machinist Mate compartment to find two empty bunks to sleep in for the night.

"Even when you're a drunk family man you have good ideas, Jay. I don't know how you do it."

"Another benefit of beer drinking, Andy; inspirational, yet free flowing," chuckled Jay.

It was the end of the quarter and the captain needed to burn the oil. The boilers were ready to steam the ship out to sea for a short, unscheduled six-day cruise to nowhere. Once out to sea the other two boilers were fired up. Now each fireroom had their two boilers fired up feeding steam to the turbines. The turbines were turning the twin shafts attached to the gigantic propellers. With only two boilers fired up the ship could reach a maximum speed of about 28 knots. However if you had all four boilers fired up the ship could reach a super speed of 33 knots. Not efficient but faster. The firerooms were suffocatingly hot when all the boilers were fired up. The firerooms were deafeningly noisy when all four boilers were fired up. The boilers were straining, groaning, and breathing. They moved, expanding and contracting with each order from the captain for more steam. Burning the oil, that's what it was all about for the captain. Fear, that's what it was all about for Andy and Jay. Later, the boys would understand how important burning that oil was to the captain. Anchors await.

Chapter 17: <u>A Birthday Bash</u>

It was Andy's birthday. 21 years old. To celebrate, a few of the snipes decided to hit the strip-big time. They agreed that they'd split the cost of his wining and dining, and all the lukewarm beer he could drink. Plus they would spring for all the Shorty's Chili dogs he could stomach, as long as it didn't cost any of them too much.

"We should get him a whore," Gritman suggested.

Maloni wasn't into this part, "Sure. You gonna pay for it?"

"I don't know," Jay said. "Andy's not really into whores."

"Bullshit. Everyone's into whores," Gritman replied. "After all, if we chip in, he won't have to pay for it, so if paying for it is his hang up, he doesn't have to worry. We'll have it covered."

"I don't think that's it. He just isn't into them. He's more the college girl type. He likes the idea of brains and personality as well as body parts and sex. But not whores."

"Aw, he'll get into it. We'll surprise him and line him up with one of the dancers at the Big Blow." Gritman was not going to give his idea up easily.

The Big Blow was a topless bar on the strip. It was actually called the Thar She Blows Club. The name supposedly had nothing to do with what everyone thought it did. It was allegedly named in honor of whalers and the whaling profession. However, Charleston hadn't seen any whaling business for a very long time, if ever, as the

216

City Council frequently pointed out. The City had been trying to close the club down for a long time, but so far had not succeeded.

A quick stop at the locker club transformed them into pretend-civilians. After beers at the Dixie Inn and burgers at the American Lunch, they headed for the Big Blow.

The Big Blow was crowded. It always was, even at noon when it opened with its first shows of the day: the matinees. Now, at 1900, things were starting to jump. The bar housed three types of people: the dancers, the large squad of muscular redneck bouncers, and the customers. The dancers were either young and ugly or, old and ugly. The young ones tried to look older; the old ones tried their damnedest to look younger. They sported an assortment of scars, stretch marks, and tattoos. The dancers were like snow flakes, no two looked alike. Bored with the daily bump and grind, they went through the motions, trying to squeeze the last dollar out of the fools sitting in front of the stage, eyes wide and tongues out. The Bouncers, in crewcuts and black tee-shirts, were all big and could easily keep order, even without the help of the ominous looking flashlight-nightstick each had hanging from their belt. Several of the storm troopers even had notches in their flashlight-nightsticks.

The only thing scarier than the dancers and the bouncers, were the customers. There were the assorted derelicts who came to ogle and fantasize while they drank $1.00 beers. Never a cover charge. Most were sailors, either young boots or old lifers (the young ones trying to act older, the old ones trying to act younger). But the real scary customers were the civilians (not the bikers who made up a significant percentage of the audience; they were too cool to be a problem). It was the other group, the sleazy, weasel-faced rednecks who sat by themselves in the shadows. They were always trying to bum money from the sailors, trying to hustle pool games, and hassle the dancers. They were the ones to keep an eye on.

The only beer sold was Heineken. Bruiser, the 350 pound piece of muscle who owned the place figured that by serving Heineken, he could advertise his hog bar as a classy place, plus make enough money to move to Florida. Bruiser was a semi-retired biker who liked to flash his set of brass knuckles at whoever was around. If

217

that didn't impress whoever he was talking to his .357 Magnum did. There wasn't much trouble in the Big Blow. When a drunk did something Bruiser didn't like, the reaction was usually swift and painful.

Standing guard behind the bar, eyes busy, keeping an eye on everyone; he eyed Jay and Andy's group without interest. At the bar, they ordered beers and moved to a table to watch the show.

Three hours later, they were sitting around a small two bedroom apartment three blocks off the strip. They had met two dancers from the club who had invited them back to their place. Jay had no idea how they had talked their way into the situation, but it had worked, whatever it was they said. The girls weren't too bad; not the greatest, but passable by strip standards. Andy was drunk. He tried his best to stay awake, but was losing the battle. After an hour of relatively meaningless conversation and little else, the girls announced they had to go out for awhile and meet their boyfriends. Jay and the boys tried to talk them out of leaving but it was in vain. They offered to go along, but changed their minds when the girls told them that their boyfriends were bikers who got insanely jealous.

"Ya'll can wait around if you want, we won't be gone long. Should be back around midnight. We'll party then," they promised. "Don't forget to lock up if ya'll decide to leave." And out the door they went.

"Sure we will," Jay said sarcastically.

Andy was on the couch, half asleep. "They're going out to score dope. That's what that was all about," he proclaimed. Andy usually knew what he was talking about, even when he was drunk and half asleep.

"Maybe," Jay added. "But I'm not sticking around here in case they decide to bring their boyfriends back. I think we're getting set up. Things could get real messy here. Let's just get going."

"You guys go ahead. I'm going to take a little nap and then I'll join up with you." Andy was losing ground fast.

"Come on, man! You best not stay here." Gritman cautioned. "Let's go. Come on!"

"No, no, no. It'll be alright. Go ahead. I told you. They're out scoring dope or fucking some johns. Doesn't matter. I'll wait around for the dope and party with them." Andy passed out on the couch.

"Oh, great," Maloni groaned. "We've got to wake him up."

"Forget it." Jay had been through this before. "First of all, he won't wake up. He's out for a while. Second, if he does wake up, he'll be wild. You've never seen him getting woke up when he's all fucked up. He gets crazy wild. Out of control. It's not pretty."

"What'll we do? Leave him here?"

"Yeah, for now," Jay answered. "We'll let him sleep it off for a while, and come back to check on him later. He may even wake up on his own in an hour or so. Whatever we do, we'll need to get him out of here before the girls come back, in case they bring their boyfriends with them. That'd be a real disaster. In the meantime, let's go back to the strip for a while.

"Sounds like a plan to me," Maloni agreed, heading out the door. They headed back to the Big Blow. Jay kept an eye out for the girls who had just left them. He was curious about how tough their boyfriends looked. They were nowhere in sight. The crowd had grown considerably bigger, drunker, and louder than it had been three hours before. It looked like it would be real easy to get into a fight. They sat at a corner table, had a few beers and watched the show until Jay finally stood up. "We better go check on Andy," he said. "I have a feeling something could go wrong here if we don't leave right now. You coming?" he asked the group.

"Ah, I was thinking that maybe you don't really need me just to wake him up. I guess I'll just stay here and watch the show and wait for ya'll to come back." Gritman was either horny or chickening out. Jay suspected the former.

"Maybe I'll stay here too and wait for you," Maloni said.

"For Christ sakes, a chicken shit and a gritdog in heat!' Jay said.

Gritman just laughed. 'Ya'll come back now-hear?" His eyes never left the naked dancer.

Maloni changed his mind thinking this could be a better show, "I'll go with you." The two of them headed back to the apartment.

As soon as they left the strip, Jay noticed the quietness. It was like being in a calm, peaceful suburbia. Almost. But as they approached the apartment, Jay noticed two things: too many lights were on and the front door was wide open. This isn't good, he said to himself. They went on, slowly, into an empty apartment. Empty rooms, empty couch. No Andy. To make matters worse, it looked like a war had been fought in the living room. Furniture was tipped over. Books and magazines cluttered the floor. It was a mess.

"Someone got here first. Someone tried to wake him up," Jay observed, "I don't see any blood, though. That's a good sign."

"What happened? Where do you think he is?"

"Since he's not sitting here all beat up or lying out in front of the building in a bloody heap, the bikers must not have gotten him. My guess is that either the cops or the shore patrol have him." Jay thought a minute. "Or, he got away and is on the run. When he's drunk nobody can outrun Andy."

"On the run?" Wayne asked. "From what? What did he do?"

"Who knows?" Jay answered, looking around the apartment. "Anything's possible. Maybe nothing happened. Sometimes it's only in his head where it's happening."

They headed up the strip. After going two blocks, they came up to a squad car. Jay went up to the officers and asked if they had seen anyone who looked like Andy.

"No. Why?" a cop drawled suspiciously.

"Nothing. Just lost a buddy of ours."

The next block over, they saw two shore patrol walking toward them. Jay went up and asked the same question.

"I don't know. Maybe," one answered.

"Maybe? Maybe what? Either you saw him or you didn't." Jay was getting tense.

"Another shore patrol team got in a fight with some drunk sailor in an apartment and had to haul him out. They got him in a van over there." He pointed down the street. Maybe he's still it."

They headed over to the van. Two shore patrol were leaning against it.

"Hey!" Jay called out. "Do you have someone in there?"

"What's it to you?" a second class with his hat pulled almost over his eyes responded. He wasn't used to being questioned while on duty.

"Looking for a friend of ours. I need to talk to him. He's about 6 foot or so. His name's Andy Mathers. He's a fireman."

"Yeah we got him. Thinks he's a tough guy. He went off on the two of us, but we got him …ah…calmed down."

"Yeah," the other SP added. This one was a tall mean looking muscleman. He laughed. "Nothing like a hard nightstick to calm an asshole like that down." He struck the palm of his hand with his club. He obviously liked his job.

"I need to talk to him," Jay said. "Its important."

"No way. Get outta' here before we run you guys in too."

"For what?" Jay wanted to know. "Just because I want to talk to him? You going to calm me down to?"

The muscle man tensed. "Beat it."

"Come on, man. I need to talk to him. It'll only take a minute. I've gotta' get the car keys from him," Jay lied. They still didn't have a car. That was part of the whole problem. They never could get enough money together to get a car. Actually, Jay just wanted to see if Andy was okay, and to find out what had happened at the apartment. Besides, he didn't have anything else to do and he was in no hurry to go back to the ship. "Come on. Just a minute or two."

"No way." Muscleman was standing firm. The Second Class was wavering. "Well, I don't know…"

Jay moved toward the side door of the van. "What happens if I just go on in?"

"We'll lock your ass up."

"No you wouldn't because I would already have locked my own self up. Its like I'd be turning myself in for no real crime. How would you explain that to your boss? Huh?" Jay went on, mimicking. "Well, sir, this guy here, we arrested him because he wanted to get arrested and locked up in the van so he could talk to his buddy for 30 seconds. We just couldn't keep him from getting in the van that everyone else wants to stay out of, so we just arrested him and put him in the van he wanted to be in anyway. We weren't sure what to arrest him for, but we arrested him anyway. I guess we lost control, Sir. You guys'll look pretty stupid," Jay added. "You know, losing control and all."

He pulled open the side door and jumped inside. "I'll be right back," he promised, slamming the door shut. Reflexively, he tried the door. From the inside it was locked. He was able to get in but not out. Oh well, Jay thought. Maybe this wasn't the smartest move.

"Hey!" He yelled at Andy, who was half sitting, half crouching in a corner. Jay looked around. "Nice place you have here." It was dark and hard to see inside the van. Pretty dismal, he thought. "So what happened?"

"Nothing much." Andy sounded preoccupied. "They tried to wake me up."

"So I figured. They beat you bad? I can't see jack shit in here. Turn around. What kind of battle scars you get?"

Andy turned around, zipping up his zipper.

"What the hell are you doing?" Jay asked, but he knew the answer.

"Had to take a piss, and those two apes wouldn't tell me where the fucking facilities are."

"Christ! In the van no less. Most animals don't usually shit in their own cage."

"Yeah they do and what the fuck. So what else would you have me do? Soil me own linens?"

"God, it stinks in here. Sure you didn't shit too?"

"Not yet."

"Hey stupid!" One of the SPs yelled in to Jay. "We've been talking and decided to take you in too. How do you like that?"

Jay ignored him.

"I won't be here long," Andy said. "They'll be chauffeuring me back to the ship soon. I'll get my hand slapped and life'll go on. What can they do? Put me in the bilges? Big deal." Andy wasn't too worried about things at the moment. He didn't look too injured either, except for a bruise on his cheek and a slight cut on his head. He sounded halfway sober, but Jay knew better.

"So what happened?' Jay asked again.

"Hey asshole!" the SP tried again. "You screwed up! Your ass is grass now!"

Jay continued to ignore him.

"What did you do, lock yourself in here?" Andy asked. "You just jumped in here and locked yourself in?"

"Yeah, I guess so."

"Wow. That's pretty nuts."

"Yeah. I guess. I think I blew their minds. They don't know what to do about me. So what the hell happened?" Jay persisted.

"Not real sure," Andy shook his head. "but from what the SPs said and from what I figure, I was sleeping on the couch, minding my own fucking business when in comes this chick who lived there with the two girl scouts we had met earlier. She sees me on the couch, doesn't know me or why I'm in her apartment, and freaks out. So she does what any good girl scout would do, she calls the cops. But I guess they figured it had to be a sailor involved so the SPs show up too and they all tried to wake me up at the same time. All I know for sure is, first there was something hurting my sides and head. Then I realized someone, no several someones had sticks and they were using my body for a pinata. So, I just started swinging, grabbing, and hitting anything that moved. That seemed to slow down the party a little. I was just trying to go for the light, like a moth. Inside the house was dark and it was hard to see. The front door was open and it was light outside from all the streetlights. I almost made it. I had a lamp or something, and got in a few good licks on the way to the door, but two big motherfuckers got the best of me in the end. And here I am."

"Yeah, I kind of figured that. I saw the place. It was a mess. It looked like a tornado had hit it. You okay though?"

"Yeah, I'm alright. Just a few cuts and bruises, and these two lumps on my head."

"That's it, asshole! Get out of there now!" The door flew open. Both SPs reached in and grabbed Jay, pulling him out of the van. "Get out now and we won't file charges. We've got to go on a call and then drop your friend here off at his ship. Get lost or there will be real trouble."

223

"I guess this means goodbye. I'm not going to get arrested. I don't get to ride in the nice SP van," Jay taunted.

"Get the fuck out of our sight," one SP yelled, shoving Jay down on the sidewalk.

Jay figured he had better cool it. "Happy birthday," he said to Andy. "Did you like this little surprise party?"

"It was a blast. The best yet," lied Andy.

The SPs jumped into the van and roared off.

Andy got a ride to the ship, two weeks of restriction, a $50 fine, and a bruised ego to match his bruised body.

The next day in the fireroom Andy thought Jay and the others looked worse. He did get more sleep than they did. They all looked like death warmed over. Nobody showed much enthusiasm making the coffee. Even Gritman, he only wiped off a couple of the cups.

"Man, you guys must have been to quite a party last night. Who's birthday was it anyway." Andy was feeling relatively chipper.

A collective 'fuck you' was all he got.

Then the Chief bounded down the ladder.

Anchors await.

Chapter 18: <u>Sick Bay Day</u>

"Chief Bronski, I request permission to go to the doctor."

Bronski looked at Jay. "What the hell do you mean? Doctor? What doctor? You mean Sick Bay!"

"Ok. Sick Bay it is. I need to get something checked out."

"Yeah, you should be checked out. How about by a shrink? Have him check out yer head. And while you're at it, take Mathers with you. You both need a shrink."

"Chief, when I get out of here, I'm going to be a shrink. I've seen enough loony people in this Navy to be an expert."

"You're an expert, alright. An expert smart-ass. Why do you need to go to Sick Bay?"

"Well today my head and my stomach hurt, but it's really my legs. They keep falling asleep on me. Every night. When I wake up, it takes awhile to get out of bed because they're so numb."

"Your legs, my ass!" Bronski yelled. "It takes you so long to get out of your rack because you're just plain lazy! But you know, if they're asleep you should get them an alarm clock of their own so's you can wake them up on time. Like about 0500."

"No. Really. They're screwed up. They're numb and sometimes I have trouble getting down the ladder to the fire room. They're numb right now and I've been up for two hours. There's something wrong with them."

Bronski eyed Jay. "There's something wrong, alright," he agreed. "But I ain't so sure it's your legs. This wouldn't have anything to do

225

with the fact that you baby snipes are scheduled to clean out the fireboxes this afternoon, would it?"

"No way. I love cleaning out fireboxes. You know I wouldn't even ask if it wasn't important. I figured you'd want me to go and get them checked out, you being so concerned about your men and all. Besides, if I can get this straightened out, I'd be able to get up and down the ladders quicker and work faster in those fireboxes."

"Yeah, and if bullshit was music, you'd be a brass band," Bronski glared at Jay. "But I'll tell you what. You can go on to Sick Bay, but you gotta' go to the base hospital. Our Sick Bay is closed down today. Our own doc's on a couple days leave. And when you get to the base Sick Bay, you see the doc quick. And you come right back. And when you come back, I'll have saved #2 boiler just for you. And you and your lazy, tired legs can clean out the firebox all by yourselves."

"Gee, thanks, Jay grimaced.

A half hour later, with Bronski's signed chit in his pocket, Jay was on his way to the base hospital. A sailor couldn't go anywhere on the base during working hours without a chit. Just like school, Jay thought. You had to have a hall pass just to get out of class. A gray security truck passed him, the driver eyeing Jay over. And hall monitors to boot, he thought to himself.

It was good two mile walk from the Jetsomn to the base hospital, sick bay or whatever it was. Jay took his time. He didn't like going to the doctor. He had never had to go to a hospital for any kind of extended stay before and hoped he'd never have to. He hated doctor appointments. The waiting rooms drove him crazy. He hated waiting, and on more than one occasion, had walked out of the waiting room and skipped the appointment if he had to wait for what he felt was an unreasonable amount of time: usually 5 minutes. But he went today because he was really having problems with his legs. And it was probably good he was going to the base hospital. He figured that his leg problem was a more serious problem than the ship corpsman could handle. Probably circulation, he thought to himself. It wasn't real bad but it was bothering him. Besides, it did get him out of the fireroom, at least temporarily. Maybe Bronski would forget about his threat to put

Jay in #2 by the time he got back. Probably not, but Jay could always hope. Maybe he could stretch this out for all day. Maybe he could even get out of the Navy if it was serious enough. By the time Jay got to the hospital, he had all but convinced himself that he was a prime candidate for a legitimate medical discharge. What a great daydream!

This would be Jay's first experience with the base hospital. He hoped it would be better than the time two months ago when he had to go to the Ship's sick bay. At that time, they were at sea, somewhere off the coast of Florida, busily keeping Miami safe from the communists or something. One morning on watch, Jay had gotten sick and lost his breakfast in the fireroom. Jay never got seasick so he figured it was either the flu or the cooks were trying to poison him. He figured the latter was the most likely because: a) Jay hardly ever got sick. Or b) when he had first come on board, Jay had worked in the galley for two weeks. He knew that the cooks and their helpers exercised their creativity and their sense of humor by adding various things to the food to be served. Hidden and disguised in the food, most of these things were never meant for human consumption. Anyway Jay was remembering his first encounter with the ship's sick bay.

It was when they were out at sea, Jay yelled down at Freeze who was sitting on his ass on the lower level. "Hey, Freeze! I'm sick!"

"Tough shit. You're just hung over."

"Freeze, we're at sea. We have been at sea for a week. How the hell could I have a hangover?"

"Get back on watch!"

"I'm sick. I puked."

"So what? You are a puke."

"So I'm up here on the upper level watching a water level gauge. You're down there on the lower level watching your boys sweat. There's a lot of open grating between me up here and you down there. Puke follows the law of gravity. You figure it out."

Freeze only had to think for a minute. "Get yer' yankee ass to sick bay!"

Jay headed toward the stern of the ship to the small room that served as sick bay. There were five others already in line. Jay took his place and began waiting. As impatient as he was, this was a hell of a lot better than the fireroom any day. Sick bay was supposed to open at 0900 but the good doctor didn't arrive until forty five minutes later. The good doctor was really a second class corpsman; a burn out who looked like he had used plenty of drugs himself and not all for medicinal purposes. Rumor was that he had been a corpsman with a company of Marines in Nam. He had stopped giving a shit about much of anything about the time he returned to the states. Rumor was that he had gotten in some trouble and was destined to remain at E-5 for the rest of his Navy career. He was the third most popular sailor on the ship, the most popular being either the barber or the mailman (depending if you asked the officers and lifers or the enlisted men). The payroll clerk was the second.

The Corpsman had a long, difficult to pronounce name that no one could remember, including himself at times, so everyone called him Doc. Doc was the name stenciled on his pressed dungarees. Whatever name he originally had was lost, on record only in official Navy records. He was from California and kept pretty much to himself when on the ship. He was seldom around when the ship was in port. He supposedly had a model/surfer chick in Charleston who he shacked up with. Jay was a little skeptical about this; he could not imagine any model/surfer chicks in Charleston. Doc kept his own hours and nobody messed with him.

By 1030, Jay was at the head of the line. He was let in the "office." The small room was filled with an examining table, a small desk, two chairs and a refrigerator. Two large cabinets held supplies; the unlocked one housed bandages and other safe items. The locked one, Jay assumed, held medications. A Jimi Hendrix poster was taped to the door of the locked cabinet. A Playboy, J.C.Whitney catalog, and a surfing magazine nestled among the notes and Navy memos on Doc's desk.

Doc was looking at his watch. "Name? Department?" He didn't even look up.

Jay told him. Doc wrote something in a notebook.

"What's the matter, man?"

"Stomach ache. Puking."

"Asshole cooks are trying to poison you, man."

"That's what I figured too."

"Ever get stoned?"

"Sure."

"Far out." Doc reached into the refrigerator. He handed a small dark colored bottle to Jay. "Drink this up and stay close to the shitter. It'll clean you out. Don't eat anything until tomorrow. You'll be alright. And when you do eat, don't eat anything you don't recognize, looks homemade, or is a funny color. Better yet, just eat Burger King."

"We're at sea," Jay reminded him.

"Oh, yeah." "Jay looked at the bottle. "What is this shit?"

"Prune juice. All natural shit. Its good for what ails ya. It'll fix ya right up."

Jay went back to the fireroom. He was still as sick as he was before, but at least he had a bottle of prune juice to show for his efforts. He had no intention of drinking it.

But enough of this musing thought Jay, as he walked into the base hospital and was immediately greeted by a serious looking Shore Patrol who demanded to see his chit. Jay dutifully produced it. Then he wanted to see Jay's military ID. Jay handed it over.

"This you?"

"It be me alright, "Jay answered. "If it wasn't me, I wouldn't be here, right?"

"What?"

"I mean, if I were someone else, it wouldn't be me here standing and talking to you, it'd be someone else you'd be talking to and you wouldn't be looking at my ID because it would be someone else's in your hand. Since you're looking at my ID, I am obviously me. Right?"

The Shore Patrol handed the ID back. You here to see the shrink?"

"Nope. I need a leg doctor."

Jay was directed through a series of doors until he came to a large waiting room. He had to show his chit to a sterile looking sailor behind the desk, who looked at the clock and noted the time of Jay's arrival on the chit.

229

"Just like school," Jay muttered.

"What?"

"Nothing. Never mind. I'm here because my legs keep falling asleep"

The sterile looking sailor peered at Jay as if he were regarding a cockroach. "You here to see the shrink?"

"No. The leg doctor. My legs really do fall asleep."

What's your rate?"

"BT."

"That figures. Go sit down. You will be called when the doctor is ready for you."

Jay sat down in the sterile looking, empty waiting room. Where is everyone, he wondered? He looked around. Boy, he thought to himself, they must clean this place religiously on an ongoing basis. I'd sure hate to be involved in the field days around here. He looked for something to read. No Field and Stream, no Popular Science. No readers Digest. Nothing except for a few old Navy publications. What kind of waiting room is this? Typical Navy. Ten minutes passed. Jay started getting restless but reminded himself that this was better than being in the fireroom

A half hour passed. Jay dozed off.

He awoke with a start, looking around. Where the hell am I? His legs were asleep. Then he remembered: hospital, waiting room. The waiting room was still empty. Jay often wondered if he would wake up one day and realize that this Navy business was just a bad dream. Maybe today. Maybe this is it. He looked around again. Am I awake or asleep, he wondered? He pinched himself. "Ouch, fuck!!" I'm awake. And in the Navy. Damn it.

He looked at the clock on the wall. A little after one. Shit, he'd been asleep for almost two hours. He shook his legs awake and walked up to the sterile-looking sailor who was still behind the desk. "Will I see a doctor soon? I've been here a long time."

"Anytime now," the sterile looking sailor answered without looking up.

"Like, today, possibly?" Jay asked sarcastically.

"I said, any time now." The sterile looking sailor again looked at Jay like he was a distasteful bug. "You will be called when the doctor is ready."

Jay decided he didn't like the sterile looking sailor. "Nice uniform," he offered. "Momma iron it for you?" No answer. Jay sat back down and tried to be patient.

At 1430, the sterile looking sailor looked up and yelled Jay's name. Jay had been dozing and jumped out of the office chair with a start. "What the hell do you want?" he yelled back.

The sterile looking sailor looked surprised. "Uh, the doctor will see you now," he said. "Come this way."

"About time. Hey are you really a nurse?"

"No, I'm training to be a medical records clerk."

"Wow." Jay said excitedly. "Sounds exciting. How do you handle all the action? All the adventure? All the danger? Join the Navy and see the X-rays."

The sterile looking sailor ushered him into a small room. "Wait here. The doctor will be with you shortly. Take off your clothes."

"Not on your life."

The sterile-looking sailor turned to go. "The doctor won't look at you unless you disrobe."

"I really do like your uniform," Jay continued. "It looks so...so starchy. So chic and so....so sterile-looking. You're a credit to the Navy."

The sterile-looking sailor left, shutting the door on the cockroach as forcibly as he could without actually slamming it.

"But your bedside manner sucks!" Jay yelled after him.

A half hour later, the door burst open and a big bear in a white uniform came in. The bear had bright red hair and a neatly trimmed beard. His name tag announced that he was Lieutenant Commander Moore.

"West!" It was a statement, not a question.

"Yessir."

The bear read some notes he was holding. "What's the problem? Legs falling asleep?"

"Yessir.'

"When?"

"All the time, but mostly at night when I sleep."

"Um-hum." The bear nodded to himself.

"I thought that maybe my circulation is bad or something or my nerves are messed up," Jay suggested. "Or..."

The bear interrupted him. He wasn't interested in what Jay thought. "At night? When you sleep, you said?"

"Yessir."

"Do you dream when you sleep?'

"Sure. I mean, Yessir."

"Do you ever dream you are running?"

"Uh, I don't know. Maybe." Jay had to think a minute. Where the hell was this conversation going? He had no idea. "Yeah, I guess maybe sometimes I am running and sometimes walking in my dreams."

"Then that's it!" The bear announced. With a voice that one would use to explain something to a first grader, he explained Jay's problem to him. "You see, when you sleep, you dream. When you dream, you run or walk. When you use your legs like that, they get tired. Then they fall asleep. But the problem is they fall asleep after the rest of your body does so they have less rest than the rest of your body. So they re still asleep when the rest of your body wakes up."

"What?" Jay almost yelled, but then he remembered he was talking to a bear of high rank. He caught himself. That's the craziest thing I ever heard of, he prudently thought to himself. "That doesn't sound quite right," he said carefully.

"Son, I'm a doctor. And I'm an officer. You wouldn't be questioning me, would you?" The bear was smiling, but Jay swore he heard a threat in there somewhere.

"Oh no, sir."

"Good then. It wouldn't hurt to exercise your legs some. Get them in better shape for all that running. Walk more. That is all," he concluded and turned to leave.

"Sir would you please sign my chit and note the time I leave?" Jay asked. He wasn't about to ask the sterile-looking sailor to sign it for him.

"Certainly, son." The bear scribbled something illegible. "Here, I even gave you an extra half hour to get back to the ship. Have a little fun on the way." He winked at Jay, turned, and plodded out the door.

What the hell? Fun? Jay couldn't believe it. A half hour of fun? On the base? What is with this guy?

Jay got back to ship just as Andy and Maloni were coming out of the fireroom. It was almost time for supper chow.

"Hey, asshole," Andy greeted him. "Got out of a little work, huh?

"You guys all done?"

"Yeah."

"Even with #2?"

"Yeah. But it was weird. Bronski didn't want us to do it for some reason. He was also waiting for you all afternoon. But finally he decided he wanted to get them all done today so he busted our asses. I supervised as much as I could."

"I would have figured as much. Your face must match you ass. Those SPs really did a number on you the other night."

"Yeah, fuck you too. So how did it go at the hospital?"

"Ok. I had a good nap and ran into a bear."

Andy looked at Jay. "You drunk? On drugs? Or just need to see a shrink?"

"Not quite. You wouldn't believe it."

Chapter 19: <u>Meals on Wheels, Money, and More</u>

It was easy to get tired of Navy food. Being stuck on the ship all day didn't provide much opportunity for dining out. Reveille typically greeted the crew at 0630. After coming to life, they would wander to the mess decks where coffee, bug juice, and breakfast awaited them. Coffee was in demand 24 hours a day on the Jetsomn. Bug juice: a deep red, industrial strength Kool-Aid type of drink, full of sugar and god knows what else, was also available 24 hours a day. The two coffee urns and two bug juice machines were never shut off. When either ran out, there was hell to pay until they were refilled.

A typical breakfast consisted of unlimited cold toast, with freezer burnt, freon tasting butter, institutional bacon, sausages, and eggs, any style (cook the snot outta' them lifers would command). Coffee and bug juice completed the buffet. Lunch usually consisted of unlimited bread with freezer burnt, freon tasting butter, institutional hot dogs (no one dared ask what they were made of), hamburgers or lunchmeat sandwiches, and the coffee and bug juice. Supper was usually a little more substantial. Unlimited bread with freezer burnt, freon tasting, butter, and now for the final full meal of the day, we always had an offering of unidentifiable casseroles that were attempted, and traditional meat and potatoes. Coffee and bug juice rounded out the menu. Supper was not as well attended as the earlier meals. Only those with duty, no money or those who had no where else to go typically stuck around for supper. At sea, the crew was treated to a fourth meal of the day. "Mid-rats" were available for those who were changing watch at midnight. Mid-rats would consist of a lunch type meal, often including unlimited bread with freezer burnt, freon tasting, butter, and anything left over from any previous meals. Mid-rats also included the mandatory coffee and bug juice. The daily meals of steak, shrimp, and lobster promised by the recruiter were rare, if ever to be found.

While in port, the crew could expect an evening visit from a privately run mobile canteen, fondly dubbed throughout the Navy as the "Roach Coach." When the announcement, "The Roach Coach is on the pier" came over the ship's PA system, sailors would file out to the truck and stand in line for institutionally wrapped sandwiches, snacks and over priced soda. The Roach Coach was under the command of an enterprising retired navy lifer who, on too rare an occasion, would have a well-developed woman selling the food. Sales skyrocketed if the weather was real hot as she was usually in halter and shorts.

At 1700 one Wednesday, Andy and Jay were standing in the supper mess line. The line was going nowhere; they hadn't moved for 15 minutes. It was a busy night for the cooks; everyone had decided to eat on the ship that night and had decided to do so at the same time. No one was moving. Something had broken down or the cooks had run out of something on the mess line.

"This sucks," Andy said to no one in particular.

"Think about this," Jay had been entertaining himself with his thoughts while waiting. "What's with these words like mess, chow, bug juice, roach coach, egg snot and all that? They all refer to something related to food. It could make you lose your appetite if you think about it."

"So what? I try not to think about it. Actually, I gave up trying to figure things out around here."

"We need something different. I'd kill for a bag of Burger King shit right now."

"Yeah, even shit sounds appealing when I think of Navy food," said Andy.

"No, really, I'm talking hamburgers, Whoppers, french fries, the whole nine yards."

Gritman was standing behind them. "Yeah," he added. "I could go for Burger King."

Jay turned to look at him. "Hey! You've got a car. You got gas? Fuck this mess line. Let's make a Burger King run."

"No money."

"I'll buy if you'll drive."

Gritman thought a minute. "Ok. Its better than waiting here for god knows what."

Jay pulled Andy out of the mess line. "We're leaving. Going out to eat. But don't tell anyone or they'll all want to go too. Or worse yet, want us to bring something back for them."

Gritman agreed. He didn't want too many people riding in his car. He actually didn't want too many people to know he had a car on base. Others would want to be taken somewhere or borrow it and he just didn't want the hassle. He was fine with Andy, Jay, and Maloni knowing about it and two riders were ok, but three would make the car ride too close to the ground. With too much weight in it, Gritman figured it wouldn't look like the 67 Camaro muscle car it was. So, the whole gang didn't get to go anywhere altogether, just a couple at a time. He only had it for a few weeks until his brother got moved into his new place back home then he had to return it.

The closest Burger King was five miles from the base. Surprisingly, it wasn't on the strip, but on a respectable street with a lot of gas stations and other fast food places. Jay had his heart set on Burger King and was not going to be distracted by MacDonalds. The other two agreed with him.

They were still in dungarees; all three forgetting that they could only leave the base in dress whites or working whites. Dungarees were forbidden off base unless the sailors were on some ultra important mission and accompanied by a President, an Admiral or at least a Chief, with a chit.

They were stopped at the gate by a stern looking Marine who quickly reminded them of the rule. He had no sense of humor and was not about to let them off the base in illegal dungarees.

"Shit! Now what?" Jay asked.

"Swing back to the ship, I'll run in and grab some dress white tops for us. We'll have to put them on and hide our legs somehow," said Andy.

"This is getting to be a major production," Jay complained. He was hungry and craving Burger King. "What a dumb ass rule. Everyone else in the world gets to walk around in jeans and work shirts but not us. They're afraid we might be mistaken for normal people. Another rule without a reason."

"Normal people don't have their names stenciled on the front of their shirts or the back of their jeans," Andy reminded him. "Or stenciled on their underwear for that matter. And then there's the business about the hair. Don't worry, even in civvies, around here we'd never be mistaken for normal people."

They changed clothes, put a blanket over their legs, and told the guard they were chilled. He waved them through the gate. They got to Burger King in record time and ate in style, loading up on Whoppers and fries.

"Life is good," Jay observed.

"Beats the ship's food."

"No bug juice."

"No loss, and we have real honest to goddamn it, Coke and Pepsi and all the rest of the shit that goes with it. This is the real world."

When they returned to the ship, some of the others asked where they had been. Jay was surprised they had even been missed. They admitted they had gone to Burger King.

"Why didn't you tell me? I'd have gone too!"

"How'd ya get there?"

"I wish I'd known; I'd have asked you to bring something back." And on and on and on…

Andy and Jay left the compartment and went out to the fantail. "Burger King is a popular thing," Andy commented.

"Yeah. Are you thinking what I'm thinking??"

"I'm thinking we could make some money here. Maybe enough for a car. Maybe we could start our own slush fund (slush fund: short term loans to fellow sailors until payday, rates were $5 for $7, $10 for $14, and on and on)."

"Really. A 'we fly, they buy' proposition. We take orders, jack the price of the food up a little, run to Burger King, and deliver the food for a slight fee. You know, for delivery and handling."

"It could work," Andy said. "We would charge so much an order, say 20%. We make a buck on a five dollar order. Twenty bucks on twenty orders. Not as much as the ship loan scams where they get $7 for $5 or $14 for $10 but still good enough money, and we could expand to that," Andy reemphasized.

Jay was getting into it. "We could hit the whole ship, take orders, and make a couple runs a day. We could come out pretty good on his deal."

"Slow down a minute. Let's start small. We don't even have a permanent car."

"Yeah, that would be perfect for deliveries, a station wagon, more room and all."

"This stinks. We need a car."

"But this is not all that bad. I think you're right, we could buy an old car." Jay considered their dilemma for a minute, "How about Gritman? He's got a car here. Right now, even though its temporary, and he's already sort of involved. Its a fast car and we can get the food back here quick, while its still hot."

Gritman was initially leery because his car would no longer be a secret. "It's not a secret anymore anyway." But the money interested him and it didn't take him long to decide, he was all for it. Jay and Andy would take the orders and all three would distribute the food once they returned to the ship with the real food and all the fixins'. Gritman would be reimbursed gas money from the profits. The rest of the money would be socked away for new ventures.

They named the business JAG' Foods (for Jay, Andy and Gritman). Andy made up a menu that also served as the order form. Prices were listed and a 20% delivery fee was included. The minimum order was five dollars. Payment was made in advance. They guaranteed the food would be delivered hot by 1800 hours. Andy talked one of the Yeomen into making a lot of copies of the order forms on the ship's mimeograph machine. They distributed notices around the ship. They would take orders five days a week, starting next Monday. There would be no weekend services.

At 1630 the next Monday, they started taking orders. Jay went up one side of the ship and Andy the other. Forty five minutes later, they met back on the fantail. Between the two of them they had thirty five orders and $195.00.

"Looking good," Andy commented. "Not bad for the first night."

They took off in the Camaro, promising to return with the food by 1800 hours. However, they soon realized they weren't going to be able to make the deadline they had promised. They lost time changing clothes at the Locker Club. Then they really lost time at Burger King. They got there at 1730; 5:30 was a peak time and the place was really busy. The kids working couldn't handle their huge order that fast. Andy and Jay watched the clock hit 1800, then 1815 then 1830. At 6:30 they left the restaurant with bags of food crammed into the back seat with Jay. They still had to stop and change at the Locker Club before they could continue on to the ship.

It was after 1900 when they finally were able to deliver the food and it was cold and getting soggy. Their new customers were not happy. They felt that they'd been ripped off. They threatened never to be taken in by this scam again. Cold food wasn't worth it.

Later that night, the three staff members of JAG' Foods had a meeting on the fantail.

"Well, it was a good idea while it lasted," Gritman said.

"It's still a good idea. We just have to figure out a better way to do it," Jay responded.

"Yeah, agreed Andy. He'd been thinking about things and had come up with some ideas. "Here's what we'll do. First, we shut down for one week to rebuild the business with some changes. Give them a week and they'll want us back. Begging us. And we'll be back, bigger and better. Believe me, there's still a big demand out there. They want something besides the shit they serve around here for supper. Especially when they see us on the fantail, after they've eaten the ship's shit, stuffing the burgers and fries down our throats."

A week later, they were back in business. During that time, they had gotten numerous questions about the venture from their shipmates. Others had started to forget how pissed off they'd been about the cold food. It seemed that the demand was still there. Andy and Jay made the rounds once again, pushing for another chance to take food orders. This time, they guaranteed hot food by 1800 hours or the money would be cheerfully refunded. To help facilitate this, Jay had called Burger King and explained their proposition to the manager. Jay could guarantee him a lot of business if they could accommodate their order at exactly 5:15. Jay also wanted each individual order double bagged to help keep it warm and then placed in large cardboard boxes so the orders would be easier to carry. When the manager initially hesitated, Jay told him he really didn't want to have to deal with MacDonalds. The manager quickly agreed to everything Jay asked for.

They also decided that only two of them would go to Burger King; the third would stay behind, ready to help distribute the food when it arrived. Changes of civvies were kept in the Camaro. Gritman and his passenger would change clothes in the car on the way to the main gate.

There were only 17 orders, totaling $105.00, the first day but Andy was optimistic. "If they see we can deliver when we say we will, they'll buy."

He was right. Within a week, they were taking an average of 45 orders, averaging $250.00, a night. The delivery was fast and the food was hot. The customers were happy. Within two weeks, they added a noon run. Empty Burger King wrappers and bags filled the ship's waste cans and the dumpsters on the pier. Unfortunately, some idiots threw their wrappers overboard so wrappers and bags were seen daily in the water surrounding the Jetsomn.

'We may need some help," Jay suggested one day. "This is almost getting too big for the three of us." His business partners voted down the idea, even though several others had asked to be involved.

They raised the handling fee to 25%. Everyone was happy and business was booming. They were taking almost 100 orders a day. Burger King was making money. JAG was making money. The crew loved it; even many of the lifers were regular customers. Things were too good to be true. They jacked the surcharge to

30%. Business surged. They expanded into the loan / slush fund business, with Gritman's large presence acting as their enforcer.

Gritman's brother was having trouble relocating and this only prolonged the good fortune of JAG. However, trouble finally caught up with JAG after about two months into the venture. It was on a Tuesday noon run. Andy and Gritman had picked up 40 lunch orders and were heading back to the ship. They slowed at the main gate, expecting to be waved through as usual. Most of the guards had gotten to know the Camaro and some of them were even customers from time to time.

Today, however, a new Marine had just come on duty. He stepped in front of the Camaro with one hand held up, staring at them from behind aviator shades. His right hand rested on his holstered .45.

"Oh, shit." Andy said. "Just what we need. A new, gung-ho motherfucker. We're running late as it is."

Gritman came to a stop and stuck his head out the window. "What's up biggen'? Can we go through?" "What is your destination, sailor?"

"Our ship."

"Present your ID."

"Sure," Gritman flashed his ID. "But let's hurry it up. We gotta' get going."

"And you sailor?" The guard turned to Andy.

"Me? I'm a communist fuckin' spy. What do you think I am?" Andy was getting pissed, and sorry he couldn't keep it to himself. "My IDs in Russian. You couldn't read it anyway."

The guard wasn't amused. "Please step out of the vehicle."

"No way! We're late getting back to the ship. We gotta' go!"

The Marine turned his attention to the boxes of food in the backseat. "What's all this? Looks like contraband. This vehicle will need to be searched thoroughly before entering the base."

"Are you shitting me? Look, this food is for the crew. They'll be really pissed if we don't get it to them. Like, right fucking now!! Call the ship. Call the Jetsomn! They'll tell you its ok!"

"Sorry, sailor. The only call I will be making is to muster up help to search this vehicle."

Gritman was getting real tense. He wouldn't even get gas money out of this deal. As the Marine stepped away from the car and into the guardhouse to make his call, Gritman floored the Camaro, laying two strips of rubber for 20 feet past the main gate. By the time Gritman got through all four gears, he and Andy were flying by the piers at 90 miles an hour.

"Holy shit!" was all that Andy could think to say. This was an awesome display of Camaro power, and on Gritman's part, even though it was driven by his tightfistedness, it was daring.

Minutes later as they approached the Jetsomn's pier, they had two gray security trucks in hot pursuit, red lights and sirens going. Gritman turned onto the pier and slammed on the brakes while alternately stepping on the gas, stopping in a 180˚ power slide in front of the ship. He and Andy grabbed the boxes of food stuff and dashed across the Quarterdeck. The Officer of the Deck had been watching their approach and ordered them to stop. But, as they stepped across the Quarterdeck, Jay was waiting. He grabbed the boxes and ran off to distribute the food. It was all still hot. No refunds. Thank god.

A crowd was gathering on the pier. Two security police, two shore patrol and several officers from the ship moved in on Gritman and Andy. The Captain and XO arrived on the scene. They initially focused on Gritman, deciding that he was the most guilty as he was the larger and probably the driver. To make matters worse, on this day, Gritman had decided to save time by keeping his dungaree pants on and throwing a Hawaiian shirt on. He was out of uniform no matter which side of the gate you looked at him from. Andy was temporarily overlooked. No one even thought about Jay who was still distributing the food.

When all was said and done, Gritman was charged with wearing an improper uniform, reckless driving, speeding, fleeing an officer, and endangering government property (himself). They tried to nail him with illegally entering the base, but that was dropped. However, they revoked his parking privileges on the base, hoping that they'd never have to see the Camaro again on base. They caught up with Andy and tried to charge him with being a Russian spy, but they couldn't make the charges stick as he proved to be unable to speak Russian. He tried, but just couldn't do it. Nyet, nyet is all he would divulge.

During the course of the investigation, the JAG Burger King business came to the attention of the Captain. He consulted with the XO and the two of them consulted with the ship's cooks. The cooks had always taken an affront to the alternative menu (even though it meant less work for them as the mess decks were actually empty sometimes and that meant they could sneak home more food for themselves). The captain decided that there was something inherently wrong with the JAG business, even if he didn't really know what it was.

In short order, Gritman, Jay and Andy were in front of the Captain and the XO. The Captain sat back in his chair, looking stern. The XO did the talking. He wasted no words informing them that their little business venture was detrimental to the ship. Productivity, he said, was lost every time they made a Burger King run. They also affected the morale as the cooks were upset because fewer sailors were eating meals on the ship. In addition, locals were complaining that Burger King wrappers were polluting the harbor. Lastly, the XO concluded, the wrong message, that Navy chow was substandard, was being given to Burger King, the public, the guards at the gate, and the sailors on the ship. The XO went on to order the three of them to cease and desist immediately.

They were dismissed. Andy, Jay and Gritman filed out of the room and set about ceasing and desisting immediately. So much for free enterprise. However, Gritman's brother was finally relocated and demanding his car back immediately, and the boys had managed to stash away $800. Jay said he could guarantee them a car with a license plate for $500. Andy said they would keep $300 to ensure that their newest business venture, the JAG Slush Fund Fun, could stay afloat. Gritman was now made a full partner because, as the enforcer, Andy and Jay had come to realize the importance of enforcing contracts in the loan business. Ironically, this capitalistic venture, though not legally sanctioned by the Captain, was tolerated. It was de facto! Even some low level officers did business with the JAG Slush Fund Fun. Anchors await.

Chapter 20: <u>The Heavy Chevy</u>

It was mid August, the air was laden with that soaking South Carolina humidity, and it was *hot*. Andy had pissed Maloni off the night before. It was a cruel joke, but Andy could be impulsive, and when he was, it usually had negative consequences for someone. They had been in a little bar on the strip slugging down the cheap brew mixture of Schlitz and Ripple when the Shore Patrol made their swaggering stroll through the bar. They were always present, ducking in and out of local establishments, ensuring that all sailors were good customers and better gentlemen. As the SPs exited, Andy, in his best Irish accent, couldn't resist. The door was still open so the SPs heard it all, "Aye mates, hows about puttin' a sweet kiss on' me wank here?"

The two SPs were back in the bar so fast it surprised the holy shit out of Andy. The bar became silent, you could hear the foam disappear from the draft beer. The SPs hadn't seen who said it, they just heard it. And they knew someone in the bar was guilty. Maloni had had just enough to drink to allow the power of suggestion to rule. Andy leaned over, and in something above a whisper, said to Maloni, "Oh shit, Maloni, they think you said it."

It was hot. Too hot to think straight. Maloni leaped off the bar stool and high tailed it for the back door. Problem number 1: it wasn't a back door, there was no back door. Problem number 2: it was the bathroom door. The SPs quickly retrieved their man and, just as quickly, handcuffed Maloni. He was led kicking, screaming, and cursing (screaming and cursing at Andy, but also at the 'stupid fucking shit-for-brains, cum-drinking, wank kissing dick-faces' who were hauling him) out of the bar. Yes things were hot these days.

Today the thermometer read 102 at the car lot where Jay and Andy (minus Maloni who now was in custody and restricted to the ship) were wandering down rows of cars in a swampy, off the main road, dumpy establishment. The little building that served as an office was also probably the home of the proprietor. A fat, balding, sweat drenched salesman waddled right behind them, talking nonstop with his thumbs stuck in his suspenders that kept his pants from falling to his ankles. He had a nervous habit of hiking the pants up, letting go, and the suspenders fulfilled their purpose.

"Buddy's the name. Cars are my game. My sole purpose in life is to fix you boys up in a classy set of wheels. Yessir, I'm Buddy-yer good buddy. My sole purpose in life is to see you boys happy and ya'll be happy when your cruisin' down the road in your new wheels and when yer happy ol' Buddy here's happy, we can all be happy. So whaddaya looking for? Convertible, muscle car, sports car?"

Buddy was smiling a plastic grin that he had been born with. He peered at them from under the yellowed, sweat stained brim of a white ball cap that proclaimed MAYNARD'S USED CARS. He chewed on the stub of a pencil that was brown from the spittle of chewin' tobaccy. He hitched up his stained, sweaty pants that had been drooping groundward, exposing the top of the crack of his fat, sweaty, pasty white ass, and then waved his mit at the rows of cars. "Look at these beauties. A-1 shape every one of them. Not a lemon in the bunch."

"Looks like a junkyard," Jay offered.

"Like I said, not lemon in the bunch," Buddy responded. His plastic grin started to look more like a sneer. "Ya'll a couple of Yankees, ain't ya?"

"Why yes, I guess we are," Jay answered, "with Yankee money. These pieces of shit are all beat up. You have anything that looks halfway decent? And if I did want a lemon I wouldn't come to a junkyard!"

245

"Yankees, and sailors to boot! Ain't I right?" Buddy sneered.

"Why yes, I guess we are," Andy answered this time, in his best Scarlet O'Hara falsetto, "I do declare, its so hot today Jay I can smell the sweat of this horse's ass from way over yonder.

"Why, that is hot Scarlet, my dear," said J. 'Rhett Butler' West?

"Why Mr. Butler," continued falsetto Scarlet, "it is so hot that this po' gennleman here is fannin' his own piss in a feeble effort to cool his fat little ol' self. His odor is absolutely putrifrying in this heat."

"Whoa der Scarlet, honey, you might upset the little fat round sweaty southern son of a bitch."

Andy and Jay were hot. They were tired of smelling this lump of shit. They were getting impatient and about to leave. "Wait a minute boys. There's no need fo' all this shit talk," said Buddy.

Andy looked over Buddy's shoulder at an ancient office / house with fake brick siding, ripped and falling off the old unpainted clapboard siding underneath. Andy knew for sure now that the building housed the car lot office, and served as home for Buddy. Just as sure as the TV antenna that was stuck at a strange angle on the roof was emitting black and white horizontal bars across a little black and white screen in the office / home. A fading sign over the trailer announced that this was Maynard's Used Car Lot. 'Maynard's Real Deals on Wheels! Quality Cars at Low Prices! The Working Man's Friend! The Soldier's and The Sailor's Friend! God Bless America!' The hot asphalt felt like it was burning through the soles of Andy's cheap tennis shoes. He was getting hotter and he knew his dislike for the salesman would not ease up, but he would try. "Listen Buddy or Maynard, or who ever the fuck you are. You shouldn't give a shit who or what we are. If you behave yourself you may make some bucks here. If you don't want to, then fuck you." He turned to Jay. "Ah, fuck it. Come on, let's get out of here and get a cold one. Fuck this junkyard, these beat up cars and this fat, stinky, ass-crack redneck."

"Crack what? Y'alls the fuckin' crackers..." In an unprecedented display of quickness, Buddy caught himself, and his sneer melted back into that plastic smile. He couldn't forget that he hadn't had a sale in at least a week, and maybe he *could* make a few bucks off these boys. "Hold on there. I was just funnin' with ya. Come on now, have a look around. I know I got something here that you fellers could use."

"What do you have that runs?" Jay asked.

Yeah, besides your mouth, thought Andy.

Buddy snorted indignantly and spat a brown wad of slimy tobacco in the yellow dust just off the crumbly asphalt.

"What do ya have for under $300 bucks?" Jay continued. "Any pickups?"

"Nope. Nothing that cheap. All's I got is quality cars. But I'll tell ya what. For jes a few more bucks I can sure fix you up. I got a lot of real nice cars for jes a little more than that..."

"How much more?'

"For a grand, I can have you tooling around in something really sharp."

Andy had it with Buddy's bullshit. "That does it! Fuck this. It's hot, I'm hot, these pieces of shit are probably hot too, and I'm going to find an air-conditioned bar."

"Fine with me." Jay started heading for the street.

"Now ya'll jes hold up a minute, wait, uh..." Buddy was beginning to sputter and the perspiration was now dripping off the third of his three chins. A light went on in that dim shithouse of a head and Buddy looked like he just remembered something. "I jes remembered somethin'. I do have a car that's reeel close to what you're lookin' to spend.'

"How much?" said Jay.

Buddy looked like he was stretching the neurons in his brain, and he half muttered aloud, "Hmm... Er.... Ah, 500 bucks."

"For-fucking-get it!" Andy still was thinking about a cold beer.

"Hold on," Jay interrupted. "Lets at least look at it." He really wanted a car. Almost any car would be fine at this point. Gritman's brother's car had really spoiled him. Jay was really sick of the Enlisted Men's Club, the strip was getting old, the Flying Dutchman was too risky, and the bus rides were intolerable. The last trip to the E. M. club almost ended in disaster. They were stealing hamburgers from the trays just outside the kitchen and pissing on the carpet under the table. If they hadn't left when they did, they surely would have been found out by the bartender, or the Shore Patrol that wandered in out of the club. They needed to get way away from the base. On their own power. They needed a car.

Buddy led them to the back row and proudly pointed at a 61 Chevy station wagon.

"A station wagon? I don't want any fucking station wagon!" Andy looked like he was getting stressed out and would be soon capable of killing, or worse. He might get so pissed he'd push ol' Buddy's button, and fuck up any chance of buying a car from him.

"I don't know," said Jay. He was thinking.

"Just look at this gem." Buddy was on the trail of a sale "No rust."

"No shit. Lots of dents though."

"They're mostly small. Whaddaya expect for 500 bucks?" Buddy opened the hood. "Look!" He announced. "A big V-8."

"A little 283," Jay retorted. "How's it run?"

"Like a top. Like a goddamn top."

"But of course it does. I want to test drive it."

"Uh, okie dokie," Buddy agreed, but was hesitant.

Jay opened the door and they were greeted by the worst smell either had ever smelled. It was at least 200 degrees in the closed up car. Whew, the smell. It was worse than the dump. No, it was worse than a dead rat in the wall. No, it was worse than the alcoholic breath of an old wino, after the alcohol had left by the same orifice through which it had entered.

"Holy shit! What the hell died in here?"

"It'll be alright," Buddy reassured them. "We'll just open up all the windows, air it out, cool it off. It'll be fine. Its jes been closed up for a while. Take it out. Drive it around. You'll see. Its a hell of a car. I *swan*, it's a hell of a car," Buddy was doing his best to be persuasive.

"It's a hell of a car alright. What the hell is *swan* anyway?" Jay took the keys from Buddy. He took a deep breath and slid behind the wheel. He turned the key and after a few seconds the "big V-8" came to life with a belch of gray-blue smoke.

Andy took a deep breath and got in on the passenger side. Andy had just enough hillbilly in him to know about *swan*, "*Swan* means swear Jay. He's jes' tryin' to make you real cumfy."

"Yeah, well fuck his *swan*. Sick bastard. Swan-fucking, sweet jesus!"

"Rhett, darlin', I jes ain't in to that sickness either," replied the effervescent falsetto Scarlet. "Ah shit, don't get your underwear in a wad Jay. He probably hasn't really fucked a swan, ...umm maybe a one winged chicken, but no *swans*." Andy noticed the headliner was completely gone. There was a large brown stain on the driver's seat and the back seat had most of the stuffing pulled out.

Several miles and a couple beers later they could almost breathe again. The humid South Carolina air coming in all the windows helped a little. "It doesn't run all that bad," Jay commented. "I kind of like it."

"We look like a couple of old farts in this thing," Andy complained. "What self respecting girls would want to be picked up in this garbage truck? Think of our image."

"What image?" Jay asked. "Remember, we're in the Navy, so we can forget any image that might attract normal girls. Our image isn't so hot with or without the car. But at least we now have wheels and can forget about the bus and cabs. We can drive it wherever we're going, then just walk away. Pretend we got out of a Porsche you shithead."

"Ok. We have wheels alright but I still think we could do better."

"Think about it," Jay responded. "It'll serve our purpose and this thing is pretty inconspicuous. Its cheap and insurance won't cost much. We're almost to our limit, anyway, we don't have some huge bankroll. Besides, a jacked up high powered muscle car may attract chicks but it also attracts cops. We won't attract any attention in this."

"You can say that again. No more attention than any short haired, Yankee sailors without a clue about what they are doing, or where they are going than they otherwise would. The oil, man look at those blue fumes. Its going to cost us as much in oil as it is in gas. Maybe more"

An hour later they returned. Buddy had been drinking something too, but it was a little stiffer than beer. After some serious negotiation and occasional name calling, Jay and Andy owned an odorous green Chevy station wagon. Buddy had tried his best to stick with the original $500 price, but Andy got on a roll. He used a combination of feigned ignorance, mockery, melodrama, intimidation, confusion, and shucking and jiving. The price went down to 375 bucks. Buddy didn't stand a chance once Andy got on a roll. The plates came with the car. This impressed Jay. "It'll make us look more like locals. Or at least, at first glance anyhow."

They got in the car, papers in hand. Andy leaned out the window in Buddy's direction. He smiled at the salesman, and, sounding like he was confiding a big secret to his best friend, kindly said, "You know Buddy, you gave up too easy. We would have paid you the 500 bucks if you hadn't come across like such a fucking cracker dickhead." Then Andy gave him the middle finger salute.

Buddy looked like he had just been bitch-slapped, but somehow recovered quick enough to scream, "Fuck you sailorboys and your slimy Yankeeassholes! Get outta here before I pound sand up yer asses!"

"What did you say?" Jay wasn't sure he had heard Buddy right. "You're gonna pound what up our whats? You? Both of us? A lard ass like you? You shitting me?" He looked at Andy. "Do you believe this jerk?"

"I think he's smoking way too much weed, or maybe he's a pervert, and you know, does weird things with his ASS," Andy suggested, loud enough for Buddy to hear every word.

"I ain't no preevert!" Buddy was red-faced. He was sputtering, brown saliva dripping from all three chins. It looked like a brown waterfall, in slow motion. "But the laugh's on y'all assholes. That car's as-is. No warranty! It's all your problem now! FUCK Y'ALL!"

"We figured on that, you little teensy prick".

Buddy started laughing and coughing and choking all at the same time. "Ya know what that smell is from? I'll tell ya! The old owner was a wino who died in the swamp-right in that there car. He sat in there for days, rotting away befo' anyone found him. He'd shit his pants and the critters were starting to feed on him.

And ya'll wonder why it stinks! It not only stinks-its haunted too! The car's possessed by his ghost. You'll see! Good luck you Yankee assholes! You're gonna need it!" Buddy was almost screaming. By now he was bright red and looked like he was going to have a heart attack or a stroke.

"Let's get out of here," Jay said. "We've got places to go." He was getting worried that Buddy was going to die on them right on the spot.

The car still stunk, but the freedom of having their own wheels helped overcome it. First stop was a car wash. All the doors open, they spent two quarters on the outside, and two on the inside. At the second stop they gassed up, bought air fresheners, a styrofoam cooler, ice, more beer, and a case of cheap oil. They were on a drive to nowhere particular, but that didn't matter. At least they were going somewhere in their own car.

"Wait a minute," Jay said before getting back into the car. "I've got to fix something. He went to the back bumper and knelt down by it. Curious, Andy joined him.

"What the hell are you doing?" Andy couldn't believe what he saw. He stared at the two new bumper stickers on the car. "America-Love it Or Leave It" and "Support Your Local Police" now decorated the chrome bumper.

"What the hell are you doing? Have you lost your mind? Now we do look like the rest of the local rednecks."

"Think of it as camouflage, a disguise, a diversion," Jay said. "We're now undercover. We'll blend right in with the rednecks and nobody will mess with us."

"Man, it looks to me like you're selling out."

"I'm not doing anything of the kind. Use your head. These don't mean a thing but they may make our life a little easier down the road. And the next stop is the local Salvation Army store so we can buy old mechanic shirts with someone else's name on 'em."

Andy started to see the point. "Makes some sort of sense, I guess. Incognito, maybe we can get into a little less trouble like this. Or push the envelope and see if we get into a little more," he was musing and at the same time trying real hard to hang on to some final wispy shreds of his image.

They got into the car and headed out on to the highway.

"We're really making progress," Andy said. "Now we DO look like two redneck old farts in this bus." He opened a beer, drained it, then opened the second. Andy always did it like this. He figured it gave him an advantage. He felt he was already one up on whoever he was with. He put the second beer in a paper bag, felt red under the collar, and took a swig of it. "Not bad, wind on your face, beer, red is a nice color."

"Cheer up. Speaking of buses, this means our bus riding days are now over," said Jay. Jay hated buses. Jay really hated busses. "Do you think Buddy was bullshitting us about that story?"

"About the wino? I don't know. Could be true. I suppose that could have happened. Something damn sure made it stink in here. I can still smell it. Your ass seems to fit the winos stain. Maybe you're next. Anyway, we can't use this damn bus with girls. Not yet anyway."

"I bet that old fat bastard made it up because he was so pissed off at us. At you mostly. As usual, you didn't leave him any way out. You always push people too far. I bet he made it up. He had to."

"Yeah," Andy thought the smell was bad enough for the story to be true. "That's right Jay, the dumb motherfucker, the stupid as a stone motherfucker, just made it up. You know, kind of on the sperm of the moment type thing."

"Yeah. He was dumb, ...so he just made it up? This is hard to swallow, I just don't know."

"Its a bunch of bullshit Jay. You can't believe a slobbery old shit like him. He had stains all over his clothes. Hell, he had stains from food before it went in, and I 'swan', he had a couple stains on his ass from food after he cut it loose! A good day for him is when he farts, and its dry. Maybe this was his favorite vehicle for one winged chickens, and then one day after an exciting hen and too much Wild Turkey he just passed out and shit *hisself.* That could explain that stain you're sitting in."

"What! Oh, yeah, nothing to it." They glanced at each other. Jay shrugged. "Hey you wanna' drive?"

"No, I'll let you wear out the seat stain. And I don't want to start up the Burger King runs again. We're doing well enough with our loan fund business, and it seems to be more widely accepted than the food runs. Go figure, the loan fund business really is illegal and the food runs are perfectly legal." Andy turned to survey the back seats. "No spooks back there," he reported.

"That's good," laughed Jay. But he kept catching himself checking the rearview mirror image of the back seats all the way to the highway. You know, thought Jay, these station wagons are heavy. This is a hell of a lot of weight going down the road. The 'heavy chevy'.

They finished the night with some cheap Burgundy wine ending up in a ditch full of rain water somewhere in Columbia, South Carolina. Jay wanted to know how they got there. Andy couldn't tell him. He didn't remember much of anything after stealing the wine from the old man in a little tiny grocery store and heading out on the highway toward the University of South Carolina, and, all those college girls. Wine, the thoughts of university women, and the tunes on the radio blasting out in the night as the cool air rushed in through the windows was all that Andy could recall.

Their heads had a dull heavy ache, they were in no shape to try to pick up girls, but their spirits had been lifted. They just barely had enough money to get a tow truck, get out of the ditch, and get back to Charleston. The boys first adventure with the 'heavy chevy' wasn't too productive, but it was heady and carried with it a feeling of a fleeting, even though a little on the fuzzy side, kind of freedom. A 'heavy chevy' equals a lighter anchor weight.

Chapter 21: Graduate School

"Accelerated Boiler Training!" Andy laughed. "It's graduate school for snipes. We're going Ivy League!"

Andy had just returned from Maloni's Captains Mast when Jay told him about the school. At the mast Andy told the captain that it was he, Andy, who caused all the trouble in the bar that night. Andy explained the whole story about cat-calling the Shore Patrol and tricking Maloni. The captain listened patiently. Then he said he understood and he thought highly of Andy for coming forward with the truth. However, it was the behavior of Fireman Maloni *after* the incident that needed changing. He didn't fine Maloni, but he restricted him to the ship for another week. Maloni was pretty torked by the whole thing. Oh well, thought Andy, Maloni just got pissed on, he has every right to be pissed off, but soon his bladder would empty, all would be urinal white, and Maloni would forgive Andy (but not forget the incident). What's Jay rambling on about?

"....isn't that a contradiction of terms or something?" Jay asked. "Imagine, a graduate degree in boilers. Better yet, a Ph.D. in Fireroom studies. Doctor West, here, specializing in what makes boilers tick and fixing what ails them."

"Actually, this whole ordeal is like a four year long shop class in hell."

They had gotten their orders, which stated that they would be attending a three week long training program in Norfolk,

Virginia. They were to report on base at Norfolk at 0800 next Monday morning, ready to learn everything they would need to know in order to become boiler experts and possibly advance to BT3. It seemed that the Navy had big plans for BTFN West and BTFN Mathers. However, Jay and Andy were not enthused about the situation. Being BT3 meant that you had to be a manager of something. So far, Uncle Sam had given them the distinct impression that he didn't want the two of them in charge of anything.

"It'll be great," Andy tried to sound enthused. "It'll be a chance to get off this tub and out of this day to day routine."

"Sounds ok," Jay agreed. "But come on-Norfolk? It's as bad as Charleston, but worse. Sailors and whores. Whores and sailors. The only good thing about it is that I have a friend stationed there. Howard. He's in subs but has an apartment off base with some other guys. I think he's around and I'm sure he'll let us stay with him. Think of this in terms of an apartment, new women, and civvies. We could be living a halfway normal life, even if it would be temporary."

The rest of the week took forever. They had a serious inspection during the week. Some Admiral from Atlantic Command Service East (ATCOMSEE) was motored around on a little boat by a coxswain. He never actually stepped on a ship. He just motored from one pier to the next looking at all the sailors in their dress whites lining the rails from the bow to the stern of each ship.

The boilermen weren't supposed to be a part of the inspection, partly because they're greasy and nasty, but also because repairs were being made to the boilers for a short cruise while Jay and Andy were away at school. Although this was originally the situation, things change. Important things, like, there weren't enough sailors on our ship to stand at parade rest in dress whites from bow to stern. So they were told to get into their working whites, keep on working, and at the last minute come up the hatch to fill a 20 foot space on the main deck with other sailors in white at the rail for the Admiral.

The problem was that boilermen do not maintain any working whites because it is ridiculous to think snipes can work in whites. Maybe yeomen, radiomen, sonarmen, or whatever, but not boilermen. We have dungarees that, if lucky, are covered with coveralls to keep some of the filth away. Well, after much rummaging around, the forward fireroom boys came up with enough white uniform tops, but not enough pants, socks, or shoes.

So at the appropriate time, the boys filed up the ladder, through the hatch, and in line at the rail. A more ragtag bunch has probably never before, or maybe since, been assembled for inspection by an Admiral. Luckily the rail was solid from about four feet to within inches of the main deck where the boilermen filled in. Some had no white pants, but wore dungarees. Others had no suitable shoes or socks and actually went barefoot. Still others wore rust stained or soiled covered (hats) or shirts. Gritman's height prevented him from standing straight. He had to endure parade rest with his knees bent in order to keep his dungarees below the rail. Goofing, grabass, and goosing one another was rampant.

The only things that kept the unruly ragtag boilermen from getting in trouble were: 1) the Admiral really never got close enough to distinguish individuals, and 2) the officers and chiefs were all together on an upper deck.

All the week's shit was over and Saturday finally came. They had to stick around because Jay had watch duty from 4 to 8am that morning. When he finally got off of watch, he showered and then woke up Andy. Half an hour later, they were in the heavy Chevy, heading for the locker club.

Standing in front of the locker, they eyed up their collection of civvies. "I think we should splurge and buy some new clothes. This stuff is pretty ratty," Jay commented.

"Yeah, agreed Andy, fingering a hole in his worn but as of yet unwashed jeans. They stopped at Pamida where they each dropped 50 bucks on new jeans, shirts, and shoes. They unceremoniously tossed their old clothes into a trashcan and turned the heavy chevy toward Virginia.

It was nice day. Sunny, but not too hot. The Chevy ran fine and the smell was tolerable. Things were looking good. Jay had gotten a hold of Howard earlier. The sub was in port for the next two months. Howard assured him that they were more than welcome to stay at the apartment. Two of his roommates would be gone, off to Groton, Connecticut for training, so he had plenty of room. They wouldn't even have to sleep on the floor. And, Howard assured them, he'd be more than happy to show them around Norfolk.

The trip went fast and without incident, until somewhere north of the Virginia state line. The Chevy's engine started knocking and white smoke started rolling out of the tailpipe. Andy, who was driving, didn't like what he was hearing, so he turned up the volume of the radio so he wouldn't have to hear the knocks. He looked at the rearview mirror and watched the huge clouds of smoke billowing behind the car. That doesn't look good, he said to himself and tilted the mirror so he couldn't see it. The knocking got louder; Andy responded by turning up the radio even louder and slugging down another beer.

"Jesus Christ!" Jay had been dozing but he awoke with a start. What the hell are you doing?" He turned down the radio just in time to hear a couple of the last engine knocks followed by a loud bang.

Lots of smoke poured out from under the hood as the engine died with a shriek and a final metallic groan. They had been on a four lane interstate and were just rolling into a toll booth. The Chevy came to a pathetic, oil leaking stop next to the booth, smoking like a fire in a tire factory.

A grumpy old man in a nondescript, faded uniform yelled from inside the booth. "50 cents! And get that piece of shit out of here! I can't breathe." He was coughing from the smoke that entirely filled his small space.

Andy tried to start the engine. It refused to even turn over. "I think I killed it," he said.

"Sounded like you threw a rod."

"Yeah, that's it! You wanted a hot rod, well, here you go. I think we can find your hot rod somewhere on the road under the car."

"Knock it off, this is serious." Nothing made Jay more tense and irritable than car trouble. He looked around. "Now what do we do?"

The old man started yelling at them again. "I said get that piece of shit out of here! And give me 50 cents!"

"Fuck you. I'm trying. Do you think I want to be here? Do you think I want to be sitting two feet from your window, looking at your ugly fucking face and listening to your yelling?" Andy didn't like being yelled at.

The hell with ya'll." The old man was no longer coughing, but he was still mad. "I'm gonna' get a wrecker and have them drag you and that piece of shit outta' my sight."

Jay looked behind them. Cars were lining up behind the dead Chevy. "Fine with me," he said, "the sooner the better." Several cars started honking their horns. "Call the wrecker. And see if they'll bring some beer with them, we just ran out."

Fifteen minutes later, the wrecker appeared, hooked up to the Chevy and dragged it out of the toll lane and over to the side of the highway. The driver, big bear of a man, asked them where they wanted the car taken.

"Good question." Andy and Jay looked at each other. They hadn't thought about it.

They popped the hood. The engine compartment was filled with left over smoke, oil and water. "Its shot," the driver announced. "Deader than hell."

"No shit," Jay responded. "Look, I don't care where you take it. Its no good to us now and we sure as hell ain't paying to have it fixed."

"Well, ya' gotta' do something with it. Can't let it sit here. Its still ya'll's car."

"How far to your garage?" Andy asked.

"Bout five miles yonder," the driver waved a thick arm down the road.

"How much to tow it there?"

The driver thought a minute. "What with road services and all, 25 bucks."

"25 bucks? That's 5 bucks mile!"

"Yup."

"That's highway robbery."

"Yup."

"Tell you what,' Andy said. "We'll sell you the car for a hundred bucks. Give us 75 and we'll call it even."

"100 bucks for this piece of shit? You're nuts."

"Sure," Jay added. "All it needs is an engine. You must have a spare 283 sitting around. Throw that baby in her and you'll have a decent car. Drive it or sell if for a profit. You won't make a million bucks but you'll make out like a bandit."

The driver was thinking. 'I don't know," he said. He thought some more. He walked around the car. "He's interested," Andy whispered to Jay.

"Yeah, don't push him."

The driver looked back at them. "$50 to boot."

"Deal!" Andy and Jay replied in unison.

"Can you give us a lift to your garage? We need to call a guy to pick us up."

"Sure thing." The driver was happy about the deal he had just made.

At the garage, Jay called Howard collect. They discovered that they were only about 50 miles from Norfolk and Howard said he'd be there in an hour or two.

It turned out the driver's name was Jake and he owned the garage. He seemed to do a pretty good business. The lot was lined with cars and trucks in various stages of repair and disrepair. Today was his mechanic's day off, so he was handling things alone. He dropped off the Chevy and almost immediately got another wrecker call. "Long as your here for a spell," he said, "ya'll may as well make yourselves useful. Stick around the place and answer the phone while I'm gone. Tell them I'll be back directly. I can't pay ya, but there's beer in that," he gestured to a beat up soda machine. "Help yourselves." He roared off.

Andy opened a beer and leaned back in a chair in the office. "Things could be worse," he observed. "At least we got a little money out of that car."

"Yeah. And you know, we never paid the toll."

By late that afternoon, they were sitting in Howard's apartment. Jay sized the place up. "Subs must pay pretty well," he commented.

"Not really," Howard replied. "It really helps splitting things four ways. Besides, one of the guys is screwing the landlady. She's got the hots for him so we get a break on the rent whenever she's happy."

"We have a whole night and day off," Andy said. Feels almost like a normal weekend for a change."

That night, Howard showed them around. Just like Charleston, Norfolk had its own Strip. Same looking bars, only more of them. Same looking whores, only uglier. Same looking tattoo parlors and pawn shops. Same old shit, different names and faces. There seemed to be twice as many cops and Shore Patrol. They stopped in several bars and drank, pretending they weren't in the Navy, on a Navy base, or on a Navy strip. Still, it was painfully obvious that they were drinking beer with other sailors. The evening was similar to one in Charleston in many ways, but there was one big difference. They went home to an apartment, not a ship. So what if they hadn't been successful in bringing any girls home with them. At least they were going to sleep in civilian beds in a civilian apartment.

Before they turned in they had to quaff a few more brews and (although the boys wouldn't admit to it if confronted) swap a few sea stories. Howard caught them up on his shenanigans. They were different types of stories from Jay and Andy's' stories. When his sub went out sometimes they didn't see the outside world for two or three months. That was quite sobering.

So Jay decided not to waste the night's buzz from an abundance of Schlitz on sobering experiences. "Howard, you gotta' hear this."

"Now hear this, now hear this," piped in Howard.

"No, really, Howard, check this out. They changed the BURNAVSHIPTECH Manual for 710 FRAM Type Destroyers because of us."

"What the fuck is this NAVSHIPBUR bullshit?"

"No, no, wait, it stands for The Bureau of Naval Ships Technical Manual for our kind of ship. All ships have one. And subs too, I guess. Anyway, it's like a blueprint for the whole ship. Huge fucking book. I saw one once. Not a big seller, not on the New York Times list, but when you have to work on some piece of the ship you gotta' have this book.

So we come back one night. Real late, like around 3:45 am or something. Right before the quarterdeck boys go off watch at 0400. You know, man they are tired. Tired of the watch. Tired of watching every drunk sailor on the ship come back from liberty. Tired of watching each other. Man they are dog tired, and that's probably what saved our ass. After coming aboard, we passed into the companionway (hallway) to go back to our racks. Then, quick as shit, Andy pulls all three ship alarms: General, Nuclear, and Chemical. The combination of all these sirens and whistles going off at same time created instant extensive confusion. Andy was yelling run, run. We made it to the aft fireroom inside hatchway, climbed a little way down, and stood on the ladder watching all the confusion. We were at floor level, even with people's ankles, looking up at this hysterical scene. People were yelling orders, running to there battle stations, and getting dressed as they were running. We thought the mass confusion was great entertainment. The next day we got our ass chewed out royally, but because no one saw us actually do it (they could only place us in the area at the time of the incident) they couldn't do a damned thing to us. The Boiler Officer said it was a total FUBAR (fucked up beyond all recognition). That's supposed to be worse than a SNAFU."

A collective bunch of, "Ha, ha, ha's, and yuk, yuk yuk's."

"And," continued Jay, "then they get an order to weld a bar across the alarms and place a lock at the opposite end of some hinges. All ships had to do this. It was put in all tech manual books too. We don't get authorship credit or even a footnote, but Andy here changed the whole U.S. Navy's fleet with one flick of his wrist. That's powerful man!"

"Then there was the time we had to clean off this sludge barge. We were told to do it with a firehose. It was a particularly hot Charleston afternoon, so fucking around with water can be kind of refreshing" Jay said, as he proceeded to regal Howard with more of their bullshit. "First we pumped all that stinking sludge on the barge, spilling some on the top."

Andy added, "That's some shit, Jay. You got more on top of the barge than you did in it."

261

"Yeah, well, anyway I'm hosing this sludge right into the bay with 90 psi pressure and Chief Bronski comes around the corner on the ship. I realize he's perspiring too, and also within firing range. You can tell he realizes this too, but it's too late. I pretended to slip and fall, and accidentally aim the fire hose on the Chief. It hits him square and his glasses and hat go flying in one direction while his coffee cup goes in another. After he got his soaking wet ass up off the deck all he could do was curse, sputter, and yell for someone else to man the hose. He's a stutterer, but not that time. It all came out clear, crisp, and no repetition. *'Sailor, shut that fucking fire hose off'.*"

More collective, "Ha, ha, ha's, and yuk, yuk yuk's."

"Yeah, then one time we accidentally bumped a battle lantern and it fell from the top floor to the bottom deckplates where Ensign Swells was trying to show everyone what a smart fucking engineer he was. The lantern hit him right on the head and by the time he looked up, there wasn't anyone around. Just a little present for Ensign Swells, but he never ever visited the boys in the fireroom again."

Another round of collective, "Ha, ha, ha's, and yuk, yuk yuk's."

"Jesus," said Howard, you guys seem to be having a little more fun than we are."

Jay went on, "Yeah, well it isn't planned. Stuff just seems to happen. Hey Howard you wanna' have a wine séance?"

"No, shit man, it's already 0430 hours. I need to get some sleep."

"Okay, but it's really 4:00 a.m.," corrected Jay.

"Goodnight, and fuck you very much," replied Howard.

Jay and Andy expected Accelerated Boiler Training to be the most god-awful, boring experience they could ever imagine. It would have been if it hadn't been for Chief Moose. They reported on base promptly at 0800 Monday morning. Class started at 0830, right after morning muster. Roll call was taken, and they were inspected to make sure they were appropriately dressed for the occasion. They stood in ranks with about 30 other young BTs in their dress whites, waiting for their professor to enter the classroom.

"Just like college," Jay said, looking around.

"Oh, yeah, exactly like college. But no girls."

"No long hair. No beards."

"No dope."

"No parties."

"And everyone is dressed alike, acting alike. What a drag. Can we leave if he's not here in ten minutes?"

"I don't think so."

So they waited, and waited and waited. Suddenly the door flew open and in charged the instructor. He was well over 6 and a half feet tall, and big. There's a lot of muscle on this one, Jay thought to himself. He must work out. A square head topped by a crew cut. He looked like a pro wrestler. Talked like one too.

"Top of the morning to you fuckers! Today is your lucky day. I'm in a good mood cuz' I got some pussy last night and if I stay in a good mood, I may not kick your lily white asses today." Then he laughed loudly, at himself. "Alright gentlemen, now that we've got that out of the way, here we go. Chief Moose is the name; boilers are my game. I hate boots. I hate snot nosed know it all kids. I hate officers. I even hate some lifers. I'm a bad ass, and you, are stuck with me. If you don't fit those categories, there may be some hope for you and we should get along fine. Don't fuck with the bear and he won't fuck you" He laughed again. "Alright! Lets see how your mommas dressed you for the first day of school."

He started down the first row in a perfunctory inspection. He stopped short in front of Andy and Jay, "Holy Shit!" he roared. "Someone here smells like a goddamn brewery." He glared at them. "What the fuck did you two do last night? Drink all the goddamn beer in Norfolk? Leave any beer for the rest of us?"

"Sure did, Chief," Andy quipped. "Hey, one thing led to another and it ended up being a late night. But here we are, Chief, bright eyed and bushy tailed."

Chief Moose stared Andy squarely in his blood shot eyes. Oh-oh, Jay thought, good bye, Andy. He could see the shit squaring up, ready to hit the fan.

But suddenly, Moose started laughing. "Well, goddamn it, at least brush your teeth. You won't get any good looking pussy to kiss with that breath," he roared. "And that's a genuine Chief Moose dating tip!" Laughing, he moved down the line of men. Andy glanced sideways at Jay, Jay shrugged.

Chief Moose was as subtle as a bulldozer. He came across as a hard ass but he seemed to enjoy himself and laughed a lot. He seemed to like to kid with Jay and Andy.

"We're the teacher's pets," bragged Andy. "Never been one of those before."

"Never had a teacher like Moose before either, I bet," jay said.

"You've got balls giving us homework, Moose," Jay complained a week or so later.

"Fucking A, I got balls and that's Chief Moose to you, boot! But you know what?" He eyed them up with a grin. "I don't give a fuck if you do the homework or not, as long as I feel you know what you need to know to keep the Navy happy, and keep your asses alive."

"What happens if we flunk, Chief Moose? Do we get expelled from the Navy?'

"BTFN Mathers," Moose roared. "If you fuck with me I'll come roaring down your fucking stack like Jose fuckin' Greco! Nobody flunks my class. I'm the best teacher the Navy has. I am the baddest mofo' in the land!"

The three weeks went fast. Chief Moose knew his shit, especially in terms of boilers and mechanics. He was funny, in a crude, in your face way. He was used to getting his way and was gung ho, but a part of him seemed to take the Navy a lot less seriously than his peers. But the job, boilers, that was serious. He knew how to teach the boys so they wouldn't blow themselves up. However, if he wasn't laughing at you or with you, odds were that you were in deep shit.

"He's weird enough," "Andy commented one night to Jay. "Maybe he'd make a good college professor."

"Yeah, like Harvard or Yale. He'd fit right in," Jay said sarcastically. He thought about it a minute. "Could you see that? Moose in an Ivy League School. That would be something."

The class ended that Friday. They had to wear their dress uniforms and stand at attention for the graduation ceremony. Chief Moose looked out of place in all the formality. He awarded them their certificates and shook their hands.

"Get back out there, do good, and don't die on the job," he muttered to them as he went down the ranks. He gave them a wink and continued on down the line.

Chapter 22: Going Greyhound

Graduate school had ended. Jay and Andy's orders sent them right back to the ship in Charleston. The loss of the heavy chevy finally hit them. They hadn't had to worry about transportation while in Norfolk. Howard had access to cars and they went from bar to bar in style for the entire three weeks. However, now they were faced with having to get back to Charleston and not having the wheels to get there.

"We need another car."

"I don't' know about you, but I'm just about out of money. Can't afford a car right now. We'll have to figure out another way to get back to South Carolina. Then the JAG Slush Fund Fun can build, and eventually, we'll have wheels again. It practically runs on its own. I'm sure Gritman is keeping the money rolling in."

Howard had told them that he would gladly have taken some time off for a field trip to drive them back, but he had pulled duty Sunday night. So that was out. They had to be in Charleston by 0800 Monday morning.

They sat at Howard's apartment and sorted out their options. There weren't that many.

"Stealing a car is out," Jay stated.

"Now wait a minute, don't be so hasty. I'm starting to backslide on that issue."

"No! I mean it. It's way too risky."

"Ok. Ok. Let's hitchhike."

"That'd be alright but it's supposed to rain all weekend. Big thunderstorms. That'd make it real fun waiting for rides alongside the Interstate.

"How about the bus? Greyhound is cheap."

They settled on the bus, only because they could wear their civilian clothes and pretend that they were civilian tourists. Besides, there weren't any other good alternatives, that's all there was.

By noon on Saturday, they were at the bus station. After bidding Howard farewell, they boarded the bus and settled down in seats in the back. The bus was fairly empty so they each got a double seat. Andy sat behind Jay.

The bus pulled out on time and headed south. After a while, it stopped in Asheville and a half dozen passengers got on. A middle-aged black man headed down the aisle and plopped himself into the seat next to Jay.

Jay and Andy were the only white people on the bus.

"Hey there," he looked at Jay and smiled.

"Hey. How ya doing," muttered Jay? He neither wanted nor expected an answer. He didn't feel sociable. He was reading a good book.

"Not bad," was the answer. "The name's Rudy. You in the service?"

"Yeah. Navy. The name's Jay." Jay was friendly by nature but didn't want to talk as the book he was reading just got interesting.

"That right? I was in the army. But they kicked my as out for ... ah...personal reasons. Pleased to meet you, Jay. I have a feeling this'll be a good trip. I like military fellas'"

It will be if you'd shut the fuck up and let me finish my book, Jay thought to himself.

Jay tossed sidelong glance at his neighbor. It seemed to him that this guy was drunk. As if to confirm this, Rudy pulled a small bag from a larger bag he had carried on and took a big swig of what was obviously a booze bottle hidden inside.

"Here's to the Navy," he offered. "Want some?" He shoved the bottle toward Jay.

Drinking an unidentified bottle of booze at 10 in the morning and toasting the Navy of all things, did not appeal to Jay. "Thanks, man, but no thanks."

"Suit yourself." Rudy seemed hurt.

Rudy talked and talked about his Army days (or somebody's army days). He repeated himself several times. Jay tried to concentrate on his book but was constantly distracted. Shortly, Rudy started asking Jay some questions that seemed a little personal. "You married? Got a girlfriend? Ever had syphilis? What's it like to be on a ship with all guys and no women... and on and on and on."

Rudy was getting on Jay's nerves in a big way. Jay ignored him. Finally, Rudy stopped talking. Jay thought he had passed out. He looked like he was out for the count. Great, thought Jay, now for some peace and quiet. He continued reading his book.

Ruby's head was down on his chest and he was slouched on his side, leaning against Jay. Suddenly Jay felt a hand on his knee. He brushed it off. The hand came back, a little higher up. "Hey!" Jay pushed Rudy away. Rudy stirred and muttered something unintelligible. He seemed to really be passed out. However, the hand soon came back to Jay's thigh.

Son of a bitch! Jay thought. The asshole's pretending to be asleep and is trying to put the moves on me. "Hey!" he said again, a little louder. "Move it on over and don't touch me again." He gave Rudy a shove to the opposite corner of the seat.

"Oh, sorry." Rudy pretended to wake up.

Several miles later, he was back to his old tricks. Jay was getting worried. This had to stop. After pushing Rudy's hand off his thigh for what seemed like the millionth time, he turned around to Andy "Hey," he whispered, "I could use some help up here."

Andy had been watching the show and thought it was funnier than hell. He raised his shoulders in an exaggerated shrug. "So who's your new friend?" he asked innocently.

"Goddamn it! It isn't funny."

"Who says so? It's the funniest thing I've seen in awhile. It's more interesting than my book. Anyway, so what's the story? Do you like Rudy?"

"Fuck you, asshole! I thought we were friends."

"We are. Just not that *kind* of friends. Better get back to Rudy, I see his hand gliding back over to caress the inside of..."

"Fuck You!"

"Not me big boy. I don't care how much money you have, you ain't stickin' that big thing in my asshole," crooned Andy.

"Yeah, well kiss my...uh grits!"

Jay looked around the bus. It had filled up with passengers. Some of the ones sitting nearby were snickering at Andy's remarks. Jay, for the first time, just realized that he and Andy *were* the only white boys on the bus. Oh great, he thought. I can't openly get in this guy's face. I can't slug this guy. I'll get the shit knocked out of me and maybe start a riot in the process. Jay felt alone and stuck.

This went on for a few more miles, until the bus pulled into a small town to let a some passengers off and let new ones on. Jay's new friend pretended to wake up again. "Where are we?" He rubbed his eyes. "I gotta' go take a piss. You gotta' go?" he asked Jay.

"I'd rather fill up my bladder and blow up like a goddamn balloon first," Jay answered.

"Oh, oh well, you don't have to be rude about it. Just say Okay." Rudy stood up. "I'll be right back," he said giving Jay's knee a final pat. "Save my seat,...honey." He headed off of the bus.

Like hell, thought Jay. He wasn't sure what he was going to do but he had to do something. He turned around again to face Andy. "Move up here, damn it. This is going to get out of hand real soon."

"Not on your life sugar bush. Your buddy would just want to sit on my lap."

"Fuck you! What am I gonna' do? This is a sticky situation."

"Don't worry," Andy reassured him.

"Don't worry?" Jay yelled. Several passenger's heads turned. "Don't worry? Look! I'm not homophobic or anything, but this is really getting on my nerves. This bastard's trying to hump me where I sit! He's bigger than me, and, to make things even more interesting you and I are the only honky boys on this bus. And you have the balls to tell me don't worry!"

"Now, don't get hysterical big boy, *but* do keep my balls out of this. Calm down. It'll be alright. Just wait. Trust me. Oops, better turn around. Your boyfriend's coming back."

"Fuck you to hell and back! Thanks for nothing. Just wait, something bad is going to happen here."

Rudy sat back down next to Jay. Before he could say anything, the driver approached him. He had been walking down the aisle, checking the tickets of the newly boarded passengers.

"Got your ticket, friend," he asked Rudy?

"Ticket? Why? You already saw my ticket. I've been on this bus since Asheville. I'm going to Charleston with my buddy here."

"I'm not his buddy," Jay piped in. He saw a chance. "As a matter of fact," he continued, "I don't even know this guy. He just now..."

The driver interrupted Jay. "I need to see your ticket, friend, we have to get going," he said again to Rudy.

"Really! I've been on this bus the whole time. I just now got off to use the facilities."

"Maybe you did and maybe you didn't," responded the driver. "But I have too many people on this bus to keep track of who's doing what. All's I know is I saw you get on the bus just now and I need to see your ticket. If you got on in Asheville, you must still have your ticket with you. Just show it to me and save us both a lot of trouble."

"Alright, Captain, if that's all it takes to make you happy." Rudy was getting cocky and the driver didn't appreciate it. "Here's your fucking ticket," he said, reaching into his back pocket. He stopped short. "What the hell? Wait a minute! Where's my ticket? It's gone! It was here, honest. Maybe I dropped it. It's lost!"

"No ticket, huh? Then you're going to have to get off the bus!"

"Damn it! I have a ticket. Or, I had a ticket. It's just gone. It's lost. It's stolen! That's it! It's stolen!"

"No ticket, huh? Off the bus, right here and right now."

"My ticket was stolen!" Rudy yelled out into the crowd that had gathered.

"Who would steal your ticket?" the driver wanted to know. "Now get your ass of this bus! I've got to get going. I'm already behind schedule."

"Sell me a ticket then. I'll buy a new one."

"Sorry, can't do that. The station just closed." The driver was getting impatient "Now get off of this bus before I call the police."

"Go ahead Captain," Rudy responded, "Call your fucking cops. Have them search that white boy. He's got my damn ticket." The liquor was definitely doing his talking for him.

The driver turned to Jay. "You said you don't know this guy?"

"No sir!" Jay answered very quickly. "Never saw him before. He just got on and said something about hoping he wouldn't have to show a ticket." Jay did his best to sound helpful. "I think he's drunk," he added.

That was enough for the driver. He hoisted Rudy out of his seat and escorted him down the aisle and out the door. The bus roared off, leaving a fuming Rudy at the curb.

Jay finally relaxed. He turned around to Andy. "What a lucky break. Man, I didn't know how I was going to be able to ..." Jay stopped talking and stared. Andy, smiling an evil smile, was holding a greyhound bus ticket in his hand.

Jay knew but he had to ask. "Ah, that isn't your ticket in your hand, is it?"

"Guess not," was the reply. "Got mine right here." He tapped his pocket. "Seems like I found this one here, just lying around.

Actually, the ticket in question had slipped out of Rudy's pocket before the bus had stopped at the last stop. Andy saw it, and had discreetly picked it up, thinking that somehow it could be of use in their situation. It had worked out better than he had ever imagined.

Eventually, the bus pulled into Charleston. Andy cashed in Rudy's ticket. They took a cab back to the ship. Andy, with his new found riches paid the taxi. As they unpacked their gear, Andy looked at the certificate Chief Moose had given him for completing the advanced boiler course. "My graduate degree," he announced. "Now I've got the world by the balls. We've got it made now, for sure."

"Yeah, right." Anchors, await.

Chapter 23: <u>Key West</u>

When the USS Jetsomn left port, which was too often as far as Jay and Andy were concerned, the boilermen were always ALL present. Others seemed to be able to miss a cruise once in a while, but not boilermen. They were short rated and none could be spared. The ship also left sometimes when it was not scheduled to leave and the boys believed it was to confuse the commies. Obviously, confused commies were desirable to unconfused commies.

Jay learned later from one of the supply clerks that the real reason we left port, unannounced to the world, was so the Captain could deplete the fuel oil that propelled the ship. Run the ship out to sea for a couple of days, train the men, burn up any extra fuel, and keep the commies confused. With this method the Captain's fuel oil allotment could be almost depleted at the end of each quarter. With this calculated madness in his mind, the fuel oil allotment would not be decreased by bureaucratic budgetary mathematical madness. The Captain was not about to allow this ridiculous reduction because of zero based budgeting, maintained by pencil pushing, paper shuffling, bureaucratic boobs.

This helps to explain the time Jay and Andy saw BT1 Freeze, who was ordered by the Chief, who was ordered by the Boiler Officer, who was ordered by the Engineering Officer, who was ordered by the Captain, to pump several hundred gallons of fuel oil into the ocean. The Captain couldn't burn it so he had to dump it. The ship was at least three or four hundred miles offshore and the ocean was deep at that spot. Nobody would ever know, the ocean would swallow it, choke it down, disperse it, and the Captain's quarterly allotment of fuel oil would remain intact. Use it or lose it policy.

But Maloni was not here for this unscheduled cruise of confusion from Charleston to Key West. Maloni was missing. He had somehow enlisted the support of the American Red Cross, a local congressman, and some favor owed someone in someone's family. Then bingo! He suddenly qualifies for a humanitarian leave in order to deal with personal problems back home. A distraught girlfriend, maybe a baby too, damned hormones, or most likely, hormones damned.

Anyway, Maloni wasn't there. Andy, Jay, and Gritman would have to face Key West without the antics of Maloni. The ship pulls out to sea smoothly. The short-staffed boiler rooms go to the usual six hours on watch and six hours off. The dull routine begins again. One week later they see the beautiful aqua waters of Key West. Gritman couldn't figure it out. He knew we were traveling about 300 plus miles a day, and by sea it's less than 1,000 miles to Key West. So, why seven days? Burn baby (oil) burn, burn baby (oil) burn.

As always, no one is given the itinerary for port until the last minute. So as the ship's two monstrous propellers are straining in opposite directions to help the tugs get the ship parallel parked at the dock, the Executive officer blurts out the schedule for shore leave over the ships loud speakers. The level of noise in a boiler room is constant, stone deafening at best. Dozens of pieces of machinery screaming, banging, hissing, and whining. Some are topping out at over 200,000 RPMs. The loudspeakers in the boiler room have the same tone and pitch as the ones in a Japanese prison camp from a John Wayne World War II movie. "Now hear this, now hear this. All hands will be granted one-day shore leave. Friday night leave will be those whose last names begin with M thru Z. Saturday night leave will be those whose last names begin with A thru L. Shore leave for each night begins after ship's work hours at 1700 hours and ends the following morning at 0400 hours. Tolerance is zero. The USS Jetsomn will depart Sunday at 0700 hours."

"WHAT DID HE SAY?" Gritman shouted.

Jay screamed, "I'LL GO UP TOP AND ASK SOMEBODY!"

They're splitting the crew in half, thought Andy. He remembered hearing about it during one of the card games from one of the older sailors. They claim its for the crew's safety. Like in Tunisia, or Istanbul, where a US ship hadn't been for twenty years, or the locals were pissed at the US and were throwing rocks, or worse. But this was Key West, 1970, supposedly part of the US of A. Nobody gives a shit about Castro, 90 miles away; impotent, not important. It must be the end of a bureaucratic quarter and the ol' mans got to get rid of some excess fuel oil. Let all of us piss ants have a nights leave ashore, and then get back out there to burn, or worse, dump more fuel oil. Andy's mind was working overtime to put the situation in a better light.

Chief Bronski had the snipes shut the boilers down and go to dock steam. It got quieter. Eerily quiet, like sound no longer existed. Still everybody yelled because sound doesn't stop when the noise does: ears tell the brain to tell the mouth to yell to get past the noise, the ringing and hissing noise that's *only* in your head. Silence can be deafening too (silence was no 'old friend' here Mr. Simon and Mr. Garfunkel). Also, not to mention its still about 120 degrees in the fireroom. It is bilge oil, piss, sweat, stink fucking hot, down in the fireroom. Jay explains to Andy exactly what's going to happen. "Who goes first?" asks Andy.

"M thru Z," says Jay.

"That's weird, but it'll work. For us. Me and you Jay. Jay West in Key West. Hmmm, sounds pretty good. Too bad for Gritman. That fucking Captain. I bet him and his closest shit lip ass kissers get both nights ashore. We'll see him later about that, that much is certain," murmured Andy.

"What's that you're sayin'? yells both Jay and Gritman.

"Nothing, nothing. Jay, we got 15 minutes to split. Let's go aft and get cleaned up. Sorry Gritman, maybe we'll see you tommorrow."

"Shit yeah, ya'll see me tommorry. That'd be my turn."

Andy and Jay are on the run to their lockers and the showers. "Jay, wear a set of civvies under your uniform...shit, wear two of everything underneath, except shoes." Thank God for Admiral

Zumwalt, thought Andy, he had relaxed standards and when they went ashore they could wear civvies unless otherwise commanded. He allowed hair, a little, and beards and mustaches too. It made them look a little more like civilians, and it helped keep them from getting spit on by hardcore peace freaks, sometimes.

"What the hell...?"

"Just do it!"

At 1700 hours Andy and Jay were three layers thick with clothes, but on the outside they looked good in newly pressed dress whites. In a hurry, they saluted the ensign, got permission to go ashore, and then crossed the quarterdeck and boarding ramp. Land. hot damn, mused Andy, it is good to get the feel of land under your feet. Even when the ship was tied up to the dock you could still feel the ocean move. Even just a little. It takes a little while, but then the land quits rolling too. But ashore. It felt good. Two short blocks, then they were out of the gates, marine guarded gates, of the US Naval Base, Truman Annex.

Andy and Jay had no idea where to go, maybe left, maybe right. They knew right away not to go across the street to the 'Gate Bar'. Jesus, that's fucking original, thought Jay, a Gate Bar right across from the gate. There was a group of locals, men, boys, greasers, whatever, probably locals gauging from what they were shouting. "Hey assholes stay away from our wimmin'. We catch you wid 'em, then we whip yur punk asses. You hear?"

"Let's go left Jay, and stay away from wimmen, at least theirs."

"They're talkin' to you Andy."

"Fuck you, come on, we don't need this shit."

Just a few blocks later they could hear music. Loud music. "I can't stand these clothes any longer Andy. Its really fucking hot here. Let's get out of 'em."

They ducked a few feet down a side street. It probably didn't matter because almost every house on both sides of the street were boarded up, empty and unpainted. It was kind of strange. Like something out of the twilight zone. "Yeah, I brought a pillow slip. We can stuff the extras in here, but be careful with the uniforms. Roll them up like they taught us in boot camp. We may need them later."

The juke box in the bar was blaring "Wipe Out" by the Ventures. It was a different sort of bar than either had seen before. It was called the 'Green Parrot' and it was full of military, all branches, but tonight mostly sailors. There were also some locals, unusual looking, but still not out of place. There weren't any windows, just rectangles cut out of the wooden walls with the cut out part on hinges and hanging down. They could let it down when open for business or pull them up when closed. You could stand outside, see inside, drink beer, and not have to be part of the mass of sailors on the inside. After all, Andy and Jay were in civilian clothes and didn't want to be confused with the sailors. The locals, by the look of some of them, had been in the sun for long periods of time, and some had on white rubber boots while others just wore bib jeans. Andy figured they must be some sort of fishermen. They weren't bothering the sailors. They were just watching the whole spectacle with more than a little bemusement.

The spectacle *was* the sailors, all 50 or 60 of them. They played one song on the jukebox. Wipe Out! Every time it ended, another coin would go in the juke box and the same song came out. In the corner on a table, not on a little wooden stage or little wooden box, or, up in the air in a cage, was a go-go dancer. She wasn't very tall and she could keep up with the fast pace of the drummer in "Wipe Out".

After watching this for awhile, three or four beers, Andy had it figured out. The dancer was pretty, with a cute, kiss-my-ass smile that still carried enough innocence, along with the twinkle in her blue eyes to keep your interest. Her light blonde hair fell past her shoulders and she could keep her hair and all her body parts moving in different directions in perfect rhythm with the song. It was fast, real fast. It kept the sailors whooping and yelling, drinking more beer and liquor, and the bucket at her feet was filling with dollar bills.

But she was working the boys. This wasn't her first dance. She had a skimpy, light blue velvet or fake fur, bikini. All the body parts were perfect, before you had any beers. She had the tan lines in all the right places and her tiny high heels gave her that extra bounce that's so important for that occupation. But, the gimmick that pulled it all together was the left bra cup and strap. The strap just wouldn't stay up, and with the fast pace of the song, there wasn't much time for adjustment. The strap, hanging and slapping, allowed just a tiny peek at that delectable darker shade of that portion of her breast, ...in the ever-falling cup. Her cup truly could have runneth over. But it didn't. Not after the tenth time "Wipe Out" blared across the barroom. Not after the twentieth. Not ever. The sailors were in no condition to understand the little lady had it all under control. The same song kept playing, the same cup seemed to keep falling, the same sailors kept drinking and leering, the sane locals kept their distance, and the galvanized bucket kept filling up, and the cup never fell down.

At some point Jay told Andy he had to move on to something else. Andy was carrying the pillow slip bag full of their extra clothes as they moved on down the street. About a block later they turned right and Andy saw his vision. It was the only car on the block. A small, white, two door, Toyota parked on a side street around the corner from the local five and dime. By now the sun had gone down and there were few street lights to illuminate area or the idea that Andy possessed. He threw the bag to Jay. "Oomph," sputtered Jay, "what the fuck you doin', Andy?"

"Just hold the bag, look around, and be quiet." Andy opened the door, slid in behind the steering wheel and began the usual search. In the ashtray? Under the floor mat? Nope, but laying up on top of the sun visor, hidden from view, was the key to a short ride of freedom for the boys. Andy turned the key and the engine turned over. The lights worked, the muffler was just a tad loud, but there was a quarter tank of gas showing on the gauge. "What are you standing around for Jay? This isn't something you haven't done a dozen times before. Get in, we need to move out of here!"

"Yeah but that was always back in Charleston. At the 'Flying Dutchman'. Only when we needed a ride home. We just borrowed the car for a ride home. Not really stealing..."

"Come on and get in. We're just, like you always say, borrowing the car for the..."

"Andy we don't need a ride. We're just a few blocks from the ship, not a few miles. Besides, I'm not ready to go back to the..."

"Come on, pleease, just get in! We aren't going back to the ship. Not now. Not tonight. Maybe we'll go back Sunday, early, before the ship pulls out. Come on, let's go."

Jay got in. Slowly at first, but then he got into it, as always, and began to get caught up in the moment. "Well I'll be dipped in shit if I didn't know better. ALRIGHT! We get two days leave. Just like the officers. This is cooler than shit. Man, wait till the guys....hey, what if we get caught, Andy?"

"Caught? By who? Superman? Pinky Lee? Barney Fife? Matt Dillon? There can't be more than a couple of local cops around here. Dude, didn't you see all those boarded up houses, the people in the bar, and no local businesses lit up on a Friday night? What's with that? It looks like if it weren't for the military and the fish, there wouldn't be anybody on this island. I bet there's only one cop on duty tonight, and I bet he's drinking coffee, or eating donuts, or watching 'Ponderosa'. Maybe he's doing all three at the same time. Anyway, nobody knows the trouble were in. Just remember Jay we're only borrowing the car. Just for the weekend. We'll even bring it right back where we found it, and maybe put some gas in it."

Jay seemed to be okay with that. Now we have to find a bar, thought Andy. A bar without any sailors. Its not easy finding something when you've never been there before. But, this is an island, and if you just keep driving, down different main streets we'll eventually find us a local bar. Maybe we went over a bridge, a rise in the road, but something seemed different. There was more space, fewer buildings, and hey, there was a glow. There was something not to far away that had lights. Yeah, it was a bar. Only a few cars out front, but when they went in, the place was nearly full. Regular people, men, women, even a couple of rug rats playing pinballs. The boys found an empty spot at the bar and moved to it.

They were about to order, when, from just a couple spots down the bar they heard:

"Hey swabbies' can I buy ya a beer?"

"What do you mean swabbies?" said Jay.

"Well, lets see. You have funny hair cuts, your skin is whiter than hogfish meat, and your shoes are black and shiny. So, if you're not off the ship that's just pulled in then you buy me a drink."

"Ya caught us fair and square," said Andy, "I'd love a Schlitz!"

"Yeah, me too, but I like Bud." said Jay."

"Slide two for the US Sailors Joe. A Schlitz for the funny lookin' one with the big mustache and, I think a Budweiser for his queer buddy," said the big hairy-bellied patriot. All his buddies nearby had a little laugh at Jay's expense.

Everything has a price thought Andy as he collected his Schlitz and moved toward the patriot. "Thanks a lot sir, my names Andy and..."

"Cut the sir shit, you're not on the fookin' ship right now. They call me 'Snatchum'." Snatchum stuck out a big hairy paw and Andy pumped it. "Glad to see some new sailors around here with some new stories. I want to know if the whores in the Med (Mediterranean) still give you a good ol' fashioned blow job for five bucks."

The boys hadn't been to the Med yet, but Andy had heard enough from some on the ship who had, that he thought he could bullshit his way through. "Yeah, it's still 'fucky sucky Joe, five dallahs."

Big hairy Snatchum started laughing so hard his belly was jumping up and down hitting the bottom edge of the bar, and he lost his wad of chew. It landed on the bar. "You hear that Joe? Its still five dollars. Hey Andy, is it still the same ones in every port," he asked as he retrieved and repositioned his chew?

"Yeah, almost always the same. One gets pregnant every once in a while and then they go home, or somewhere..., anyway there always seems to be enough to go around. Its still the same, if you want to know where you're going next, you ask them. They fuck the officers too and the officers want to make sure they're taken care of so they tell 'em where to be next. Andy figured he was doing alright. He had Snatchum's attention. He had something else too, an odor. It was on his right hand. The one he shook with Snatchum. It was like bad fish...or...the morning after an all niter with one of the 'ladies' on the strip back in Charleston. What the fuck does Snatchum do for a living thought Andy. Must be some sort of fisherman, Andy hoped. Anyway, he started drinking with his left hand.

The night wore on, blah, blah, blah. Andy found out how to get off the island and that there was a Navy Air Base called Boca Chica. After that there was a string of islands all the way to Miami.

At some point, Andy and Jay bought a case of Shclitz and a case of Bud. They talked the bartender out of a big bag of ice and backed out the door saying toodles to Snatchum and his friends. Glad they had run into regular people that liked them even though they were in the military. Then they headed on down the road.

Snatchum gave good directions and they had ice cold beer in the back floor boards, a full tank of gas now, and a very pleasant balmy breeze blowing across their faces. The radio didn't work. Nothing seemed to matter though, they had their freedom and knew other sailors were ending theirs. "One road in and one road out, ya can't fuck up," Andy remembered Snatchum saying. They never met any other cars on the highway. Not one car passed them. They passed the sign to the 'Boca Chica Naval Air Station. This was the best drinking road Andy had ever been on. The boys were laughing about the evening's events, putting away the cool ones, and just generally loving the feeling of the freedom they were defending.

After only a few miles though Andy was getting tired and he found a clearing to pull over onto. This might be that Sugarloaf spot Snatchum had talked about. "Let's sleep in the car tonight. I'll take the front seat and you, Jay, can have the back, with all the beer."

"Jeez, thanks a lot. Aren't you afraid I'll drink the all the beer?"

"Nah," said Andy, "but I want you to try. Try to loaf a little. See ya' in the morning...sugar, uh, bush, yeah, that was it."

"Fuck you!"

"No way Jay. I don't care how much money you got big boy, like I said before, you ain't stickin' that thing in me."

"Piss off and shut up!!!"

The breeze was cool and sleep was easy. Early in the morning, before the sun rose, the breeze abandoned the boys. Soon thereafter they were joined by others of the animal kingdom. Mosquitoes swarmed in the open windows, hundreds, no thousands, shit millions. Smack smack. "Son of a bitch after son of a bitch." Smack smack.

"Turn on the fuckin' lights Andy! What the hell is going on?"

The dome light revealed that the entire roof liner had gone from a cream colored cloth to a living, moving black mass. They were so thick they were breathing and spitting out the damn things. Andy started the car and took off. Jay was thrashing at the insects and they were leaving through the windows, but the liner was turning red, and black where the dead ones were sticking. At some point, Jay decided to shake up unopened cans of beer and spray the mosquitoes out. This pissed Andy off, he hated the thought of beer not being consumed in the normal manner.

After several miles Andy decided he had turned the wrong way when he took off earlier. The sun was coming up and it was beautiful, pinks, golds, purples, reds, oranges, but it was in his face ("one way in and one way out"). He could remember Snatchum telling him. He turned the Toyota around, the mosquitoes pretty much under control, and he was thirsty.

"Give me a beer, please, motherfucker. Jay, you alright?"

"Yeah, but the shit is hot Andy."

"Warm Jay, warm."

"You're a sick bastard Andy."

"I know, but its harmless and I enjoy it. Besides, we're going to have a nice breakfast. Free. And warm, like the beer."

"What the hell are you talking about?"

"First we'll change back into our uniforms and wipe all the extra bugs off our faces, then just show our military IDs at the gate, and we'll be in like Flynn. You ready Jay? Warm meal? Stolen car? You up for this?"

"Umhmp, shit, piss, dammit! Yeah, right now I could eat dog food I'm so hungry!"

"What? Hey look, there's water everywhere. Let's pull over and we can wash up a little before trying to get on that air base."

They pulled the car over by a bridge. There wasn't much of a shoulder on the narrow two lane highway, but there wasn't much traffic either. After sliding and scampering down a small embankment by the bridge abutment, Jay saw some of the clearest cleanest water he'd seen since Wisconsin. The water looked about four or five foot deep, they stripped down, and dove in. Immediately resurfacing and screaming because the salty water was burning the hundreds of bug bites on their face and arms that they had just received when the wind had died down. They hopped out, cursing the stings, and used the old set of civvies to dry off. Then they donned their sailor whites and took off for the air base.

Once at the gate Andy slowed the car and gave both military IDs to the somber marine guard. While checking the IDs the other marine crossed behind the car to get a better look at the passenger. "What's wrong with your face sailor?"

Jay hated these Marine guards and Andy hoped this wouldn't set him off. Andy looked at Jay's face and it looked like the worst case of chicken pox and/or measles he'd ever seen. Andy also wondered what he looked like. "I got pimples real bad, you want to pick on me too," snapped Jay. Hmm, real fucking clever response thought Andy. Yeah, classic Jay.

"No! Uh, I mean no. Uh, I'm sorry. Uh...." the marine hurried around to the other side again and hid in the gate house booth. The other marine returned our IDs and gave us that chest high salute which means you can pass through. As he pulled away Andy could see in the rearview mirror both marines were laughing hysterically. And, when he looked in the mirror he saw his face and was painfully reminded of why they were laughing.

Now they had to find the chow hall. They couldn't see the airstrip form here but there was a sailor on the first corner and they got directions from him for the chow hall. It must have been about 0800 and on the way to the chow hall Jay spotted the local EM club. It was proudly named 'The Anchor'. "Well we'll just have to check that out later." Jay wasn't real interested in anything except food and didn't comment any further about 'The Anchor'. Pulling into the parking lot for the chow hall, 'The Galley', they could see and hear the airstrip. The planes were loud. Deafening, worse than the fireroom.

Inside they had no trouble making it to the metal food trays, utensils, and...the chow. It was no different than on the ship. It was the same piles of greasy bacon, curiously linked sausage (linked side by side, as opposed to, end to end), piles of greasy hash browns, and mounds of cold toast. There was real butter available and, unlike the ship's butter, it didn't have that freon taste (hmmm, no leaky refrigerant pipes here, thought Andy). Then the two cooks, "How you boys want 'em? Scrambled? Over easy? Medium? Or fry the snot out of 'em." Maybe all the cooks went to the same school, thought Andy.

There was no limit on how high you could pile the food or how many times you returned to the chow line. The boys didn't leave until they were as full as a three day old tick on the back of an old country coon hound. Then they found a spot down the road and watched the jets roar in, right over head, just barely touch down, then head up for the sky again. They were laying on the warm hood of the car and the bright sun felt good on their bug bites. Andy retrieved one of the beers from the pool of water in the back floor boards. It WAS hot. Fuck this, thought Andy, as he downed the hot beer in one long pull.

"Hey Jay its gotta' be about 1100 let's go check out The Anchor, shoot some pool, and put away some cold ones. Who knows maybe even find some cool babes there."

"Good idea, but, you know you're full of shit on the chicks."

"Yeah, I know, you got that A-fuckin' straight there."

The Anchor was dark, no windows, low light, seascape and sailor shit painted everywhere, and the standard moldy carpet. It had one pool table and Jay put his quarter on the rail. He was pretty good and sometimes he made the drinking cheaper. Jukebox on one wall, bathrooms near the exit, and a U shaped bar. It was before noon and Andy saw about fifteen military at the bar. Probably about the usual Saturday brunch crowd. Unusual though was the mix. On a Navy base it was normally just sailors, but here you had Army, Air Force, Marines, and Navy. They found two empty stools and ordered up.

It didn't take long, even in this dimness, for a comment on their appearance. A stocky young man with glasses in Army fatigues said to Jay, in a deep gravelly voice, "Looks like you guys been out on the skeeter range without any protection."

"Yeah, they ate us up pretty good last night. We ran into a huge cloud of mosquitoes," said Andy as Jay moved over to the pool table. "Why is every branch of the military represented in this fine establishment? I've never seen this before."

"Well you got the Navy, naturally, and you always have the Marines around to protect the Navy, whether they want protecting or not. The Air Force comes here to practice same as the Navy fly boys, and then us Army folks guard the radar installations so we can check on Castro without any interference from the commies. Then there's always the spooks, but you can't see them, cuz they're always invisible or the CIA would make 'em visible and then they'd just be kooks and get themselves run off. Wooooooooooo!" He was waving his arms around like a ghost as he said that.

"Sounds pretty complicated to me. I think I'll just have another beer. Can I get you one, uh..."

"Brad's my name and bein' a short timer is now my game. I only have two months left and I'm outta' here, if I survive. And yes I'll have a shot of schnapps."

"What are you talking about, 'if you survive'?"

"Well I just got back from two years in Korea. Learned to speak a little Korean, but I only use it when I'm drunk. I got a likin' for kimchee. That's rotten cabbage from under the ground and out of a dirt hole. Put it with some hot peppers and you got some real fine salad there. It's the only way you can get that Korean beer down. I didn't much care for the Korean pussy though. They all got straight pussy hairs, not curly you know."

"No I didn't know, but thanks for the information. Especially about the salad. Maybe it'll come in handy some day."

"Probably not," growled Brad, "but at least ya know. Yeah, after two years over there with those weirdoes they send you back here a little early so you can reacclimate yourself. Reassimilate, or whatever, you know, get used to the curly ones."

Jay had two extra beers lined up on the rail so Andy went over and picked one up. He didn't like Budweiser but the price was right. When he returned to the bar he inquired of Brad about the surviving part. This looked like pretty good duty. It was on land. It was an agreeable climate. And, the locals liked you. At least, once you left the gate area. "What do you mean 'survive'?"

"Well, they only send out one of us at a time to guard the radar domes. It doesn't matter what time of the day or night because the skeeters are just as bad any time out there. So they issue you a flashlight, a rifle, one round of ammo, and one can of skeeter spray."

Astonished, Andy said "one round of ammo? Why not, at least one whole clip?"

"It's a humane issue, not a security issue. The skeeters are real bad here. You know that, just look at your face in the mirror. The deal is, if you run out of skeeter spray, then take the one bullet and blow your fuckin' brains out! Ha ha ha ha! Hee hee hee!

Brad liked telling that one. The rest of the afternoon was spent swapping jokes and stories, playing pool, and just having fun. The other military people all had a little different perspective on some of the similar situations we all found ourselves in. It was good for Andy and Jay to hear all of it.

It was getting to be early evening. Jay had quit playing pool. Andy could hear something that sounded like Korean and it was coming out of Brad's mouth. Jay said he had the beer all iced down. Andy wondered aloud how long ice would last in hot water, but Jay said he found an old piece of rebar, a larger bolt, and more than one rusty spot in the old Toyota's floor board. Thus, for now and evermore, water would drain from the Toyota's back floor boards and only iced beer would remain. Jay could be quite resourceful at times. Andy's dad always said an educated man can make do with what he has.

Then when they changed back into their second set of civvies and Andy looked in the mirror at all those 'skeeter bites' he remembered something else his dad had said. "Son if you're going to be dumb, you have to be tough." Then, as he walked away, sometimes his dad would pause, turn around, and say, with a friendly smile, "son, you'll need to be real tough."

Okay so two tough guys were on their way back to Key West. The guards at the gate to the air station were different. They had undergone a watch change and they don't check you on your way out anyway. It was a great ride back, but Andy kept wondering why the road seemed so narrow.

They hadn't been to the beach. Jay said to find one and Andy obliged. The sun had just set and the boys were watching the same beautiful colors as they had that morning. What a sunset, all the same colors as this morning, and it seemed to last forever. The stars came out, there was a breeze, no mosquitoes. But something was missing. They felt better, the beer was ice cold, but still something wasn't there. Then it was. Two young ladies were walking up the beach toward them.

"God I wish I didn't have all these bites on my face, and shit, they do look like pimples," said Jay.

Andy told him not to worry they wouldn't look at them anyway, and if they did it was night time. Maybe you couldn't see those little bites at night. Jay seemed to feel better about it. The girls got closer. There was something different about the way those two girls talked. It was a foreign language, but Andy had learned some Spanish and it wasn't Spanish. Weird, it sounded similar, but softer with a gentle lilt.

Andy couldn't stand it any longer. They were only about ten feet away. "Oye, do you, 'dos mujeres quiere cerveza muy frio' (two young ladies want an ice cold beer)?"

In perfect English one of them said, "We sure would."

They turned out to be sisters from Brazil. After introductions and some small talk Jay gravitated away with the older sister, Elizabeth, and Andy was left, infatuated, with her sister, Samantha. Andy learned they were in Key West with their parents who were looking for a new home. Their parents were Americans, but had worked in Brazil, raising their family there. Thus, their Portuguese conversation.

Andy couldn't get over the captivating presence of Samantha, her precocious, yet innocent smile. She was intellectual, but also as soft and warm as the tropical evening breeze. She had long silky dark brown hair, and unlike Andy's temporary blemishes, her skin was soft and creamy, eyes twinkling in the moonlight. Andy asked her to say something in the Portuguese language and she spoke a few sentences. This was intoxicating to Andy. Each time she smiled it brightened the glow in her face. Andy knew he was in heaven and had found an angel. They talked for what seemed to be hours. She's was the nicest, most interesting, and most captivating female Andy had ever met.

There's something about the sun, surf, and sand that makes a person tired, a healthy tired. Andy fell asleep in her arms under a palm tree on the sand. He heard the gentle crashing of the waves, felt the soft balmy breezes of ocean air, and saw the dim light of a distant moon in his mind's eye as he drifted off.

When Andy awoke, it was slow and peaceful, as if he had slept the sleep of a full night. He was rested and calm, but alone. He looked over where Jay and Elizabeth were, and Jay was alone. The sisters had left. Were they ever there?

The moon was high and they needed to put the car back where they found it. Andy woke Jay and they returned the car, then walked back to the ship. Along the way Andy found himself wondering if the sisters were real or had he dreamt it all. He confirmed it with Jay. "Yes Andy it really happened," he said, "but now we have to face the fiddler. You know, the captain. Remember, Don Juan, we're in the Navy."

"No sweat Jay. We just go on board as usual. Everybody's asleep and nothing will happen until the morning. Then the chief will write us up and we'll go to Captain's Mast. I'll give the captain a cock and bull story about somebody slipping something in our drinks and we don't really know what happened, and we're just glad we made it back before the ship pulled out. Then, he'll lecture us, fine us a $100, and restrict us to the ship for two weeks. Then two weeks later when the ship pulls into port, we'll go to the Flying Dutchman, get drunk, borrow a car, go back to the base, walk to the ship, sleep it off, and eat breakfast. Its that simple Jay." Just knock 'em down and get back up and do it again, thought Andy.

"Sounds like a plan. A damn good one! Yeah, and next month we travel to the Med to see what we can do there. Spain, France, Italy, and Greece, hell, there's no telling what we'll do or see. I like the way we're thinking Andy."

"Remember, its all for freedom and in the defense of democracy."

Two days later the boys found themselves on the bridge (that's the room high up on the ship where the captain drives the ship while sitting in a huge shiny brass and leather throne). Its very formal up there, with a whole mess of polished brass, and yessirs up everyone's ass. Very formal, especially for snipes who rarely leave the stink and sweat of the bilges.

"No Captain, it's a heavy burden, a real weight sir. We were wrong and its my fault...." said Andy, with a straight face, as he attempted to blurt out his whole line of bull shit.

The Captain was taken aback with such a quick, and seemingly sincere and unsolicited admission. He stuttered, "Well, er, uh, at least you're honest about such indiscretion and blatant disregard for the rules and regulations of the US Navy. I'm not going to get into a long lecture here, but both of you boys know....blah, blah, blah.....(for thirty minutes longer). I'm going to fine you each $100 and restrict you to the ship for ten days. Dismissed!"

Andy and Jay were relieved. Now they were looking forward to the Mediterranean Cruise. They knew they couldn't completely remove the weight all at once. However, they were learning that piece by piece, little by little, that all you had to do was nudge it a little. Each time you put a little effort forth, you could chink off a little iron. Then, the weight was eased, just a little. When you did that you had fun, you found your freedom, and each time, you learned a little more about yourself.

Chapter 24: The Weight is Aweigh!

As the time grew shorter for the upcoming Med cruise, Jay grew less and less enthused. Andy, on the other hand was getting more and more fired up. Six months, half a year, that's a long time, Jay worried. They both liked the prospect of seeing new places. Unknown and unexpected foreign ports were appealing, but for Jay, the idea of being so tightly tethered to the ship did not appeal to him.

"The ship, like it or not, is basically our home, anyway," Andy said for about the hundredth time. "We have a little more than 18 months left and to spend six of that on a vacation is almost to good to be true...."

"Vacation, my ass! We'll be on the ship most of the time and any time we get off the ship, you know they'll have us on a pretty short leash. That leash will be like an unbreakable anchor chain because they know we'll embarrass the shit out of the US Navy without it."

"Don't fret too much Jay," Gritman piped up, "sides ya'll got the ways of the ship down to a science. We got plenty of money cuz our slush fund is healthy and we ain't no threat to the bigguns. We jes loan to our own. When we git off the ship we have money, there'll be those whores they talk bout, new nightspots where no one knows us, and sometimes, a warm beach with yourapeon wimmun and no tops on. Titties showin'."

"Gritman," reminded Andy, "there's a good chance you don't want to see the underarms next to those titties."

"What? Oh yeah, ya' mean they might have pubes there. Yeah, but I think I could see past that."

"Well we want to change Jay's outlook and you're got the right train of thought, but don't forget about unlimited beer and maybe a new herb or two. You just have to lighten up a little Jay."

The powers that be were in high gear and there was an immediate and commanding priority to get the ship spotless, newly painted, and all machinery in shipshape condition for the big cruise. It seemed everything had to be fixed, washed, painted, and repainted. All at once! If it didn't move: PAINT IT! Eight hour days turned into 12 hours. Liberty was getting scarcer and it sounded like it may be nonexistent in the final few days before departure. The boys needed a night out to rethink things.

Gritman and Maloni went to their favorite titty bar and Jay and Andy went to the Palm Room, both bars were on the strip.

"I'm not looking forward to this as much as I was."

"Yeah," said Andy, "that's pretty obvious. Just remember, its gonna' be real cool seeing these new places. I've been to a lot of places here in the states, but never abroad. Good word Jay, abroad. Just keep saying it to yourself. Abroad. A broad. You'll be okay. You'll love it if its half the fun the others say it is."

"Ha ha, and if 'ifs and buts were candy and nuts everyday would be Christmas', asshole. This shit is serious! I just don't know. We'll be living, eating, drinking, shitting, farting, belching, and sleeping with all these assholes 24 hours a day, 7 days a week. 24 / 7, I just don't know. The stinking fucking ship will be our only home."

"It is right now and we're doing just fine. You forgot pissing and probably other stuff too, but you have to remember what Gritman said? We've accomplished a lot already and who knows what's just around the corner."

"Yeah, well I think, I don't know...."

"It'll be okay. We have to go, we have no say, no control, no options, and no good way out unless you want to do something stupid, like go over the wall."

"Nah, we're at war. Deserters get shot during war time, UCMJ. We learned that in boot camp." Jay was feeling resigned and just a little down.

Andy was definitely more optimistic, "We'll come through it just fine, you'll see. We got places to go, new sights to see, and new people to meet. And all the time we just get closer to getting out. Well, faith and begorrah, speaking of new people. Look at who just crossed the threshold of the Palm Room."

"Oh god," moaned Jay, "your grandmother. Now I have to listen to your phony Irish accent."

A fairly new addition to Andy's circle of intimacy was a lady known only as 'Love'. She wasn't as old as Jay let on, but she definitely was older than Andy or Jay. Love was short, attractive, and would do anything for Andy. She had a sister who was a little younger and she definitely had the hots for Jay. Her moniker, appropriately, was 'Hope'. Andy told Jay that Chastity had to be somewhere near, but right now Jay didn't want to hear much of what Andy was saying.

"Love, my dear, come hear and let me see you, closer. You have a beautiful new bob and blond streaks to set it off. You look great with short hair."

Love giggled a lot and this drove Jay nuts.

"Can I get you a drink? Two Ripples barkeep. Jay, don't be a clod. Sweet Jesus, get Hope something. Maybe she'd like to play pool. You know you need you're stick chalked."

Hope was thirtyish, and reddish hair, with a strong set to her jaw, nice figure, and she wasn't a giggler. She didn't add much to conversations either, but Jay needed that right now.

Jay and Hope sauntered off to the pool table with two Ripples and Andy and Love engaged in what was now becoming a regular routine. A little small talk, a few drinks, a quick dance or two, back to her place, then she'd bring him back to Shorty's and the main gate.

Back on the ship Jay and Andy hit their racks quickly. It was late, but Jay had trouble sleeping. The compartment was especially hot. The small fan near his rack only blew hot humid air on him. The Ripple, beer, greasy hot dogs, and distorted memories of Hope didn't help. Jay figured Andy had a cast iron stomach, no gag reflex, and now was capable of regretting very little. Jay tossed and turned. He was thinking about a lot of things, but mostly the Med cruise. He wasn't so sure he really wanted to go, but there really wasn't any choice. Finally, mercifully, he dozed off into a fitful slumber.

A hand roughly shook his shoulder. "Get up! Time for watch!"

"Huh?" It was dark, the red glow of the compartment lights cast an eerie glow. Jay rubbed his eyes. No one was around. Whoever woke him up was gone. "What watch? We're still in port," he said to no one.

He shook his head. The noise of the generators and the general noise of the ship told him otherwise. What's going on? He climbed up the ladder and looked out the hatch. What the hell? They were at sea.

"West! Git yer ass in the fireroom. You have a six hour watch in 10 fuckin' minutes!"

Jay looked around but whoever yelled at him was already gone. He got dressed and went on watch. He stared at the water gauge, trying to keep from dozing off. It was also extremely hot in the fireroom and the vents were blowing even hotter air down the hatch from the deck above. It seemed like an eternity passed before someone came to relieve him. Gritman.

Gritman grinned at him and sat down without saying anything.

"What the hell is wrong with you?" Jay asked. He was not in a good mood.

Gritman just grinned back.

Fuck him, Jay thought. Two can play this game. I wont say anything either. He wandered down to the mess deck for some mid-rats. Jay ate a cheese sandwich by himself. A few other sailors were also eating. Jay didn't recognize any of them. That's strange, he thought. He left the galley and climbed up a ladder to a higher deck. Halfway up he slipped and started falling backwards, falling.... falling...

Jay woke with a start! Where was he? In his bunk it seemed. The air was hot and there was no sound. No generators, no noise of the ship underway. No red lights, only a white light burned on the other side of the compartment. They were not at sea. Jay looked at his watch, 0330 hours. He had slept for only a ½ hour. Just a dream. He turned his back and tried to go back to sleep.

It seemed he was sleeping for just a few minutes when an alarm sounded. "This is not a drill!" a metallic voice shrieked from the ship's intercom.

He pulled on his clothes and joined others on the deck. They went to their assigned battle stations. What the hell?

Russians, he was told. A Russian destroyer was closely shadowing them and the Captain had turned on it and was going to confront it. Holy shit, thought Jay, putting on a battle helmet and holding a fire hose. Andy appeared from somewhere below.

"Do you believe this shit?" Jay asked. "What the hell are we doing here?"

"Got me. I hope we don't do anything stupid."

The lights of the Soviet ship could be seen on the horizon. They seemed way to close. You could see other sailors on that ship. They looked scared shitless. Then our ship turned about and lined up sideways to the Soviet ship. Guns and missiles turned toward each other on both ships. Orders were given to lock and load. It was deathly quiet.

The lights and faces of the other ship got closer. There was a lot of activity on the Soviet ship, but it was difficult to know what they were doing. This is the big time, thought Jay. He wondered what the Russian sailors thought. He didn't dare say anything. He was scared, and mad, and tired. Man, was he tired! He didn't know what to think, let alone what to say.

They sat that way for what seemed to be forever. All of a sudden the Soviet ship turned and appeared to steam off in a different direction. No one around Jay spoke for quite some time. Finally, word was passed to stand down. The 'lock and load' order had been cancelled, the Russians had turned away and left, and everything was back to normal.

Back to normal? Jay thought. Back to normal? We had a serious fucking stare down with the Russians that almost ended up in monstrous shoot out at the O K corral, a gunfight of total death and destruction, and now, all of a sudden, everything's normal? What the hell?

Jay woke up in a sweat. He had been dreaming again. Russians, gunfights, but it was only a dream. Still, Jay was nervous and irritated about the dreams. He had to get better sleep or he wouldn't be worth a shit in the morning. Then he remembered he didn't care if he was worth a shit in the morning or not. It would just be another typical day in the fireroom.

Jay closed his eyes again. He tossed and turned and finally dozed off again for the third time that night.

He found himself staring at the wall by his rack. The noise of the generators was back. The ship was underway again. Going to the Med. Jay knew they were halfway across the Atlantic but he had no idea how he knew that. The wall he was staring at was actually the hull, the skin that separated Jay from the sea. It was well under the waterline. By Jay's rack, it bulged inward from some past minor collision with a pier or something. Jay had noticed the bulge when he was first assigned the rack. He watched it regularly to make sure it wasn't getting any worse or leaking or something. Now Jay could see water seeping along a riveted seam. Not a lot of water, but water nonetheless. We're leaking. Holy shit! Here we are in the middle of the ocean and we're leaking.

Jay jumped up and went looking for someone, for help. No one was in the compartment.

"That's strange," he said to no one.

He walked the main deck. The ship was slicing quietly through the water. The moon was full and green streaks of something were flashing and streaming by in the ship's wake. Phosphorus, Jay remembered someone telling him. Some chemical interaction with salt water and something, and something. It was all so surreal, this fluorescent light show. Jay watched the show for a long time before remembering his mission. The ship was sinking, slowly, but surely, it was sinking, surely. He needed to tell someone.

He went to the mess decks. It was full of sailors, some he recognized, some he didn't. "Who are these guys?" he asked himself. He was looking over unfamiliar faces now.

"The ship is leaking," he announced. "There's water coming in by my rack."

No one responded. They were all listening to a radio or something.

"Hey really! There's a leak. Someone needs to take a look at it."

"Pipe down!" An unfamiliar Chief shouted at him. "There's no leak. You're wrong. This ship can't sink. The US Navy doesn't sink. Go back to bed. You're imagining the whole thing. There are no problems!" Jay stared at the Chief. He looks like Larry, the recruiter who got me into this mess. Can't be him. Jay told himself, "No fucking way!"

"That's right," chorused several other voices from the group. They ignored Jay to a man, all of them were engrossed with the radio. Jay went closer so he could listen to the radio too. It seemed that a sailor was missing from an aircraft carrier in the vicinity. No sign of him, he was presumed overboard.

"We are going to help with the search come daybreak," said the unfamiliar Chief.

"He jumped," someone said from the crowd. "Did himself in. Couldn't take it."

"No way, he was tossed over cuz he pissed someone off," said another. "He's a goner. He's a goner, no one could survive a fall from a carrier. Poor fucker."

"He must have had it coming. You don't want to piss off your shipmates.," someone else opined.

Fuck my shipmates, Jay thought. He turned and headed back to his compartment, convinced that the water would be rushing into the ship by now. The lights were all out except for the red lights along the passageway that lit the way with an eerie glow.

Suddenly, the intercom announced that a big storm was coming. The wind picked up and the sea started to swell and roll. Immediately, the ship started rocking back and forth. Bouncing between the bulkheads, Jay finally made it to the compartment. The ship pitched sharply and Jay almost fell down the ladder. But, he did make it to the bottom unharmed and saw that the compartment was now full of sailors trying to sleep. The ship was pitching so much that the men were falling out of their racks. Jay made it to his bunk and crawled in. The seam was still seeping but at least the water wasn't pouring in – yet. He wrapped himself in his sheets and secured himself in his rack to keep from being tossed out by the rolls of the ship. Others around him were violently seasick and were puking in their beds, on the walls, and on the deck.

"This is absolute shit!" Jay yelled, but no one responded. They were too ill.

Some amount of time passed and then the intercom came alive: "All hands on deck for refueling!"

Jay looked at his watch. It was midnight. What the fuck?!? Refueling? In the middle of the night? In the middle of a storm? He struggled out of his sheets, fumbled for his clothes, and finally made it on deck. He was the only person there except for the unfamiliar Chief from the mess decks. God, he sure looks like Larry, jay thought to himself again. He wanted to avoid talking directly to the unfamiliar Chief.

The Chief turned to Jay, "Alright! Its you and me. Everyone else is sick. There all a bunch of pussies. We gotta' fuel this bitch ourselves. We can do it!"

A huge ship, an Oiler, had pulled alongside. The wind seemed to have increased. Both ships were rocking and rolling in the high waves. They were way too close to each other.

"We're gonna' hit her for sure," Jay said. "There's no way this is going to work without us all getting killed." He thought of the leak by his rack. "We're on a ship that's sinking," he added. No one responded to him.

A line came across and was secured by someone Jay couldn't see on the deck above him. This was followed by a large cable. The cable carried a huge flexible hose which was going to carry the fuel oil to the ship.

The fuel hose hit the deck and sat there. Jay tried to lift it but couldn't. "This sucker must be a foot in diameter and it feels like it weighs a million pounds," he yelled over the wind. No one responded.

"There's no way we can do this," he yelled again. "This is fuckin' crazy! I quit!" He turned around and looked for the Chief. No Chief. No one even on deck. All alone.

"So now what? Fuck you all! I'm going back to bed!" He started for the ladder.

Again, Jay awoke with a huge jerk. He was soaking wet with fresh sweat. He was disoriented, groggy, and nauseous. "No way," he muttered to himself in the silent compartment.

"Pipe down," came a voice in the darkness.

Jay laid still, assessing things. No noise. No generators, no movement. He slowly realized he had been asleep, and had yet another wet dream. Yuk, yuk. Damn it! Damn these dreams. He groped for a flashlight under his mattress and flicked it on. The wall next to him still bulged, but it was dry. No sign of water, even along the seam. His light flicked off. Jay felt agitated and anxious. Those were some really weird dreams, he thought. He was extremely tired but very tense from the dreams.

"Now I'll never get back to sleep," he muttered. Jay thought for a moment. "Maybe its better if I don't even try." He dug his flashlight out again and found a book to read.

That morning Jay and Andy sat on the mess decks, Jay picking his way through breakfast, while Andy woofed his down like a dog.

"You look like warmed up shit," Andy observed.

"Bad night. No sleep. Lots of weird dreams. You wouldn't believe it. We were heading for the Med and it was one nightmare after another." Jay briefly told him about the leak, the overboard sailor, the Russian destroyer, and the refueling in a big storm. "You wouldn't believe it. I sure hope its not a sign of things to come."

Andy was uncharacteristically empathetic. "No shit sherlock! That is really weird. Really weird. Now you gotta' hear this. I just found out that the boilermen are going to be restricted to the ship for the last two days before we leave for the Med."

"I knew they were going to fuck us like this!"

"No! No! No! We are going to fuck them."

"Okay, what now. This ought to be real good," groaned Jay.

Andy told Jay that right after breakfast he was going down into the forward fireroom and get the #2 fuel oil pump diaphragm (a wafer thin, special metal mixture). There were no others in supply and they would have to special courier a new one down from

Norfolk. It was rumored that the ship might leave a day or two early because of a fear of too many AWOLs. Andy figured getting the diaphragm would prevent the ship leaving early.

"How will you get it and not get caught if its so valuable? And who says this does us any good?"

"Yesterday I heard the Chief telling that ass kisser of a boss we have that that pump better be fixed by the end of today or he was going to bust him. He also told asskiss not to lose that diaphragm because there wasn't another one, except in Norfolk. Somebody is riding the Chief's ass pretty hard or he wouldn't have been so rough on his main butt wipe. Anyway, when no one was looking, I got the diaphragm and put up in the bulkhead where you can't see it. Its one of the last things you put back in the pump so they wont miss it until much later."

"So what?!?"

"Soooo, you go powder your mug in the head and I'll go get the diaphragm. Then we meet in the aft companionway and walk off the ship. When we get down the pier away from the ship I pitch the diaphragm in the ocean. Then we go to the Palm Room, call our sweeties and meet them for two nights of R & R."

"You are nuts Andy! You are one fucking nutcase. How do we get off the ship?"

"We tell the O.O.D. (Officer On Duty) that we're going over to the Tender to get a box of rags and some all-thread. They don't give a shit about snipes after rags, all-thread, or anyone going to the tender. So we cross the quarterdeck, walk right on past the Tender, and toss the diaphragm. Then we change clothes and head out the main gate. Come back two days later. The Captain gives us two weeks restriction to the ship and a small fine. It is the same M.O. as in Key West. Once you have pattern that works all you do is replicate it. According to the others that have already been to the Med it takes the ship two to three weeks to get there, depending on storms and weather conditions. Besides, the first port is Rota Spain. That's just another fucking Navy base."

"Aw shit, I don't even like Hope and you want us to spend the last two nights here in the good ol' US of A with a couple of ancient haggy bags. Damn, the Captain's going to take some money from us too."

"That's okay, its not our money anyway. The others just give us money when we loan it to 'em. Its free money. Lighten up Jay.

"Oooooooh......"

"Hey, they have a nice apartment, good music, cook good food, and then there's always dessert."

Jay acquiesced, barely. They left the ship. Everything went according to plan. Within two hours the boys were showered, slouched into a couple of easy chairs, listening to some smooth Smokey Robinson tunes, and smoking some big fat cigars. The two aging angels were hovering over them, waiting on them hand and foot, and Jay had to admit it was better than putting together a greasy fucking fuel oil pump.

"Okay Andy, we got the pattern down. I think we can do it...I mean the Med. I believe we know how to take the burden, our load...and lighten it." The rest of the night went well.

However, the next morning wasn't according to plan. There was a loud knock at the door. Then another series of knocks, louder this time. Love opened the door and was greeted by a big burly Charleston County cop.

"Sorry to disturb you this early ma'am, but we're looking for a couple of sailors by the names of Andrew Mathers and Jay West."

Andy was closer to the door than Jay so he wrapped a sheet around himself and went to the door. "Is there something I can do to help you officer?"

"Yes. Step outside and come with me. They want your presence back on the ship."

Andy tried to explain that he had to get dressed and he was going back anyway. The cop just said, "you can do that outside on the front porch son." So, Love passed his clothes through the half opened door while Andy explained that he didn't know where Mr. West was. But Andy could see into the rear of the house, in the back bedroom. What he saw was a dresser that was visibly bumping and shaking. He knew Jay was hiding there, and he knew Jay was scared, but he also knew Jay was going to have one more night of freedom.

The cop handcuffed Andy and returned him to the ship. He was ordered to the boilerman's compartment and told not to leave except for chow call. He was then to report to morning muster and would be dealt with at that time. The Chief, with veins popping from his neck, explained it would be better for Fireman Mathers if Fireman West returned before they pulled out for the Med. Further, that he would personally be at the Captain's Mast in order to get some kind of explanation from Mathers about the difficulty in getting the #2 fuel oil pump back together. "I expect full cooperation from you at that time Mathers because I know you had something to do with that. If it isn't a satisfactory one, I will personally throw your worthless ass overboard on the way to the Med. Understand me?"

"I certainly do Chief."

Down in the compartment everybody wanted to know what he and Jay were up to and where was Jay and blah, blah, blah.

Andy just wanted to read his book, but he knew they wouldn't quit pestering him until he gave them something.

"Tomorrow at the morning muster Fireman West will be escorted to the ship by two beautiful ladies of the night. Night angels, gentleman, night angels."

"Aw, you're just as full of shit as you ever were Andy." That seemed to be the general consensus, and Andy was left alone to read his book.

The next morning all the boilermen, enginemen, machinist mates, their respective petty officers, and the Chiefs were assembled on the fantail getting their days orders. This was followed by a speech from the Engineering Officer, "As you all know, we are about to embark upon a wonderful patriotic voyage that....

Then the melodic sounds from a car radio interrupted the speech, "...I know you're gonna' leave me, but I refuse to let you go...," all eyes on the fantail turned from the Engineering Officer to a white and gold four-holer Buick convertible that had come to a stop just a little beyond the ships quarterdeck. From the ship it appeared as if Fireman West surfaced, like an ASROC missile, from between two gorgeous women within the Buick. He emerged from that car exuding a confidence and a nimbleness usually reserved only for young on-the-move officers. He wore on his face a smile that couldn't be drug down by any chain or anchor the Navy had.

As he crossed the quarterdeck and gave a smart salute to the colors, a quiet murmur arose from those on the fantail and it swelled into a loud cheer. Jay was ready, eager, and he bellowed, "anchors aweigh my boys, anchors away!"

Printed in the United States
95561LV00003B/150/A